The Corrupt Shadows

The contents of this work, including, but not limited to, the accuracy of events, people, and places depicted; opinions expressed; permission to use previously published materials included; and any advice given or actions advocated are solely the responsibility of the author, who assumes all liability for said work and indemnifies the publisher against any claims stemming from publication of the work.

All Rights Reserved
Copyright © 2023 by Michael G. Dunkley Jr.

No part of this book may be reproduced or transmitted, downloaded, distributed, reverse engineered, or stored in or introduced into any information storage and retrieval system, in any form or by any means, including photocopying and recording, whether electronic or mechanical, now known or hereinafter invented without permission in writing from the publisher.

RoseDog Books
585 Alpha Drive, Suite 103
Pittsburgh, PA 15238
Visit our website at www.rosedogbookstore.com

ISBN: 978-1-6461-0320-1
eISBN: 978-1-6461-0389-8

The Corrupt Shadows

by

Michael G. Dunkley Jr.

PITTSBURGH, PENNSYLVANIA 15238

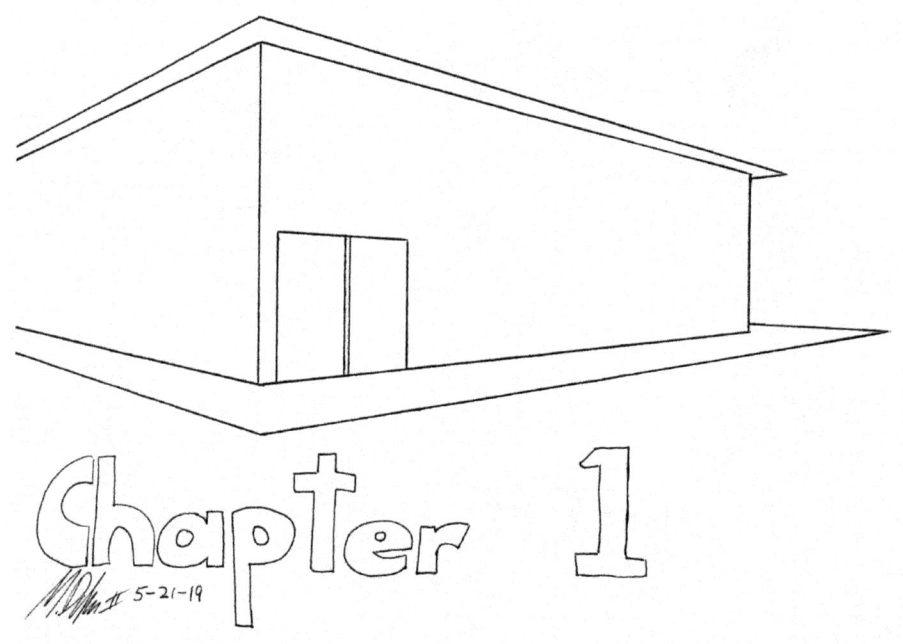

Chapter 1

Chapter One
Unsettling Terms

The sun begins to set and the street lights are slowly turning on. The light posts line the street from end to end. One light is already on, the one in front of those trees that are obviously in desperate need of trimming. Just about every street has one, the light that seems to stay lit all day and night. The street at this time of day is very quiet. No people in sight and the only sounds come from the swaying trees. The business day is over and everyone has gone home. The sound of the lamps and their bulbs click. The whisper of the wind slowly blowing, the slight breeze keeping small things moving. One by one, the lamps light up the street alongside a small building. The structure is set back on the end of the street. The yellow colored illumination makes the walls of the building look different from its true color. Browns look like grays, and blues look like greens. The color of the light is chosen to prevent blindness over time. A small safety measure no one even knows about. The roof is flat with a slight pitch. The old-style brick work is a look not seen very often, making it appear older than it really is. Its masonry perfection outweighs the modern look being captured by builders today. The architect's ultimate intention was to make sure the structure would last the test of time. Inside this small one level building is Eric Colewell. Eric, the security guard for BIO-TEC, is sitting in the middle of an archive room. He is a middle age five-foot, ten-inch, 250-pound man. Eric is slightly overweight with two bad knees from playing football as a young collage kid. He is basically an overpaid secretary without the responsibilities. No ringing phones and no massage taking. The most action he's seen was the locate hoodlums defacing the walls on the outside of the building. These acts of vandalism, Eric contently had to clean up. Their destructive behavior warranted the local police to roll threw once and a while. The lobby and the main archive room are mostly kept dark. The only light hangs over Eric's head, so he can read the newspaper. Reading the paper from the day before, Eric always felt a day behind in the world. Maintaining the night shift was hard. He spent most of his spare time catching up on his sleep. Eric was going to be there, perched on that chair all night until his replacement came. The life of a security guard is not all that glamorous, but it pays the bills. One of those jobs to justify a means to an end. Like he would allow the wheels in his life to turn without going anywhere. Eric spins around in his chair like a five-year-old with nothing to look at but those four plan green walls. A tone of green one would never think to entertain painting in their own house. The color, no matter how dull or plain, fit the surrounding. The dark brown, almost black rubber trim followed the floor and ceiling. Tall gray file cabinets line almost every wall. Four draws high and three feet wide, the cabinets stored some very important files. If he hadn't been being paid so well, he might have considered a new job. He sat there looking out the glass door through the doorway and into the street. Eric stood up from his seat. His knees and legs felt heavy. Eric needed to stretch his legs a little. He walked to the door and continued peering out into the street. His thoughts preparing himself for the next act of war from those local hoodlums. At this point, he was just trying so hard to fight boredom. The feelings of being there the whole night in that same spot got old fast. Standing also stopped his butt from getting sore, too. His mind began to wonder. Eating would sure past the time, maybe he would eat his well-prepared dinner early. Leftover ribs from his neighbors picnic the day before was the only thing he had to look forward to. Along with some rice, potato salad, and two rolls, he was going to eat like a king tonight. After standing at the door and his face almost pressed up against the glass for a few minutes. Eric turned around and started walking back to his desk. "*There is nothing out there,*" he thought out loud. The sound of someone knocking on the glass made him stop and hesitate. His first thought was those kids from last week were messing with him again. They must have nothing better to do than to harass the guards. Eric snapped back around in an effort to catch them in the act, but he saw nobody there. He approached the door again slowly, someone running by in the darkness got his attention. Eric pulled his flash light out from his utility belt and pointed it through the glass up and down the sidewalk outside. Suddenly, there was an explosion breaking the glass, knocking Eric off his feet. He fell backward onto the floor. It was so hot; the wooden door frame was on fire. Eric lay there on his back in the middle of all the glass. The thought of what may have caused this was his first concern. Frightened, he quickly checked himself to make sure he still had all his limbs. Then he looked up and saw him. He could see a black metal man step through the flames. The man looked right at him. His eyes glowed red and his hands were on fire. It was him, this metal man caused the explosion. Without thinking twice, Eric pulled his gun out and fired a shot at the metal man. The bullet bounced off the dark metal like he was a tank. The bullet deflected into the wall, having no effect on the metal man. Before Eric knew it, his gun became very hot. It almost burned his hand and he had to drop it onto the floor. It was the metal man, he was somehow able to control fire and its heat. Outside on another remote side of the building, a red car pulls up to the sidewalk. The long, gray sidewalk, dark and empty. The four-door dark red car slowly crept in the middle of the street. Trying to keep itself in the shadows. It's new-like red glossy finish unappreciated in the darkness. If it didn't just come from the show room, then it was apparent that the owner devotes a lot of time to its maintenance. The black tinted windows too dark to make out its occupants. The large chrome-colored rims glisten in what little light there was. The tires looked brand new, but that couldn't be further from the truth. The almost blue tinted head lights went out and the dark passenger window rolls down, ajar. This thick white smoke begins to flow out like steam from the top of a train. A smoke trail sails around the car and along the building like fog. Almost like it was being guided. It settles over the sidewalk, and the cloud then forms into a woman. The driver door opens and Liset steps out. They are both completely unaware of what is already happening on the other side of the building.

"Jean, are you sure this is the place?" she asked as the smoke consolidated into Jean.

Michael Dunkley, Jr.

The man looked right at him. His eyes glowed red and his hands were on fire. It was him, this metal man caused the explosion.

"I don't know, but this is the address!"

"How are we getting in mow-mow?" Liset asked impatiently.

"Hold on, girl, I'm thinking!" Jean now stood with both hands on the wall and her head up against it, trying to hear anything. She backed up and turned her arm back into smoke. Jean reached through the thousands of tiny macroscopic holes in the cold, brown brick wall. The rest of her body slowly followed. Like a ghost, there one minute, gone the next.

"Jean, what about me?" Liset tried to grab Jean before she went all the way through. "Wait for me!" she said, slapping her open hands on the tough brown bricks. Like a child throwing a fit because she can't have her way. For Jean, communication was never her strong suit. Having a conversation with her could be hard sometimes. In a moment, Liset will realize she may have overreacted. Liset stopped and turned her back to the wall. She folded her arms and started pouting like an unhappy little girl who just dropped her ice cream. "Can't believe she just left me here!" Liset said out load.

"Come on, drama queen!" Jean said as her smoke hand came out from the wall's surface. Jean's trail of smoke wrapped around Liset's arm, turning her entire body into smoke as well. They both flouted between the brown bricks an into the back-left corner of the archive room. They were in a small corridor with a big, gray fire exit door behind them. Jean reformed alongside Liset.

"You need to tell me what you're doing before you do it! Wait, do you smell that?" Liset asked.

"Smell what?" Jean snapped.

"It smells like something is burning." Suddenly, the fire alarm rang out, followed by the blue flashing lights. The alarm was loud and deafening.

"Look over there!" Liset yelled. She was pointing at the front entrance. Thick, black smoke was starting to flow into the main room. Jean immediately turned herself into smoke and flew up, traveling just below the ceiling. Liset ran through the door way and jumped, sliding across a few file cabinets. She was going so fast and in such a rush, she almost didn't land on her feet after hitting the floor. When Liset reached the front, she found a man lying in the middle of the floor. The man was shaking in fear. The small fragments of shattered safety glass covered his body, as well as the whole corridor. He seemed to be very afraid and was staring at someone standing in front of him. Liset glanced up to see him; it was the shadow from her nightmares. Flashbacks of him in that gas chamber and the screams she would hear at night haunted her. Liset fell to the floor in a fetal position, rocking back and fourth.

"Dark Shadow!" she yelled. He turned his attention to Liset. Jean flew down and formed herself in between Liset and Dark Shadow.

"You better back off!" shouted Jean. Dark Shadow made some quick motions, moving his hands in a circular motion clapping his pomes together. Without a word, he channeled the hot flames from his hands at the both of them. A stream of fire shot at them like a flame thrower. Jean quickly grabbed Liset's arm and turned them both into smoke again. The fire traveled straight threw them and hit the security desk. When they reformed, Dark Shadow was gone, and the man lay passed out from so much smoke inhalation. For what seemed like 20 minutes, the fire sprinklers finally kicked in and water started showering over everything. It was too little, too late. The rest of the building was starting to go up in flames. It was time to get out of there before the fire department showed up.

"Liset, Liset, snap out of it!" Jean yelled, dragging the man out the front door and onto the sidewalk in front of the building. The water managed to make the doorway accessible again. "We have to get out of here, girl!" Jean pulled Liset by the arm to her feet and dragged her to the car. Liset was still in a state of shock, she was like a mindless zombie. "I'll drive." Jean sat Liset in the passenger seat of the car and ran around to the driver side. Safely in the red car, they rolled away from the building just before the police made their appearance.

"We're going to need help," Liset whispered. It would seem Dark Shadow was back and out for revenge. There are many rumors appearing in social media and reports all over major cities about the dark color metal man. Mostly about his path of destruction and the lives he has affected. It has gotten Silver Shadow's attention, and he has been working closely with Lacey Carson. She is his inside source, and he has helped her solve some very important cases over the last few weeks. By putting a spot light on BIO-TEC and their operations, Silver Shadow and his team decide to start tracking Dark Shadows movements to see if there is a pattern. He will have to pay Lacey a visit, she is at the office and about the go home for the night.

"Okay, Jasson, that's it for me. I gotta go home and get some sleep," Lacey said as she waved good-bye to her coworker. It was late in the day and she was tired. The large carpeted room was practically empty. Only a hand full of lights were on in a sea of gray cubicles. Those were the people still working on things they hadn't finished throughout the day. The same people that have poor time management skills because they spend way too much time around the water cooler talking. Or the type that run back and forth to the coffee maker to pour themselves their third cup. Lacey is a hard worker, and for a while, felt a little unappreciated. Waving to Jasson, the only person she could trust, was the only thing to her that would justify her hard work. The path from her corner office to the elevator lead through the large room of slackers.

"Okay, Lacey!" Jasson said, waving back from his desk. "I'll see you tomorrow." Lacey walked past Jasson's desk as she always did and got into the elevator. The interior was cranberry colored with white tile floor and light brown marble trim. The metal hand rail was always clean and shiny. Lacey sometimes found herself zoning out, looking at the rail wondering who she should thank for keeping it so nice all the time. The buttons were also kept pristine. She couldn't help from noticing after hitting the three button. The elevator went down to the parking garage. The ride always seems to move so smooth. The low playing music entertained Lacey on her short trip down. She got off on the third floor. The first three floors of the building were all parking, making it easier for all the workers to get to where they had to be. Her purple car sat alone on the parking level. The car was a good distance away from the elevator. She made her way to the car with her high heels making the only sound. She struggled to find her keys in her over stuffed bag. Her footsteps echoed through the structure. Her tan button up trench coat over one arm and her black laptop bag on the other. Today, she was wearing her black blazer with matching skirt. Her purple heels matched the purple silk blouse with white pin strips. Underneath her well dress professional attire, she was still wearing the necklace given to her by her mysterious hero and partner. The parking level was kind of dark. It could be a very scary place if you're alone there at night. Those bulbs on the ceiling not offering much light. Finally standing in front of her car, she heard the sound of a glass bottle falling over behind her. Lacey snapped her head to see were the sound had come from. Still peering behind herself with one hand in the bag, she grasped her keys. When she turned back, Silver Shadow was standing on the other side of her car.

"Hello, Lacey."

"Oh, geez! You scared the heck outta me." Lacey looked around to make sure no one saw her talking to him.

"I'm going to need your help."

"You just skip the small talk and get right to the point, uh!"

"Yes, time is short," Silver Shadow expressed.

"Okay, what do you need?" Lacey replied.

"I need all the recent stories and appearances of the metal man cataloged and compiled." Silver Shadow reached out and handed her a data dish. "Put everything you find on this, please."

"Alright, I'm going to need a few days," Lacey insisted.

"Of course, thank you," said Silver Shadow. As Lacey reached for the disk, she dropped her car keys. She slipped the disk into her bag and bent over to pick up her keys off the ground. "So, how do I call you when I'm done?" she asked, standing back up.

"Just press the button on your necklace."

"Well, I'm going home." Lacey glanced down to unlock the car door. "Do you want a ride somewhere?" she said, looking back up. Silver Shadow wasn't there, he disappeared like a magician. "Of course you don't. I hate it when he does that!" Lacey said aloud. Silver Shadow makes his way down the side of the building and to the next street. On the roof of a small four-story apartment building, SGD aircraft is waiting. Using the old fire escape, Silver Shadow heads to the top. The aircraft hovers there in cloak mode with the stairs flouting from its door. Climbing aboard he makes his way to the cockpit.

"Silver Shadow, incoming message from Shadow HQ," said SGD.

"Patch it through," replied Silver Shadow as he sat down in the pilot's chair.

"Affirmative!" A video link came up on the hologram panel; it was Poison.

"I just made contact with Liset and Jean. They have some news about your brother," she said.

"Where are they?"

The Corrupt Shadows

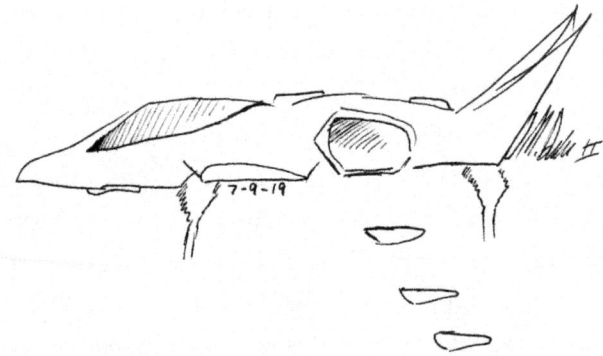

On the roof of a small four-story apartment building, SGD aircraft is waiting.

"I am inputting their GPS location on your HUD. It should be coming up now." A ringing tone sounded with a blinking marker had appeared on the small mini map.

"Ok, I'll pick them up on my way back. Get the rest of the team together," Silver Shadow answered.

"I'll see you when you get here."

"Okay, Silver Shadow out!" The SGD aircraft headed for its new location. The GPS showed Jean and Liset's position wasn't too far away. With the steps retracted and the aircraft already raised to the right height, it took off. After a few minutes, the aircraft hovered over the red car blocks from the big fire.

"We have reached the distention," SGD stated.

"Good, where are they?" Silver Shadow asked, looking on the screen showing the whole outside of the aircraft.

"My sensors indicate they are directly below us in the red car," answered SGD.

"I'm going down. Once I'm clear, lower your altitude and stand by, we may have to dust off quickly."

"Affirmative!" Sliver Shadow walked to the back of the aircraft, opening the deploy ramp door. He ran down the ramp and leaped off onto the roof top of a nearby building. He could see and hear the fire trucks racing to the blazing fire. Silver Shadow approached the edge of the roof and peered over the side, looking down to the street. Just below him was a new looking red four-door car with dark tinted windows. The driver side door opens and Jean stepped out.

"Down here!" Jean yelled, waving to him. She could just make out Silver Shadow's head on the top of the building. Silver Shadow shock his head okay. Before climbing down to the street level, he looked over his shoulder to see SGD still hovering above him. Silver Shadow touched the side of his head where his communication device was.

"SGD, meet us street side," he whispered into his com link.

"Affirmative!" the aircraft answered. Silver Shadow climbed down from the roof using a series of ladders and ledges. Jean walked around to the other side of the car, opening the passenger side door.

"Help me with her," Jean said, pulling Liset out from the passenger seat. Finally standing in front of the car, Silver Shadow stopped for a second.

"What happened to her?" Silver Shadow asked. It seemed she was in some kind of shock state. She was motionless, not looking Silver Shadow in the eye or saying anything that made any sense. She was uttering words in no particular order to herself with limited volume. Jean and Silver Shadow could barely hear or make out the words. Like a mental patient off their meds. Even Silver Shadow couldn't understand what she was saying.

"Shoot, I don't know." Jean answered.

"Let's get her some place safe." The aircraft was already waiting with the door open behind them a few yards from the car. "Okay, Liset, your chariot awaits!" Silver Shadow scooped her up in his arms and carried her to the aircraft, Jean followed. Something was off, he felt like someone was watching them. Silver Shadow stopped right in Jean's path to the open aircraft door. She walked around him without even thinking why he had stopped in the first place and climbed into the aircraft. Silver Shadow turned around, looking to justify his gut feeling. Jean glanced back to see him just standing there with Liset still in his arms. He was standing the middle of the street holding Liset like a child, one step from boarding the aircraft.

"What!" Jean snapped, already up in the aircraft. Silver Shadow felt eyes watching them, a spy investigating them. Silver Shadow could not identify it, this presence he was feeling. The presence felt familiar, then it was gone.

The Corrupt Shadows

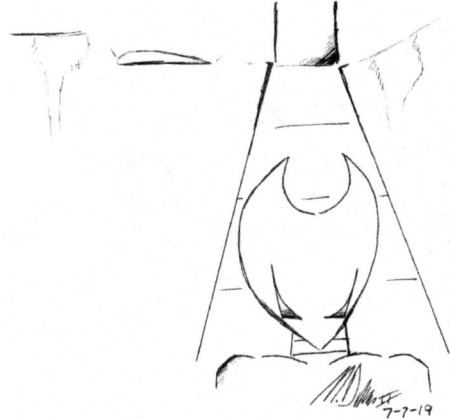

Silver Shadow could not identify it, this presence he was feeling. The presence felt familiar, then it was gone.

"It's nothing! Let's go, SGD, we're out of here," Silver Shadow said, taking that last step into the aircraft. The aircraft returned to cloak mode as the steps folded up and headed for home. Silver Shadow put Liset into a chair while Jean sat down next to her. It was going to be long ride back to the Shadow Dome. It would be best if they made themselves comfortable. Silver Shadow kneeled down beside her and took one last hard stare at Liset's face. She was lost somewhere in her own mind. Seeing there was nothing he could do for her right now, he stood up and headed for the cockpit to check in with SD. Silver Shadow sat in the cockpit chair.

"SGD, take us home," Silver Shadow instructed.

"Affirmative, Silver Shadow," SGD answered. Silver Shadow sat back in the chair with a bit of relief. The anxiety of getting out of there without being seen is always a factor to consider. The feeling of being watched fueled the anxiety like gas to a flame. It had faded for now. "Silver Shadow, my sensors have picked up an accident on the road northwest from our current location." Silver Shadow sat up in his chair and snapped out from his thoughts.

"Bring it up on the mini map," Silver Shadow ordered. The hologram map in the center consul lit up and showed Silver Shadow how far they were from the seen. "Change altitude, adjust our speed, and prepare the towing cable."

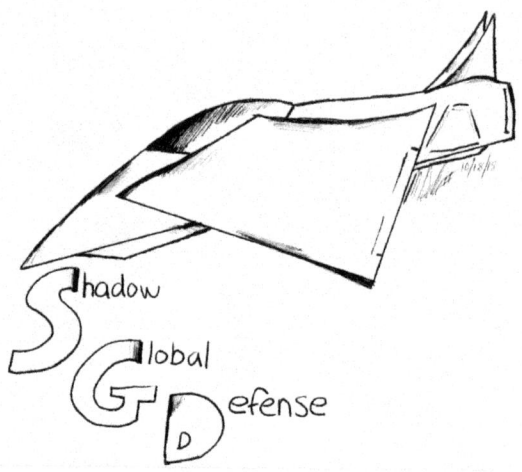

Silver Shadow said, taking that last step into the aircraft.

"Affirmative." Silver Shadow could see on the mini map that the location was very isolated. If the proper emergency response team knows about the accident, it could be a long time before they even reach the seen. Silver Shadow quickly sat up in his seat.

"Alright, SGD, how long before we reach the scene?"

"Twenty-three and a half seconds."

"Okay, take it off auto pilot. I can fly us the rest of the way."

"Yes, Silver Shadow," SGD answered. Silver Shadow grabbed the controls and flew the aircraft lower.

"Which way?" he asked.

"Follow this road another 300-feet. The accident is on the bridge." Silver Shadow could see a location marker on the HUD blinking. They were in the mountains below some heavy fog. A long, narrow black road with the double yellow line in the center was just 60-feet below them. Silver Shadow flew the aircraft low above the road, carving a path through the air. He could finally see some dark black smoke and a large bus hanging off the edge of a wide bridge. Silver Shadow began to slow down the aircraft.

"Switching to hover mode."

"Affirmative."

"SGD, run diagnostics on the bus and find me a safe point to hook the cable to."

"Affirmative, running diagnostic." The aircraft slowed down and was now hovering behind the bus 15-feet away. The bus only had the front two wheels off, hanging diagonally. "Diagnostic complete. The best point of contact is here," SGD said, high-lighting the place on the bus through the HUD.

"Copy, SGD," Silver Shadow answered. He reached over to his right and pressed a few buttons arming the toe hook. As the aircraft hovered, a small door on the outside open. An arm with a very large hook emerged. Silver Shadow flew the aircraft steady as he aimed the hook. He pulled the trigger on the joystick controls and the hook shot out from the bottom of the aircraft. Silver Shadow hit his mark on the back of the bus with no effort. "Okay, SGD, we got a big fish, let's reel it in."

"Affirmative, Silver Shadow."

"Divert all secondary power to rear jets," said Silver Shadow, holding back on the controls. The aircraft began pulling the bus slowly back from the edge.

"Silver Shadow, my sensors indicate the emergency team will be here any minute."

"Copy, cut the cable and return to cloak mode, SGD."

"Affirmative, Silver Shadow." The aircraft disconnected the cable and turned invisible. Just as the fire trucks arrived, the shadows were gone. Silver Shadow sat back in his seat once again with a sigh of relief. He looked forward to being home.

Meanwhile, Poison sits at a table alone in the laboratory, using this time to do some research of her own. The capsule she discovered in her old apartment was under the microscope in front of her. The machine on her left had a sample of Poison's pink liquid, along with a scraping of the residue from the inside of the capsule. Poison wanted to find the truth, comparing the two samples to see if they were related in origin. She stared into the microscope, examining every detail of the capsule. *"This must have been what held the experimental medication,"* Poison thought to herself as she sat back in her chair. Trapped in thought, a sound interrupted her. The DNA analyzer had found a match. The results appeared on the screen in front of her. Poison leaned forward. *"It's a match, the two are the same,"* she said to herself. The truth was hard to bear, her heart dropped. Poison sat back in her chair again, motionless. When you sit somewhere by yourself long enough, you can hear and feel everything around you. Your able to recognize sounds in your environment. Some sounds give you comfort because you know what it is, or in this case, who it is. Poison could hear all the sounds around her. Her whole body still and comfortable. Her mind blank and thoughtless with every one of her senses. She closed her eyes to feel everything around her. Poison's comfort and relieve came from the sound of the underwater pressurized hanger. The long drawn out sound of the heavy door closing once the aircraft was completely inside. Or the vacuum-like sound of all the water trapped inside being removed. Then there is, of course, the footsteps and the kind of low-pitched screeching sound that comes from the hanger door when it opens. After the hanger door opened, Silver Shadow walked in carrying Liset, Jean trailed behind him. Poison jumped up out of her seat and ran over.

"Is she going to be okay?" Poison asked.

"She is in shock." Silver Shadow sat her in a chair. Poison followed Silver Shadow over and knelt down in front of Liset.

"Liset, can you hear me?" Poison asked, waving her hand in Liset's face. She just sat there looking at Poison. "Come on, you are going to need some rest." Poison grabbed her hand and helped Liset stand up. She moved slowly and carefully, being guided like a lost dog on a leash. Poison took her to one of the spare rooms they save for guest. Silver Shadow and Jean watched as they left the room.

"What happened?" Silver Shadow curiously asked, turning to Jean.

"We ran into your twin, that's what happened!" Jean indicated.

"Did you two have anything to do with that fire I could see three blocks over?"

"No, talk to your boy! Your twin did that and almost killed a security guard. He would have barbequed us if I wasn't fast enough!"

"I have to find him before it's too late," Silver Shadow suggested.

"Well, after tonight, I'm not sure I want to run into him again! He scares me and I'm not usually afraid of anybody!" Jean replied. Silver Shadow is worried about what Dark Shadow might do to other people. He is a reckless shadow who needs answers and guidance. Shadows, when first born, are nothing like human babies. Aside from their obvious appearance and defenses, their brains operate on a completely new level. Everything they experience, like love, sadness, companionship, and hate, ultimately defines how they will interpret the world around them. Given the way Dark Shadow was treated in that horrific glass cage, chained up like some sort of animal, it's no wonder he is filled with such hate. Can Silver Shadow show him how to love, show him how to let go of the hate that drives him? Can Dark Shadow accept his brother's help, or will he push Silver Shadow away? Joy in life can sometimes be hard to find. There is often more bad in this world than good. Some good can still be found, like the union of two shadows meeting again in what seemed like a life time ago.

"Aunty Jean!" a voice yelled from across the room.

"Is that who I think it is?" Jean shouted back.

"Yeah, he is getting big," said Silver Shadow. A young shadow stood in the door way. The height of an eight-year-old child with a head shaped like an upside-down triangle. It was folded, leaving a straight round edge with two sharp points in the back, and those red eyes to complete the look. A spitting image of his father and a voice to match.

"It's me, Tyton, Aunty Jean!"

"Oh, come here, little man!" Jean said, holding her hands out. Tyton ran over to Jean and wrapped himself around her. "Look at you, you've gotten so big. How long has it been?"

"Almost a year, Aunty."

"Yeah, and all that boy talks about is when is Aunty coming back to see him!?" Silver Shadow said. "He doesn't grow like a normal shadow. Because he is half human. His growth is in between a human and a shadow. He'll grow faster than a human but slower than a shadow."

"What about his mind?" Jean asked.

"He can still learn just as fast as a shadow, and he also seems to be able to remember everything from the time of his birth to now," Silver Shadow explained.

"Wow, that's good!" Jean replied. Tyton looked up at her.

"Yeah, but I have no power, Aunty," Tyton scowled.

"What are you talking about, Daddy just said you can remember everything. I can't even remember what I had for breakfast half the time," Jean said, still hugging him. The two of them continued to embrace, swaying a little back and forth. Everyone could see Jean loved him like her own son. She was like a second mother to Tyton, loving, protecting, and making sure he would learn right from wrong. From the day she first laid eyes on him, she seemed attached to him emotionally. Lingering around him just a bit more than the others. Having him in her thoughts and more concerned about his well-being.

"But, Aunty, you don't eat!" Tyton replied.

"Boy, nothing gets past you, uh!"

"Nope, Father says I'm the first of my kind!"

"He's right! Listen, little man, don't worry about your power, it will come in time, okay!" Jean said, finally letting him go and kneeling beside him, bringing herself to his eye level. She could sense he was a little discouraged.

"Okay!" Tyton said, shaking his head. "Hey, do you want to see my room?"

"Not right now, baby, maybe later," Jean answered.

"Tyton, I think it is time to do your training classes, okay!" Silver Shadow interrupted.

"But Aunty just got here," Tyton said, wrapping himself around Jean's hips again as she stood back up. Jean glazed back down at him, looking into his eyes and putting her hands on his face. Her hands on either side, making him focus on what she was about to say.

"I'll still be here when you're done, okay!" she said slowly.

"Alright!" Tyton said, letting go. He slowly turned around and walked across the room to the hallway. Silver Shadow watched as he left. He turned to look at Jean. She began sitting down in the chair next to her. Jean's body language said something was troubling her. Silver Shadow moved closer to her, he sat down beside her.

"You okay?"

"I had a son once. I wanted a baby so bad. I went to fertility doctors and took a class. I always wanted to be a mother. It was the only thing I felt I was good at."

"So, what happened?" Silver Shadow carefully enquired.

"I went and had artificial infestation done and I got pregnant. I was filled with so much hope, I finally thought this was my chance to care for someone other than myself."

The Corrupt Shadows

"Did you have the baby?" Sliver Shadow asked, hanging on to her every word.

"Yes, made it all the way up to my ninth month. But the baby was still born, much like Tyton there. When I saw him there, helpless in that incubator, I remembered. It brought up some feelings I had hoped I would never feel again. Feelings I tried to bury deep inside. Only difference was my baby never woke up. It was a boy, just like him. I used to lay awake at night every year on his birthday, wondering what he would be like. I think he would have been a lot like Tyton."

"Is that why you two were at the BIO-TEC archives."

"Yes, BIO-TEC was the company I went after everything had failed. You know, I think they are the ones that killed my baby. When I found out I was part of the same program Poison was, I wanted to know more about it! That baby would have been the only reason to give me a whole lot of pills. I would have taken anything if I thought it would help the baby. They used my desperation against me. My one and only real chance of having a family die with my son. When my baby died, a part of me died with him. They took everything from me. I think in a way Tyton saved me, gave me a reason to keep looking in all this bad for some good."

"My offer to help is still on the table. Together, we can learn the truth," Silver Shadow suggested. Poison walked in; she had heard Jean's whole story. She felt Jean's pain as if it was her own. Poison can better understand why Jean was so close to Tyton.

"I couldn't help but hear your story, and I think it would help you a great deal to find out the whole truth. If anyone can help, it's Silver Shadow."

"What if I don't want to know!" Jean said snappy. She was back in defense mode. Those emotional walls she built around herself came down, if only for a moment. Silver Shadow took her hand and looked deep into her eyes.

"If you really didn't want to know, you wouldn't have gone to the BIO-TEC archive looking for information." Jean lowered her head. Silver Shadow was right. Jean knows now all they want to do is help. She doesn't have to fight this war by herself. Jean just sat there with Silver Shadow and Poison around her for a minute.

"It's too late!" a voice said. Silver Shadow and Poison turn to see Liset roaming back into the lab. She could barely walk, Poison rushed over to help her.

"What are you doing out of bed?" Poison asked.

"I could read his mind, he is filled with so much hate!" Liset ranted.

"Who's mind?" Silver Shadow replied.

"Your twin. The darkest shadow is what he is. He hates everything and everyone!" Liset yelled. She staggered, trying to balance on her two legs like she was on stilts with her hands held out. Liset looked like a drunk preacher spouting her message of warning and caution. Too weak she fell into Poison's arms. Everyone in the room was puzzled, Silver Shadow had an idea.

"I'm taking her back to bed," Poison said, attempting to usher Liset back to the spear room.

"Let me know when she wakes up," Silver Shadow said. "Jean, why don't you get some rest, too!" he implied. Jean looked at him for a second, then she got up from the chair.

"I'll see you later," Jean said. After their talk, he seemed to have an understanding. Silver Shadow has learned Jean will open up but not to share. Only to relieve her own justifications and concerns relating to her past life. She will only let one person see in, maybe unfold from her shell to relieve some stress. Silver Shadow is the only one she can talk to because he is the only one who will keep her vulnerabilities a secret. Instead of parading her emotions around for everyone else like a puppet show. The only one who will listen and not judge. At the same time, maintain her trust and confidence. Silver Shadow was left sitting there when the elevator came up, CD pocked his head into the lab.

"Silver Shadow, you're going to want to see this," he said, waving at him to get in the elevator. Silver Shadow got up and rushed over and stepped into the elevator.

"What do you got?"

"I'll show you, come on!" CD replied. The two of them went down to the control room. Cyber Ball was already there watching a news report on the main screen. *"On to our top story tonight, BIO-TEC has just announced in a press conference the addition of a new division. BIO-TEC Max Force will be another branch of their company geared toward advanced prosthetic limb for the military and their troops. President and founder of BIO-TEC, Vincent B. Sundice, has said he will reveal more about this new division at a later date."*

"CD, we've got to learn more about this new Max Force division."

"Agreed," CD replied.

"I want you to follow up on Mr. Sundice, find out more. Report back as soon as you have something," Silver Shadow requested.

"I'm on it!" CD left heading to the weapons room as the news program continued. *"In other news, more sightings of what people call the metal man have been reported. This metal man seems to be responsible for countless destruction. Fires also have been breaking out all over the city. The police have no viable leads at this time."* Cyber Ball and Silver Shadow just stood there, watching the rest of the news cast on the large center screen. Without a word, Silver Shadow turns in frustration and heads for the elevator, shaking his head. CB turns around in time to see him get in.

"Hey, Silver Shadow, I didn't know you made the news!?" Cyber Ball joked.

"I didn't, that is my twin's bad press!"

Chapter Two
New Complications

Lacey made her way down what was an extremely busy hallway. Her corner office was at the end. She just needs to sit down for a minute and enjoy her already percolating pot of coffee. The juice that makes her shake the afternoon sleepiness. The news station was hopping with people running all over the place. The station was always busy but never like this. It was like Lacey could see the world beginning to change. She always had an eye for this sort of thing. It's what made her a good reporter. Not just some hack trying to run down a story on their way to the top, stepping on whoever was in the way. A person who checks the facts and hears all sides of the story without passing judgment. It was already starting, that title wave of change. The biggest question was, is the world ready? The world was at a turning point, and she may be right in the middle of it. Reports of the metal man were coming in from everywhere. People calling in to the news room claiming they got a picture of this mysterious man. Every one of them trying to get their picture in the newspapers and their rights to 15 minutes of fame. For as far as Lacey could see, those little blinking lights on the phones of almost every desk with some nobody on hold. Every untold story of how the sighting of the metal man changed their life for the better, or more likely, the worst. Some accepting the fact they would be too afraid to go out at night by themselves. Others just looking for the truth, the real stories they would tell their grandkids. Always confusing fact with non-fiction. The other hot topic was the newest story with BIO-TEC lunching a new branch of their already giant company. Only an in-depth story would unearth the real matter or purpose of this new division. BIO-TEC working with the military on what would seem to be a somewhat noble cause. Their reputation was already in question because of some very outlandish environmental actives. Some other reporters seem to think the announcement of this new division is a smoke screen to divert attention from some of the other more important issues. It is said the dynamic of this strong and large company is flawed morally. These are just part of the concerns from the public. Meanwhile in the background, the military is overall using the publicity to strengthen their numbers because recruiting is at an all-time low. Their advertising is geared to keeping the average solider on the battlefield. Citizens who couldn't join were now officially in, maybe standing for something bigger than themselves. With all the many things being considered and discussed in board rooms or around conference tables, one thing is for sure. More people want the truth, and there is maybe only one person able to give them that. As Lacey fought her way through people running from one office to the other, she could hear her name being called. With all the noise and commotion, the voice was faint. It was Jasson Smith, her coworker that has worked closely with Lacey on many stories since she started.

"Lacey, Lacey, here!" he said, trying to catch his breath, handing her a large folder. After finally catching up to her, he could hardly speck.

"What's this?" she asked.

"It's…the information you wanted, about the…sightings of the metal man," Jasson desperately said, attempting to get the words out while trying to breath. He was now hunched over slightly with his hands on his hips.

"Oh, yes! That's right. Thank you!" Lacey replied, putting her hand on his back. Jasson had sweat rolling down his face, now completely hunched over regaining his composure. She took the file from his hand and opened the door to her office. Jasson was still behind her, starting to stand up straight and adjusting his tie.

"Why do you need all that stuff anyway?" he asked, following her in. At first, she didn't answer. In her head, she was trying to come up with a reasonable excuse. She had trusted Jasson more than anyone in this office, but he wasn't ready for the truth yet. Or meet the shadow behind the curtain.

"I was thinking of writing a follow-up story on all the sightings," she answered.

"Oh, okay, sounds good. Let me know what I can do to help." Lacey was standing at the counter in front of the warm coffee pot. Slapping the file down on the counter, she poured herself a cup. Lacey held it to her lips, taking in the fresh smell of warm coffee.

"Don't worry, I'll let you know," she said before taking her first sip. Jasson has worked with her a long time, at some point her trust in him will be tested. Still a bit puzzled, Jasson started to walk out.

"I'll see ya!" he said, leaving and closing the door behind himself. Lacey closed her eyes and took another sip. She turned around and saw Silver Shadow standing there.

"Oh geez!" she shouted, dropping her coffee cup, spilling it all over the front of herself. "I hate it when you do that!" Lacey implied as she quickly grabbed some napkins to wipe herself with.

"I am sorry," said Silver Shadow. "Were you able to get the information we needed?" he impatiently asked.

"Yes, I haven't been able to transfer it to the disk yet." Then the door to her office popped open. Jasson poked his head in. Lacey was on her hands and knees, trying the very best she could to mop up the coffee with small, light yellow cocktail-size napkins.

"Are you okay?" Jasson asked. Lacey, looking up at him, then quickly glanced around the room and Silver Shadow was gone.

"Yes, I'm fine. I just spilled my hot coffee all over myself and ruined my favorite green blouse."

"Oh, okay!" he said as he closed the door again. As soon as he was gone, she looked around the room for Silver Shadow.

"I'll take what you have," his voice said from behind her.

"Man, you're fast. The file is on the counter."

"Thank you!" he said, picking the file up. Silver Shadow tucked it under his arm. Lacey finished cleaning herself up using the last dry corner of the napkin. Looking down at herself, checking to make sure the stains weren't visible, she could not help but wonder.

"What do you think about this new division of BIO-TEC?" she asked. When she glanced up, Silver Shadow was gone again. "I wish he would stick around long enough to have a conversation with me for once." Just because he wasn't there in the room with her doesn't mean he did not hear the question. Lacey did raise an interesting point. Silver Shadow was so wrapped up in his quest to stop his brother, he neglected all this talk about BIO-TEC's new branch. With all the things this company has been involved in, he felt there is maybe a need to keep a close eye on it. Silver Shadow made his way up to the roof. The SGD aircraft was waiting, hovering there completely invisible. As Silver Shadow approached the aircraft, the door opened and the floating stairs came out. He made it to the second step when Silver Shadow heard sounds. Still holding the file of papers under his arm, he quickly glanced around. On the other side of the roof, Silver Shadow could just make out someone standing at the edge of the building. He continued up the last step and took the file, putting it on the first seat just inside the aircraft.

"Are we leaving now?" the SGD aircraft asked.

"Not yet, hold position and scan the area," Silver Shadow ordered. In the middle of the daytime, someone else was sure to see him. He would have to make this fast, no telling what people might think.

"Affirmative," SGD replied. Silver Shadow climbed back out and down the flouting steps. He made his way over to the opposite roof side, there was a man. He had his back to him. From behind Silver Shadow could tell the man had short, black hair and was wearing a gray business suit. He may work in one of the offices below. Silver Shadow read the man's emotions, he seemed to be upset about something. The man may be ready to jump and end his life. Silver Shadow felt compelled to help. He stood beside one of the many large air ventilation units, hiding.

"Are you okay?" Silver Shadow asked the man.

"Uh, what, who's there?" the man shouted. Remaining on the ledge of the building, he turned around to investigate. Silver Shadow walked out slowly. "What the…who are you?" The man was a bit frantic and distrait.

"My name is Silver Shadow, and I want to help."

"Wait, you're that metal man everyone keeps talking about. You know, in the newspapers and on TV." The man started to calm down a little.

"It's not important who I am. What is your name?" Silver Shadow politely asked. The man turned back around to face the ledge.

"That's just it, no one cares who I am!" the man screamed down from the top of this very tall building. "You want to know my name!?" the man repeated, putting his head down.

"You know mine, it's only fair I know yours," Silver Shadow replied.

"I guess you're right. My name is Marvin Glassco. I work downstairs as an assistant.

"What do you do as an assistant?" Silver Shadow asked. He was creeping closer to Marvin with every word. He didn't want to scare Marvin, making him fall. Silver Shadow just wanted to convince Marvin no matter what he was going through, it wasn't worth his life.

"You want to know what I do!" Marvin screamed, flailing his arms around. "I'm the guy who gets the coffee. I took this job because I want to be in the news room covering important stories. Maybe have my own column in the newspaper or start my own magazine, yeah!"

"Sounds like you have many goals."

"I can't catch a break, I can't even get out from under my own life." It was clear Marvin was depressed and at wits end. Marvin looked back and saw Silver Shadow was standing right next to him. "Keep back, man, I'm going to jump 'cause I am sick of it all!" Marvin shouted.

"Okay," Silver Shadow said, starting to walk away. Marvin peered back.

"Wait, that's it?" Marvin yelled back. Silver Shadow stopped and turned back.

"If you want to jump, go ahead. I can't stop you."

"But…"

"But what? You just told me all the things you want to do with your life. You seem intelligent enough."

"Yeah, but!" Marvin was a little thrown off by Silver Shadow's actions.

"You want to write?"

"Yes," Marvin replied.

"You want to have your own magazine, right?" Silver Shadow said, walking back toward Marvin and the ledge.

"Yes, more than anything."

"How are you going to do all that if you're dead?"

"Uh, well…" Marvin turned back to the city view below. The thought of death suddenly didn't look so good anymore.

"Marvin, life is what you make it. The only person standing in your way is you!" Somewhere deep inside, Marvin started to get it. He always knew it, Marvin just needed someone to remind him.

"You're right! I have to take charge of my life." Marvin turned back around, but Silver Shadow was gone. He stepped down away from the ledge. He took one long, hard look back at the city again. From this day forward, he was going to start living life the way he wanted. His life was change for the better now. Silver Shadow always trying to help people, but sometimes they have to help themselves.

Finally, the SGD took Silver Shadow home where he devised a plan for keeping an eye on BIO-TEC. Silver Shadow found Cyber Ball and CD on the lower level in the control room.

"Cyber Ball, can you analyze this file and tell me if you find a pattern?" Silver Shadow asked, handing him the file from Lacey.

"You got it!" Cyber Ball answered. He grabbed the thick white folder that was stuffed with all kinds of different papers from Silver Shadow's hand.

"CD, I have something I need you to do also," Silver Shadow said, pointing at him. CD felt like he was kind of put on the spot. The truth was he couldn't wait to see some more action. Feeling like a spot light was on him, he got up from his comfortable black chair. He followed Silver Shadow and the two of them got in the elevator. They went up; while in the elevator, Silver Shadow seemed very serious. He said nothing, but CD could read it from Silver Shadow's demeanor. After entering the conference room, they sat down at the slowly emerging long white table. Silver Shadow started hitting a series of icons on the surface bring up several 3D hologram images. The images began showing up just above the surface of the table. The task ahead would be challenging for CD to complete on his own. CD, on the other hand, liked to bite off more than he could chew. Always up for a new challenge. Silver Shadow was there to make sure that didn't happen, to make sure CD was not overwhelmed by this task or in any unnecessary danger. A good leader can regulate and assign the right shadow for the job.

"I want you to shadow the president of BIO-TEC, Vincent B. Sundice."

"What do you think I will find?" CD asked.

"I'm not sure yet, but something is off. This new division of the company has got me wanting to discover more about its purpose," replied Silver Shadow. CD started looking over the 3D images of the building where he would find the target.

"I agree, sounds easy enough, when do I start?"

"Now! There is also something new I want you to test out for me," Silver Shadow said. He got up and took CD to the vehicle equipment room. A few weeks ago, Silver Shadow was held up tight in this room for days on end. He was working on countless projects and new tools that may help his team. There were blue prints hung all over the room. CD was kind of excited. CD also noticed something standing in the corner covered with a dark blue sheet. The room was filled with untold possibilities. Every member of the team really rely on Silver Shadow because he is a master of all things. There isn't anything Silver Shadow could not do. He is the best leader for this team and he proves that almost every day. "I want you to take this!" he said, handing CD a small, round metal plate. It looked like two metal circular plates attached together. CD held it out in front of himself for a minute. Looking at every side of it, turning it over in his hands and examining all the angles. He wasn't sure what to make of it, couldn't be a weapon, it was not a shield. Curiosity filled his mind like too much thick tomato soup being poured into a small bowl. Then came the obvious question, the one he should have asked already.

"What is it?" CD asked.

"It is a hover board, it will help you follow undetected," Silver Shadow replied. "Press the button on the side to active." CD flipped it around in his hands and found the button. He had not seen that button before because it didn't look like a button at all. It was very well hidden on the side. With one click, the round disk dropped from his hands and floated near the surface of the floor. Then it quickly turned into two floating metal disks joined by a single bar in the middle.

"Woo!" CD remarked.

"Go ahead, step on, try it out," Silver Shadow insisted. CD jumped on it and a pair of feet strap-like belts fasten each foot automatically. He started

Michael G. Dunkley Jr.

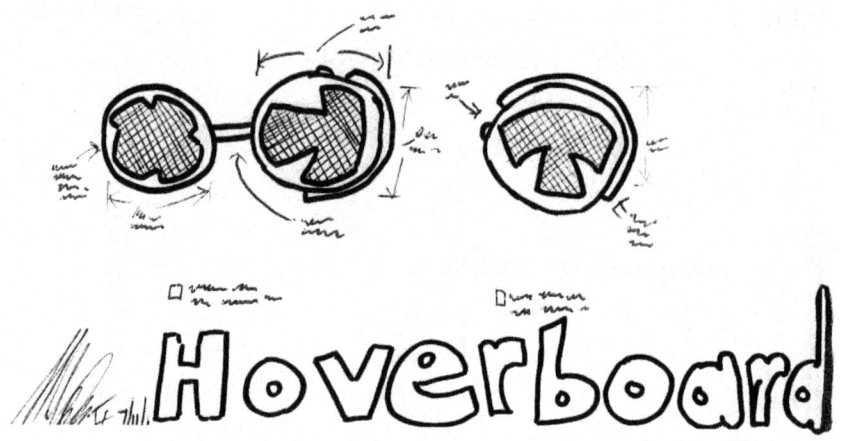

Hoverboard

With one click, the round disk dropped from his hands and floated near the surface of the floor.

zooming and floating around the room in every direction. He started circling Silver Shadow, who was just standing there watching. Having someone test his inventions always made Silver Shadow ecstatic. His team isn't just a group of shadows there to watch his back. They are his family, brothers and sisters, with possibly the same great destiny. Making more tools for the team was like a father buying his kids a new toy from the store he knows they would get lots of enjoyment out of. Silver Shadow's mind is always going a mile a minute. Thinking of new things and trying to find that next step. This hover board was a good start, but like everything else, it could always be better.

"You should have told us about these things along time ago!" CD said, coming to a stop in front of Silver Shadow. The air from CD flying around made all the papers and blueprints in the room flap like leaves on a tree in the breeze. CD looked over at the table where a few more hover boards sat. Each a little bit more different than the next.

"Does it work good?" Silver Shadow asked.

"Perfect!"

"Here, you will also need this," Silver Shadow said, handing CD a new GPS locater.

"An upgrade!?"

The Corrupt Shadows

"Yes, and be careful!" Silver Shadow said, pointing at him like a big bother warning their younger sibling. "I have no idea what you'll encounter. After grabbing your weapons, SGD will take you to a safe drop point."

"I'll let you know what I discover," CD answered.

"Of that I have no doubt!" This wasn't CD's first mission and will differently not be his last. "You should check in with the control center every two hours."

"You got it!" CD said, getting off the hover board and folding it up. He eagerly headed for his weapons locker. For some reason, Silver Shadow looked on as CD left like it would be the last time he would see him. His thoughts outweighed his feelings. *CD can take care of himself*, he thought. The real question would be, *is CD about to be in over his head!?* Silver Shadow said to himself. CD grabbed his gear and boarded SGD. The aircraft was waiting with the steps out and door open. It was parked by itself in the hanger with mission instructions uploading from SD's mainframe. CD entered, dropping some of his gear in one of the empty seats. Silver Shadow remained alone at the conference table, still going over more data. Something was off; Silver Shadow learned to always trust this feeling because it was never wrong. The elevator came up and Cyber Ball ran out.

"I've got something!" he snapped. Cyber Ball ran over to the conference table and started hitting some random icons on the surface to bring up his discovery. Cyber Ball has already transferred the whole file into SD's computer using the scanning profiler. Many pictures came up on the main screen. One of the images was a map of different sights reported Cyber Ball had put together. Silver Shadow sat back in his chair.

"What are we looking at here?"

"These are all the locations from the file you gave me," Cyber Ball replied.

"Then you found a pattern, right?!"

"A pattern, I may have figured out where he might go next."

"Where?" Silver Shadow asked.

"Well, I have only viewed half the file, but so far every sighting has taken place near or around a known BIO-TEC facility. We also now have some new locations as well!"

"We'll have to do some recon on the new ones," Silver Shadow pointed out.

"I agree but, there is still one place untouched." Cyber Ball kept moving the map to bring up more information. "Right here!" Cyber Ball was pointing to the map now on screen. Silver Shadow looked up and saw a small building blinking.

"Good job, we'll leave ASAP!" said Silver Shadow. "SD, alert all shadows to report to conference room for a briefing."

"Confirmed, Silver Shadow!" SD replied.

"Good work, Cyber Ball!" Silver Shadow remarked. Leaving the images on the screen, Cyber Ball sat down in the nearest seat.

"So, where is CD?"

"I sent him on another recon mission."

"What, you mean by himself?" Cyber Ball asked. He couldn't help being concerned for CD. Those two are like a needle and thread, can't have one without the other. They are so much alike.

"Yes, it is a simple assignment. He should be back in a while," Silver Shadow implied.

"Oh, okay!" Cyber Ball answered.

"He will check in every two hours."

"What if we are not here?" Cyber Ball asked.

"I will have a link to SD; if he misses a check in, we will know," Silver Shadow replied.

"Alright, sounds good," Cyber Ball said. He was a little less worried now. Him and CD were close like twins, both from the same world. Within a few minutes, everyone met Silver Shadow and Cyber Ball at the long table. Each shadow sat down at the long white table, one by one. Silver Shadow sat at the head with Poison on his left. Cyber Ball on the right with Liset, Jean, and little Tyton lined up alongside him. Ton sat next to Poison.

"We have a chance to stop my twin and learn more about BIO-TEC at the same time," said Silver Shadow.

"Me and Liset aren't trying to run into your evil twin again!" yelled Jean from across the table.

"Understood, I want to set a trap," Silver Shadow replied.

"So, what's the plan?" Cyber Ball asked. Silver Shadow reached down and hit a few icons to bring up the 3D image of the target building.

"This facility is much like the other archive building, except it has three floors," Silver Shadow explained.

"How do we get in?" Poison asked.

"On the roof, there are many maintenance hatches that lead to several parts of the building. Ton, Poison, and Tyton will provide sniper cover. Keep your eyes out for my twin. After we get the information we need, Cyber Ball and I will wait around to see if he shows up. It is unclear how many guards will be on patrol. The ground floor is our target, it contains all the electronic file in a system database. Once we hit the roof, I'll need Jean to travel through each hatch to determine which is the best way down. Cyber Ball, you and I will take out any guards. Jean, you and Liset will hit the ground floor and take the main computer's hard drive. It looks like this." Silver Shadow put up an image to show them what to look for. On the main screen was the hard drive. It was small, flat, and had a handle-like attachment, making it easy to remove. "If we can obtain it, we should be able to find out something about your project." Jean glanced back at Silver Shadow. That caught her attention. Until now she had been just listening to the plan without looking at Silver Shadow. To be in the dark for so long about your own past, the truth would be her release. The truth would set her free like a caged bird flying inside its tight prison from bar to wooden bar. Still skeptical she asked the only question that made any sense to her.

"What if there isn't anything on that thing?"

"If the information about the project is not on there, this hard drive will at least tell us where to look," Silver Shadow said, reassuring Jean's fear. "Are there any more questions?" Every shadow looked at one another. "Alright, gear up!" Silver Shadow ordered. The team started leaving the table going in all different directions. Before Jean could get up from her seat, she felt someone grab her arm.

"Aunty, did you hear that, I'm going, too!" Tyton uttered with excitement. He was hanging on to her arm like a flag on a pole.

"I heard," Jean answered. Jean was almost a different person when talking to Tyton. Her tone of voice was always nice and soft. Jean cared for him like he was her own. Inside she had the utmost gratitude for him. Tyton was a reminder of her own memories of the son she lost. The feelings she repressed so deep, making it too hard to even remember. With the bad feelings of lose also came the good. The first kicks of the baby inside. The long conversations she would have with the baby while sitting in the bath tub and the water from the shower running onto her belly. She knelt down beside him, holding his hand. "Now promise me you are going to listen to your mother and stay safe." Tyton stood up straight with his chest out.

"I promise!" he repeated. A voice came out from the background noise of the team.

"Come on, Tyton, we have to get ready," said Poison as she walked over to him.

"Alright, Mother!" Tyton replied. Jean stood up as Tyton walked away. She turned around to find Liset just standing there with a stare like she had something to say.

"What!" Jean snapped. Just like that, and the soft, nice tone was gone.

"Nothing!" Liset replied. "That boy loves you."

"So! What do you got to say?"

"Nothing, I just think it's cute," Liset said kind of giggling. They both made their way to the weapons room. The entire team got ready for the mission. Every member of the team, except Liset and Jean, had their own little space of specialty weapons. On the other side of the room was all the rest of the normal guns. Ranching from handguns to rifles and some rocket launchers as well. After they all geared up, the whole team gathered in the vehicle room. With SGD out with CD already, it would give Silver Shadow a chance to try out another new craft. The team all stood in the vehicle room, waiting. One of Silver Shadow's newest inventions sat before them. A pair of giant boat clamps held it off the floor. It was very tall and almost took up the entire room. Only two shadows have seen it, counting Silver Shadow. Tyton also helped his father work on it, like a side project they did together. His intelligence was off the carts, Tyton was just like Silver Shadow in almost every way. Tyton's potential is limitless.

"Hey, Silver Shadow, is this the new transport you've been working on?" Cyber Ball asked.

"Yes, it's time to field test it." Silver Shadow pulled off the tarp and revealed a large black aircraft. "I call it The Shadow Hopper." Everyone was in shock.

"That's hot!" Liset implied.

"What is it?" Jean asked.

"It is a low flying hovering aircraft. It is primarily best used over water but designed for almost any flight," Silver Shadow answered.

"It looks like a really big speed boat!" Jean replied.

"Aunty, I helped father build it," Tyton interrupted.

"Really, I can't wait to go for a ride," Jean answered. Tyton ran up to it. He was so excited to be a part of something this big.

"Father, can I open it?"

"Go for it!" Silver Shadow answered. Tyton ran his hand along the side of it like he was looking for something. He was standing at the back of the Hopper with his hands feeling the surface. Then he found the button to open the door and pressed it. A set of hovering stairs came out from the back. For a brief moment, the team stood there in amazement. Everyone began boarding the aircraft. The aircraft appeared to have two levels. There was a passenger level with six seats and a latter leading to the upper level in the front half. Silver paneling lined the floor and walls. The seats covered with soft blue felt material. Each seat arm rest had all kinds of buttons and switches. Behind the last row of seats was a cargo area with several small lockers, much like the back of SGD aircraft.

"Tyton, you're going to be my copilot, right!" Silver Shadow insisted.

"Really, me!?" Tyton said with some surprise.

"You helped me build it. I can't imagine anyone else being my copilot on the Hopper's first real flight." Before Silver Shadow could say another word, Tyton flew up the ladder to the upper level. Cyber Ball and Ton followed him. Silver Shadow turned to see Poison setting up Liset and Jean in their seats.

"Hey, see if you can contact CD when you're all set here," Silver Shadow asked Poison.

"Okay, I'll let you know," she replied. The women stayed on the lower level, it would serve as their mobile command center for now. As Silver Shadow made his way to the pilot chair, Tyton was already in his seat with his heads up display online. The control panel in front of him was all lit up with varies icons and details.

"I'm ready, Father."

"Good, looks like I picked the right man for the job," Silver Shadow said as he sat down and strapped in. "Three and four status!"

"All weapon systems up and running!" Cyber Ball answered.

"All defense programs in the green!" Ton replied.

"Tyton, would you open the hanger doors."

"I'm on it!" The big gray clamps holding the aircraft started to elevate, bring the aircraft closer to the ceiling. The hangers' floor above the vehicle room began to open. Once the aircraft was clear and fully in the hanger, the floor closed. Leaving the aircraft sitting in the hanger, it filled with the water from the outside and the outer hanger doors open. The aircraft slowly floated through the cold ocean water to the surface, just like SGD would.

"Okay, team, hang on to your seats. Tyton, activate cloak," Silver Shadow informed, talking to everyone in the cockpit.

"Cloak up!" The Shadow Hopper turned invisible. The cloaked aircraft reached the surface, bobbing up and down like a beach ball in a pool. The unstill waves causing the ride for the occupants to be unsettling. "All systems are good, Father!"

"Alright, here we go." The Shadow Hopper rose from the ocean, about ten-feet, and took off. It flew low enough to avoid detection from radar but high enough from the surface to not disturb the water. Making the aircraft invisible to any and everything. It was flying at incredible speeds; at this rate, they would reach their destination in a few hours.

"This thing is great, we'll be there in no time," said Tyton.

"This is just one of the many vehicles I plan to build," replied Silver Shadow.

"Do you think I will be able to help with them all, Father?" Tyton asked.

"I had hoped you would build one on your own."

"Really, that's great!" Tyton practically jumped from his seat. He couldn't wait to start his own project. Silver Shadow was giving Tyton a bit more reasonably. He is the fastest learner Silver Shadow has ever trained. Tyton may not have a power yet, but his skills even now are unmatched. Tyton must learn to use his abilities in the best ways.

"There are a few small ones I think you can handle. Remember what I told you, take your time and follow everything step by step. You can do anything if you set your mind to it!"

"I remember."

"Good!"

"Are there some I can look at right now?" Tyton insisted; he was eager to start.

"Yes, hold on a second," Silver Shadow replied. He downloaded some files from HQ. Silver Shadow sent a few of the files to Tyton's station like an email. A little screen icon unfolded on Tyton's control panel in front of him. The blue prints of new small aircrafts appeared on his screen.

"Wow, what, is that!?" Tyton asked, completely surprised. He was so enthusiastic; the possibilities were endless.

"It's the small spacecraft Doctor Eastin designed." Behind them, Ton and Cyber Ball couldn't help but overhear their conversation. They both looked over as soon as they heard Eastin's name.

"Who is Doctor Eastin?"

"He… Was my father. He died before any of you guys were born."

"So, he was my grandfather, right?"

"Yes, well, kind of."

"Cool," Tyton said, leaning back in his chair. He sat up and started going over the blueprint files top to bottom. He thought this is his chance to prove to his parents and the team he could do anything. When his power came, he would be like nothing they have ever seen. While Tyton was occupied with that, Silver Shadow called down stairs.

"Poison," he said over the com link.

"Yes," Poison answered.

"Any word from CD?"

"No, but I found his location. He is nearing the BIO-TEC building."

"Thank you." Silver Shadow reached over and brought up CD's location on the mini map. It displayed on his screen. He patched into SGD's com system.

"CD, come in," Silver Shadow said.

"CD here, go ahead."

"What is your status?"

"SGD is about to drop me in a safe zone."

"Good, I'll need a report every two hours. If you fail to check in, we will be coming to find you."

Michael G. Dunkley Jr.

"Copy that! CD over and out!" No matter how hard Silver Shadow tried, he couldn't help but think something was going to go very wrong.

*

Chapter Three

Close Encounters

SGD begins to lower altitude to reach the safe zone. CD is preparing to start making his way to the BIO-TEC's main headquarters. The drop zone is on the roof of an old bakery four buildings away.

"CD, we are now in position."

"As soon as I am clear, go into Alpha pattern and stay on station."

"Affirmative, good luck." CD got up from his seat and left the cockpit heading to the drop door in the rear of the aircraft. He hit the button on the side of the door and it opened up, letting the cold night air in. The air rushed into the aircraft. As the ramp lowered, a strong gust of wind drifted in, pushing CD back a step. CD was filled with an intense amount of excitement and anticipation. Not knowing what to expect and loaded for war, CD's eyes begin to glow. With one last look back into the empty aircraft, he turned and jumped. Free falling head first and his arms held out like a sky driver, CD dropped like a rock. The air was spiraling all around him as he fell. CD had the new hover board on his back. From the looks of it. he was about 1,000-feet from the target roof for his landing. He continued to fall, then had an idea. Now about a 150-feet left, he reached back and pulled the hover board out. It was time to see what this thing could do. Just before he hit 50-feet, CD pressed the button on the side of the hover board and threw it in front of himself. The hover board opened up just in time for his feet to latch on. CD looked like a bird doing a nose dive at the water after a fish. He flew low over the roof top of the building just before impact. CD sailed, stopping at the edge of the old bakery building overlooking a dark, narrow alley way. His eyes stopped glowing and the rush was over. Taking a few seconds, he hovered there in one place admiring the night time sky. *"The city is very peaceful at night,"* he thought. Suddenly, a gun shot rang out, followed by a woman screaming. CD snapped to attention quickly, glancing around to find where the sounds were coming from. The sounds interrupted the quiet night like a single pebble in a still pound making ripples. The noise echoed off everything. CD hovered across the roof toward the street side. The tops of buildings were the best place to see everything around, especially at night. The street lights lit up everything below, making it easy for someone to see down. Not so easy to see who or what was up on the top. Looking down CD saw a cream-colored station wagon under a street light. It was the old grandma-type with that famous wood paneling on the side. A classic but a little run down with old tires, possibly the original hubcaps, and a bent radio antenna. The driver door was open with a man in brown dress pants and black shoes was half way inside. The driver of the car was a woman with a blue sweater, and it would appear she was fighting for her life. Two more men on the other side of the car, both wearing black leather jackets, were trying to open the doors. The two of them recklessly pulling at the handles on the passenger and back passenger side doors. The two men were both carrying a large gym navy blue bag each with gray straps. After witnessing this, CD had to act, it was time to even the odds. The man in the driver side door was getting increasingly aggressive. CD quickly spun around like a top hovering back toward the alley way. Floating down into the dark narrow passage, CD flew out onto the street. CD stepped off his hover board and folded it up. He continued to watch the man trying to pull the woman from the car. CD stood there, the men completely unaware of his presence.

"Help me!" the woman shrieked. She was kicking and screaming, fighting every step of the way.

"I just need your car, lady!" the man said.

"No, you can't have it!" The men were obviously trying to get away from something. Was this just a simple car-jacking or was there more? CD put the hover board on his back with one hand and pulled a disk off with the other. The disk glowed orange in the darkness. CD was standing just out of the street light, in the shadows. The hostile man broke the woman free from her vehicle and tossed her into the street like garbage. She let out a yelp as she hit the black top, landing at CD's feet. Peering up at CD from the cold, wet ground, she looked a little dazed and confused. CD held out his free hand for her. The woman's behavior suggested she was not afraid as she grabbed his hand. CD helped her up off the street.

"My babies!" she screamed. All three men looked up.

"Hey, Tony! Who's that?" one of the men on the other side of the car asked. The man half way in the driver side looked up. All he could see was this metal man standing there in the shadows beside the woman. CD's eyes piercing the darkness fixed on the men, along with a strange, orange glowing dim light coming from the disk in his hand. The man climbed back out of the car. The other two men walked around the car toward CD and the woman. These men were not afraid of a little danger. They may even like to fight without backing down, accustom to get their way regardless the cost. Men who look for trouble, just so they could brag to their friends later at the local bar.

"Hey, you, do you know who I am?" the man from the diver side shouted at them. "I'm Tony Geonni!" He started reaching for his gun tucked in the front of his pants. His belt the only thing keeping the black pistol in place.

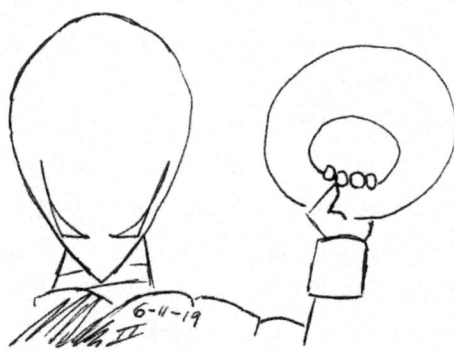

CD's eyes piercing the darkness fixed on the men, along with a strange, orange glowing dim light coming from the disk in his hand.

The other two men unzipped their gym bags and pulled out their own pistols as well. They followed Tony's lead. CD said nothing and stepped in front of the woman. This was going to get out of hand real quick. CD made sure to keep himself between the men and the woman. The men started to walk closer to CD. "Who, or what, are you?" Tony said, trying to make heads or tails out of what this metal man really was.

"They call me CD."

"Oh, yeah! What, is that supposed to stand for somethin'? What are you, some kind of space man?" His ignorance was unjust.

"Get any closer and you'll find out," CD threatened.

"Oooo, look, boys, I'm shaking in my shoes," Tony said, mocking CD. He was holding his hands out, pretending to shake with fear. This guy was clearly a mobster wanna be. With his nice dark colored clothes and his fancy black Italian shoes. The other two men placed their unzipped gym bags on the ground near the car. "And what, you're going to stop us with a Frisbee?" Tony said with sarcasm. "Look here, these are my friends, Frank, and Joe. I think I'm gonna let them pistol wipe ya until you no longer have feeling in your face."

"Oh no, no!" the woman shouted. The two men kept slowly moving closer. CD walked toward them, leaving the woman standing alone.

"Get him, boys!" Tony yelled. Still clenching the orange glowing disk, CD let the two henchmen surround him. Within arms reach, they towered in front of CD, one on the left and the other on the right. These two looked like they don't miss meals, even in their sleep. Both very large heavy-set men. This would intimidate a normal person. CD is not an ordinary man and also knows size doesn't matter. CD would have to hit them hard to put these big guys down. CD's eyes begin to glow with blue flames. In a blink of an eye, CD drops the orange disk to the ground. It was so sharp, it cuts into the street and was sticking straight up in the air like a sharp knife on a wooden floor. The one on the right makes the first move delivering a left-handed punch. CD ducks down out of the way, and at the same time, performs two double punches directly at the man's exposed gut. With so much force, the gun in the man's right hand drops to the ground while the man flies four-feet backward.

"Joe!" the man on the left yells. Joe lays there on his back, out cold. "You're gonna pay for that!" Frank threatens. He quickly threw a right-handed punch, still holding the gun in his left hand. CD blocks the punch and rolls his hand outward, grabbing Frank's wrist. CD's hold so tight, Frank screams out in pain. In one single round motion, CD does a round house mid kick to Frank's stomach. Using so much power, Frank flips off his feet and his body rolls four-yards away. Continuing in a full circular momentum rotating on one leg, CD grabs the orange glowing disk. Snatching it from the ground, CD throws it at Tony Geonni, who is now pointing his gun. The disk coasts low and up to Tony's hand, cutting the gun barrel off. Leaving Tony standing there, holding nothing but the handle grip of what is left of his gun. Making an effort to get away, Tony turns around and starts to run. Dropping the guns handle as he makes his escape.

"Oh, no, you don't," said CD as he catches the orange disk behind his back. Using his other hand, CD pulls a triangular-shaped object from his utility belt. With one click, it unfolds into a large, thick, heavy plated oval-shaped disk. It was clearly not made for cutting with the blunt round edges and no glowing color. CD whisked his whole body around in a circle and threw the heavy disk. Escaping and now ten-feet away, Tony looked back to catch the heavy disk with his forehead. He fell into a bunch of metal garbage cans, spilling the contents all over the sidewalk. CD glanced back at the woman.

"Are you okay?" CD asked. The woman just stood there, frozen. Her mouth hanging open as if she didn't know what to say. "Miss…"

"Yeah, I'm fine," she finally answered. "No one has ever stuck up for me. You really saved my life." Before CD could say anything, the woman ran past him toward the car. Cupping her hands, trying to look inside the car window, she stood at the driver side back car door. "It's okay now, it's Mommy," she said, pulling on the locked door. CD walked closer to the car. He could see two child car seats in the back behind each front seat. The space in the middle filled and overflowing with a box of random stuff. A little hand slow raised from below the car window. The small hand reached up and unlocked the car door. The woman franticly peeled the car door open and almost jumped inside. After a few minutes, the woman brought out three young children. The kids must have been in the back this whole time, frightened. It would also explain why the men couldn't get the car right away. The main reason why the woman fought so hard to stay in the car. "Are you guys alright, Mommy was so worried," the woman said, huddled over them. Holding them all close to her chest, giving them a big hug all at the same time. CD reattached the orange disk to his back. He stood there for a moment, taking in their love for one another. A parents' love for their children is like no other. The woman turned around and saw CD still standing there. "Thank you so much, Mr. CD," the woman said, holding the youngest baby in her arms.

"You don't have to call me mister," CD answered. The children just glared at CD, each little mouth open just like their mother's had done at first sight. With two boys and one girl, CD felt like the spotlight was on him again.

"Oh, right. My name is Jillian, Jillian Gracewood, by the way. I used to own the bakery there until business got slow. I fell behind on my payments and the bank foreclosed on the property. All the stuff I have left of this place is in the back of my car. You know, it's hard for a single mother to pay for a small business and raise three kids. I am talking too much? I do that when I'm nervous."

"It's okay. Nice to meet you," said CD, bowing his head. "Your children are beautiful."

"Why, thank you, CD. These are my three angels. This is Kacey, she's six," Jillian said, pointing to the young girl standing on her right. "Talyor there is four, he's a fearless one," she said, pointing to the boy standing beside her on the left. "And this little guy is Jhnoa, he just turned one." Jillian held him in her arms. His head was resting on her, keeping both eyes on CD.

"I couldn't let those men hurt you, and now I'm even more glad that I didn't."

"Thank you so much, how can I ever repay you?" Jillian said. She turned around, helping the kids back into the car. The two older ones climbed in on their own. She put them in their car seats, making sure to strap them in. Slamming the car door shut, she turned back around, tripping over the two gym bags. The bags still lay by the car on the ground. Jillian almost fell over them making her way to the driver side.

"Are you going to be okay here?" CD asked, watching her almost fall on her face.

"I think so," Jillian said, looking down. Kneeling down beside one of the half-unzipped bags, she opened it and pulled out what was inside. Huge packs of 100-dollar bills filled the entire bag. "Did you see what was in here?" she asked looking up, but CD was gone. He knew what was in the bags. CD could trust Jillian to make the right decision. It will be interesting to see the outcome of this situation. A single mother of three that used to own a bakery in a financial hole with almost no options left. CD flew away leaving the ball in her court. He flouted back up to the rooftop of the buildings, making his way to the mission. He headed for the large glass BIO-TEC building in the distance. CD will now have to track and find his target on the 40th floor of the BIO-TEC HQ. The most likely place to start looking for the president would be in the center top office. It will be a hard place for him to reach and will be heavily guarded. Finally, at the target building, CD floated around the outside of the building, going up to the top. He could see robot security guards through the windows on every floor. *"This wasn't going to be easy,"* CD thought to himself. The robots were more advanced than the ones he had dealt with before. Better armored, up linked to the main security network, and carried heavy artillery. At the top of the building were a few sky lights, that would be his way in. The triangle peaked roof was covered with the traditional dark black roofing shingles. With no flat spots, CD had to pick a good place to slip in. Hovering over to one of the sky lights, CD peered in, making sure there were no alarms or trip sensors. He stepped onto the slanted roof and folded up the hover board. As he slapped it back on his belt, he pulled a small disk off his leg. Using the small pink disk, he cut his way through the glass. CD removed the entire pane of glass. Then he slipped in, dropping onto the floor and quickly ducking behind a desk. CD was in a small office with the only illumination coming from the sky light. The hall was bright white with maroon red carpet. By looking through the glass door, he could tell it was a corner office. CD stayed low and continued to hide, looking over the office. The room was clear, the only movement came from the hall. Roaming sentry guards patrolled the halls in pairs of two. Getting to the center office would prove to be a very difficult task. The office was small with white walls and thick, soft blue carpeting. The dark brown marble desk sat in the center with a couple family pictures on the top. The draws in the desk, along with the one matching colored file cabinet in the corner, were all locked. It would be a waste of time to go fishing through this office. CD kept peering into the hall from behind the door, trying so hard to stay out of sight. If he were to get caught, the consequences would be unbearable. He had an idea; looking down the hall, he came up with a plan. *"It might just work if I could time it right,"* he thought. The ceilings in the halls are quite high. He pulled his hover board off his belt and opened it. CD stayed out of sight until the guard passed the doorway again. It would seem the guards just walked in a complete circle, passing the office every 12 or 13 seconds. He leaned on the wall as the footsteps became closer. There were two guards going to pass, walking in the same direction. The shadow of the first guard's body passed him. Then the second guard's shadow passed. As soon as it did, CD walked directly behind him with the hover board floating at his back right behind himself. He put the other guard out front in the only blind spot. As the guard continued walking around the next corner, CD stopped. With the second guard still in front of him, CD hopped onto the hover board, laying on his stomach, and hovered up to the ceiling. The robot guard turned around to see an empty hall. CD hovered there for a moment above the guard's head. The guard didn't suspect a thing and continued to roam the hall. The lights were mounted on the wall's verse on the ceiling, so CD wouldn't cast a shadow on the hallway floor. He flouted along the hallway over to the office. CD hovered just above the double doors like a stopped elevator between floors. Slowly trying to peer through the small but sight crack of the door frame. He could see movement and lights on the other side. All CD needs now is conformation the person inside behind the doors was Vincent Sundice. The guards continue walking the hall. CD hovers out of sight just before the guard came around the corner. Hiding in one of the many alcoves in the hall, CD pulls a small round device from one of the many compartments on his belt. The round device allowed him to see right through walls. Once he can see inside the room, the shadow scanner can identify facial likeness. It was Sundice, standing at his desk on the phone. Vincent was having what looked like a very heated conservation. CD decided this was his chance to put a tracking bug on his car. He might not get another chance, what better time than while he was on the phone. Tucking the shadow scanner back into his belt, he glanced both ways down the hall. Making sure the cost was clear, CD hovered back down the hall to the corner office he first came in from. Up and out the window, down along the side of the building to the parking structure. The dark blue car with personal license plates made

The Corrupt Shadows

it too easy to locate. The parking garage was dark and cold with very little light and water puddles spread all over. CD hovered there next to the side of the building four stories up, looking inside. With no cameras in view, CD hovered in through the large window spaces toward the only car on the level. In his approach, he grabbed a tracking bug from his belt. CD hopped off the hover board and laid under the front of the car. The ring of the elevator coming to the level sounded. There was only one car here. This could only mean CD's target was on the move. CD jumped from the ground and hopped back on his hover board. With the bug placed, it would be easy to track Mr. Sundice's movements. The elevator doors open and Sundice came out walking briskly. He seemed to be in quite a hurry. Sundice was five-foot eleven and about 170 pounds. He had dark combed back hair with a little white on the sides showing his age. A sharp cut chin and dark mustache completing his evil-looking face. His light baby blue eyes were the only thing keeping him from appearing suspicious. The eyes read kindness, a kindness that would fool and be misread by almost everyone. His black suit with white pined lines running down made it hard to see him clearly. The red tie just seemed really very odd. His black and white dress shoes clicked and clacked as he walked fast across the concrete floor toward his car. A brown leather briefcase swung with his left arm. His arm swung faster than a pendulum in an old grandfather clock. In a tightly grasped hand with those long fingers and clean-cut nails. The car keys in his right hand, held out enough to expose the gold watch on his wrist. It matched the tie clip and cuff links to a T. As CD hovered there, a few questions popped into his head. *"Where was Sundice going in such a hurry? Did the phone conversation have anything to do with were and how fast he was going?"* These are just a couple of things CD wanted to know. He would have to follow Sundice closely if he really wanted to find out the answer to these questions. The tracking bug only works in a limited range. Sundice got into his car. The head lights lit up almost the entire level. CD hovered down closely to the side of the parking structure. In place over the only way out, CD waited for the car to exit. After a few minutes, Sundice's blue, four-door, luxury car came out of the parking structure. CD followed it, flying high above, staying out of sight. CD looked back at the BIO-TEC building as he slowly flouted away. It seemed so much bigger from down at street level. It towered over all the other buildings, it was like a symbol of mans' lust for power. CD continued following Sundice down the street. After crossing the city, they ended up in the old factory district. *"What's here that is so important, most of the buildings in this part of the city are run down,"* he asked himself. As CD followed the car, the answer became clearer. He stopped following and hovered down to one of the narrow streets. Sundice's car rolled down another unfamiliar street. His car stopped at the end, where there was a chain link fence with bobbed wire at the top. CD hid, hovering up behind a tall tree. The tree branches were spread out and wide all around, providing him a nice place for spying from. Just in front of the gate was a white guard booth, yellow colored lights inside it. A High-Tec robot guard reveled himself from within and walked up to the car. After a second or two, it turned around and stepped back into the booth. The gates opened and Sundice's car drove in. The facility beyond the gates was massive with hovering patrol droids and search lights on every corner of the roof. Getting in would not be easy, but that's never stopped CD before. Still hiding in the pocket of tree branches, CD grabbed a branch stepping off the hover board. It just flouted there next to him. He opened up his belt and pulled out a mini camera. The mini cam would broadcast a live private feed to HQ. CD set the camera up in the tree, attaching it to the base. The thick bark of the tree was the ideal spot to put a hidden camera. With this in place, it will also help the rest of the team to discover more about this top-secret BIO-TEC facility. After tugging on it a few times, making sure it was safe and secure to the tree. CD got back on the hover board and flew down to the ground, leaving the mini cam at the top of the tree. The gate was 60 or 70-yards from the tree he was taking cover behind. The fence around the building was at least ten or twelve-feet tall. If CD was to make it over the fence without being seen, he was going to have to do it fast. He reached into his belt and pulling out something the size of a cell phone. It was a mini screen linked to the mini cam. It was able to give him live thermal images of the building. CD watched for a moment, studying the movement of the robot guards and hovering security droids. The R.G.s (robot guards) moved in pairs along just inside the fence line. There were two H.P.D.s (hovering patrol droids) covering the front and two in the back of the building. They traveled in a straight line, back and forth. CD was more concerned with the two in the front. He couldn't risk destroying the H.P.D.s because their destruction may trigger the alarm. For now, he would have to just get past them. There were several windows on the front of the building. He put the mini screen back into his belt. CD had a plan and discovered a gap in the surveillance swipes. CD jumped off the HB (hover board) and closed it up. *"This could be fun!"* he said to himself as he slapped the HB on his back. He stood under the tree below his mini cam. Steam began coming from the holes under his chin. CD's eyes started to glow dark blue. He was ready, standing in a running stance with his back pressed to the tree. CD's hands open and held out behind himself like he was hugging the tree backwards. His dark blue body highlighted in the moon light. His arms held out and feet together. Frozen there like a statue, waiting for the perfect opportunity. Then without warning, CD bolted toward the ten-foot tall fence. The rings of bobbed wire from on the top of the long fence were like the thick crust on a pizza. CD was moving at great speeds across the field of grass that lay between him and the outer perimeter. The tall green grass almost seemed to be afraid of CD, parting a path as he ran. He was within jumping range in seconds, 15-feet, ten-feet, five-feet. At the four-foot mark, he leaped into the air. His body soared up and over the fence like it was nothing. In the air, he tucked his body into a ball. As soon as he cleared the top of the fence, he pulled the HB off his back. It unfolded in mid-air and CD landed on it, hovering over the ground on the other side. Wasting no time, he flew right at the building and hovered above the first-floor windows. CD hovered there for a moment, checking to determine if he had been detected. He eyes stopped glowing and his body cooled. The guard at the front gate walked out of the booth for a minute. The robot looked around, then went back in and stood at the window. There he stayed, hovering in the shadows up high. He wouldn't be able to stay there long because the roaming guards were going to make another pass soon. The H.P.D.s would be making another pass in a few seconds. Glancing up at the second-floor window, he saw a way in. He could hear footsteps on the dark brown gravel path that goes around the whole building. The guards would be close in a second. CD hovered a little higher to the window. He took the small, light purple disk off his forearm and started cutting the glass. He made a hole just big enough to put his hand in, unlocking the window from the inside. It popped open and CD hovered inside. CD could hear the robot guards now passing his position. He quickly glanced out the window, making sure they had not seen the whole in the window. It was safe for now. CD found himself in a room; it was dark and had lots of computers set up. Light brown wood paneled walls with black tiled floor made the room feel cold and uncomfortable. The computer lab had a glass door leading to a balcony making up the entire second floor. CD quickly folded up the HB and opened the door to the big lobby. He looked out to see if he could spot Sundice. The balcony was lined with a silver rail and clear glass mid-height wall, stopping anyone from falling into the lower lobby. CD saw two robot guards escorting Sundice down a hall at the end back half of the lobby. The lobby floor was gray with matching walls. They walked up to a stainless steel door outline with yellow painted lines. Some kind of secret secure wing of the building. Sundice stepped up to a device mounted to the wall. A red light scanned his eye and the door opened. It must be a retinal identification reader. The door was huge, like a vault at a bank, and opened slowly. The two guards followed Sundice in through the secure area. The door started to slowly close behind them. Without even thinking, CD sprung from the computer lab where he was hiding. CD jumped over the rail of the balcony down to the first floor. In mid-air, he threw out the HB and flew over to the door just in time. He stopped the stainless steel door from closing. It was time to see what Sundice was doing here and what he had planned. Behind this door may lay the answer to why Silver Shadow had him following Sundice in the first place. CD, still holding the door, stayed low and slowly folded the hover board up behind his back. He peered in, looking into a long hall. No one saw him yet, he still had the element of surprise. He could see the two robot guards and Sundice walking down the hallway. They were at least 17-feet away. CD ducked in the door, closing it softly behind himself. A well-lit all white round hallway-like tunnel leading to a large room was the only thing keeping him from finding out the truth. CD walk slowly and carefully down the catwalk-like floor toward the end of the tunnel. He couldn't help but feel like a rat in a maze. CD could hear some sounds coming from the next room. It was two men talking, one of them was Sundice. He could not place the other voice. The other voice had a demanding tone. CD had never heard it before, he would need to get closer. As CD neared the end of the tunnel, he saw a small stair case. It went down into a very big circular room. Some laboratory equipped with all kinds of machines CD had never seen before. The voices were coming from the corner of the room behind some of the large equipment. He snuck to get a look at the mystery voice. CD made his way over, he stood on the other side of some large file cabinets. The voices were talking just on the other side. The two men continued to talk, which turned into an argument.

Before CD could piece together what they were discussing, the mystery voice said, "Wait, we have an intruder!" Without even thinking about it, CD hit his distress beacon on his belt. He glances over his shoulder and the two robot guards grab each arm, picking CD up right off the floor. CD tried to struggle free, but the guards just held him more tightly.

"So, there are more shadows out there," Sundice said as he revealed himself. He walked out from behind the large machines. Now Sundice stood right in front of CD, face to face. "You are a magnificent specimen," he remarked, looking at every inch of CD's body. CD played along because knowledge has always been more powerful than skill.

"Who were you just talking to?" CD insisted, still trying to break free. Sundice had this sinister look on his face. He peered backward over his shoulder.

"Why don't you show yourself? It is only a matter of time before they learn about you." Another shadow came out from around the corner.

"Who are you?" CD asked.

"The name is Skade!" the shadow answered. He was like nothing CD has ever seen. Skade had three arms, he had two strong-looking arms with normal hands. The third arm was tucked under his right arm and had a two-foot long hook. It was like a stinger from a scorpion. To complete his already enhanced body, he had a long, highly advanced mechanical snack-like tail instead of legs. The tail started at the hips, and he could slither across the floor. He was about seven-feet tall. Skade towered over Sundice standing behind him. Sundice stepped out of the way. Skade slithered closer to CD, keeping his third arm with the stinger tucked under his right arm. He hunched over and looked CD in the eyes.

"We cannot allow you to escape," Skade said, trying to intimidate CD.

"I don't think that decision is up to you!" CD answered. Skade's sharp-looking third arm unrolled from his body. It slowly edged closer to CD. Skade held the very pointed tip under CD's chin.

Michael Dunkley, Jr.

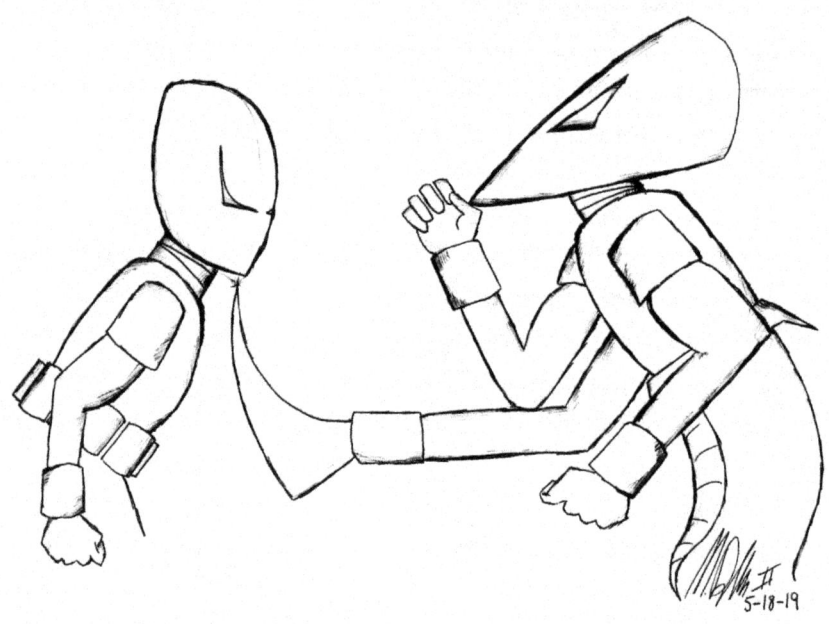

Skade held the very pointed tip under CD's chin.

The Corrupt Shadows

"It would be very disappointing if your friends didn't come to help you." Skade glanced up at the two robot guards holding CD. He shook his head at them and they started to drag CD away into another room.

"You think there are more?" Sundice asked. Skade snapped around to face him.

"Molric has seen them. They will come to save their friend and we will be waiting." CD was taken down another hall where there were more rooms. He was being dragged by his arms. They entered another small room. It was all white with nothing in it. In the middle of the room were four blue glowing circles in the floor. CD tried to shake his arms free as the R.G.s (robot guards) dragged him into the center of the blue circles. These guards were much stronger than the ones he had encountered before. Every time CD moved, they would just tighten their hold on him. The R.G.s drop him and then took a step back, then a blue force field went up all around CD. It was then he realized it was a holding cell. Round and narrow like a telephone booth, the cell didn't give CD a lot of room. The two robot guards walked out and the door closed behind them. CD looked down at his distress beacon; it was no longer blinking. The force field must be jamming all signals, keeping CD from calling SGD. The one thing about being a Shadow Runner is knowing when to fight and when to be patient. He sat down on the floor in the middle of his cell, folding his legs Indian-style, and CD went into a deep mediation. He could count on the team to help. All he would have to do is wait. This new team of bio engineered shadows may have been stronger, but their over confidence will be their greatest weakness. Even now as CD sits there alone, events were in motion. SGD had received his distress alarm and was in route to deliver a report to Silver Shadow. The well-placed camera is still streaming live footage to SGD's systems. Direct action was needed to insure CD's safety.

"SGD to Shadow Hopper."

"This is Sliver Shadow, what is your mission status, SGD?"

"My sensors have picked up CD's distress beacon."

"What happed?" asked Silver Shadow.

"Status is unknown. CD followed the target into an unconfirmed facility. Some voices were pick up by the beacon before commutation was lost," SGD answered.

Michael Dunkley, Jr.

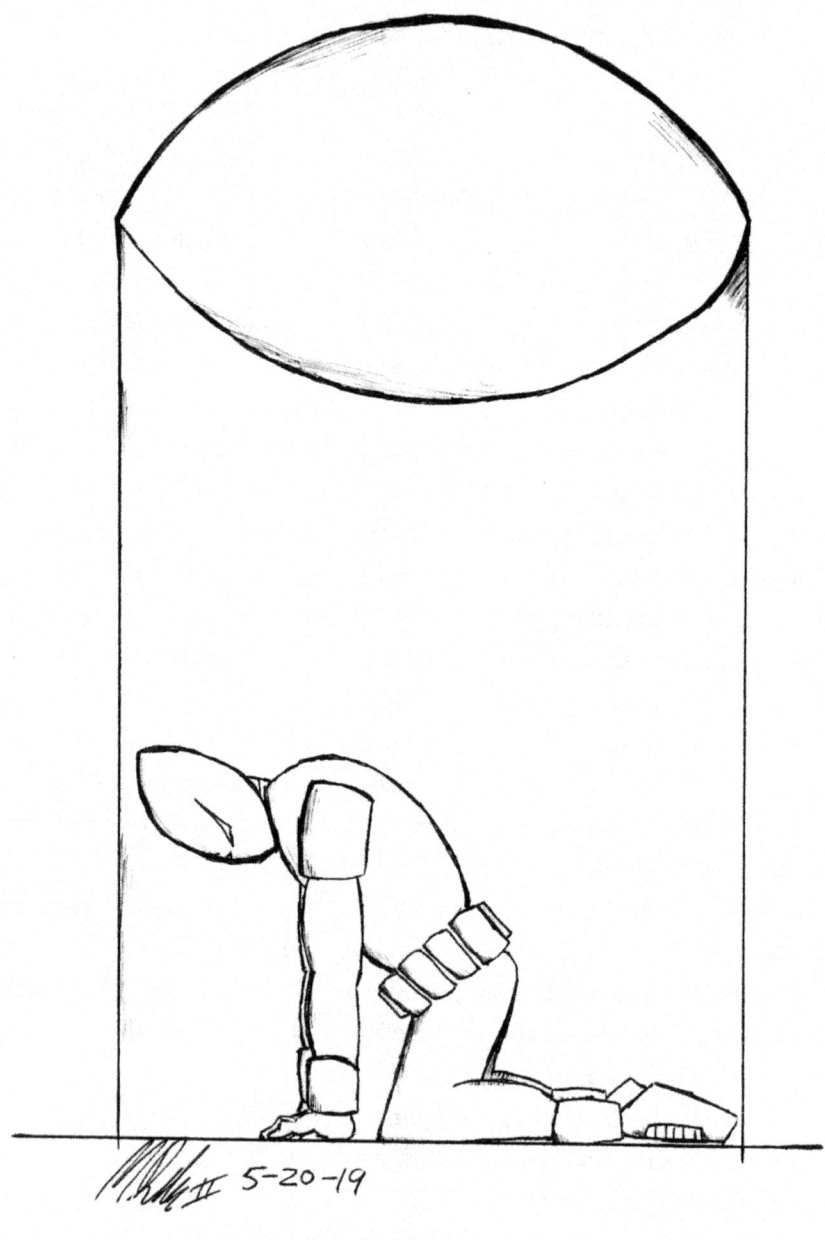

It was then he realized it was a holding cell.

"Who's voices?"

"The voice analysis indicates one CD, Vincent Sundice, and the other was unknown."

"We are in route, give me your location."

"Updating the Shadow Hopper's GPS now."

"Copy, be there in 13 minutes," Silver Shadow said.

"Affirmative!" SGD answered. Silver Shadow made an executive decision in an instant. CD's life meant more to him than tracking down his evil twin brother. Grabbing the pilot stick, Silver Shadow turned the SH (Shadow Hopper) around, heading to the new location. Tyton, his copilot, just looked at him.

"Father, where are we going?"

"CD is in trouble. Go down and tell the others to gear up." Tyton jumped from his seat.

"Yes, Father!" Tyton said, running down to the lower level. Cyber Ball and Ton just glanced at each other. Silver Shadow peaked over his shoulder at them.

"Cyber Ball, log in with SD, try and find out what you can about the facility."

"I'm on it!" Cyber Ball answered.

"Ton, link up with SGD's systems, we will use it for the extraction," Silver Shadow ordered.

"You got it!" Ton replied. The first thing on Silver Shadow's mind was getting CD out. They have been in far worst jams than this. Yet somehow this felt different. The third unknown voice could be the reason for that. Was BIO-TEC making more powerful shadows? They most certainly had the experience in completing the task. If so, what was their plan? There is only one way to find out for sure. After what seemed like the longest 13 minutes, the SH reached the facility.

"SGD, I have designated a safe drop zone. We can converge with you there."

"Affirmative, Silver Shadow!" SGD answered. After a few minutes, Silver Shadow brought the Shadow Hopper in for a landing at the DZ (drop zone). As soon as the aircraft came to a stop, Silver Shadow turned around in his chair to face Cyber Ball and Ton.

"What do we got so far?"

"The data from SD didn't really give us much. There is no records or even blue prints on file," Cyber Ball answered.

"Wait, looks like CD set up a remote camera on the base of a tree in front of the facility," Ton interjected.

"We can use that! Sent it downstairs, time for a briefing," said Silver Shadow. After setting the autopilot, the three of them went down to the lower level of the SH. Everyone was already sitting down, ready to find out what was so important.

"CD is in trouble and it may be some kind of trap," Silver Shadow suggested.

"What are we going to do?" Poison asked.

"We'll spilt up into two teams. Ton, Poison, and Liset will take the Shadow Hopper to one side of the facility. You will provide sniper cover for us."

"Okay," Poison agreed.

"Liset you up for this?" Silver Shadow asked.

"I'm good," she replied.

"Cyber Ball, Tyton, Jean and I will jump from SGD onto the roof. Once we're in, we will locate CD and escape. Snipers, you will have to cover our movements from the outer fence." Everyone shook their heads, they knew what had to be done. "Gear up, we only have a few minutes." Everyone got up from their seats and began to prepare themselves. Ton went over to the gun locker and grabbed a sniper rifle. When he turned back around, he saw Liset standing there.

"You remember how to use one of these?"

"Yeah, it's been a while since the training," Liset answered.

"Here." Ton handed her the one in his hand. "Start by looking into the scope," Ton said as he put it in her arms. He stood behind her, showing her how to stand and point. "Now, if there is anything you want to shoot, make sure you can see it first."

"Okay," she said, peering into the scope. Ton went and grabbed another rifle from the locker. Silver Shadow was in the back loading his M4 when Jean approached him.

"Let me get this right. You expect me to jump from a moving airplane." Silver Shadow just stood there knowing the best answer to her angry question.

"No, I expect you to float down in smoke mode," Silver Shadow replied.

"Right, I knew that!" Jean said, shaking her head. Without warning the ship shook like a giant person just sat on top of it. A voice sounded over the intercom.

"SGD in position." The SGD aircraft landed on top of the hopper and was now attached. The two aircrafts were made to attach to each other in mid-flight or from a stationery location. This would allow the aircrafts' occupants to transfer from craft to aircraft. Silver Shadow walked to the back and hit a small green button on the ceiling. A hatchway opened and a ladder came down. Poison walked up to Silver Shadow; he was already helping Tyton up the latter.

"You two, be careful," Poison encouraged.

"Always," Silver Shadow said reassuring her. Cyber Ball followed up the ladder after them.

"Don't worry, I'll keep them out of trouble," Cyber Ball remarked, looking back at Poison. She was standing at the bottom of the ladder holding onto the side, like a mother seeing her son leave her side for the first time. This wasn't the first time, just a more unplanned time. Or maybe the first time Tyton would be put in danger. Too many things could go wrong. Poison would rather be by Tyton's side when it happens.

"That makes me feel a whole lot better." Poison's sarcasm was noted. Jean turned herself into smoke behind concerned Poison.

"I'll keep an eye on him," Jean's voice said as she flouted around past Poison.

"Thank you." Her thank you was heartfelt.

"You're welcome," Jean's smoke replied. The ladder went up and the hatch slowly locked closed.

"They'll be fine," Ton said, walking past Poison. She was just standing there, still looking up at the hatch. SGD's aircraft disconnected from the Shadow Hopper lifting off. Ton made his way up to the cockpit to take the controls. Poison and Liset followed him up and sat down. They each loaded up their guns. The SH sailed to another DZ on the other side of the building outside the outer perimeter. It was go time, the moment to remind each other what being part of a team meant. The Shadow Runners were now more than a team, they were a family.

57

Chapter Four
The Entrapment

The night was warm with a good breeze. The softly blowing wind makes the trees sway just a little. It was as if the trees were dancing to an unheard song. The full moon was their stage light. In the center of it all was a well-fortified gray glass building. The tall mechanical guards patrolled around it in a foreseen pattern. Two aircrafts approached the facility from the same direction, headed straight toward it. The low flying one was the Shadow Hopper. The other was SGD, setting itself up for a bale out over the top of the building. The two aircrafts flew swift and silent through the night air like a pair of giant paper air planes. Ton is flying the SH (Shadow Hopper), accompanied by Liset and Poison, together, they form the sniper team. They are tasked with providing over watch on the outside of the building. SGD is carrying Silver Shadow, Tyton, Jean, and Cyber Ball, the rescue team. Their primary objective is to infiltrate the building and extract CD. The mechanical guards below unaware of the events that were already about to unfold. This team of shadows defined their race. It just may be the way they have been able to live alongside the human race for so long in secret. Everyone puts a small communication device just under their ear.

"You ladies ready?" Ton asked Poison and Liset as he brought the Shadow Hopper into the first position. They both said yes at the same time. "Poison, you're up!" The back door to the SH open. Poison stepped to the edge, sniper rifle strapped tightly to her back. They were flying low, about ten-feet or less from the ground. "Go!" Poison looked down and jumped. She landed on her feet with a tucked roll that turned into a slow run. Poison was quick at finding herself a safe spot to hide. She glanced up at the SH as it kept going passing right over her. "Okay, Liset, you're up!"

"Okay, let's do this!" she said with some excitement.

"Get ready... Now go!" Liset jumped out, hitting the ground very fast, landing on her feet with a roll. As the SH passed over her, Ton could see her in the process of laying down with her sniper rifle out and ready. She may have been a little inexperienced, but she was learning from the best. Within a few seconds, Ton landed the Shadow Hopper and was covering his assign side of the building. "Sniper team in position."

"Copy, Ton, infiltration team hitting the roof in ten seconds," Silver Shadow replied. SGD was in the final approach descending toward the building. Silver Shadow exited the cockpit into the back half of the aircraft. Everyone was lined up at the open back ramp. Cyber Ball was first with Jean behind him. Tyton was at the back of the line in front of his father.

"This is my first real jump!"

"We're not jumping from very high, it should be easy," Silver Shadow implied.

"I know, it will still be fun," Tyton replied. The green light in front of them on the side lit up. The small team jumped out one after the other. Cyber Ball landed first, followed by Tyton and Silver Shadow. Jean turned into smoke as soon as her feet left the ramp. Her mist trail floated around the outer edge of the building's roof.

"Jean, find us a way in," Silver Shadow whispered. "SGD, go to flight pattern Delta!"

"Affirmative, Silver Shadow!" SGD answered. The aircraft back bay ramp quickly closed and hovered higher. The light from the inside of the aircraft was like a night light, it disappeared from view in the black sky. SGD soared out of sight, flying into some cloud cover. Cyber Ball began glancing around the roof, making sure their landing was still undetected. Silver Shadow had his M4 in hand and Tyton was ducked down behind some large air-cooling units. Tyton lost sight of Jean for a moment. It was a black, flat roof with a ca- pable of big air conditioning units. The surface of the roof was covered with light brown gravel-like sand. At the other end was a light blue steel door. Cyber Ball felt like something was wrong, he could hear a sound. It was coming from the other side of the door. Silver Shadow and Tyton had already heard the sound, too. The red dot of Silver Shadow's M4 laser sight sat in the center of the door. Silver Shadow and Tyton both hid, taking cover beside something in the shadows. Cyber Ball just stood there, he pulled a racket from his right leg. His left hand hit a button on the ammo tubes mounted to his chest. A hovering bomb ball came flouting out, and he unfolded the racket in his hand. Cyber Ball held his ground with his right hand held high in the air. Cyber Ball was poised there like a bull fighter waiting for the bull to charge. His fist gripping the racket as if it was the only thing stopping his body from falling from an edge. Like it was holding all his weight. It was almost as if to let go would be to fall off a high cliff. The door swung open; it was Jean letting the team in.

"Will you put that thing away?" Jean whispered, waving at the team to come in.

"Sorry!" Cyber Ball apologized, folding the racket up and tucking the bomb ball away.

"You always look-in to hurt somebody or blow something up!"

"Have any trouble getting in?" asked Silver Shadow as he emerged from his hiding place.

"Nope! Not at all!" Jean answered.

"Watch yourself!" Silver Shadow said as he waved to Tyton, signaling to follow closely. He kept his M4 pointed at the door way while making their way over to it. In front of them was a white stairway with polished white linoleum floors. It was well lit and almost bright enough to see your own reflection in the sheen of the wax coat on the floor.

"Jean, can you go ahead?" Silver Shadow whispered, taking the lead. She shook her head yes. In a flash, she turned into smoke and flouted over their heads, seeping through the cracks in the walls. Silver Shadow glanced at Tyton. "Stay close."

"Okay," Tyton whispered back. Silver Shadow took point leading the team down the stairs, keeping his weapon aimed in front like a swat leader. The three of them traveled in a straight line. Silver Shadow in front, Tyton in the middle, and Cyber Ball covering their backs. He put out another hovering bomb ball, it floating around in front of him like his best friend. At the bottom of the stairway was a long hall leading to an elevator. Jean formed herself behind them.

"You guys still up here?"

"Did you find CD?"

"I didn't find him, but the guards look like they're ready to kill us. I've never seen so many guns before!" Jean replied. She was starting to panic a little.

"What do you mean?" Silver Shadow questioned.

"They are super High-Tec. I think they're waiting for us!"

"How many?"

"Shoot, I don't know, 100, maybe more!" Jean replied.

"How many floors are there?" Silver Shadow impenitently asked.

"Four floors and a basement I can't get into."

"They must be holding CD down there."

"Agreed, but how do we get down to him?" Cyber Ball asked.

"Tyton, you're with me. Jean, see if you can clear the basement entrance. Cyber Ball, you think you can take care of the guard problem?" Silver Shadow questioned.

"Permission to use deadly force!"

"Weapons free!" Silver Shadow answered. Jean disappeared into the floor under their feet. Cyber Ball stepped into the elevator and hit the down button. Silver Shadow and Tyton stayed there. They watched Cyber Ball as the doors closed. Once the elevator went down, Silver Shadow forced the elevator doors open with the back of his gun. The two of them both looked down into the elevator shaft.

"Get on my back," he said to Tyton. Silver Shadow strapped the M4 to his chest. Tyton jumped onto his father's back. Silver Shadow reached and grabbed the cable to the elevator as it continued to go down. Sliding down the ruff steel cable, they both landed on the top of the elevator in the dark shaft. Cyber Ball was in the elevator below them, alone. Tyton leaped from his father's back and knelt down, peering inside. He used some small hole in the maintenance hatch to see into the elevator. Tyton could see Cyber Ball standing there in the center. The elevator reached the ground floor with a ping sound. The doors open to a hallway filled with robot guards. They all turn and looked at Cyber Ball standing there by himself. Cyber Ball's eyes began to glow. He started rapidly hitting the buttons on his chest, releasing hovering bomber balls all around himself. The elevator filled up with the tennis ball-sized flouting bombs. In one motion, Cyber Ball pulled the two sticks from his legs, unfolding them into the rackets. Before the guards could let off a single round, Cyber Ball was hitting the hovering bombs through the air. Bouncing them off the walls and the floor. The sounds of explosions were going off continuously. Cyber Ball was like a conductor standing in front of an orchestra waving his arms back and forth. Cyber Ball's bomb dispersal was an art, and he was conducting a masterpiece. His precision swings were destroying every target. Each strike part of a carefully calculated plan. His hovering bombs were extremely effective, hitting every intended hostel. Tyton continued to watch with his face glued to the small vent holes on the top of the elevator. Silver Shadow pulled him back a little, all the targets were destroyed. After the smock cleared, there was nothing left. Sliver Shadow opened the vent cover and jumped down, Tyton climbed down right behind him. Cyber Ball folded his racket up, still standing in the door way. He turned and looked back at Silver Shadow, who was sort of admiring his art.

"Good work!" Silver Shadow confirmed.

"Thank you!" Cyber Ball replied. The glow from Cyber Ball's eyes began to fade. The hall was filled with nothing but scrap metal. Body parts of the robots scattered all over the floor. Black charred spots marked up the relatively new white walls where the explosions hit. Cyber Ball stepped aside as Silver Shadow made his way through the door and down the hall. Tyton followed closely behind his father. With his weapon still drawn, Silver Shadow glanced back at Cyber Ball.

"Cover us!" Cyber Ball shook his head okay. They must have been on the main floor. In the middle of the hallway was a guard station. It wasn't much, just a small, white podium-like stand. There were five doors and a set of double glass doors leading outside to the parking lot. They were both blocked by a heavy metal gate rolled down from the ceiling. At the end of the hall was another elevator. Silver Shadow's instincts sensed a trap. It was like they were being tested. Smoke emerged from the elevator doors in front of them. It was Jean and she appeared very quickly.

"A group is coming!" she shouted. Her voice broke the already uneasy tension. Starting to feel more like a hamster in a metal box, Silver Shadow began to push Tyton back. He was following him closely, and a father's first thought is always of their children. Silver Shadow glanced back at Cyber Ball and he was already taking up a defensive position in the hallway. Rackets unfolded, and in hand, several hovering bomb balls already floating round himself. The hall was very narrow, they would most likely have to fight their way out. Going back the way they came was an option, but Silver Shadow wasn't leaving without CD. Before Silver Shadow said anything, Jean floated past him, grabbing Tyton's arm, pulling him behind the guard station. The ping sound rang out and the doors revealed four odd-looking men standing there. They weren't robots, they looked like shadows. If this was true, who were they, and more importantly, where did they come from? The only thing Silver Shadow could do was to protect his team and save CD. He pointed his weapon at the unknown shadows.

"Silver Shadow, at long last we finally meet!" said one of them as he stepped forward out of the elevator and into the hall. His head was shaped like a large metal bow tie almost. Everything about him indicated he was the leader of this group. Whenever meeting an unknown group, it is almost guaranteed the first one to speck is the leader. He was tall and muscular, at least six-foot four and about 210 pounds. He must have been left handed because of where his hand gun sat on his belt. The letters M and F in some kind of symbol was engraved on his chest. It was small and off to the left over his heart. It sat on his chest like a badge of sorts. Silver Shadow wasn't very surprised he knew his name. He was more concerned with some of the obvious attributes of the other shadows behind him. One of them looked like he had mufflers for arms. These large spikes ran along the top middle of his head, like a big chain saw. The other appeared to have half the body of a snack and a third arm with a sharp hook instead of a hand. The last one seemed to have no feet at all. He just hovered there like a small jet-propelled aircraft. At the time, Silver Shadow didn't realize everything he had observed about them was only one of the many problems his team was going to face. "My name is Molric."

The Corrupt Shadows

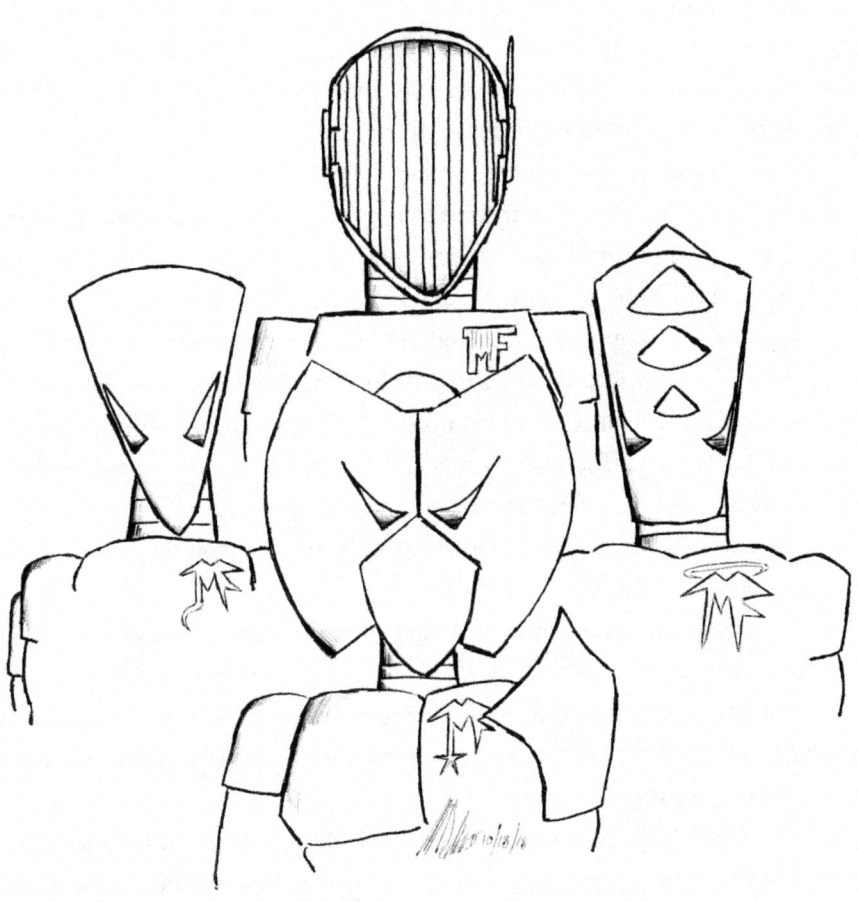

"My name is Molric."

"What have you done with CD?"

"He is safe, for now. He can remain that way. All you have to do is surrender," Molric commanded.

"What are your intentions?" Silver Shadow bluntly asked.

"We want the boy!" Silver Shadow looked back to where Tyton was hiding. Tyton poked his head out from behind the guard station. Cyber Ball was a bit farther back and ready to release some more bomb balls into the air. Silver Shadow turned his attention back to Molric.

"You will have to go through us first!"

"Soufual, Rojet, Skade, retrieve the boy alive!" Molric shouted, pointing at the guard post. Silver Shadow started shooting at Molric. The one he called Soufual ran to the left. The half snake man called Skade slid to the right. The hovering Rojet flew up to avoid the bullets. Molric started running directly at Silver Shadow. After watching the rounds from his M4 bounce off Molric like paintballs, Silver Shadow stopped shooting. Molric ran over Silver Shadow like a linebacker on a football team at full speed, knocking him to the floor. Silver Shadow's weapon few into the air and slid across the floor.

"Go, I'll cover you!" Cyber Ball yelled to Jean and Tyton. He started hammering the bomb balls down the hall.

"Take my hand, little man, time to get you outta here," Jean said to Tyton.

"But my father!"

"Don't worry, he'll handle this. He wants you to be safe." Tyton glanced up at her as he saw his father laying on the floor. Molric was now standing over Silver Shadow.

"Watch out!" Tyton yelled. Soufual was right behind Jean. He was pointing his muffler-like arms at her. Jean quickly turned into smoke as he spread his flamethrowers at the back of her head. As she ducked out of danger, she floated to the side and formed around his arms. She pulled the two mufflers together and held them up over her head. With one step under Soufual, Jean flipped him up and over onto the guard post. Soufual's body flew on his back, hitting the top of the five-foot podium with a thud. He rolled off and slid across the white linoleum floor. "Nice one, Aunty!"

"Come on, boy, let's get you somewhere safe!" Jean peered back at Cyber Ball. He was trying to fight off the snake man Skade. Jean grabbed Tyton's wrist and turned them both into smoke. They flew down the hall into the elevator through the vent holes. They then travelled up the elevator shaft and onto the roof again.

"Tyton, hide up here," Jean said as they both reformed. Letting go she started to turn away and head back down to help the team.

"Wait, where are you going?" Tyton asked.

"I'm going to help the others, stay here! I'll be back for you," Jean insisted. Tyton ran and hid in an air ventilation duct. The air shaft was small, but Tyton had no problem fitting inside. He tried to go slow and carefully. Every move he made caused the thin duct work to bend and flex with each time he shifted his weight. The team could be in some real trouble. It would seem Silver Shadow and his team have met their match. The power of these new shadows was almost too much. Molric stands over Silver Shadow like he was a freshly swatted fly.

"For someone who is as smart as you, why go through all this? It would have been easier to just give me what I wanted." Silver Shadow appears to be out cold. He is much smarter than Molric realizes. Silver Shadow is capable of great power and could very easily take care of these new shadows. Instead Silver Shadow decides to learn more about his enemy. "I am a little disappointed. I thought you would have put up more of a fight. Soon your boy will be my prisoner and your friends outside are being taken care of as we speak," Molric continued to brag, hunched over in Silver Shadow's face, not knowing he was just buying more time. Molric looked up and Soufual was on his feet. Rojet and Skade were in a stand-off, getting ready to tag team and fight more with Cyber Ball. "Soufual, find and finish off the woman."

"Yes, sir," he replied.

"Rojet, bring the boy to me," Molric ordered.

"Y-e-s, s-i-r," the robot answered. Rojet hovered past Cyber Ball and Skade into the elevator. Rojet hovered in the center of the elevator for a second scanning it. He looked up and saw the vent hole at the top. His infer red vision could see the trail of smoke that was left behind by Jean and Tyton. He busted through the much too small maintenance hatch, creating a bigger hole, nearly destroying the top of the elevator. He hovered silently up through the shaft to the roof. At the same time, Cyber Ball stood his ground and prepared to face off against the snake man Skade. He put the second racket back onto his leg, folding it up, and released two more hovering bomb balls into the air. One floated behind him, the other in front. Skade made the first move wiping his metal snake-like tail at Cyber Ball's head. Ducking back out of the way, Cyber Ball quickly spun around, hitting a bomb ball at Skade's chest, knocking him off balance. Without knowing it, Cyber Ball may have discovered these new shadow's weakness. He could see there was a little damage done to Skade's metal armor. Skade went back on offence, lifting his right arm and swung his shaped large-like blade. It was like the reaper's sickle cutting the air around it. Cyber Ball dodged it, and before he knew it, came the one, two punch. Right hand, then the left. Cyber Ball blocked them both with his rackets. Skade's punches were strong and quick. There was only one thing left, and it came at him just like Cyber Ball had anticipated. Skade swiped his tail low in an effort to sweep Cyber Ball's legs out from under him. Cyber Ball did a tucked back-flip over the tail high into the air and hit the second hovering bomb ball at the same spot. It hit Skade in the chest again. Skade went down, smoke was coming from the burn marks on his chest. They were shadows, but their armor was nothing like the originals. Skade let out a loud shout. His metal snake-like tail flapped across the floor like a freshly caught fish on a wet dock. It flailed and thrashed around a bit. It was now that everything made more sense, clearly these shadows were no match. Skade was in fact a race of the shadow, but Silver Shadow and his team were clearly more highly trained. Molric and his band of inbreeds seem to be rather clueless to how their bodies worked. The new shadows have not even reached their full potential. Their mind and body must first achieve a high level of discipline and work together as one. Molric looked up and saw Skade was down. He was still standing over Silver Shadow. Soufual was standing a few feet from Cyber Ball with his muffler-like arms pointed at him. Out came the most intense flame Cyber Ball had ever felt. Before it hit him, Cyber Ball dove and rolled out of the way. He landed on one knee and quickly released two more bomb balls. Just as Soufual stopped the hot flamethrower bust, Cyber Ball hit the two bomb balls. One bounced off the wall and landed inside the hole of the right arm. The other straight into the left hole. Soufual was disabled for a minute. He couldn't use his flamethrowers without setting off the bomb balls that were now jammed in his arm valves.

Suddenly, Jean formed in front of Soufual. She pushed him back a few steps, followed by a strong, low round house kick. She knocked him onto his back and he slid along the glossy floor.

"No one messes with my nephew!" she declared, kind of standing over him. Molric started to draw his gun. Then he glanced down, and Silver Shadow swung his legs around, sweeping Molric off his feet and he fell backward. Molric quickly recovered by tucking into a roll and back onto his feet. In a blink of an eye, Molric finally drew his pistol and fired one round. Silver Shadow ducked and flipped toward him, kicking the gun from his hand. The gun landed three-feet behind Molric.

"Looks like I may have underestimated you."

"It would appear so," Silver Shadow replied. At the same time, Rojet continued his search of the roof for the boy. Hovering up the stairs and through the door, Rojet's movement was very fluent, like water. He glided smooth through the air. Floating from one point to the next, searching. Tyton could hear Rojet hovering around, scanning for him. Rojet was getting close. Peering through a very small crack, Tyton could see his head. Rojet's head was round and kind of shaped like a motorcycle helmet. The visor was made up of several panes of high-Tec glass. Tyton saw the little pieces of glass changing color. The panes of glass stretched around his whole head. As he conducted each scan in different visions, the panes of glass would move. Rojet continued scanning the roof and the air vents along it. Tyton stayed hidden, desperately waiting for him to pass so he could move. Before Tyton knew it, an arm busted through the thin aluminum vent and pulled him out. Tyton fell out and down onto the roof gravel. There Tyton laid on his back with the large robot now hovering over him.

"Y-o-u a-r-e f-o-o-l-i-s-h t-o h-i-d-e f-r-o-m m-e!" Rojet threatened. Without wasting a second, Tyton did a flip up from his back onto his feet. Tyton turned around and bolted for the exit door. Just above his belt, Rojet shot out a little grapping hook with tow cable. It wrapped around Tyton's leg and tripped him, making him fall face first into the light brown roof gravel. The tow cable started reeling Tyton in, bringing him closer to Rojet.

"D-o n-o-t t-r-y t-o e-s-c-a-p-e!" Rojet instructed. As it dragged him, Tyton got an idea. He flipped over on his back and the cable continued to drag him closer. Tyton may be young and have no destined powers as of yet. He will still always be the Silver Shadow's son and a quick thinker.

"You want me, you got me!" Tyton yelled. He jumped to his feet and ran as fast as he could directly at Rojet. Before he could react, Tyton jump kicked Rojet right in the head. Rojet fell back into the air ducts. The ducted work molded to Rojet's body as he fell. Rojet sat in the frame like an arm chair in a man cave, sitting right in front of the television awaiting the big game. Tyton reached down and untangled his leg. He ran back through the door. Rojet was down for now but not out for good. It would only be a matter of time until he was operational again. Tyton jumped down the stairs and reopened the elevator door leading to the shaft. He quickly clenched the elevator cable and slid down it to the top of the elevator again. After looking over his shoulder a few times on the way, Tyton jump through the broken maintenance hatch hole and landed out of sight into the elevator. The doors were still open. He slowly peered around the corner. He could see Molric and his father standing at the opposite end of the hall. A trail of smoke breezed past them, down the hall, and over both of their heads. *"That must be Aunty Jean,"* Tyton thought. Molric didn't see her go by them. The smoke went past and over them through the crack of the other elevator Molric and his team came from. *"Where was she going in such a hurry?"* Tyton looked on as his father and Molric battled it out. Then something or someone caught his eye. There was some movement coming from one of the doorway alcoves. It was Cyber Ball deploying some more bomb balls into the air, getting ready. The bombs free floated around him like balloons. Tyton decided to move to where Cyber Ball was. He would be safer there, and Rojet was going to coming down from the roof at anytime. It wasn't that far from the elevator where he was hiding. Tyton would have to run past Soufual and Skade. Before even considering making his move, he glanced at their limp bodies on the floor. They both showed no signs of life. *"They can't be dead,"* he thought. Tyton was going to have to make this quick. He peered back at his father and Molric. While they were still fighting, Tyton made his move. Hugging the wall, Tyton crept toward Cyber Ball. He slowly passed Skade first. He was half way there when he felt something grab him. It was Soufual, he had his leg. The grip was too strong, Tyton couldn't break loose.

"You're coming with me!"

"Let me go!" Tyton yelled. Silver Shadow looked back and saw Soufual holding onto Tyton's leg. Skade's tail began moving around. Cyber Ball was ready to slap a bomb ball at Soufual's hand. Before he could, Soufual stood up and held Tyton in front of himself like a human shield.

"Be very careful with that. We wouldn't want you to hurt the young boy," Soufual said with a snicker. He had a good grip, and Tyton was struggling. "Hey, I may even forget this inferno bomb is suck in here and blow us both up!" Soufual suggested, shaking his muffler arms near Tyton's head. The bombs were still jammed in there pretty good.

"Father, help!" Tyton screamed. Cyber Ball stood there, ready and waiting for an opportunity. Before long Skade was back on his feet, or tail in this case. Rojet hovered down from the elevator. Once again, the two teams were sort of at a stale mate.

"You see, Silver Shadow, you can't beat us. Admit defeat and no one else has to get hurt," Molric commanded. Silver Shadow turned and faced him.

"There is one thing you seem to have forgotten," Silver Shadow replied.

"Oh, yeah, what's that!" Silver Shadow's eyes started glowing, Cyber Ball's eyes as well.

"My son isn't yours to take!" Suddenly, the elevator behind Molric rang out and the doors opened. Molric snapped round to see CD standing there. His eyes were glowing, too. He was holding a large disk in his hand, it was glowing just as bright.

"Mind if I join this party?" CD requested. He through his disk as hard as he could. It curved around Molric and Silver Shadow, past Cyber Ball, and cut both Soufual's arms right off at the shoulders. Tyton sprung free and ran toward Cyber Ball. The disk landed in the wall next to him. Soufual fell to his knees, his arms lay on either side of him. Before they could grab Tyton again, Cyber Ball launched four bomb balls at Skade and Rojet. They both were hit in the head, the other bombs hit them each in the chest. The bombs hit with such intensity and power, their limp bodies hit the floor like rag dolls. Before Molric could react, Silver Shadow flipped over his head, grabbing Molric's shoulders. He flung Molric six-feet down the hallway into the open elevator. CD jumped and rolled out of the way. Molric's body hit the back inside of the elevator so hard, it left an imprint. His body slid to the floor. Silver Shadow started waving his hands around in a circle. The air around him in the hallway and around the team started flowing like a mini cyclone. Using the air, Silver Shadow forced the elevator doors close. The doors slammed close hard and buckled a little under the presser and force. As quickly as it had started, it was over. Some of the lights in the hall were flickering on and off. Silver Shadow's eyes stopped glowing, and he slowly kneeled down to one knee. His hands clanged tight and arms folded across his chest. An intense steam spread from the holes under his chin like the smoke from a locomotive traveling at full speed. A strong hissing sound followed with the smoke. Silver Shadow stood up, he turned around and glanced back at the rest of the team. They just remained there, checking each other, making sure everyone was alright. Molric was sealed in the elevator, and his team was scattered all over the hallway. Just then a smoke trail emerged from the sealed elevator shaft in front of Silver Shadow. It flew over to Tyton, Jean formed in front of him.

"Are you okay?" she asked.

"Yes, Aunty, thank you."

"Alright!" Silver Shadow interrupted. "Let's get out of here!"

Silver Shadow's eyes stopped glowing, and he slowly kneeled down to one knee.

Chapter Five

Hasty Escape

Outside the facility, the rest of the team waits. Liset is very still, laying there alone in the darkness in the prone position on her belly with the sniper rifle bipod legs dug into the ground. Liest almost looked like a real pro-sniper. Patiently waiting for that one good, clean shot. She held the sniper rifle in her hands very tightly. It was a bit heavy for a person of her size, but she seemed to handle it nicely. Every few minutes, she would look through the scope in Ton's direction. Just so she wouldn't feel so alone. The feeling of loneliness in the dark could be overwhelming at times. She would keep pointing her weapon in Ton's direction to make sure he was still there. It was to remind herself he didn't leave her side. Still no communication from the others inside. The buildings thick walls may have been blocking their signal. Worry started to set in, the mind wonders when you're lying in the dark with nothing to do but wait. *"What was taking so long? Was everyone inside safe? Maybe they ran into a problem? Was CD okay?"* She asked herself these questions for which she had no answers. The trees around her swayed in the night time breeze. In the distance, she could hear footsteps. Liset stood up with the sniper rifle looking through the night vision scope. The sound of brushing leaves came from up above her. Before she could look up, someone dropped down behind. They jumped from the top of the tree she was standing in front of. She felt someone wrap their arms around her tightly, lifting her up off the ground. Someone was holding her around the chest, pinning her arms at her side. Their grip from behind was too strong.

"Hi sweetheart, I've been watching you," said a deep voice. "The name is Nethal."

"What, boy, you better get off of me," Liset shouted. She was trying to shake free.

"I've got orders to kill you. Now hold still, this is going to hurt a lot!" Liset felt something sharp under her chin. She stopped struggling instantly. Too frighten to move anymore, she carefully glanced down. A large hook-like blade was probed against her neck. A million things ran through her mind. She barely had time to adjust to her new life. Liset doesn't want this to be her end. She started to struggle more. A part of her had already given up. It was in this moment she realized. If she wanted to live in this new life, she was going to have to fight for it. Her fear of death turned into anger and aggressiveness. Before she could break free, a shot rang out. Liset looked up, Ton was in the distance, trying to get a clear shot. The sharp hook was no longer at her neck. She felt Nethal's grip around her weaken just a little. If she was going to break free, now was her chance.

Someone was holding her around the chest, pinning her arms at her side. Their grip from behind was too strong.

"I'm not letting you go!" Nethal whispered into her ear. His voice was a little shaky, weak even. He must have been hit with Ton's first shot. Liset became frustrated, time to prove herself.

"Yes, you, are!" she yelled. Liset slipped out of his hold, pushing Nethal back two steps. She took one step forward with her right foot, then did a spinning hip round house kick backward with her left leg. She hit him across the face, sending Nethal flipping over the tree stump behind them to the right. He landed in a small ditch. "What!" she continued to boast. "Say something now! I ain't your sweetheart!" she shouted at Nethal's limp and unconscious body. Ton ran over to make sure she was okay. When he reached her, Ton picked up her sniper rifle.

"Good work," he said, handing her the rifle. Before Ton could say anything more about her excellent performance, they hear gun fire. The shots were coming from where Poison was positioned.

"Hey, she might need our help!" Liset uttered. Ton just gave her a look, he didn't have to say anything. The two of them darted through the bushes toward the sounds. They came to a small clearing behind the facility. Poison stood at one end with a wave of robot guards storming her position. She was caught in a very intense fire fight. The gun fire sounds soon fill the dark and hollow night air. Poison was cut off with two groups of robot guards pushing closer to her position. They were heavily armed with fully automatic weapons. The robot guards were keeping a constant bombardment of gun fire on Poison. Shooting in small bursts and rotating when reloading. Without help and their shear numbers, Poison would soon be overrun. Armed with only her sniper rifle and back up pistol, it was difficult to keep them at bay.

"Could use a little help here!" Poison yelled. Ton immediately went down to one knee and started taking out as many as he could. He glanced over and saw Liest laid down on her stomach, covering from left to right. The three of them were holding the robots back, but they just kept coming. Without warning Ton was grabbed from behind and quickly thrown backward three-feet to the ground. Poison turned around and saw this four-arm shadow standing over him. She began to run over to push him away. Before she could, another shadow ran up on her left and did a sliding tackle across the slightly wet grass. Poison fell, dropping her weapon. Liset peered over in time to see

Ton fighting off a four-armed shadow. Poison was picking herself up off the ground.

"My friend and I suggest you stay down. My name is Cotolek, and my man over there is called Carben-Arms." Before Poison could respond, Liset ran up, holding her sniper rifle by the barrel over her head.

"And my name is Liset, don't forget that!" she yelled as she smacked the stock of the gun on the back of Cotolek's neck. He didn't even move, he snapped his head around.

"You have no idea, little girl." Like a reflex, he back handed Liset across the face, knocking her off her feet. By the time he turned back around, Poison was up. She did a roundhouse kick starting low, spinning on one leg like a top. Cotolek went down to one knee. In the same motion, Poison swung all the way around, kicking him in the face. At the same time, Ton was fighting with an extremely strong opponent.

"You can't stop me, I will crack you in half!"

"You say that like I don't have a choice," Ton remarked.

"Believe me, you don't!" Ton stood his ground. Carben-Arms charged at him like a bull running at a red colored cloth. Ton put his hands out and grabbed him as he got within arm's reach. Once Ton had Carben-Arms, he dropped to the ground on his back. With a short roll and a push off with Ton's feet, he flung Carben over his head, sending Carben up and onto the grass flat on his face. Ton glanced back over his shoulder to see Poison standing there.

"You good?" she asked, walking over to him.

"They're down, for now," Ton answered. Ton and Poison walked over to Liset, who was still laying on the ground. Poison extended her hand.

"How about you. Are you okay?"

"That guy tried to knock me out," Liset replied. "Next time I'll use something bigger!"

"I think that means she is fine," Ton interjected. Liset grabbed Poison's hand as she helped herself up. In a few seconds, another wave of robot troops emerged from inside the building. Just as the troops exited the doors, an explosion went off behind them. The doors almost came off the hinges, swinging into the wall twice. A dark blue disk came out slicing everything in its path.

The disk cut a path through the crowd of robots like a sharp blade in a wheat field. It flew out, curved around, and landed in the solid concrete wall. The disk stuck there like a pencil into a ceiling tile at the office. It came to a stop on the outside of the building next to the doors. After the smog cleared, Silver Shadow, Tyton, Cyber Ball, and CD ran out. The two teams met each other in the middle of the clearing. The robot troopers' bodies lie all around them in small piles. They were like little hills of scrap metal in a junk yard. Some parts still smoking and sparking from the damage they had sustain. Flickers of light in the night from the sparks like fire flies. A mechanical hand or two lay on the soft slightly wet grass, fingers still moving.

"Are you guys okay?" Poison asked.

"Yes, but there are more guards following us," Silver Shadow replied. He had his M4 in hand, the barrel was steaming. Silver Shadow dropped the empty clip right from his gun onto the ground. He quickly slapped another full clip in. Everyone knows what to do. Cyber Ball rapidly punched more hovering bomb balls out from his chest. Tyton ran and stood behind Poison, hugging onto her. CD pulled two more small, red colored disks from his shoulders. Ton and Liset grabbed their rifles and took sniper position on each side of the group. Poison took Tyton back further from the group behind a large rock at the end of the clearing. They both hid there, waiting.

"Hey, where's Jean?" Liset asked. Before anyone could answer her question, the double doors open again. A large number of robot guards ran out, there must have been 20 or 30. The whole team started shooting as they came out. Silver Shadow realized they may have bitten off more than they could chew. They may be in danger and the team was taking heavy fire. The large group of robot troopers were not easy to take down. Silver Shadow observed the way these robot troopers use cover fire. The way they would advance on the team's position. It was a little overwhelming. The team was doing the best job picking off every robot as they desperately tried running in different directions. Every member was shooting at this mob of robot troopers. Tyton was the only one not shooting, instead he was hiding behind his mother. Running low on ammo, it was time for some backup. Silver Shadow stopped shooting and pulled the communicator from his belt. They only had to hold out for a few more minutes.

"SGD, provide air cover on our position!" he shouted. With all the shooting from the robots and his team, there was so much noise. There was no time for mistakes. "Ton, get the Shadow Hopper for our extraction."

"I'm on it!" Ton said. Bullets were bouncing all over the place. In an effort to avoid getting hit, Ton stayed low. When he turned around to head in the direction of the Shadow Hopper, he noticed something. The other two shadows were gone, nowhere in sight. Without more time and given the present situation, he didn't worry about it right now. The group of robots were getting closer to the team. Then there was a light over them, it was SGD hovering above them. It wasn't long before the only sound was SGD's mini guns unloading hundreds of rounds. The tracer flashes lit up the night sky, mowing the wave of robots down like grass. SGD's mini guns were the lawn mower. Ton flouted up in the Shadow Hopper with the back gate down.

"Everybody in!" Silver Shadow yelled. In an instant, the whole team was aboard, except Jean.

"Where's Aunty?" Tyton asked. Silver Shadow just stayed on the ground just outside the Hopper. It was like he was waiting for something. Pointing his weapon in every direction each time, looking through the scope.

"Are we ready to go?" Poison asked.

"Not yet!" Silver Shadow shouted. The noise from SGD's mini guns made it hard to hear. SGD was whipping out any remaining robot troopers trying to approach the team. Plus, the air from the Shadow Hopper was swirling around him. He was focused on the doors and anything that came out. Then a trail of white smoke floated out; it was Jean. She flew to the Shadow Hopper, and inside, Silver Shadow followed. "Okay, let's go." Silver Shadow said, hitting the button to close the back ramp. The back-ramp door to the Shadow Hopper closed and it took off. SGD continued covering the teams escape by lunching several air to surface rockets. As more robot troopers came out, they try to return fire, but SGD went into clock mode. SGD hovered to a higher altitude and flew away just before the rockets hit the doors. The explosion rocked the building and destroyed the rest of the robot troopers. A concentration of smoke and concrete dusk filled the night air. In the distance, a dark black pillar of smoke could be seen for miles. The mission was over and would more than likely shed some light on the truth. In the SH, everyone seemed to relax. The trail of white smoke streamed up to the cockpit. After stowing his weapon, Silver Shadow followed it. Before he could go up the ladder, Liset jumped in front of him in the middle of the aisle. Her hands on the seats on either side of her. Silver Shadow stopped and looked at her. She was clearly blocking his path with no intention of moving.

"What did you do with Jean? I'm not movin' till you tell me!" she insisted. Silver Shadow looked up at the ladder. Jean formed in the cockpit and popped her head down through the hatch hole.

"I'm right here, girl, shut up!" Liset turned around, peering up at Jean like a confused puppy.

"Oh, okay… Well, where were you?"

"Don't even start, I was looking for some stuff. And don't act like you were even worried about me!"

"Well, next time you go running off some place, you better tell me first!" Liset demanded with her hands on her hips.

"Uh ah, why? You afraid I'm going to leave you behind. At least I know how to use my powers. Did you ever stop to think you would, too! But it only works if you learn to accept what you are now!" Jean argued.

"I'll remember that the next time you need my help," Liset said as she turned her back to Jean. She walked back to where she was sitting. The entire team just looked on without saying a word. Silver Shadow could see there was something deeper going on with Liset. In the past, Silver Shadow thought if he just give her a little time and space, maybe she would come to him on her own. There is still a way he could help. For now it would have to wait. He climbed the ladder up to the cockpit. Jean was sitting down at Silver Shadow's station to show him what she found. It was the reason why she took so long getting back to the Shadow Hopper. The reason CD was released from his cell. Silver Shadow glanced over at Jean.

"Were you able to hack the network?" Silver Shadow asked.

"Yes, and I sent it all to SGD's hard drive like you showed me," Jean answered.

"Hopeful we will find something useful."

"I'm not so worried about what they have done. I'm more worried about what they plan to do," Jean replied.

"As am I. Get some rest, we'll be at the HQ soon," Silver Shadow insisted.

"I'm beat, don't got to tell me twice." Jean peeled herself from Silver Shadow's chair and headed to the ladder. Jean was so tired, going from solid to smoke mode took a lot out of her. Fazing and changing Tyton to help him took its toll on her body as well. No matter how hard she tried or what she had now become, Jean will always be half human. The human half will continue to have its limitations. The only flaw was there are no restrictions on the human spirit. The rest of the team, Poison, Tyton, CD, and Cyber Ball, were stowing their guns and gear. Liset was sitting in the back under one of the lights by herself. Jean went over and sat beside her. They both just kind of sat there next to each other with their heads down. Their relationship is like two rocks hitting one another, fighting to see who was stronger. For Jean it was a test of strength and knowing the truth. For Liset it was being included in every aspect. She hated being the only one on the outside looking in. Each of them with their own set of core values and one-track opinions. Their opinions based on some form of the facts they have learned. The rest on pure fiction. The truth was, they could only be strong together. Having one without the other would be like a half of a shadow. Jean's roll is of the big sister watching, protecting, and sometimes pasting judgment. Liset plays the little sister, making mistakes. Never asking for help until it is almost too late. Looking hard for a solution when the answer is staring her in the face. Their arguments only addressed Liset's fears of a younger sister being left behind. Her fear of self-worth and having no place in her older sister's life. It was now Jean's job as the big sister to reassure Liset's confidence. There is always a roll for her to play in the master plan. Jean can be harsh, saying what is on her mind. Using the brutal truth like a weapon to keep everyone out, no matter what. Liset is the opposite, trying to maintain normal, holding onto what was instead of what is. Hard headed and always assuming the rules don't apply to her. Saying one thing and doing another. She keeps herself lock up, afraid to let anyone in. Something her and Jean both share but go about it in much different ways. Liset fears other people might not like who she really is. She seems to have a more difficult time accepting herself. Keeping herself sealed up like a note in a bottle. Coming out her face, showing those claws when necessary, and using people like equipment from a tool box. Contently burning bridges rather than taking care of those friendships. Now being like everyone else is not what she had in mind. It means she will have to share this life and have something in common with other shadows. Jean, on the other hand, has embraced her new life. She sees this opportunity to become more than what she had been. Learning more, and at the same time, staying true to herself. They sat there for a while, Liset broke the silence.

"I can't do this."

"Do what?" Jean snapped, still mad.

"Be like this, I want to be normal again," Liset remarked. There was distress in her voice. "I want my old life back."

"It's too late for that. Get over it! This is who you are now. This is who you were meant to be."

"I don't want it!" Liset cried.

"Too bad, you got a second chance. Would you rather be dead?" Jean suggested.

"No!"

"You better make the best of it. You need to relax and get your head on straight, 'cause I need you."

"What, so I'm supposed to just forget about everything?"

"Yes because we might not have been this way if it wasn't for that company. The people who did this to us are still out there. I need you to stop crying and help me find out who they are," Jean explained.

"Then what?" Liset asked.

"You and I make them pay."

"After we pay them back. How will we live?"

"We just have to help as many people as we can. Something tells me who ever made us and took our lives away is still doing it; they probably didn't stop with just us," Jean implied. Liset sat back and thought about it for a minute. Jean was right, this shadow thing might not be so bad. Not everyone gets a second chance. It had crossed her mind that there were others out there. More shadows like them; she will just have to accept her fate.

"How are we going to find exactly who did this to us?" Liset asked.

"Leave it to me; for now you get some rest," Jean answered. Liset made herself comfortable in an effort to fall asleep. Jean looked around, the rest of the team had their own method of relaxation. Tyton was on his laptop designing something. Jean could see the 3D image floating over the meeting table. Poison, his mother sitting next to him, catching some winks herself. Cyber Ball talking to CD, expressing how much he missed him. He wasted no time bringing CD up to speed on current events. Before they got out of there, Jean hacked the building's computer mainframe, sending all the files she could to SGD hard dive. Little does the team know in those files lay many secrets. The truth about the newest division of the BIO-TEC company and their plans. Back at the facility, Molric and the rest of the Max Force team collected themselves. Their first encounter with the Shadow Runners didn't go as they planned. They did learn from their mistakes and will come better prepared next time. The building was nearly destroyed. Molric began his damage report, as the leader he would take the heat for their failure. At BIO-TEC HQ, Vincent Sundice muddles at his desk, awaiting Molric's arrival. He had already heard the bad news and eagerly awaited Molric's report. The doors to his office opened and two robot guards escorting Molric came in. Sundice noticed Molric was carrying a small, metal gray case.

"Guards, wait outside," Sundice ordered. Molric stood there in the middle. The two guards turned around and exited the office, closing the doors behind themselves. Sundice's office was very large for one person. It was like a small apartment with thin maroon-red carpet and polished wooden paneled walls. You could see the whole city through the large windows that stretched from floor to ceiling. Off to the left, there was a full bathroom with doors next to it. The doors lead to a walk-in closet where Sundice hung most of his suits. He now sat at his desk in the front middle of the room. It was big with a bunch of buttons on the surface of it. A small flat screen was mounted on the top right side. The desk was made of wood with a dark brown undertone varnish and had a shining stain finish-like marble. Two house plants sat on the floor behind him on each side. In front of the desk were two black leather arm chairs. "Sit down." Molric sat down in front of him. Sundice's body language seemed to say he was displeased. Sundice got up from his tall brown leather chair behind the desk. He turned around facing the window, just looking out. His arms folded across his chest. "I must say, I am a little unhappy with Max Force's performance. I had hoped for a better result."

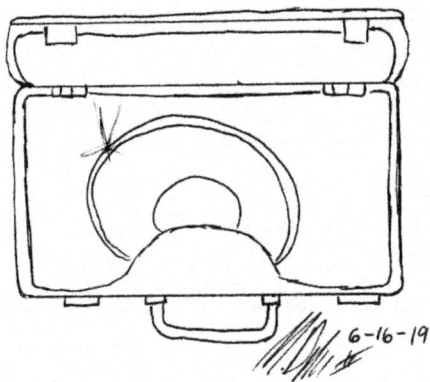

Sundice reached out and opened it all the way. A dark blue light glowed from inside. It was the disk CD had left lodged in the outside wall of the building before they escaped.

"Sir, if I may, we failed to obtain the boy. We did, however, learn a great deal more," Molric added.

"Is that all, commander?" Sundice said, still starring through the glass, keeping his back to Molric.

"No, sir, they left something behind." Sundice turned around to face him. Molric was putting the gray case onto the desk.

"What is this?"

"It is something that will help us understand their technology." Molric popped both locks and open the case slightly. He slid the case across the desk. Sundice reached out and opened it all the way. A dark blue light glowed from inside. It was the disk CD had left lodged in the outside wall of the building before they escaped.

"Excellent, your teams first encounter wasn't a total loss. You have a new assignment. I want your team to deliver the contents of this case to our weapons development and research laboratory."

"Max Force will leave as soon as the repairs are complete." Molric grabbed the case, closing it and stood up. He proceeded to head for the door of the office. Sundice turned back, facing toward the windows again. He said something before Molric reached the doors.

"Commander," Sundice called out, stopping Molric in his tracks.

"Yes, sir," Molric said, turning back around, standing straight up at attention.

"I don't want a reason to deactivate the Max Force team. I will not tolerate failure again."

"Understood, sir!" Molric left the office with a bad feeling. Having this disk might bring trouble for the Max Force team. Silver Shadow and the Shadow Runners never do anything without a reason. Maybe the disk was left behind on purpose. After returning to HQ, the team took some time to unwind. Ton, CD, and Cyber Ball started running some training exercises in the training room. Poison was finally teaching Tyton how to defend himself. She started with simple hand to hand combat techniques. Something all mothers should be teaching their sons. Jean was getting some much-needed rest. Liset sat alone in the dark on her bunk. She was very still, virtually listening to the sound of her own heart. A little illumination coming from the doorway and hall lights that were always lit. Silver Shadow came down the hall and approached her living quarters. He stuck his head in, discovering it was dark.

"Are you okay?" he said from the hall.

"Oh, hey. Yeah, I'm fine," Liset replied. Her bed panel was extended from the wall. Liset sat on the edge curled up in a ball with her arms wrapped around herself, holding her knees up.

"I can't help but notice you're having a hard time," Silver Shadow suggested.

"I want to be normal, but I guess it's too late for that now, uh!"

"I'm afraid so. My instincts tell me your ability is going to be your greatest power and your biggest weakness."

"What do you mean?" she asked puzzled. Liset didn't understand Silver Shadows's riddle.

"If you just open your mind, you could achieve anything. All you have to do is believe in yourself. Acceptance is the key."

"Yeah, I know. Do you think you can you help me with that?" Liset asked.

"Come with me," Silver Shadow said. He took Liset out to the lab. Then he sat her down in a chair and hooked her up to a machine. After a few minutes, he stood back a little, "Shadow Dome, run CT scan on brain waves."

"Yes, Silver Shadow," the AI answered. After a few more minutes, the computer was done. "CT scan complete."

"So, what just happened?" Liset asked.

"Watch, SD, bring results up on main screen." The big screen in front of the chair and the station open. Part of the wall opened as the screen behind showed Liset's results. It showed Liset's brain in a 3D image. "Every shadow has a very unique power. When a human becomes a shadow, the genetics always enhances any natural ability or attribute. A normal human brain is displayed on the right. Yours is on the left. Notice the difference?" Liset sat up from the chair, looking at the screen, trying to make sense of it all.

"Wow, there is so much more going on in my brain."

"Now, with the right training, you should be able to make the most of your natural abilities."

"You think so!?" Liset asked.

"Yes. SD, set up new simulations for Liset. Form classes on disk," Silver Shadow ordered.

"Yes, Silver Shadow. Compiling list now," answered the Shadow Dome. A loading bar showed up on the bottom of the screen. It only took a few seconds. "List complete. Ejecting disk from drive port A now." Silver Shadow stepped away from the chair and went over to the opened disk drive.

"You ready to take control of your power?" he asked, pulling the disk from the drive. Liset glanced up at him. She got up from her chair.

"I'm ready."

Chapter Six
No Choices

A convoy makes its way down dark and secluded streets. Four vehicles in total form a long line, traveling closely to one another. They leave very little space between end to end. A black car with dark tinted windows is leading in the front. Behind that is a black armored van with large off-road tires. The Max Force heavy duty square armored truck is in the middle. It is made out of an old armored truck used to export large amounts of cash from banks. Now loaded down and painted gray with the BIO-TEC logo on the side, it was the perfect vehicle for Molric and his team. Another black car matching the first one follows at the rear. The armored truck was clearly being escorted by these vehicles. All the vehicles in this convoy were dark colored, making them kind of hard to see at night. From above each only appeared under the yellow tinted street lamps. The armored truck fit Molric and his team like a glove. Molric sat in the back, clenching the gray case that may hold the Shadow Runners' secrets. The inside of the truck was cold, dark, and dense. From inside, behind those thick armored walls, sounds were muffled from any street noise. Making it a silent ride for most. The only light coming from the small holes on the back doors. The windows were odd, shaped like port holes on a cargo ship. As the convoy traveled on the highway, the windows would just let a little light in. Every time, like a flash, would reveal the team. Sitting shoulder to shoulder, on long benches inside. The benches were made just like the walls: dense, cold, and strong. The glow from their eyes made it possible to make out each member of this dangerous team. In the darkness, each glow had a slightly different color and shape. The convoy approaches their destination and begins to slow down. The sounds of the main entry gate to the facility could softly be heard. A metal clicks, followed by a low-pitched screeching sound. The driver checks in with the guard at the post in front. They had arrived at the weapons development laboratory code named Otilum. The vehicles all came to a stop in front of the main entrance. Molric stands and opens the back doors, lets his team out. After stepping from the armored truck and making his way around it, Molric stopped to stare at the front of the facility. The Max Force team lined up. They stood there for a minute and took a long hard look. In Molric's mind, there were unclear thoughts of what uncertainties his team would encounter. The men in the other vehicles got out and secured the area. They formed a circle around the Max Force team line. The building was in the middle of nowhere. Nothing but sand and short brushes for as far as the eye could see. The structure itself looked more like a military concrete bunker. It also wasn't very tall, indicating that there could be more underground levels. The building matched the sand in color as well. The half-bared build surrounded by sand like it had been born there, or just emerged from the ground like a plant. Three men came out from the double glass doors that were mounted to big black glass windows. Just above those doors was long rectangular windows stretching the whole length of the building with more black colored glass. Behind those long glass windows is an observation room. The room covered all of the top floor. The guards on patrol could see anything coming at the building in all directions. On the roof was a communications array for satellite feeds and up links to headquarters. The three men approached Molric, greeting the team. They walked up in a line. They all had standard issue military desert camouflage. They all looked the same, except the one in the middle, he had a different kind of uniform. He also had a hat instead of a helmet. He must have been the one in charge of this place. Molric could tell by the ribbons and badges on his chest that he is the rank of major.

"Commander Molric, we were told to expect your team's arrival. My name is Major William Docard."

The Corrupt Shadows

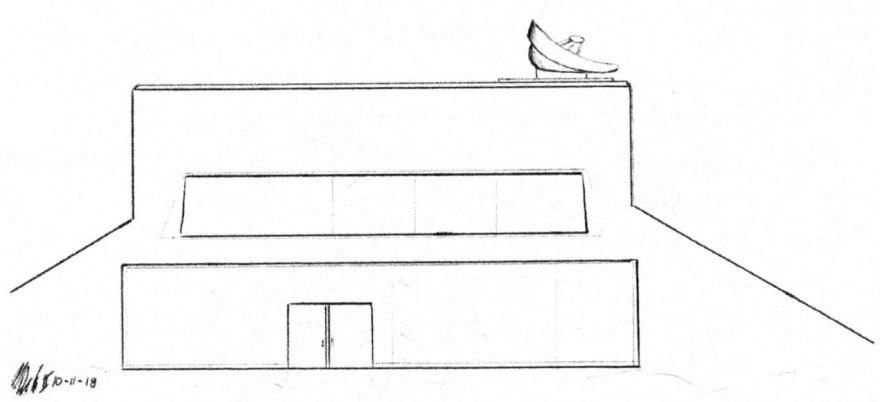

They had arrived at the weapons development laboratory code named Otilum.

"Major, I'm carrying something of great importance."

"Yes, I know…" the major started to rebuttal.

"Then you should know I'll feel better when I have put this case in the right hands." Major Docard stopped for a second and just starred at Molric.

"Yes… Yes, of course. This way," the major reacted holding his hand out and stepping aside. Molric had a strange first impression of the Major. It was easy to see the company doesn't let him out much. Molric could remember back when he was just starting out. Some of the military personal he served with always complaining. He heard them mention they would stay at a signal post for sometimes years before being rotated. The rotations on reassignments could be rough going and tough to deal with. The major here seemed to be more like a star stuck fan than a leader. The way he acted, the way he showed the team in, everything. Or the major had other orders and he was a little nevus of what Molric would do to him if he caught wind of some kind of trap. It was the only other way to describe the major's actions and demeanor. As the team walked into the complex, Molric began to wonder. *"What do they really do here?"* BIO-TEC kept this place a secret, even from him. Whatever this place is, it was well guarded. The team was led by the Major in and they were escorted by about a dozen guards. After opening the glass doors, they entered the first room. It was a large lobby with big dark brown tile and white wood paneled walls. In front of them was a guard post with a desk and metal detector. There stood five guards armed with heavy state of the art fire power. The weapons were like nothing Molric had seen before. All the base personal had bright yellow badges, so they wouldn't have to be checked. As soon as the guards saw the Major, they all stepped aside. One of them hit a button near the desk and the metal detector folded into the floor. It created a clear path for the Major and the Max Force team as they walked through. The team walked down a wide hall to a big cargo-sized elevator. Cameras on the ceiling followed their every movement the whole way, right from the time they entered the glass doors. Molric took notice right away. He had an eerie feeling about it. Before the group reached the elevator, the huge gray-colored doors opened. Six robot guards stepped out and moved three to each side. They stood in the hallway and waited. The Major turned around and pointed to one of the many human guards still following to stay. The group of human guards stopped. The Major,

Molric, Soufual, Skade, Rojet, Cotolek, and Carben Arms entered the elevator. The big gray elevator doors stayed open. The interior of the elevator walls was made out of mirrors, nothing but reflections all around. Molric noticed there were no buttons on the inside. The Major pulled a key from his belt. He inserted the key and gave it a half turn. The doors shut and the elevator began to move. Molric glanced back at the others. They were as uneasy about this as he was. Molric gave Soufual the be ready for anything look. Being the leader of an elite unit like the Max Force team means your teammates rely on you. You come to count on them to support you and your decisions. They have been together for a long time, like a family. The looks they give one another tend to mean more and can be understood easier. They know the team comes first and the leader will honor it. The team will watch each other's backs till the end. It's like a code they live by and sometimes die for. It's not always easy to do, and it is even harder to live by. Those who have not fought in a war or served in a combat unit can never really understand. It's not about the war or the fight you're in, it's about the teammate next to you. Fighting and doing their part to make sure at the end everyone can go home. Putting all the bad behind them and maybe finding some peace. In the grand scheme of things, Molric was like the number two. The only person he had to report to was Sundice. If Sundice was already talking about dismantling the Max Force unit, it meant BIO-TEC might already have a replacement team. These things were bouncing around in Molric's mind. He is a soldier who wasn't thinking like one. He was supposed to be a grunt that just followed orders, but Molric is too smart for that now. Sundice is like his commanding officer. At some point, he would have to disobey orders. It would also mean Molric could no longer trust the orders being given. He would have to evolve and become his own leader looking out for his team. This action could not only be dangerous for him but for his team as well. There is nothing more important to him than the survival of the team. His thoughts were interrupted when the Major turned around to faced him.

"Now that we are safely underground, I will take the case." Molric peered back at his team before handing over the case.

"It's all yours," Molric remarked.

"Thank you, commander," Docard replied. "Now I will show you where your team can rest." The elevator finally stopped and the doors open. The Major walked them out into what looked like living quarters. The floor level they entered was large. It had two rooms on either side and one at the end. There were two bathrooms in the back and a large meeting table in the middle. Security cameras were in almost every corner, as if to say the team couldn't be trusted. "You and your team should be comfortable here."

"How long until we can expect a briefing?" Molric asked, testing the Major's answer.

"Four hours, commander. Get some rest." Major Docard turned around, the case still in hand, and got back in the elevator. The Major had a sly smirk upon his face. Molric's theory about what was happening may have been right. The Major was definitely hiding something from them. In this building, the whole team felt like prisoners rather than guests. The thought of trying to call the elevator crossed his mind. Molric will now face some hard choices, and in doing so, he will now have to tell the team what might happen. Molric will also have to depend on them more than ever. The dark blue glowing disk was now in the hands of the BIO-TEC Max Force division. Regardless what happens to it, this is a good thing for the Shadow Runners. It was no accident the disk was left behind. If Silver Shadow was going to find out what BIO-TEC was up to, he would have to go fishing. In the last few days, their team has analyzed every and all known BIO-TEC facilities. It wasn't long before Silver Shadow would have to find all the new locations. The BIO-TEC company is expanding more every day. With new laboratories, offices, and test sights popping up everywhere. The plan to find these new places was already in effect. The disk has an advanced tracking locater attached on the inside of it. CD and Cyber Ball now sit in the control room of the Shadow Dome, tracking it. CD is searching for his blue disk signal. While Cyber Ball is reviewing all the raw data from SGD system hard drive, the Shadow Dome's AI computer is breaking all the information down into easier to read formatted files. The system is decrypting each file. The elevator comes down and Silver Shadow steps out.

"How is it going?"

"Slowly, there is about 75 terabytes of data," Cyber Ball answered.

"How long will it take for SD to finish decrypting the information?" Silver Shadow asked.

"At this rate, 72 hours, at least."

"Keep me posted," Silver Shadow replied. He turned around to CD, who was sitting in the chair next to Cyber Ball. "Did you pin point where the disk signal is coming from?"

"Not yet. I set it on a timer, so the disk could past through bug sweeps. I still have a few minutes before it starts relaying a signal. No matter where it is, we should be able to track it." The two of them stood there motion less for an instant. CD set up the main screen in front of them. A red beacon popped up on the world map. SD immediately tracked down its location. Its search program narrowed it to an area, then known nearby street. It stopped on a small one-level structure.

"Silver Shadow, take a look at this," Cyber Ball insisted, trying to get his attention. Silver Shadow turned back around.

"Find something?" he asked.

"SD is still cycling through all the data, but I've started reviewing the processed files."

"What did you come across?" Silver Shadow impatiently asked.

"The military record and profiles of all the Max Force members. Check this out," Cyber Ball said, scrolling down the files on his screen. "Turns out they're all former military. The leader, Molric, was chosen from birth to undergo a secret military project."

"Does it have a name?"

"It doesn't say, but whatever it was, it must have worked. The file says something about a human ageing experimentation. By the time he was 20, he had been in every branch of the military."

"Meaning what?" Silver Shadow inquired.

"It says here he achieved the highs rank in every branch. It would make him the youngest military expert on earth. We're talking urban tactical warfare, C.Q.B, advance weapons, pilot training, and combat sniper experience and the list goes on."

"He must have been brain washed from the beginning," Silver Shadow implied.

"I guess so," Cyber Ball answered.

"What about the others?"

"Well, Soufual is an ex-fighter pilot. He went down in a crash and burned 90 percent of his body. He was a volunteer for this advanced shadow program."

"What else?"

"Rojet is a super self-learning A.I. It can fly at mock three. Repair itself with anything in its environment. It is also equipped with ten different spectral imaging. That includes ex-ray, night, and thermal vision," Cyber Ball described.

"We wouldn't want it to be too easy." Silver Shadow remarked.

"Nethal is an ex-army ranger. He saved six men in his unit by jumping onto a live grenade. He survived but lost his left hip and five of his left lower ribs."

"They all must have wanted a second chance. BIO-TEC gave them one and took everything human about them away."

"There's more. Skade was a marine trooper that stepped on a mine and lost his legs. Listen to this: "*When subject was asked what upgrade he wanted, all he kept saying was the word snake.*" It would explain why he had a mechanical snake tail," Cyber Ball said, reading right from the profile.

"You're right, what about the others?"

"Looks like Cotolek was a navy sniper. He was sent on a mission and was captured. He was held for almost a year before he escaped. Four men went in and he was the only survivor. After he got back, his commanding officer gave him a choice of his next assignment. He chose special teams," Cyber Ball explained.

"What's the story with the last member?" asked Silver Shadow, pointing to the screen.

"The last one is a bit of an odd ball. They call him Carben Arms or CA for short. He was a jungle commando stationed on a deep cover black opps mission. He joined the program after hearing he would be the strongest combat commando ever."

"A fairy tale only a fool would jump at. Now we know what we're up against. It might be a little easier," Silver Shadow replied. Cyber Ball glanced at him and shook his head. They both turned around to see if CD found anything. Cyber Ball got up from his chair and stood behind CD next to Silver Shadow. The two of them stood over CD like a pair of nosy birds in a tree looking into the house from the outside. CD continued his search being very diligent. He wanted to be sure the signal was coming from such a small building in the middle of nowhere.

"The disk is defiantly there?" Silver Shadow interrupted him, viewing the screen.

"Yes, I also learned the building has more floors underground," said CD.

"It's new?"

"Yes, and satellite photos show more activity started only three weeks ago."

"It just opened."

"Exactly!" CD remarked.

"So, what now?" Cyber Ball questioned.

"We scout it," Silver Shadow answered. "Find out what you can from the rest of data, Cyber Ball."

"I'm on it!" he replied, turning around and getting back into his chair, sitting himself back at his computer, and got started working vigorously.

"CD, map out the building. See if you can find us a safe way in and out. Research the purpose of this new facility and what makes it so special."

"Okay, you got it!" CD ensured him. Silver Shadow walked away from them and boarded the elevator. They were both given their tasks and CD and Cyber Ball working hard to make sure to leave nothing out of the plan. Silver Shadow went to the main floor in the elevator. On the way up, he started to think about the place the disk was taken to. *"What was this place used for? Why was it kept so secret? Would it shed any light on where Liset and Jean came from?"* Images like memories started flashing through his thoughts. Silver Shadow had a hard time getting the barrage to stop. They came so fast and made his head hurt a little. After a few minutes, he began to almost control them and slow the flashes down. It was then, he realized, he wasn't seeing memories. He was seeing the future. Things that had not happened yet. He tried to focus on what he had seen, trying to make sense of it all. Silver Shadow was interrupted when the elevator came to a stop. He stepped out of the elevator and saw Liset coming into the main room at the same time. Liset had come from her room. She had just finished her intense training. She started using her mind to talk to Silver Shadow.

"I CAN'T HEAR YOUR THOUGHTS, BUT I CAN TALK TO YOU," Liset said using her rediscovered power. Silver Shadow just stood there looking at her.

"YOU'RE NOT THE ONLY SHADOW THAT CAN DO IT," Silver Shadow replied. He could use telepathy, too. There was just never anyone he could talk to before. Liset was shocked, all this time she could have been using her abilities.

"You're a telepathic, too?" Liset asked.

"Yes, I have always been. You can't just talk to any shadow. The power doesn't work that way. Their mind has to be open, too."

"You were never able to talk to me like that before."

"Your mind wasn't open before. Your anger and frustration prevented you from your best possible potential," Silver Shadow explained.

"What do you mean?"

"I'm going to have to agree with Jean. You spent too much time on who you were. Instead, you should be more concerned with who you want to become. Imagine what you could do if you focused." Silver Shadow walked to the center of the room. Liset was a bit apprehensive, worried that maybe she would hurt someone with her new power. She started to use what she had learned, determined to focus her efforts. Her voice ran through Silver Shadow's head stronger than before.

"I HOPE YOU'RE READY!" her voice said. Liset's eyes began to glow. The eyes gave off a green misty glow with smoke to match. Before Silver Shadow knew it, things all over the room started flying at him. He was doing his best to move out of the way, but glass beakers from the table next to him flew very fast. He ducked down behind a lab counter. Silver Shadow was extremely impressed with Liset. He was peeking over the top of the counter. She had finally opened her mind and enhanced her abilities. For an instant, he felt proud, a leader who could give each member in the team clarification and wisdom. Liset was still picking things up off the counters at random. It would appear she had exceptional control of her power now. Silver Shadow decided to put Liset to the test. He reached over and grabbed a hand full of test tubes. Silver Shadow started throwing them at Liset. There was a silver metal tray in front of Liset on the table. The tray flew off the table and floated in front of her. Liset used it to deflect the glass objects Silver Shadow was throwing. The objects stopped flying at Silver Shadow and the metal tray fell to the floor. Liset's eyes were no longer glowing. Silver Shadow stood up from the counter he was taking cover behind. Liset was just standing there, white smock sprayed from the vents under her chin. Then she collapsed to the floor. Her body dropped like a bag of rocks. Silver Shadow ran over to make sure she was okay. He picked her up and put her in a nearby chair. After sitting her down, she woke up.

"What happened, I was starting to get the hang of it," she asked.

"You have unlocked your power. It may have been too fast and too hard on your mind all at once," Silver Shadow suggested.

"I need to practice more, like you said," Liset said, holding her head.

"Remember, your body is a little different, your mind is limited. You will only get stronger in time. Don't over load yourself because the next time you black out might be your last."

"Okay, I'll remember that," Liset replied.

"How does it feel to control your power?" Silver Shadow questioned.

"It's, like, crazy, you know?"

"I was once told the mind is the greatest weapon. Now you know first-hand and knowledge is also a terrible thing to waste." Liset looked over Silver Shadow's shoulder and saw Jean standing in the doorway. She walked over to the both of them.

"About time you got your head outta the clouds. Now, how did it feel?" Jean asked.

"That was hot! Is this what it felt like when you discovered your powers?"

"Yeah!" Jean replied.

"I feel like I just busted off a huge weight!"

"Hello!" Jean shouted, snapping her fingers. "And all you gotta do now is practice every day."

"You know I will, trust. I'm never going to have to get the TV control again!" Liset replied. Silver Shadow kind of laugh a little. That wasn't quite what he had in mind when he said practice.

"Okay, Liset, try and get some more rest. I'll have SD set up more training simulations for you," Silver Shadow suggested.

"Silver Shadow, you're needed in the conference room," Shadow Dome interrupted.

"Alright, SD, I'm headed there now," Silver Shadow answered.

"Thank you, Silver Shadow," Liset said as he walked away.

"For what?" he asked, stopping and glancing back at her.

"For putting up with us," Jean glanced at her, like what? "I mean me," Liset corrected herself. "For believing in me and for your help."

"No thanks needed, but you're welcome!" Silver Shadow said, darting back into the open elevator. The doors closed, leaving Jean and Liset there.

"Come on, girl, after the day you've had, you deserve to rest. These shadows keep weird hours," Jean implied.

"You said it! I need my beauty sleep."

"And you know what happens when people mess with my sleep!" Jean added.

"I know!" Liset answered. The team was finally at full strength. With Liset learning more about herself and Tyton achieving the highest weapons training, the Shadow Runners are the most elite team. Silver Shadow made his way down to the conference room to check on CD and Cyber Ball. They must have discovered something by now.

"What do we got?" Silver Shadow asked, stepping off the elevator and walking into the room. The two of them were standing at the center table. A few images were on the main screen. CD had ten or more 3D images projected above the surface of the table. Some video surveillance and the others were snap shot pictures he was using to create a time line.

"About half way done with the data. It also looks like there are plans for more advanced shadows."

"Good work," Silver Shadow said, sitting down in his chair at the head of the table. "Let's narrow it down and see if we can figure out where the information is going. Maybe we can find which facility the shadows will be born and housed," he insisted.

"I'll check it out," Cyber Ball answered.

"Silver Shadow, you might find this as interesting as I do," CD interjected. Using his hands, CD moved all the snap shots around. He waved his hands up in the air, putting all the images into some kind of order. The main screen is motion activated, making it easy to move things around on screen. The images almost told a story. On the main screen is a thermal image of a large numbered convoy. They were clearly traveling between known BIO-TEC facilities.

"What are we looking at?"

"It's a convoy. Knowing how the BIO-TEC company works. This is how they travel from complex to complex," CD replied.

"I gather that much."

"Judging by how many vehicles are in this convoy, it's safe to say they are transporting something important," CD implied.

"I agreed."

"Good. Remember the virus we planned into the BIO-TEC system?"

"Yes!" Silver Shadow answered, getting more and more interested.

"With the virus, I'm only able to access some of their network. This way it can remain undetected. Sixty-three minutes ago, the complex's silent alarm was tripped. There was an intruder and the base was put on high alert. Five minutes later, the alarm was turned off and base personal caught the intruder. I was able to obtain an image of the intruder." CD turned back to the time line of pictures. Using his hands again, he pulled one of the images out of order. It was Dark Shadow in the snap shot.

"They captured him?!"

"It would appear so, or maybe he let them catch him. Now this convoy is leaving the facility and I think I know where it's headed." Silver Shadow, captivated by what was transpiring, he didn't speak for a moment. Slouched in his chair, with his head down just a little. He was clearly thinking and planning the right course of action.

"We're going after him, right?!" Cyber Ball blurted out, breaking the silence. Cyber Ball and CD stood there at the end of the table like two kids. Waiting to hear the answer to the sleepover question that always seemed to pop up during the summer. Like two kids standing there awaiting the answer from their parents. This situation was different, of course, and this decision would affect the team.

"Well, are we going?" CD reiterated. Silver Shadow glanced up at them both.

"We almost have no choice."

Chapter 7

Chapter Seven
Misread Decoy

Molric lays in his room, one level below the ground floor in the Otilum facility. The walls all look the same, the bunk was hard. It reminded him of the military barracks. He has been all over the world. So many places all seem to remain the same. Fighting, winning or losing, surrounded by death. After all that, Molric finds himself here, leading a team of some of the best operators he has served with. The small room mine as well have been a prison cell. There was no difference. The bed felt like a bench with a thin cushion and all the doors are just missing the bars. Giving this a lot of thought, Molric was more uneasy about this whole situation. He awaits patiently for his briefing, ready to go on the next task. Cotolek approaches the doorway.

"Hey, better get to the meeting table."

"Next assignment?" Molric diligently asked.

"Yes," Cotolek answered. Molric got up from his bunk, thrusting himself in the direction in one motion. He made his way out into the center of the meeting room just outside his door. His team was already sitting at the table. A small screen emerged from the middle of the table. It was Vincent Sundice on a live video link giving the Max Force team another chance. Molric stood at the head of the table. The screen rotated toward him. Molric could tell, by the expression on his face, something had happened.

Michael Dunkley, Jr.

Molric stood at the head of the table.

"Approximately 68 minutes ago, an intruder was apprehended in another one of our newly built facilities. I'm sending your team there to provide security."

"What's the objective, sir?"

"Make sure the detainee doesn't escape. Make no mistake, this is your last chance, commander," Sundice implied.

"Yes, sir, I understand," Molric answered.

"Report to me when your team arrives."

"Yes, sir," said Molric. The screen went black and proceeded to fold back into the table. The rest of the team didn't really understand why this was their last chance. They, too, began to think Sundice had something more planned. There was something he wasn't telling them, another angle he was playing. As the team gathered in the open elevator, Soufual approached Molric.

"What does he mean it's our last chance?"

"When I showed him the disk before, he said if we fail again, he would dismantle the team. We must consider everything we do is a test with a pass or fail. If we fail too many times, our little team is no longer useful."

"What?!" Soufual reacted.

"In my experience, that's code for destroy," Molric replied. Cotolek over heard them.

"No room for error on this one," Cotolek interjected as he passed them to enter the elevator.

"That's right, we'll just take it one step at a time," Molric suggested, stepping into the elevator. The doors close and the team went to the ground level. The armored truck was backed up to the main entrance with the back doors open. It was running and waiting for the team. Everyone loaded up and the three-vehicle convoy left Otilum's front gates. The Max Force team sat eye to eye in the back. The back was completely isolated from the robot driver. It was late after hours. All the human guards must have all gone home for the night. It would explain why they now had a robot driver instead of the human guard. Molric saw this as an opportunity to bring his team up to speed. If they were going to survive whatever Sundice had plan, they would have to do it together. Molric broke the maintaining silence.

"From here on in, things could get intense."

"Meaning what exactly?" Nethal asked.

"Based on the last few convections with Sundice, it has become clear to me he has something up his sleeve."

"So, what are you saying?" Carben Arms impatiently insisted.

"He might want to destroy us if we're not careful!" Soufual interrupted.

"So, what do we do?" Cotolek enquired.

"Without knowing what Sundice has planned, there is very little we can do about it. I know we can no longer trust Sundice's orders. Consider every assignment suspicious."

"So, we've got to watch our backs now!" Nethal suggested.

"Let's just get this assignment done. Then we can look further into Sundice," Molric insisted. The convoy continued onto the prison facility. The team had arrived before the prisoner. This building was complete with 20-foot high three-feet thick stone walls around it in the shape of a square. Four guard towers, one on every corner. A robot guard greeted the team. The whole complex sat low in the middle of a huge valley. It was like a big bowl with white tipped mountains and lush green grass in every direction. One dark gray gravel road making the only path between the tall hills. The small stone fragments flying and kicking up light brown dust when vehicles traveled along it. The sky was perfect, the sun was beginning to set, making it light blue and purple. Small white clouds that looked soft enough to cuddle and fall asleep with. When the armored truck rolled up to the main gates, Molric was the first one out. In the distance, the team could see another large numbered convoy approaching the prison. The long narrow road made it easy to spot.

"Skade, make your way to the control room."

"Got it!" Skade answered.

"Cotolek and Rojet, check in with security to find out where the prisoner is going to be held. Nethal, scout the outer perimeter," Molric ordered. "Soufaul, Carben Arms, you're with me." The team had their assignments, and the prisoner convoy was getting closer. Nothing could have prepared Molric for what he was about to see next. Ten robot guards marched out from the complex. The convoy stopped in front with only Molric, Soufaul, and Carben Arms standing there. A car, then two vans, an 18-wheeler with trailer, two more vans, and another car made up the vehicles in the prisoner convoy. All the smaller vehicles pulled up in a straight line off to the side. The tractor

The Corrupt Shadows

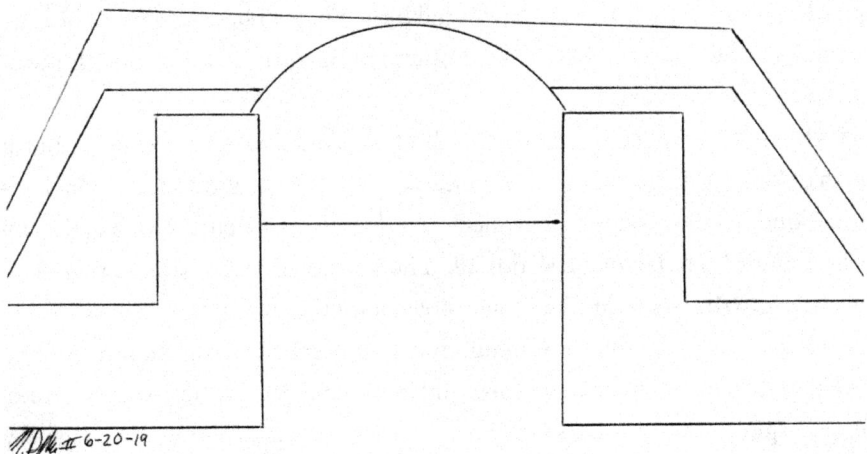

Four guard towers, one on every corner.

trailer made a circle, turning itself around and backing up in front of the main gates. Molric began counting the number of robot guards as they emerged from the vans, cars, and the cab of the truck. Forty-six in total. They must have been afraid of whoever this prisoner was. Their fear was displayed in their numbers like a school of fish against a large predator. Maybe they went a bit overboard as well. The robot guards line up in two lines outside the end of the trailer. The whole trailer unfolded like a blooming flower. It's open breaking down to one single platform and the end extended out into a ramp. Inside was one prisoner with five guards attached to every one of his limbs. Four guards, two on each side and one behind him. They all had long poles hooked to the prisoner, and his hands were bounded in front of himself with metal covers over his fingers.

"It can't be!" Molric said out loud. He looked like Silver Shadow, but it wasn't. At least it couldn't be, he appeared to be a little different. He had another kind of color to his body. The Max Force team watched completely surprised, their body language said it all. The guards carefully walked this Dark Shadow into the base complex. They moved him slowly as if they were carrying something fragile. Molric, Soufaul, and CA (Carben Arms) followed. The group walked through the main gates and into a courtyard. There were no trees, instead light brown dirt and sand. Then they walked under a gray stone archway into the prison itself. Three hanging lights lit a long, cold narrow hallway leading to a steel cell at the end. The dark metallic gray iron bars could be made out from the doorway. The hallway floor was covered with the same sand from outside. The walls were constructed with heavy dark brown colored stone bricks. The group walked down toward the iron cell. Just before reaching the cage, the cell door opened. It made a screeching sound as it crept ajar. The group move slowly pushing Dark Shadow into the center. The robot guards still holding him at pole length like a dog catcher from animal control. He stopped in the middle, all the guard's poles detached and the guards backed up holding their rods. The cell door slammed close as Dark Shadow glanced back. He had been in this position before. There was nothing they could do to him now that would be any comparison to what he had endured before. The guards folded up their poles and stationed themselves along the entire hallway. Leaving Molric, Soufaul, and Carben Arms just standing there, kind of dumfounded.

The Corrupt Shadows

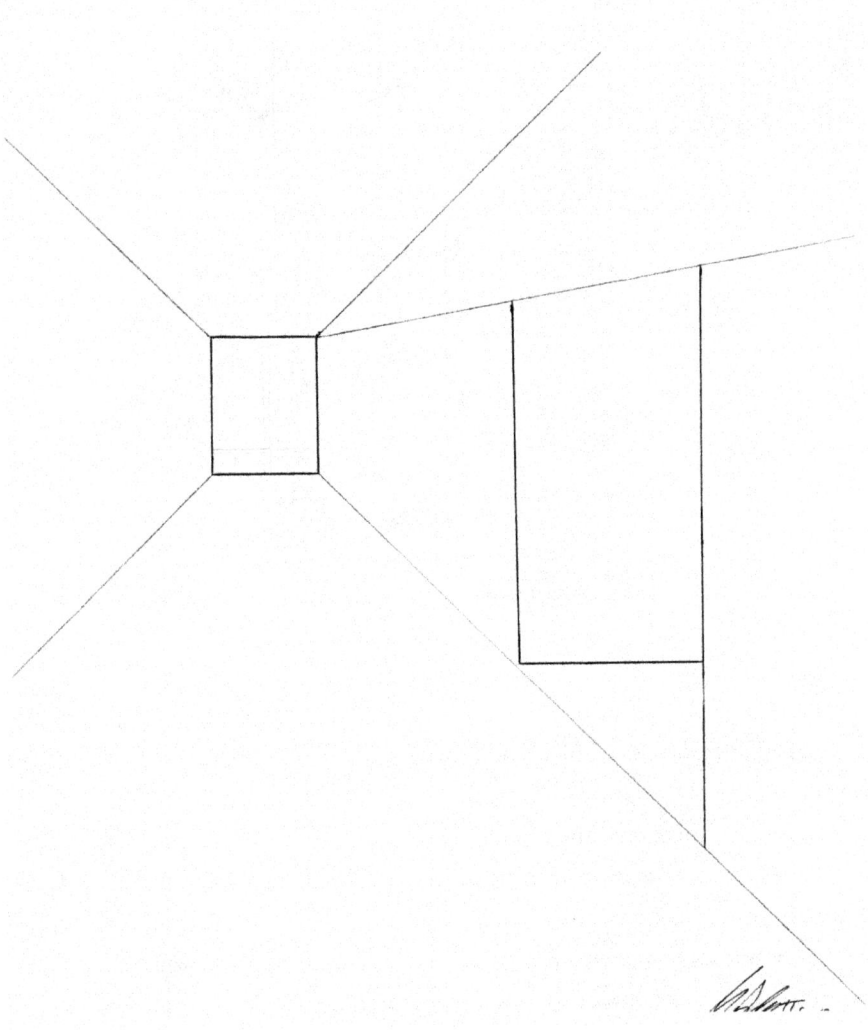

Three hanging lights lit a long, cold narrow hallway leading to a steel cell at the end.

Leaving Molric, Soufaul, and Carben Arms just standing there, kind of dumfounded.

"So, you're Molric," Dark Shadow said as he turned around to face his captures.

"How do you know my name?" Molric replied a little puzzled.

"I was there. Where do you think they got the technological from? I know about all of you."

"You know so much about us, but we know nothing about you."

"In time you'll know more. By then it will be too late and your team will have suffered for it," Dark Shadow said, turning his back to the three of them again. He still had the covers over his hands and shackles from head to toe. Molric glanced back at Soufaul and Carben Arms. They were just as puzzled as he was. Then it hit him like an anvil in the cartoons. He figured it out, what Sundice's plan was.

"Let's go," Molric said as the three of them started walking away. Molric was walking fast.

"You have no idea what you're up against! There're so many shadows you haven't seen! So many more to come!" Dark Shadow uttered. His deep voice echoed through the hall. Its demeanor behaved like a conscience coming full circle, bringing all fears to life, making Molric face the truth. Molric may have an idea of what he was talking about. Time for a team meeting to put all his ideas on the table. They walked down the hall and turned the corner, heading into another narrow corridor with several doors. At the end was a meeting room with an intercom on the wall.

"All MF team members to the meeting room," Molric paged. The team began to assemble, first Nethal, then Skade, followed by Cotolek and Rojet. "I think we are being played," Molric insisted. Everyone looked at one another.

"Molric, what do you think is going on?" Cotolek asked.

"I think their plan is replacements!"

"You think Sundice is planning to replace us?" Skade enquired.

"I think he already has. If we want to know more, that prisoner will tell us."

"Does he know what the plan is?" Nethal questioned.

"He knows something!" Soufaul interjected.

"We have to find out, and fast," Carben Arms suggested. Suddenly a loud alarm started going off, something was going on. The prisoner was trying to escape. The team ran out and down the hall one by one. Sounds of gunfire could be heard in the background of the very loud fire-like alarm. Max Force turned the corner to see six robots shooting at Dark Shadow. He was still in his cell but maybe not for long. The bullets were going into his cell and bouncing off him like little pesky flies. His armor was getting stronger with each hit. He was throwing himself into the metal bars, slowly breaking through. Dark Shadow stopped when he saw Molric and his team standing at the end of the hallway. He looked right at Molric as the guards continued shooting. Dark Shadow's eye began to glow. Molric had seen this once before, he needed only one time to learn from his mistakes.

"Watch out!" he yelled. Dark Shadow held his shackles out in front of himself. The covers on his hands flew off, sailing between the bars hitting two of the guards, knocking their heads completely off their bodies. Their hollow domes fell to the floor rattling as they rolled. Dark Shadow broke the chains from his legs and his body began to heat up. The surface of his body was red hot. The bars melted before him, and he stepped through the hole. The last four guards tried to stop him with bullets. Their guns almost had no effect, he was too strong. The bullets melted as they made impact with his hot armor, like chocolate on a red-hot grill. Dark Shadow may be stronger than his brother Silver Shadow. He slowly let the guards surround him as Dark Shadow patiently stood in the middle of what would be their last attempt to stop him. One guard did a low sweep at the back of Dark Shadow's leg. Before the guard could bring his foot to make contact, Dark Shadow lifted his leg, and at the same time, kicked downward, hitting the guard in the chest. There was so much power in his kick, the guard hit the floor and slid into the wall, shattering its body. Sand from the floor sailed in the air for a second. The heat and force had the limp robot body make spare parts fly down the hallway. The robot's damaged body slid so far and stopped at Molric's feet. The other three guards wasted no time starting their attack. One in front of Dark Shadow tried a high kick to the face. Dark Shadow caught his foot in midair and pulled him closer. With one swing at the knee, he broke the leg in half. Before the robot guard could break free, Dark Shadow kicked the other leg, forcing it to bend the wrong way. The guard fell back onto the floor. Without hesitation the guard behind him threw a punch. Dark Shadow ducked out of the way and grabbed his arm. Using his arm like a lever, Dark Shadow flipped the guard over his shoulder. At the same time, the last guard swings his arm in an effort to clothes line Dark Shadow. Before impact, standing on one leg, Dark Shadow rotates his whole body with the direction of the punch. Before his body came completely around, his leg swings heel first into the back of the guard's head. The guard spun and tumbled onto the floor. Molric and his team still standing at the other end of the hallway, they are the only thing left standing in the way of Dark Shadow and his freedom. "We have to stop him!" Molric yelled. Carben Arms unfolds all four arms and ran at Dark Shadow full speed. He bolts past the rest of the team, Dark Shadow's eyes continued to glow. Carben Arms runs like an out of control Mac truck speeding its way at a brick wall. Dark Shadow walks at him, keeping himself calm and revered. He puts his hands out as they

The Corrupt Shadows

meet in the middle. One set of Carben Arms's hands locked like dead bolts on a door around Dark Shadow's body. The other set of hands around Dark Shadow's neck. Dark Shadow's core temperature began to climb, and the fingers around his neck start to melt. Dark Shadow moves his hands to Carben Arms' wrist in their power wrestle. The two are locked in, a kind of pushing war without either side giving in. At this very moment, the team realizes Dark Shadow is far more superior than them. Carben Arms tries to break free as he watches his hands slowly melt like butter in a frying pan. His armor and synthetic hands now dripping like clay from their hold. Carben realizing he has met his match. trying to break free. His efforts are futile and useless; Dark Shadow's grip is too tight. Soufual tries to help followed by Nethal. Before the two can reach him, Dark Shadow pushes Carben Arms back a little, making him change his stance. With Carben's feet in the right position, Dark Shadow sweeps Carben's legs and does a hip toss, flipping Carben back down the hall. Soufual spays so much fire at Dark Shadow in front of himself. He loses sight of him in the flames for a second. Before Soufual can react, Dark Shadow runs at him through the fire. The hot flames seem to part in half just for him, as if he was controlling them or moving them from his path. Dark Shadow emerges out with a straight up and down jump kick. Dark Shadow plants both feet into his chest, pushing Soufual, and at the same time, lunching himself off backward. Soufual flies down the hall and Dark Shadow flips backward, landing on his feet. Nethal leaps over Soufual in time to see Dark Shadow flying at him with his arms out. Dark Shadow wraps his arms around Nethal's head and neck. While still in the air, he swings his legs off to one side of Nethal. In the same motion, he lands on his feet, body throwing Nethal down the hall. Rojet hovers over Nethal's body and Dark Shadow's hands glow red-hot. Rojet makes the first move by cupping both hands together, swinging down from over his head. Dark Shadow moves to one side and grabs Rojet's wrists with one hand. He puts the other hand on Rojet's chest and holds it there firmly. Skade starts to creep forward behind Rojet, ready to engage Dark Shadow. Rojet's chest began to get hot, before he could do anything. Rojet started to malfunction and smoke emerged from the creases inside his shoulder plates. As Skade gets closer, fire shoots out of Rojet's back, Dark Shadow had burned a fist-size hole through Rojet's chest cavity. Skade puts his hands up to protect his head from the hot flames. Dark Shadow throws Rojet's body to the ground. Before Skade knew it, Dark Shadow was standing in front of him. Skade swiped his mechanical snake tail followed by a one two punch, right then left. Dark Shadow jumped, ducks, then came the large hook arm. Dark Shadow grabbed it just before it takes out his head. Clenching it tightly, he breaks the hook off, disconnecting it from Skade's arm. It made a muffled sound as it clinked, bouncing around on the sandy ground. Then Skade swung the tail again, but this time Dark Shadow ducked back just out of range of it. As it passed Dark Shadow's face, he let go of the broken hook arm and snatched the end of the tail. With as much force as he could, Dark Shadow pulled the tail, making Skade fall onto his back. Then Dark Shadow snapped the tail like a wet towel in a shower room. The tail clapped on the ground of the hallway, breaking every important part. Skade couldn't move at all and his mechanical tail lay there on the ground. Alongside it were some small metal fragments from the inner workings. Dark Shadow glanced up and saw Cotolek running at him. Cotolek threw a punch at his head. Dark Shadow caught his hand and misdirected the punch. In the same motion, Dark Shadow spun with the punch around and elbowed Cotolek in the back of the head. The impact had so much power, Cotolek's head impaled the stone wall. The life ending sound was so loud, only silence could be heard after. Cotolek's motionless body hang there like an unbalanced picture frame on the wall. Molric was the only one left standing between Dark Shadow and the open doors at the end of the stone prison hallway. He was pointing his pistol at Dark Shadow's head.

"If you escape, my team and I will be destroyed."

"There is so much you don't know. Your team is obsolete. Did you think Max Force was the only team of shadows Sundice was developing!?" Dark Shadow replied. Molric started to lower his weapon.

"What do you mean?" Molric questioned. Without warning Dark Shadow was already running at him. Before Molric could raise his gun back up, Dark Shadow hit him like a stampede of wild buffalos. Molric fell to the ground and blacked out. When he came to, Dark Shadow was gone. Molric pulled himself from the ground still weak. He took a moment and stood in the open entrance way looking outside into the courtyard. The night desert breeze flowed like a soft whisper through the hallway. Molric glanced back over his shoulder with regret. The Max Force team lay scattered along the hallway; they have failed again.

Chapter Eight
Contingency Foresight

Silver Shadow stands alone riding the elevator in the Shadow Dome. He finds himself at a cross roads with his brother, Dark Shadow, out there in the world alone. Now it would seem he was in danger and Silver Shadow is in a position to help him this time. Maybe too little too late for his evil twin brother because his mind is in a dark place. Tortured and mistreated, hate fueled with vengeance is all he knows. He despises the human race so much, Dark Shadow is willing to sacrifice anyone who stands in his way for retribution. Hate can be like a prison for the mind stopping one from seeing things clearly. Dark Shadow might be stronger as well. Silver Shadow will have to break through to him in order to bring Dark Shadow back. He could do so much good instead of inflicting pain on others. And what's his end game, it is still unclear what Dark Shadow's goal is. The elevator reaches the main level and Silver Shadow steps out. The room lights up just for him after being dark. Silver Shadow made his way across the laboratory and into the hall, leading to some of the living quarters. Walking slowly he heads for the last room at the end of the hall. Doctor Eastin's grave room, the place he would end up when he was trying to clear his mind. The hallway lights turn on as he walks. Silver Shadow passes the threshold and sits down in the middle of the floor. It's the room, the mood, like a church sanctuary. Calm and peaceful at the same time. The single light in the tiny room shines down on him like a spot light. No matter where Silver Shadow went, this room always seem to help him center himself. Silver Shadow sat there for a good minute, looking at the large, flat silver metal door. The sheen of the door made Silver Shadow's unclear refection. The glossy appearance gave away his eyes. Truth stared back at him. Silver Shadow sat there Indian style with his hands together like he was paying, flat palm to palm with all the fingers lined up. He put his head down.

"This is going to be a war no matter what I try to do," Silver Shadow said out loud in an effort to talk to the only father he's ever known. "The human race will find out about our kind. I feel it will not be a matter of if but when. They won't expect us on any level. They are not all the same, we will need help, human help. I need a secondary plan, a plan B. I wish there were more people I could trust…" Before Silver Shadow uttered another word, something opened. Silver Shadow looked up and saw a little compartment had open like a CD drive door. The little mini flat edged draw was slightly above Eastin's metal grave plat. Sliver Shadow stood up to investigate. Looking over and down into the little compartment, there was a small flash drive. He reached in and pulled out the square, black object. "SD, did you know about this hidden device?"

"Negative, I was unaware of any device. It would be no surprise to me if there were more things throught-out the dome hidden for you. If there was one thing Doctor Eastin did well, it was plan ahead."

"You're right about that, SD," Silver Shadow answered. He took the flash drive in his hand and closed the little draw. Turning around Silver Shadow proceeded to walk out of the grave room and back down the hallway. The single motion sensitive light turned off as soon as he left the grave room. Walking at a semi-fast pace, Silver Shadow made his way back to the laboratory. *"How could I have missed this?"* Silver Shadow thought as he played with the flash drive in his fingers. He approached the main computer in the laboratory. Finding the end and plugging it in the port, the computer screen went black. A long list of names appeared in a green font. There had to be about 30 names on this list. At the bottom right hand side of the screen was an arrow icon. Using the touch screen, Silver Shadow hit the arrow with his finger. Another list appeared in a red font. He recognized some of the names right away. *"This must be the people he couldn't trust."* The list included the other three scientists Eastin had worked with on the previous project. Doctor Junior Northberg, Doctor George Southland, and Doctor Duncan Wester. Silver Shadow didn't know their full names, but now he would not forget them. The only thing left for Silver Shadow to do was check out every name on these lists. He could hear the footsteps of someone behind him. Silver Shadow quickly turned around; it was Poison.

"Hey, you, what are you doing?" she asked in a soft tone of voice. Poison had just woken up from laying down. She walked over to him from the doorway and put her arms around him, hugging him from behind, resting her head on his back.

"I found something…" Silver Shadow paused for a second and returned the favor by hugging her back. "My father left this for me to find." Poison let go of his body and stepped back a little. Silver Shadow turn to face Poison and see her reaction.

"Say what?" she was surprised, like it couldn't be true.

"I found this small flash drive in a hidden drawer in my father's grave room." Silver Shadow turned back around to face the computer screen again. Poison could tell this was a very sensitive subject for him. By just talking to him about this, his whole demeanor changed. He started to show her the list of names. Poison stepped closer to the computer to see for herself.

"Are you going to check this out?"

"Of course, there's a reason my father left this for me. Finding and rescuing my brother will have to wait," Silver Shadow implied.

"How can I help?" Poison asked.

"There are too many names for just one shadow to check out, so…"

"So, we split them up, right?"

"Yes," answered Silver Shadow, "pull the team together and have them assemble in the conference room. There are a lot of things we should talk about."

"Okay," Poison said, shaking her head. She walked away from Silver Shadow, who was still studying the list. Poison approached the intercom on the wall in the corner of the room. "All shadows to the conference room for a meeting," she said over the loud speaker. Poison's voice could be heard in every room of the Shadow Dome. She walked back over to Silver Shadow and put her arm around him. He was rattling on the keyboard. Silver Shadow was in his own world, this new secret really had him worked up before Poison could say anything to comfort him.

"SD, run a search on all names on this list."

"List confirm, searching," SD answered. Silver Shadow looked at Poison.

"Okay, let's go tell the rest of the team."

"Alright..." Poison grabbed his hand. As Silver Shadow began to walk away, she pulled him back in front of her, face to face. "Are you okay?" Poison asked, looking deep into his eyes and grabbing a hold of his other hand.

"Yes," Silver Shadow answered, trying to look away. Something was clearly bothering him about this whole thing. They stood closer, their chests were torching.

"Are you sure?"

"Why didn't he just tell me? I miss him so much." Silver Shadow pleaded with his eye, started to glow a little. He was pouring all his sadness and frustration out all at once. "There is a hole now and I feel more lost than ever."

"I know, my love," Poison consoled.

"Does the pain ever go away?" Silver Shadow asked.

"Not really, it is only replaced."

"Replaced, with what?"

"Me and your son. Your father would have wanted you to go on, teach your son everything you know. Show him life in a way only a father can."

"I wish he were here to see Tyton."

"He is, inside you and inside of me. I love you and Tyton, I always will. That is what your father wanted for you. To be loved, to feel love," Poison said. She let go of his hands and gave him a huge again. She embraced him tightly, holding him for a few minutes. Silver Shadow hugged her back, letting off a large heavy breath releasing a weight off his mind. His eyes stopped glowing and a rush of hot air flowed from the vent holes under his chin. They both let go of each other at the same time. "Feel a little better?"

"Much better, thank you, my love."

"Come on, let's go tell the team what you have discovered," Poison said, pulling Silver Shadow by the hand toward the elevator. She dragged him into the slowly opening doors. As they went down, Silver Shadow and Poison stood in the center of the elevator holding hands, looking at each other every few minutes.

"Silver Shadow."

"Yes, SD?"

"The list search is complete," acknowledged SD. "I was only able to find a location on one name so far."

"Okay, thank you. Send all the information to the conference room computer," Silver Shadow ordered. The elevator stopped Silver Shadow and Poison stepped off to see the conference room was filled with the rest of the team members. Tyton was sitting at his unofficial spot at the conference table with his laptop on the right side to the head of the table where his father sat every time. Jean stood behind him, watching over Tyton's shoulder work on another project. CD and Cyber Ball standing next to where they would sit talking about tactics and strategy. Ton, in his seat close beside Liset with his arm around her. She was enjoying the attention petting Ton's wrist draped over her.

"Okay, team, listen up.," Silver Shadow said loudly, standing at the head of the table. Everyone stopped what they were doing and began to take their seats. Poison sat in her chair on the left of Silver Shadow. Ton, then Liset and then Jean sat along the left side of the table. Tyton sat across from Poison with CD, then Cyber Ball the right side of the table. "I found something my father left for me. The search and rescue for my brother will have to wait," Silver Shadow explained. He put his hands flat on the table and put his head down for a second. He leaned hard on the table, and by his body language, everyone could see this was hard for him to talk about. Silver Shadow lifted his head back up. "I have discovered two lists of names, human names!" Everyone except Poison had a slight reaction. Silver Shadow moved his hand along the table and started hitting some icons on the surface. The list along with all the information displayed on the main screen at the end of the table. The team all had the same question on their minds. Only Tyton was the first one to say it out loud.

"What does this mean?"

"This means we might have to fight a war, and we will need all the help we can get. The humans will find out about our kind. I've seen what they become when they are afraid."

"Why two lists?" CD asked.

"Yeah, and why are they in different colors?" Cyber Ball added.

"The list in green are humans we may be able to trust, friends to my father. The ones in red are humans we may want to avoid," Silver Shadow suggested.

"So, what do we do now?" Liset asked. Before Silver Shadow could answer, he glanced over Liset's shoulder and noticed Jean was looking at the list hard. Like maybe she had recognized some of the names from the red list.

"Now we spilt the two lists up and check every name." Silver Shadow was still looking at Jean. "Are you okay, Jean?" he asked. She didn't answer, Liset spun around in her chair.

"Jean...Jean!" Liset said louder.

"What!?" Jean snapped turning her attention back to the room and glaring at Liset.

"Did you even hear us talking to you?"

"No, what!?"

"Do you know those names or something?" Liset asked, pointing at the wall screen.

"One or two maybe, why?" Jean argued. Liset turned back to Silver Shadow. Jean gave him a look like she wanted permission to check out this lead.

"I am going to split up the green list and have every member vet six or more names. Tyton, you will be with me," Silver Shadow said. Tyton shook his head yes like he agreed. "Jean, you and Liset will check out the red list. Start with the names you know or have seen before."

"How?" Liset asked.

"SD will give a location on most of the names."

"What do we do when we find them?" Jean snapped. It had become clear to Silver Shadow one of those names may have something to do with Jean's past.

"Take their picture, under no circumstances are you to interfere or interact. We will need to learn more about them first. It will help us understand what the bigger picture is."

"Fine!" Jean said loudly, folding her arms over her chest and putting her head down a little. "No promises," she uttered under her breath. Liset gave Jean an elbow nudge after hearing what she said.

"Father, can we use my new Shadow Finder to save and upload the images?" Tyton implied.

"I was just going to ask you if it was done. Now I think this would be the perfect time to test it out." Tyton got up from his chair and walked over to the vehicle equipment room. The team watched him from the table.

"Are there any questions?" Silver Shadow blurted out, getting everyone's attention again and breaking the short silence. The team looked at one another, they all had their jobs and knew what to do. "No?" Silver Shadow asked, giving the whole team one more chance. Tyton came walking out from the vehicle equipment room carrying a shoe box-sized metal crate. He placed the crate on the table.

"Okay, there is enough for every shadow to have one," Tyton said, opening the lid. The whole team got up from their seats and gathered around Tyton.

"So, this is what we should use to take the pictures with?" Liset asked.

"Yes, each device is linked up with The Shadow Dome," Silver Shadow explained.

"I also designed it to save the images you capture right to SD's mainframe. So, if you lose it or break it, no pictures will be lost," Tyton went on.

"That's cool, Tyton," CD said, patting him on the back.

"Yeah, because I will probably break at least two of these things," Cyber Ball implied.

"Well, try not to break this one," Tyton said, removing one from the crate and slapping it into his hand. It was a small black device that looked like a sniper's scope. It had two lenses with a little rubber hood on the back and a lens cap on the other. There were finger-sized groves on both top and bottom. A small, foldable black antenna on top like the ones found on wireless routers to send images straight to SD. There was also a red button on the side, along with a solar panel much like a calculator next to it. Tyton took another one out of the crate and held it in the air. "It's very simple. Just aim and click the red button. Don't have to worry about charging it. These things run on solar power."

"SD has found a location on Mace Lii so far."

"What about the others?" Ton asked.

"SD is still searching, but it will take some time. Jean and Liset use one of the submarines to get back to your car."

"Okay," Liset answered. "Come on, Jean, let's go." Tyton handed them each a Shadow Finder. Liset turned around and gave Ton a big hug. "I'll see

Michael Dunkley, Jr.

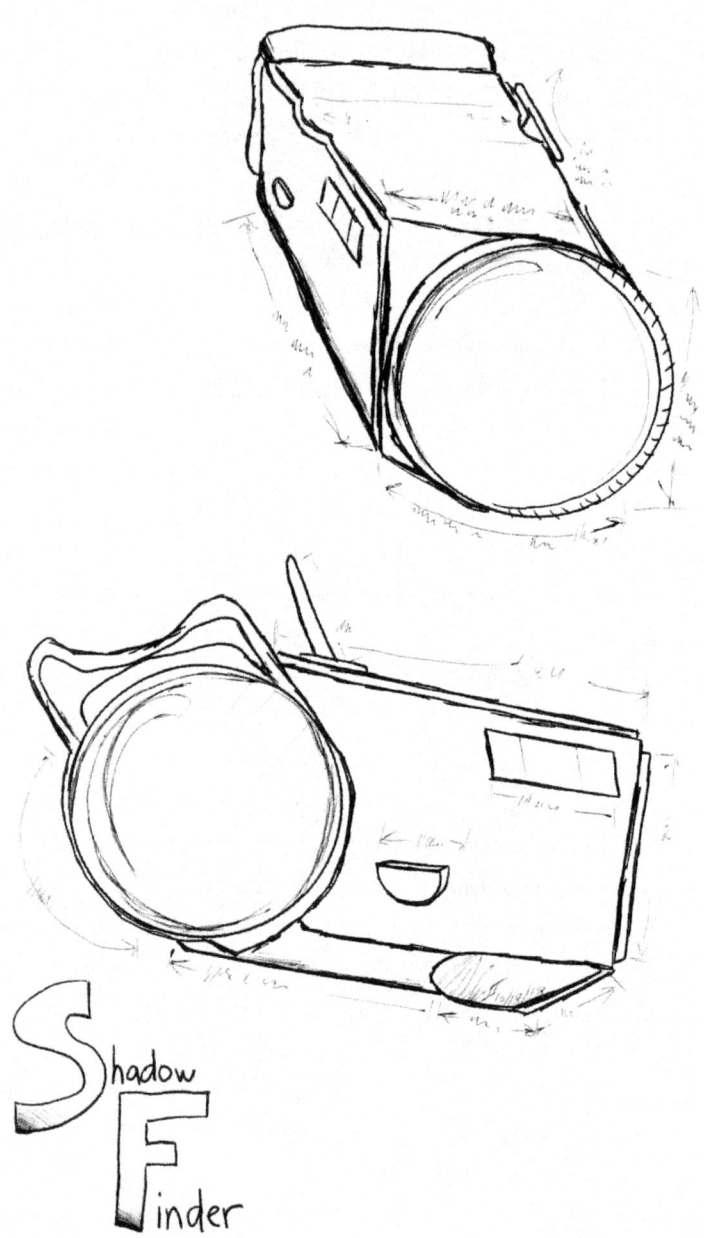

Shadow Finder

There was also a red button on the side, along with a solar panel much like a calculator next to it.

you later, okay?" Ton shook his head okay. Jean and Liset both walked over to the elevator and went down to the lower level.

"Ton, CD, Cyber Ball, and Poison, get what you need. You can use the Shadow Hopper once SD locates more names from the list."

"Alright, stay in touch, okay," Poison said, looking at Tyton. Ton and CD grabbed an SF (shadow finder) from Tyton. They both headed for the weapons room lower level. Cyber Ball was still standing there with the SF unit in his hands, glancing at all the sides and examining it very closely. He started walking in the same direction as CD and Ton, following behind them. His head down, looking at the device. It was like he had just got a Rubik's cube and he was trying to solve it. Poison was the only one still standing there. Silver Shadow approached her. He reached out and took her hands. He could see she was worried about something.

"Here you go, Mother," Tyton said, stepping in the middle of his parents.

"Thank you, Tyton," Poison answered as she grabbed the SF unit from Tyton's hand. She let go of Silver Shadow's hands and knelt down next to her son. "Try and be careful, okay."

"Okay, Mother," Tyton exclaimed as he gave her a big heart-warming hug.

"Okay, why don't you go get ready, son," Silver Shadow interrupted. Tyton let go of his mother and turn back to his father.

"What should I bring?"

"You're going to need your laptop and whatever else you think you will need."

"Right, I'll be right back." Tyton ran off to his room. Poison stood back up and grabbed Silver Shadow's hands again. She pulled him a little closer to her body. Their eyes were locked together.

"Are you ready to see your father's past? Maybe discover more about his history!?"

"There is only one way to be sure," Silver Shadow replied.

"Take it slow and remember to have an open mind," Poison remarked.

"I will, my love." Poison hugged him tightly. Tyton came back into the room.

"I think I have everything I need."

"Then let's go," Silver Shadow said, letting Poison go. She took a step back, looking at the both of them.

"Be safe," Poison expressed.

"We will, Mother," Tyton said, grabbing his father's hand and dragging him to the elevator. Silver Shadow waved to her as she stood alone in the conference room. The two of them went up and exited into the laboratory. They passed through the lab and into the pressurized hangar where SGD was waiting. They climbed aboard and the aircraft prepared for take-off. The hanger began to fill with water as the aircraft sealed itself. Silver Shadow and Tyton made their way through the aircraft to the cockpit. Walking from the back of the aircraft in the narrow aisle to the front, Silver Shadow took a seat, taking the pilot controls and Tyton sat beside him. The hanger was filled with water and the aircraft was ready to float out of the slowly opening hanger doors.

"Father, where are we headed?" Tyton curiously asked. Silver Shadow just looked over at him for a second.

"Ome, Japan. We are going to the top of Mount Mitake," Silver Shadow answered.

"Alright, who are we looking for?"

"The first name on the list is Mace Lii."

"Why do you think he was the first name on the list?"

"I think he is very important somehow. I haven't figured out why yet."

"Do you think he has seen our kind before?" Tyton continued.

"Not sure, I am still trying to figure out how he knows your grandfather," Silver Shadow answered, trying to keep up with Tyton's questions. He was very curious about everything, as was Silver Shadow. Tyton, satisfied for the moment, sat back in his seat. Silver Shadow glanced back over his shoulder and could see Tyton trying to figure it out as well. He saw it had Tyton thinking, too. Silver Shadow could tell his wheels were turning like a slow-moving clock. "Now, I have a question for you."

"Yeah," Tyton said enthusiastically, sitting up in his seat.

"I will need you to help me design an upgrade for SGD."

"What do you mean? Are we going to replace SGD?"

"No, we need to build a better aircraft. Like making a new shell for him."

"Why, this one is still really effective," Tyton pointed out, trying to stick up for SGD.

"Yes, you're right, but the team is going to grow and we will need a better way for everyone to get from place to place. When we design a new aircraft, I can remove SGD's consciousness and input it into the new aircraft."

"You had me a little worried just then," Tyton remarked. "Hear that, SGD, you're going to get an upgrade?!"

"Yes, there is always room for improvement," SGD replied.

"So, can you help me come up with some ideas?" Silver Shadow interrupted.

"Yes, I think I have a few ideas already," Tyton implied. He sat back in his seat again and started hitting some buttons on his arm rest. A small screen emerged from the back of the chair. The lightweight flat screen unfolded in front of him, attached to a mechanical arm. Once the screen had finished unfolding, Tyton grabbed it in an attempt to adjust the height. Using his finger on the touch screen, he began drawing some sketches. Silver Shadow glanced over and saw Tyton busy drawing. He turned his attention back to flying the aircraft. They were now soaring high above the clouds.

"SGD, how long until we reach our destination?" Silver Shadow asked.

"At current air speed, approximately 67 minutes," SGD answered.

"Alright, locking in location into GPS and setting you on auto pilot."

"Affirmative, Silver Shadow," SGD replied. Letting go of the controls, Silver Shadow reached over to the center console and started typing in the location. He sat back in his seat and just kind of stared out at the blue sky passing by. The thought of his father and what he would think about what may come. Eastin must have known it would start a war between the races. The humans' history seemed all too familiar. The people on this list must have a deep connection with Eastin. Silver Shadow felt a little betrayed and it was then he realized the sacrifice Eastin made. He had to give up everything about himself in order to keep Silver Shadow a secret. He left his past and surrendered his future. Silver Shadow was suddenly filled with sadness. Eastin did what any father would have done for their child. What he could see himself doing for Tyton if he had to. Suffer for them, even die to protect them. This list was the only true way for Silver Shadow to really learn what Eastin had given up. Maybe a way for Silver Shadow to thank him. Talking to his friends about what happened and getting help to overcome. Silver Shadow was still staring out the window at the sky. Something was starting to obstruct his view. Mount Mitake was slowly piercing its way through the clouds, dividing them like a knife. Silver Shadow stood up from his seat and found himself right in front of the window, looking out at a beautiful sight. Before Silver Shadow knew it, Tyton was standing next to him. They both were enjoying the view of the peaceful-looking mountain together. Before long the aircraft had reached the mountain.

"Silver Shadow, we have arrived at the location," SGD indicated.

"Thank you, SGD," Silver Shadow replied. He turned to Tyton, who was still standing next to him. "Are you ready?"

"Yes, but how will we find him? We don't even know what he looks like."

"We will have to observe and survey the area. My guess is he will be the only person living on this mountain. So, we will start with the places that are the most secluded," Silver Shadow said, walking out of the cockpit. Tyton followed closely, asking questions and drawing more conclusions. They made their way to the back of the aircraft passing all the empty seats to the drop door. Next to the door behind one of the seats was the foot locker with all the gear and weapons. Silver Shadow reached to open the locker.

"Do you think he lives up here all by himself?" Tyton continued.

"I am not sure, but that's what we are here to find out," Silver Shadow said, pulling two utility belts out from the locker.

"Right."

"Here, you will need this," Silver Shadow implied, handing Tyton one of the belts.

"Is this one mine?" Tyton asked with so much excitement.

"Yes."

"I know how this works." Tyton put the large circular belt over his head and down to his waist. It was clearly too big for him. He hit the button in the center of the belt buckle. The belt retracted, conforming to Tyton's hips for a comfortable fit. "It fits good, Father."

"Good," Silver Shadow replied. "Now, you know what all these compartments have, right!?" Silver Shadow asked, pointing to the first one.

"Yes, this one has knock out gas pellets, there is smock pellets, E.M.P. remote mine, flash light, and grappling hook with tow cable," Tyton answered, looking down and pointing the first one and working his way around to different parts of the belt.

"Okay, son, good. Here, you will need this as well." Silver Shadow handed Tyton a custom-made pistol.

"This is new. Did you build this?"

"Yes, and there are only two of them."

"One for you and one for me, right!?" Tyton said, hooking the weapon to his belt. The weapon had its own black leather hip holster with leg strap and clip at the top to attach to any belt.

"Yes," Silver Shadow answered, pulling another duplicate pistol from the locker.

"What do you call it?"

"SMP10, Shadow Marksmen Pistol. It shoots 10mm (millimeter) bullets."

"Thank you, Father."

"You're welcome. Now take good care of it. I have some more attachments we can work on together when we get time."

"Deal!" Tyton replied. Silver Shadow finished putting on all his gear and stepped up to the drop door button. He hit the big red button and the drop doors on the back of the aircraft open. The air came rushing in from outside.

"Ready!?" Silver Shadow asked, looking back at Tyton.

"Always!" Tyton replied, looking down. The aircraft was low just above the tree tops. They could see a very small clearing between the trees. They both stood there, glancing down from the edge of the drop door ramp. Silver Shadow reached into his belt and pulled out his communicator and stuck it to his chest. He turned to Tyton standing next to him.

"Follow me and stay close," Silver Shadow said, putting his hand on Tyton's shoulder. Tyton shook his head okay. Silver Shadow pressed and held the communicator button down to talk into. "SGD, when we're clear, maintain position and fly pattern Bravo, stay on station."

"Affirmative, Silver Shadow," SGD replied over the communicator.

"Okay, let's go," Silver Shadow said, letting go of the button. He turned and jumped from the ramp. Tyton leaped after him, falling through the air right behind his father. Their bodies consumed the air and pushed it out just before reaching the ground. Silver Shadow hit the ground and Tyton landed two steps behind him. Tyton looked up and the aircraft retracted the ramp, closing the drop door. SGD, already in cloak mode, slowly flew away, disappearing into the clouds. The ground was soft dark brown with tree roots running in every direction. Thick light and dark green moss covered every rock in sight. The tall narrow trees stood close to one another, making it a very dense forest. The trees had no lower branches, making them seem even taller looking. The ground had various small plants and shrubs growing. Based on what Tyton had observed already, he was sure he could make his way through to the mountain side without being seen or heard. They both stood there where they landed, ducked down a little for a few minutes. Hands held out like a runner on first base in a baseball game. Ready in sneak mode, looking around at the environment. Taking in all the natural sounds and smells. Air was a bit warm, so there might be a fog later. They did the same thing at the same time, one could tell they were father and son. Silver Shadow reached into his belt and pulled out a small, flat, circular, quarter-size device. He placed it onto his wrist and pressed the top of it. The device opened up and unfolded around Silver Shadow's wrist like a bracelet. With his fingers, he pressed the sides of the device like he was starting a stop watch. A light blue projection showed a 3D holographic map of where they stood in the forest. The image was coming from SGD. It was flying overhead, mapping out all buildings, paths, and people in the area. Without a word, Silver Shadow glanced back over his shoulder and told Tyton to follow, waving at him. Tyton shook his head okay and the two shadows made their way through the thick forest. Looking at his 3D display, Silver Shadow lead the way, following alongside a known path people walked. The shadows stayed off the path but used it as a guide to find the large temple. The Shinto Shrine was inside the temple and would be a good starting point. The structure was about a mile from where they landed. The shadows would have to make their way through lots of forest first. Silver Shadow stopped for a second, Tyton stopped right behind him. Looking up at the sky, Silver Shadow could tell they had about three hours of daylight left. Suddenly they heard footsteps on the path. Silver Shadow and Tyton quickly hid behind the closest tree. The sound came closer and words of conversation could be heard. It was people walking down the path. A small group making their way down the mountain. The sounds became louder and then they passed by the shadows and continued away. Silver Shadow emerged from his hiding place, as did Tyton. They both looked at each other and hunched down in a catcher's squat side by side. They were huddled together like they were in a football game, making their conversation quieter.

"Everyone must be going home now," Tyton whispered.

"Yes, it's getting late and it will be dark soon. Might be more, let's be careful. Look here, there is a steam we can follow," Silver Shadow answered, pulling up the 3D map again.

"Looks like it goes right to that large structure," Tyton said, looking at the 3D map.

"It's the temple."

"So, we can start looking there?"

"Yes, it might be the best place to start," Silver Shadow suggested.

"Sounds good," Tyton replied. Silver Shadow tapped the 3D map and the projected image went off. The two of them began to sneak through the forest again, keeping low and out of sight. They found the stream and started to follow it among the moss-covered rocks. The stream was good and deep, carving a trench dividing the ground with seven-feet between each side. Tress grew on the edges with their roots hanging down into the water. The two shadows moved fast, sneaking along the edge. Leaping over large rocks and between trees. Tyton was doing a good job keeping up with his father. Without warning Silver Shadow stopped dead in his tracks and Tyton froze behind him. Silver Shadow started to peer around as he crouched down, looking at something in the mud. Tyton got closer and looked over his father's shoulder. It was a bear track, and from the looks of it, a fresh one.

"Bear track?" Tyton asked, kind of amazed by the size of it. He stepped around Silver Shadow and took a knee right in front of the animal print.

"Sh!" Silver Shadow said as if he could hear something. Silver Shadow glanced over at the closest tree and saw claw marks scratched into the bark. "Watch it!" Silver Shadow said grabbing Tyton by the arm. They could hear something running through the shrubs right for them. The sound was like a heavy rock rolling down a steep hill. A heavy thumping sound with the rustling of the bushes. The two shadows turned around just in time to see it emerge from the bushes. The biggest black bear they had ever seen. It ran out of the bushes and had both shadows in its sights. Stopping right in front of them, the bear began growling at them. It stood on its hind legs in an effort to make itself look bigger. An age-old instinct used by the bear to intimidate other creatures. Silver Shadow quickly stood in front of Tyton. The bear continued to try and intimidate the two shadows. Silver Shadow and Tyton didn't move one inch. The bear started to get closer to them, growling louder and louder. Silver Shadow eyes began to glow and he moved his hands in a pushing motion. Holding his hands out in front of himself, Silver Shadow just stood his ground. The bear got back on all fours and charged directly at them. Before the bear reached the two shadows, it slammed into something, stopping the bear in its pursuit. It was like the bear ran into a glass window, stopping it from getting any closer to them. It was Silver Shadow making a shield in front of them. The bear couldn't figure out what it was. The bear circled around in place, trying to scratch it with no success. Silver Shadow held the invisible shield up, focusing hard on keeping it strong enough to keep the angry bear at bay. The bear eventually gave up and sat down in front of the invisible barrier. Silver Shadow slowly brought his hands down and the shield dissipated. The bear didn't move and continued to stare at the two shadows. Silver Shadow glanced back at Tyton, who was captivated by his father's power. Silver Shadow looked back at the bear and slowly started walking toward it.

"Father, what are you doing?" Tyton whispered, signaling his father with his hands to come back. Silver Shadow stood in front of the bear and knelt down next to it. The bear did not move and it was breathing very heavily. Silver Shadow held out his hand and the bear sniffed him. It started to lick his fingers and whine a little. The bear seemed to be in some kind of pain. Silver Shadow slowly placed his other hand on the bear's head. He scanned the bear's body, looking for the cause of the pain. He found it; something was lodged in between the pads on the bear's right paw. Silver Shadow took his hand off the bear's head and held it out. The bear put its paw in his hand. It was like the bear and him had a deep understanding. Silver Shadow gently flipped the bear's paw over and began searching. After a few seconds, he pulled a large piece of wood from the bear's paw. The bear let out a loud growl. Silver Shadow ran his hand down the bear's neck, petting it in an effort to keep it calm. The large sharp piece of wood must have been in there a while. The bear's skin was starting to grow over it. Silver Shadow threw the splinter onto the ground and rubbed the bear's paw with both hands. The bear was grateful, licking Silver Shadow's face. After a few minutes, Silver Shadow stood up and started looking for something. He was quickly checking all the small bushes around. He spotted the one he needed. Stepping over to a tree with a small plant growing from the side, Silver Shadow pulled off a few of its leaves. He stripped the little plant clean. Using his hands, Silver Shadow began mashing the green leaves together. The bear just sat there, watching. After a few seconds, Silver Shadow walked back over to the bear and sat in front of it again. He rubbed the bear's neck and gently lifted the paw in pain. Now green mush in his hand, Silver Shadow applied the green stuff like it was an ointment. It was a bit thick, like toothpaste, but it seemed to do the trick. The bear was calmer after Silver Shadow put it on.

"Okay, big guy, no more climbing trees," Sliver Shadow whispered to the bear. The bear was licking his face again. Tyton leaned over, still standing back behind his father.

"Father, we should go," Tyton inferred.

"Yes, you're right," Silver Shadow answered, talking over his shoulder. "You stay out of trouble," Silver Shadow said, standing up as the bear started to get up and walk away back into the bushes.

"You just make new friends everywhere, uh?" Tyton commented.

"I'm always looking to help."

"I know. We are the same that way."

"Two hours before dark, let's go this way," Silver Shadow said, pulling up the 3D map.

"Right behind you," Tyton replied. Silver Shadow turned the map off and lead the way. The two shadows made their way along the large stream. Before long they found themselves standing on an edge of a waterfall. They stopped for a moment to enjoy the view. It was a beautiful sight and about a 40 to 50-foot drop. Complete with moss covered rock face, tall trees growing along the sides on the way down and a nice flow of water. At the bottom, it was shallow with not much water.

"There's not enough to swim," Tyton stated.

"Right, so we jump," Silver Shadow answered. Before Tyton could say anything, his father leaped from the edge, performing a full front flip. Silver Shadow landed at the bottom and looked up at Tyton. "Come, let's see what you got, kid?!" Tyton glared down at his father, challenging him. Tyton stood back from the edge a little and turned around. With his back facing the waterfall, Tyton did a back flip from a stand still. Silver Shadow watched as his son flew over his head and landed behind Silver Shadow.

"Well done," Silver Shadow congratulated. He put his hand on Tyton's shoulder.

"Thank you, Father, but I had a good teacher," Tyton replied. The two shadows continued to follow the stream, and just before dark, they made it to the temple. The temple sat at the top of a hill with many stairs leading up to the large doors. Halfway up there was a bare wooden bamboo archway with Japanese symbols carved into the front. There were old fashion lanterns along the staircase going up with a small wall to stop anyone from falling. The lanterns had little roofs on a square box with lit candles inside, not providing much illumination at all. The two shadows stayed in the tree line halfway to the top. Using hand signals, Silver Shadow told Tyton to stop and stay hidden. They watched from the forest to see if anyone still lingered in the temple. No one for at least 30 minutes. Then Silver Shadow spotted someone. It was a short man dressed in orange colored robes. Silver Shadow looked back at Tyton and they didn't have to say anything. The two were thinking the same thing. Silver Shadow began to follow the man and Tyton trailed behind, watching his father's back. The man was old and a little slow, climbing the stairs one by one. When he reached the top, the man walked off to the right instead of entering the temple. Silver Shadow followed the man as he proceeded down a narrow path, leading to another building. This building matched the temple but was much smaller. The man made his way to the doors, sliding one half open, stepped inside, and slid it closed. Silver Shadow and Tyton were sneaking down the dirt covered path to the door. They were in a mini bamboo garden, and they could see light coming from inside the little hut. Silver Shadow made it to the door and glanced back at Tyton. Tyton shook his head yes like he was ready. His father slid the door open and Tyton followed. The two crept inside and saw the man sitting on the floor, meditat-

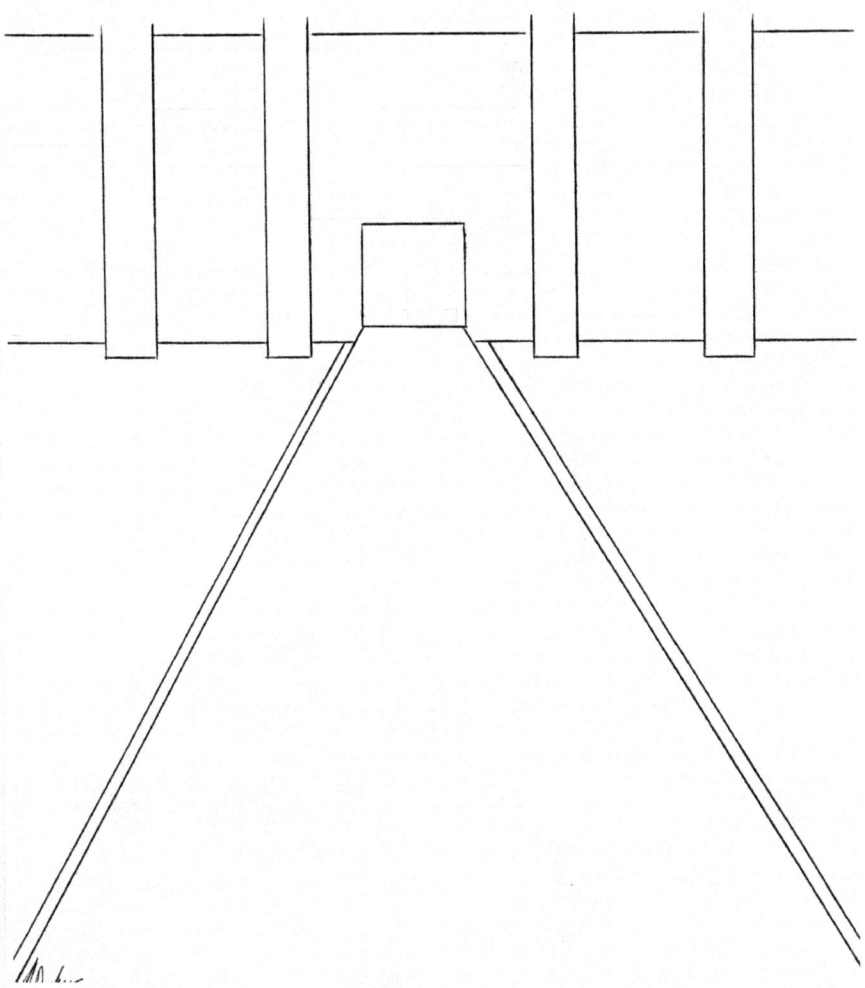

The temple sat at the top of a hill with many stairs leading up to the large doors.

ing in front of some slowly burning incense. Silver Shadow sneaked to the right corner of the room behind the man and Tyton to the left. They stayed in the shadows for a few minutes.

"Hello, my friend. I have waited a long time to meet you."

Chapter Nine
Elevated Risks

The Shadow Dome's mainframe is working overtime to find and locate the names from the list. There is always down time for the team. Each member deals with spare time in their own way. Most of the time, it means training. To be better, make themselves feel whole, or to find that missing skill needing improvement. Poison had been laying down on her stomach in the firing range using an AWM (Arctic Warfare Magnum) sniper rifle. Each time staying very still, looking through the scope, shooting off rounds at paper targets. After discarding an entire chip, she would use the auto button to bring the paper targets back. Poison finally brought herself to use this weapon, trying so hard to fight her past. The only thing stopping her from feeling discussed was the promise she made to herself to do good with her skills of long range. She couldn't miss as she brought the paper targets back, examining each one. Every shot hitting the same place, making only one hole in every paper target. She stood there, holding each one for a long few minutes, staring through the hole. The lingering thought of how many times this was a person she may have killed haunted her.

"Poison, I have located the proximity of two names," SD interrupted.

"Yes, okay," Poison answered. "Send the two locations to the Shadow Hopper."

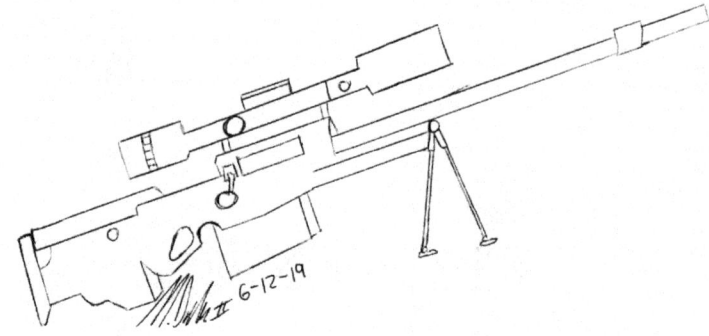

Poison had been laying down on her stomach in the firing range using an AWM (Arctic Warfare Magnum) sniper rifle.

"Affirmative, Poison."

"Which names are they?" Poison asked, dropping the paper target she was holding.

"Rick Bartos and Hector Wells. I found bank account records in their names in the same state. Also, employment history and utility bills."

"Anything else?"

"I also found the connection to Doctor Eastin."

"Really!" Poison said surprised.

"Yes, they all attended the same collage."

"Okay, I am on my way to the hanger," Poison answered after taking one last look at several of the paper targets laying on the floor. She began to walk away, leaving the AWM sniper rifle still set up on the floor beside her. Poison got about three steps away and stopped, then she turned back to look at the rifle again. Before she could convince herself she wouldn't need it, Poison picked it up and grabbed four more .300 Winchester magnum round clips from the table in the corner. She walked out of the firing range and into the weapons room lower level. She tucked the extra four clips still in her hand into her belt. Poison quickly searched the shelves in front of her for a shoulder strap. She saw one hanging from some hooks on the right side of all the shelves. Grabbing the strap from the hook, she made her way through and out into the conference room. Poison quickly walked, making her way to the elevator and stepped inside. As it began to move up, Poison attached the strap to her weapon. The elevator doors opened and Poison stepped out into the laboratory with the sniper rifle slung over her shoulder. The Shadow Hopper was sitting in the hanger. As Poison walked across the lab, she heard something behind her; it was Ton.

"SD came up with two names?" Ton questioned, coming into the lab from the hallway.

"Yes," Poison answered, turning around.

"Okay, want me to go with you?" Ton asked.

"No, I got this," she said, adjusting the sniper rifle on her shoulder.

"Okay, be careful," Ton suggested, still walking toward her.

"I will, thanks," Poison said, heading for the hanger door. She entered and closed the door behind herself, leaving Ton standing there in the middle of the lab. Poison climbed aboard the SH and the pressurized hanger began to fill with water. She stowed her rifle behind the pilot seat in the cockpit. Sitting down at the main controls, Poison established a connection with the Shadow Dome.

"SD, come in," Poison commanded.

"Yes, Poison," SD answered.

"Where am I headed?"

"Washington, the GPS has been updated. Your ETA is three hours, 14 minutes."

"Thank you, SD."

"You're welcome, Poison, good luck." Poison leaned back in the seat and hit the auto pilot. The Shadow Hopper floated through the cold water out from the hanger and to the surface. It emerged from the water slowly, cockpit first. Poison looked out and could see the sun rise, it was going to be a beautiful morning. The aircraft just bobbed up and down in the ocean for a few minutes, waiting for Poison to hit flight mode. The Shadow Dome was deep under water in the north Atlantic Ocean and the team spent most of their time there. It was like their home, but it is very easy to forget how nice sunlight can be. Poison loved a good sunrise, it always made her feel there is still hope. After almost forgetting what she was doing in the first place, Poison reached over and hit the flight button. The Shadow Hopper's engines fired up, jumping from the water and flying up into the air. Poison made herself comfortable, preparing herself for the long flight to Aberdeen, Washington. She opened the arm rest and unfolded a mini screen to review the information about her targets. The files had their names, current occupation, DMV photo, and last known address. It wasn't going to be easy to find these two needles in the giant hay stack. Poison continued to read and she slowly started to drift off. Falling asleep, sitting up right in her chair. Her arms slowly fell to each side of her seat. Before Poison knew it, the sound of the GPS telling her she had reached the destination woke her up. She looked out to see the Shadow Hopper hovering above a river under a bridge. It was mid-day and Poison didn't want anyone to see her. She quickly grabbed the main controls and set the Hopper into the water. The river was deep enough to hide the aircraft for a while.

"SD, come in."

"SD here, go ahead Poison," the Shadow Dome answered.

"I have reached Aberdeen and I have hidden the Hopper in a river."

"Copy, Poison. My sensors indicate you're in the Wishkah river."

"Right, I will check in every hour on my communicator. Poison, out," she replied. Poison avoided the obverse question. The one she was diyng to ask or hear some good news. The question about her son Tyton and Silver Shadow. Were they okay and what was their status? Like all mothers, she worried even when it seems it's not necessary. She had to stay focused if she was going to find these two people. Poison got up from her seat and grabbed her sniper rifle. The Hopper was still floating in the water under the bridge. She made her way to the lower level and to the back seat. The weapons locker is behind the last chair. Poison opened it and grabbed the small bracelet, placing it on her wrist. This arm band would track her location, communicate with SD, help navigate with a 3D map, and remote control the Hopper. Poison closed the locker turned around and used the narrow ladder to climb to the roof hatch. She slowly opened the hatch door and peered out, making sure the cost was clear. Poison climbed through the hatch and closed it. She stood on the top of the Hopper, weapon in hand. She slung her rifle on her shoulder and jumped into the water. It was only a few feet to the river bank. Poison swam till she could touch the bottom. After pulling herself from the water and reaching land, she turned around. Poison held out her arm and used the bracelet to control the Hopper. The arm band lit up and the Hopper slowly sank to the bottom of the brown mud colored murky river. It was deep enough, so no one would see it. *"It should be safe there for a while,"* Poison thought. She stood in some slightly tall grass and bushes. Poison started to walk up the river bank and saw a large sign held by two green metal posts with green frame work. Poison walked around the sign to read it. It had some writing on it, along with the name of the river. *"SD was right,"* she thought, *"the name of the river was Wishkah!?"* Poison began looking around the area. She saw a lot of telephone-sized wooden poles grouped together coming out of the water. They may have been used for an older bridge build before the current one. The bridge standing now had gray metal beams under concrete platforms with a heavy touch-looking guard rail. It looked like it was able to stop most any car from going over the edge. In the distance on the other side of the river was a few small buildings. There were small docks and boats alongside each building. *"The locates must do a lot of fishing judging by the size of each boat,"* Poison thought. Some houses sat back along the river with lots of small trees and bushes. The whole place seemed a bit secluded, too. Then she heard the sound of a car on the road. Poison quickly ducked down near the edge of the water. The car pasted without incident and Poison decided to be more careful. Poison held out her arm and hit a button on the bracelet. The 3D map projected in front of her. It showed which direction to go and what the address of the house was as well. Poison would be able to use the river as her guide for about a mile, after which she would have to wait till dark to make her way through a small neighborhood to reach the house. Poison memorized the map and clicked it off. She pulled her rifle from her back and started to make her way along the muddy river bank. Poison moved quickly and stayed low to keep out of sight. A few hours, she crept and finally reached a good spot to hide until dark. The sun was already starting to go down. In front of her were some large bushes and a little space in between them. Poison thought, *"This is a nice spot to rest."* She entered slowly with her weapon in hand. Poison wanted to make sure nothing else thought this was a good spot to hide, too. She heard a sound and snapped in the direction it was coming from. Looking through the sniper scope, she searched. Poison got her eyes on it, just a few birds chasing each other. She put her weapon down and planted herself on the ground. The birds flew away, up and out of the trees. Poison sat down with her back against a tree stump. She put her legs straight out in front of herself and laid the sniper rifle across her lap. It was nice and relaxing; there was a gentle breeze with the sun setting. *"Today was a good day,"* she thought to herself. She got to see the sun rise and set, it really doesn't get better than that. Poison's mind wondered for a few minutes; before long it was dark. The sounds of crickets could be heard and filled the night time background. Small clouds of fireflies were seen all around. *"Well, break time is over,"* Poison thought to herself. She grabbed her weapon from her lap and stood up. Holding out her arm again, she confirmed the direction she should go. The light from the 3D map lit up the small place between the bushes. Turning it off quickly, Poison moved through the brush and trees. She came upon what looked like a backyard. Chain link fence marked the outside perimeter with various children toys scattered through-out the yard. There was a small house with the lights still on. Poison moved along the fence, making sure not to touch it. The fence would make noise and she didn't want to attract any attention. Another house with a backyard and porch was next door. Their yard had no fence and the lights were off. Poison cut between the two houses and found a small road. Making it through to the over grown sidewalk, Poison stopped, making sure the coast was clear. She hid beside some tall well-trimmed shrubs. Glancing up and down the road, she evaluated the situation. Across more houses lined the other side of the road. The road was clear and had very few street lights. Poison would be able to move unseen more easily. The whole place was very quiet, like the rest of the town. Poison was used to busy streets, crowded subways, and well-lit plazas. This town might be a very nice place to get away from all the noise and pollution. Poison stayed very still for a minute, closing her eyes and relaxing her mind. She focused on listening, using her super hearing. Poison could hear things four blocks away. So many things at once, but she was able to focus on one thing at a time. Sorting through every sound at once like a radio, trying to find that balance. Poison always attempted this in the city, each time meeting failure. The city has way too many raw sounds, making it almost impossible. Poison could hear a mother and father talking about their child. Someone talking on the phone with their friend. Three teenagers having a sleep over and conversations about the boys they like. The sounds of splashing in a pool. *"Wait!"*

Poison thought. *"It's a little late to be taking a swim."* Poison stopped and tried to focus on the splashing sounds again. She could hear gasps along with the water. Without hesitation Poison darted across the road, passed between the next set of houses. Making her way across the front yard and to the back. Stopping herself quickly, looked behind both houses. She ran fast to check the backyard of the next two. *"Which way?"* she thought. Poison listened again, trying to pinpoint the source as she slung her rifle to her back. In front of her were another set of backyards. The sound was coming from the house across the next road. When she looked at the backyards in front of herself, the house on the left had a fenced in side yard. The tall unpainted wooden fence took up the space between the two houses. There was no time for Poison to go around. Poison ran along the side yard to the two backyards up to the wooden fence. With one leap, she lunched her body over it like a pole vaulter in the Olympics. She dodged a black grill and lawn chair as she ran across to the other side. Poison let herself out through the gate door, leading to the sidewalk. The sounds were getting louder, she was close. Poison quickly checked both ways before running across the road to the next set of houses. The house now in front of her had a large stone wall around it with a space for the driveway leading to a garage. The house on the left had a short dark green picket fence with trimmed hedges in the front half. Poison could hear the sound coming from behind these two houses, possibly in the next set of backyards. With a six-foot space, Poison ran straight up the middle and along the stone wall. After reaching the end, Poison turned the corner and saw her. There was a little girl in the next yard, drowning. The large in-ground pool was deep and there was an open sliding glass door on the other side. Without thinking Poison took her sniper rifle off her back, hiding it in a bush. She sprinted to the chain link fence that was around the pool and hopped over it. Poison leaped, diving into the water head first with her hands out. She swam under the little girl, struggling to stay above water. Poison quickly brought her to the pool edge, lifting her out of the water and onto the ground. The little girl began coughing up water, spitting it onto the ground. The girl was safe for now, she must have been about three-years-old. Poison climbed out of the water and knelt down beside her. The little girl sat in her own puddle, continuing to cough up water. After a few minutes, the little girl looked up at Poison with her big blue eyes.

"Are you okay?" Poison asked, softly rubbing the little girl's back. The little girl shook her head yes. "My name is Poison, you shouldn't go swimming by yourself, okay." For five minutes, they sat there together in the dark. The only light coming from the pool lamps under water, illuminating almost the whole yard in a light blue color. Suddenly the backyard lights mounted to the house came on.

"Alivia, Alivia, what are you doing out there?!" the little girl's mother said, running out through the sliding glass door. Opening the door more and quickly rushing out to scold her, the mother found her daughter sitting alone under the backyard light in a puddle of water. She quickly picked the little girl up in her arms. "Why are you all wet?" she asked, without even thinking. The mother looked around and saw another set of wet footprints leading to the grass on the outside perimeter of the pool. Still holding the little girl, she followed the wet prints all the way to the fence around the whole backyard. The mother stood there for a second, making sure no one was there. "I told you not to come out here by yourself," the mother said, putting her attention back on her daughter. She slowly walked back to the house. The mother was brushing the little girl, trying to get the small amount of water off. The little girl was moving restlessly around in her mother's arms, trying to look over her mother's shoulder to find Poison. The mother stopped in front of the door and turned back around. "Who are you looking for?" she asked, peering into the darkness herself.

"Poison," Alivia said.

"There's nobody out here, let's go!" the mother suggested. They both went back into the house, closing the sliding glass door behind themselves. Poison sat in the bushes, sniper rifle in hand, waiting for them to go back in the house. She could hear the mother lock the sliding glass door. The little girl was safe and Poison still had someone to find. She made her way past the house to the street. Poison looked both ways before crossing the road into a small wooded area. She stopped and took a knee in the middle of some tall trees. Then, she opened the 3D mini map again to see how far off course she strayed. She was one street away or two backyards from her target location. Poison glanced around and turned off the map once more. Trekking along the tree line, Poison moved around the house, following the edge of the neighborhood. She could see the street sign, *"There it is, Henry Alley,"* she thought to herself. Poison got into a position with a line of sight on the house. She found a spot across the street in some wild growing, uncut grass. Poison laid on her stomach sniper rifle in hand and looking through the scope, *"It seems quite enough,"* she thought. The stone house was two levels with a nice front yard. A fence and gate in front went around the whole house. There was a slab rock pathway leading to the front door from the side walk. In the driveway was one dark maroon colored four-door car. It looked almost new and had some odd-looking bumper stickers. Poison could tell someone was home by the one light still on inside. She focused on her hearing to see if she could tell who occupied the house and maybe what they were doing at this very moment. Poison stopped looking through the scope and concentrated. She could hear the wind blowing, a television reporting the news, and typing on a keyboard. She could only hear one heartbeat. There was just one person in the house. Poison began to stand up and make her way to the house. She slung her rifle over her shoulder and ran across the street. Poison quickly hopped over the three-foot fence and darted up to the house. She made her way around to the back door and looked for a way in. Poison peered into one of the windows and saw a small kitchen with the light off. The window was open a little. Poison removed the screen, placing it on the ground outside under the window. She opened the window further, slipping into the house next to a tall white refrigerator, rifle now in hand. She crouched down in the darkness, pointing her sniper rifle around, making sure no one saw her yet. Poison began to observe the room and her surroundings. The kitchen was very neat, everything was in place. There were no dirty dishes or things lying about the counter tops. Pots and pans hung neatly above the stove. Large wooden spoons on top were in a tall glass container. There were two doorways: one in front of her, another on her right. The one in front must have led to a living room, there was light coming from inside. Poison could still hear the TV. The room to her right was dark, but there was a little light coming from the other window. Poison crept to the right through the doorway and into the next room. It seemed to be set up as a hobby room with model air planes hanging from the ceiling and more boxes stacked on a table in the corner. Poison saw lots of the model planes all around the room, some still waiting to be opened and some displayed. The completed models had to have taken an extremely long time because each one was hand painted. The detail was extraordinary. Poison couldn't help but be a little captivated. She could see another doorway leading to a dining room. A large table with four chairs sat in the center of the room. A large light fixture dangled over the middle of the table. Poison made her way into the dining room slowly. As soon as she passed the doorway, on her right was a door slightly open. It was a small half bathroom and smelled like it was just cleaned today. The odor of bleach lingered. The house structure was set up to be a circle with each room leading to the next. Poison crept around the table and saw him. A man sitting at a computer in the corner of the living room. He was typing on his keyboard desktop. Poison could see a little over his shoulder. It looked like he was in the middle of designing some kind of plane. There was a diagram he was perfecting as he moved it around on the screen using his mouse. Poison stood there at the doorway, watching him for a minute, sniper rifle still in her hands. Suddenly, the man turned around in his chair to grab the TV remote and he saw Poison. She ducked back into the dining room.

"What the, hey!" the man yelled. He got up from his chair and snatched a nearby broom. "You'll have to kill me before I give up my air plane designs!" the man continued to yell. He was standing in front of his desk, holding the broom like a spear.

"I'm not here to hurt you," Poison said from around the corner.

"Oh, yeah, what's that thing in your hands? It's not a BB gun."

"I'm not here to hurt you," Poison repeated.

"Then come out and show yourself, or I'll call the police!" Poison took her sniper rifle and slung it onto her back and slowly walked out with her hands up.

"I'm really not here to hurt you."

"Oh, yeah, well, you look like some kind of assassin!"

"I am no assassin," Poison suggested; she hated being called that.

"I bet you're here to kill me and take all my designs. Well, can't have them!"

"I have no idea who you are or what you're talking about," Poison answered.

The Corrupt Shadows

"I don't buy that!" the man shouted. He waved the broom around like he was going to hit Poison with it.

"Are you Rick Bartos?"

"I knew it, you got my name from their hitlist, didn't you?"

"Do you know Doctor Michael Eastin?"

"Eastin? What's he got to do with this?" The man seemed caught off guard with the question.

"So, you know him?" Poison asked, still holding her hands up.

"Know him, yeah. But I haven't heard from him in almost 22 years. He sent you to find me?"

"No, his son did."

"His son? I didn't know he had any kids," the man said, starting to lower the broom in his hands. The man stood there, dressed for bed with his green striped pajamas, brown bath robe and dark blue slippers. He was about five-foot nine with black short hair and thick black frame glasses. He hadn't shaved in a few days, the five o'clock shadow around his face was starting to sprout. "He died, didn't he?"

"Yes, I'm sorry to be the one to tell you."

"I am Rick Bartos," the man admitted with some regret. His arms became limp at his side and he expressed sadness. The news of Eastin's death took its mark on his face. Poison had only known Eastin for a short time, but she was beginning to see how much he meant to everyone. "I meet him in college, and we became friends almost right away," Rick said, lowering his head down. He was filled with such sorrow and despair.

"So, that's how you knew him?" Poison asked, putting her hands down. Rick put the broom down and slowly sat back down in his black leather chair.

"Yes, he was a true friend, not just one of those people in your life you call friend. A real friend, someone you can count on always." Rick's eyes were filled with tears. "After I lost contact with him, I couldn't find him. Why did he do that?"

"He had to, I'm sorry. There were people after him, so he went into hiding." There was a brief silence, Poison could feel his pain. The moment came back, his last words to her before he died in her arms. Feeling his life slip away as she held him. The one thing in her life that Poison would never forget. Doctor Eastin was very important to her as well, a true hero in her eyes.

"Why?!" Rick cried.

"He did it to protect you and those close to him," Poison explained.

"I didn't have many friends even in college. But Michael helped me so many times. Even when he didn't have to. It's funny, he used to always call me Rickey." Poison felt Rick's pain, like Silver Shadow, he truly missed Doctor Eastin. The memories of Eastin helped make Rick smile a little. "So, why have you come here looking for me?" Rick asked, wiping the tears from his face.

"We found your…"

"Wait, we who?" Rick interrupted.

"The Silver Shadow and I…"

"Wait, hold on, who's Silver Shadow?"

"He is Eastin's son," Poison answered.

"Michael named his son Silver Shadow?"

"Yes, and it looks like Eastin left us your name, along with many others when it came time to find humans we could trust."

"Wait, you're not human?" Rick asked.

"I was, the Silver Shadow is not."

"You…you mean…he did it!?" Rick said, jumping from his chair, making it turn in circles. Rick started hopping up and down with some much joy, like he had just won the lottery or something. Poison took a step back a little.

"Did what?" Poison politely asked.

"He spent so much time trying to make it work, to make a super human, and he did it!" Rick celebrated the fact his best friend achieved his life's work. Rick stopped with his back to Poison, then he turned around. He held out his hand to Poison.

"Can I see?" he asked. "Can I see your armor?"

"Yes," Poison said, putting her hand in his.

"Amazing, it is…you are the most beautiful thing I have ever seen."

"Thank you," Poison answered, feeling a little uncomfortable, but she quickly realized Rick was happier his friend did not die for nothing. Eastin's life's work had been complete. To see it for himself brought him great joy. Before Poison could tell him more, she heard something outside. Three cars rolled up to the front of the house screeching to a stop. Rick snapped and quickly let go of Poison's hand and ran to the window.

"They're here!" he uttered, using his finger to hold down, at eye level, a section of the off-white blinds. He seems to be afraid of who might be out there.

"Who?" Poison asked confused.

"I think the same people who were after Michael. They want my designs and to silence me! I bet that's how they found me, tracking down all Michael's known associates. Anyone Michael has ever talked to could be on that list, some of which will be on your list, too!" Rick quickly ran to his computer and started saving everything. All his projects, data, and files. He put all of it onto a memory stick, already plugged into the computer. He turned around to Poison, who was looking out the window. "We have to get out of here," Rick said, pulling the memory stick out.

"I will take you with me," Poison said, looking around the room. She was trying to find the best way to escape. Poison also wanted to get a better look at the people coming after Rick. "*Who were they? Why are they after Rick? More importantly, who sent them?*" Poison thought to herself.

"What are you doing, we have to get out of here!" Rick frantically repeated.

"Okay, give me a second. I need to know more about these people," Poison reassured him. She had her hands out, examining the wall and ceiling.

"We can't exactly stay to ask them!"

"We won't have to," Poison replied, pulling something small from her utility belt.

"What's that?"

"It's an R.S.D.C.!"

"A what?"

"A Remote Self-Destructing Camera," Poison answered, holding it out. Rick stood closer to check it out.

"That little thing, it's the size of a dime."

"Yes, and it should do the trick." Poison was standing under a smock detector on the ceiling. She threw the R.S.D.C. up and it stuck to the top of the detector.

"Okay, can we go now!?"

"Yes, follow me and stay close." Poison and Rick went into the kitchen. Poison opened the window she had used to get in. Before going through it, she glanced out, making sure it was clear.

"What do you see?" Rick whispered.

"It's clear, for now." Poison started to climb out with Rick right behind her. As they crept slowly through the darkness away from the house, she stopped. Poison could hear the sounds of footsteps. The men have just started to surround the house. Poison grabbed Rick by the shirt and pulled him beside some tall bushes.

"Hey..."

"Sh!" Poison interrupted, holding one finger in front of her face. A man dressed in all black with full body armor and tactical gear walked past the bushes. By the look of what he was wearing, Poison could tell his suit had all the same features, weapons, and the same little logo on both the collar and shoulder of the shirt. They may be part of the same team that hit the original laboratory. Poison can only remember how much damage they did before. It would also mean if they were part of the same unit, BIO-TEC was involved as well. Poison started to become anger, she wanted pay back. Now was not the time, she would have to get Rick to safety first. The man stopped and stood near the bush they were hiding behind. Poison focused on her hearing, so she could tell how many there were. The footsteps gave them away, making it a little easier. *Ten maybe 12,*" she thought to herself. She could hear someone talking on their radios, giving the team instructions. If she was going to get out of here, she would have to wait until the team entered the house.

"Seven here, in position. Back perimeter is clear," the man said into the radio.

"Copy seven. Breaching team, stack up," the leader answered.

"Breaching team ready," they whispered.

"Go, go, go!" the leader commanded. Poison could hear a group of four or so hit the front door and charge into the house. If Poison and Rick were going to get out of there, now was the time. Poison used her hands to tell Rick to stay there. She creeped out from behind the bush. The man nearby had his back to her. Using the back of her rifle, she knocked him out. The man didn't stand a chance. He dropped like a rag doll to the ground. Poison glanced around to make sure it was still clear and he was the only one on this side of the house. She looked back at Rick, who was watching her. Poison waved to him to follow her. Rick quickly slid from behind the bush and looked down at the man.

"Remind me never to get you mad," he quietly admitted.

"Let's go," Poison replied. She led the way, using the same path she used to get to the house without being seen. The two of them stayed low and moved quickly through one backyard after another. Poison felt Rick starting to slow down, so she stopped. He seemed a little out of shape.

"Wait, can we rest for a minute?" Rick said, trying to catch his breath. He was falling a little behind. He stood next to Poison, hunched over with his head down gasping for air. Then he looked up, "Where are we going anyway?"

"To the Shadow Hopper," she answered, peering around to make sure they hadn't been seen or followed.

"What, what is a Shadow Hopper?"

"Come on, it will be light soon," Poison snapped, beginning to run again.

"Hey, wait up…what's a Shadow Hopper?" Rick asked again. This slightly heavy-set man was going to have to keep up if he had any hope to live longer than tonight.

"I'll show you when we get there."

"Get where?"

"The river where I hid it," Poison replied. The two of them made their way to Wishkah River. Poison found the same path she took on the way in. She wasted no time finding the river and followed it back upstream to the bridge. The sun was starting to come up and Poison would have to move fast if she didn't want to be seen. She stopped and quickly pressed a small button on the bracelet. Rick sat down next to her with sweat rolling down his face.

"So, where is it?" he impatiently asked.

"Here," Poison said, pointing to the bubbles in the brown murky water. The bubbles began to get bigger and the Shadow Hopper emerged from the middle of the river. It hovered over the water and moved close to them. The door opened along with an extending ramp, Poison and her new friend climb aboard. "Come on," she said, helping Rick inside. Once in Poison hit the big red button on the wall to close the door and ramp behind them. "Take a seat and I'll get us air borne."

"Oh, okay," Rick replied, looking around at everything. Poison made her way up to the cockpit. She sat down and started to fly the Shadow Hopper out from under the bridge. It hovered slowly just above the surface, pushing the water away from the bottom. After it cleared the bridge, Poison flew it up and out of sight, high between the clouds. She stowed her rifle next to the seat, which she neglected to do at first. Poison clicked on the auto pilot and went to check on Rick. He was sitting in one of the chairs with one of the small screens unfolded from the arm rest.

"So, Rick, I see you found the computer."

"Yeah, and call me Rickey. Only my friends call me that. Seeing how I only had one, and you did save me. I think that makes us friends, right?"

"Yes, um… What are you doing?" Poison asked, watching Rickey plug the memory stick into the side if the screen.

"I'm uploading all my designs."

"Right, well, we have one more stop to make before we go see Silver Shadow and I think I'm going to need your help."

"One more stop?! Where, why?" Rickey asked, looking up from what he was tinkering with.

"Yes, it is daytime now and I have to find another person in Kennewick," Poison said, walking away.

"Wait, who?" Rickey rebutted. Poison didn't answer him. Rickey continued hooking up the portable screen. Poison went back up to the cockpit. Sitting down in the pilot seat, she tried to hale the Shadow Dome.

"SD, come in, this is Poison, do you read me?"

"Yes, Poison, I am receiving you."

"I have deployed an RSDC number 257154 at 3:23 am. The address is 17 Henry Alley. Can you confirm solid link for trap and trace?"

"Affirmative, Poison, I have established a live fed and I have recorded all images."

"Copy, SD, I have the first target and I am on my way to the next," Poison replied. "What's the stats of Silver Shadow?"

"He has checked in and they have found their target as well. I am awaiting confirmation and location on their next check in."

"Copy, Poison out." Poison sat back in her chair and relaxed a little bit. Knowing Silver Shadow and her son Tyton were safe made her feel at ease. Those two always seem to find trouble where ever they go. Reaching over and lighting up the 3D GPS, Poison set it for the next target location. She set the auto pilot and the Shadow Hopper sailed through the cloud cover. Poison glanced at the ETA (estimated time of arrival) displayed on the GPS. *"Twelve minutes,"* she thought. After hitting a series of icons, Poison was able to view what SD had found on the next target. Hector Wells appeared to be a special mechanic. The address found was the same in the GPS, 3709 West 20th Avenue. He attended the same collage as Eastin but a year after Eastin had graduated. She continued to read the file on Hector for a while. A tone sounded, they have arrived at the destination. Poison snapped her attention to the window. She looked out to see the Shadow Hopper hovering in place high above a small light brown house. The aircraft was high, still in the cloud cover. Poison peered down at the narrow street, trying to find a nice place to land. No place to land without anyone seeing the aircraft. Cars moved about, passing the house every few minutes. Poison watched for a few minutes, she would have to go down and see if anyone was home. Poison got up from her seat and went back down the ladder. Rickey was in the same spot trying to download his files.

"Rickey, I need you to stay here while I go check the house."

"Where, you don't need me to come with you?"

"No, not yet," Poison replied.

"Okay, by the way, I seem to be having trouble getting my files to upload on this computer," Rickey said.

"How many files are we talking about?"

"I don't know, never counted them. Four hundred or more. All of them at least a gig."

"Gig as in gigabytes?" Poison asked.

"Yeah, my designs are very complex you know," Rickey answered, shrugging his shoulders and holding his hands out, palms up.

"This aircraft has not been updated to handle that much information yet, so I will set up a link with SD and you can download the data there."

"Okay, what's SD?"

"The Shadow Dome, it's our HQ."

"Oh, I knew that," Ricky said, scratching the back of his head. Poison reached around Ricky and logged into the other computer.

"SD, this is Poison, do you read me?" Poison asked, looking into the computer screen. The monitor lit up and a live feed of the control room came up.

"Affirmative, Poison."

"I have Ricky here. There are some files he would like to download to your main frame."

"Confirm, Poison, I am ready to receive data." Before Poison could say anything, she glanced back and Ricky was looking over her shoulder.

"Is that your headquarters?"

"Yes," Poison answered, jumping a little. She was caught by surprise by how close he got so quickly. "Ricky!" Poison said, trying to get his attention followed by a look that said back up a little.

"Yes, oh, sorry," apologized Ricky, stepping back.

"Plug your memory stick in this computer. When you are ready, press that icon there on the screen," Poison explained, getting up from the seat and sitting Ricky down in it by holding his shoulders. She stood behind him, making sure he heard what she just inferred. Ricky unplugged the memory stick from the computer he was originally trying to use. As he inserted it into the computer Poison set up for him, Ricky glanced back, attempting to see if Poison was still standing over him, watching him like a child and waiting for him to do something wrong.

"Verifying data from live link on memory stick number 117," SD said. "Data upload complete."

"Wow, that was fast!" Ricky implied.

"Rick, would you like to name your files to make it easier to find in my main frame?" SD asked.

"Yes, I would. Call it Falcon File 117."

"Confirmed, Rick."

"So, SD, is that what I call you?"

"Yes, you can use this name if you wish."

"What are you exactly? Some kind of A.I.?"

"Yes, I am a self-operating A.I. tasked with protecting this secret laboratory and the shadow team," SD exclaimed.

"Wow, amazing," Ricky remarked. Poison was getting ready to drop down to the house. Just before she opened the drop door, she stopped.

"I'll let you two talk, stay here and try not to get into trouble," Poison interrupted, turning around, looking at Ricky. She was already standing at the back of the aircraft. He was glued to the screen, making another new friend.

"Uh, oh, okay," Ricky said, half paying attention to her. Poison turned back around, hitting the big red button to open the drop door. The door opened, bringing in a rush of air from the outside. After thinking about it for a second, Ricky was confused. "Wait, how are you going to get down to the house, we have to be a couple hundred feet in the air?"

"Easy," Poison said as she leaped from the end of the extended drop ramp. Ricky jumped from his seat and ran to the edge of the ramp. He looked down to see Poison falling to the ground. Ricky watched terrified, he was going to see her die. Poison fell fast and landed on her feet as she always did.

"Wow... Did you just see...how did she...?!" Ricky said. The drop door closed and the ramp retracted. He just couldn't believe what he just saw. Ricky walked back to his chair and plopped down in it. "SD, are you still there?"

"Yes, Rick, I am."

"She just jumped from this Shadow Hopper from about 300-feet up," Ricky said, still in shock.

"Yes, they have performed things like this many times before. They surpass human limits as Shadows," SD explained.

"So, they do this kind of stuff all the time?"

"Yes, they are highly trained super beings by definition. They are in a classification of their own."

"Holy cow! Oh, and SD?"

"Yes."

"You can call me Ricky."

"Ricky... I like this name better," SD admitted. While Rickey and SD got better acquainted, Poison touched down in the backyard. The yard was a little small with trimmed seven-foot tall square bushes. A short light brown stone wall followed the inside edge of the yard. Poison stood in front of a flat railless wooden deck with one step leading to the back door. The green grass was cut low and neat. *"Whoever lives here likes their privacy,"* Poison thought to herself. She walked up to the white aluminum screen door. Poison opened it to get to the dark wooden back door. Using some locksmith tools from her utility belt, she was able to gain entry. Once inside Poison moved slowly. She was standing in the kitchen next to a stove. Poison stopped and focused on hearing, *"There's no one here!*" she thought. She started to glance around, looking for clues as to where the target might be. She hoped it wasn't too late. The kitchen was a mess, with a garbage can overflowing, some dirty dishes in the sink, and an old pizza box still on the counter. There were some things around the room that would suggest a girlfriend or at least a woman lives here. Like short yellow curtains hanging in the one window. A few handmade knitted things under the one plant in the corner on a round end table. A note on the tall white refrigerator starting with the words honey and ending with love you. Poison found herself standing in the middle of the room, reminded of her old life. The little things she would do for her boyfriend. Her memories were fading away like a dark rain cloud. She often compared her old life with the new. Thinking of how much she has grown and the love she shared. Poison started to move through the house from one room to the next. *"Maybe they are at work,"* she thought. *"It is the middle of the day."* Poiosn went into the living room. It was large with a fireplace and neater than the kitchen. The old brown rug covered the floor wall to wall with new looking furniture. Except for one worn down dark green arm chair, folded newspapers covered its seat. Poison continued to check out the place. There was a T-shirt in a frame hanging behind the green chair on the wall. Kennewick Lions in big yellow letters on it. Poison continued to peer around when some pictures on the mantel caught her eye. There were several small framed pictures, *"Could it be?"* Poison questioned herself. She walked over and picked up one of the pictures. It was two kids standing next to each other with their arms round one another. One of them was Doctor Eastin as a child. The face was different but very much the same. The other could only be the target, the person she was looking for. This was the connection, how Eastin knew this person, *"They must have been childhood friends."* Poison placed the picture back just as she found it and started to search. Next to the wore down dark green chair was a small square table. Papers cover the top of it. Poison checked some of the papers, trying not to touch too many of them. Some were mail but not with the same address. It was an address of a business, some kind of automotive shop. Poison held out her arm and plugged in the address, sending it to the Shadow Hopper from her bracelet. The same 3D map lit up, showing her where in town the shop was. It wasn't far from where she was now. *"This must be where he works,"* she thought to herself. Poison turned off the map and went outside through the back door, making sure she left everything the way it was when she came in. Poison pressed another button on her bracelet, calling the Shadow Hopper. The SH floated into position right over her head. The back door opened with the ramp. A thin steel cable lowered with a hook on the end. Poison quickly locked the hook in place on her belt and pressed the same button again on her bracelet. The cable began to quickly pull her up off the ground to the back door. Still in the cloud cover, the Shadow Hopper was completely unseen. Now standing on the end of the ramp, Poison unhooked the steel cable from herself.

"You're back. Did you find him?" Ricky asked.

"No, we may have to make another stop," Poison replied.

"Where?"

"I found another address, it might be where this person works. I'm going to need your help on this one," Poison insisted, walking past him on her way up to the cockpit.

"Oh, okay," Ricky said. "Hey, SD, I have to go now, but I look forward to meeting you in person."

"Good luck, Ricky."

"Thanks, Shadow Hopper out!" Ricky said into the video chat, giving the screen an old fashion salute. The computer screen went blank and Ricky got up from the chair. He started looking for Poison, then she climbed down the ladder from the cockpit. The aircraft had already traveled to the new address and Poison found a nice low-key place to land.

"Are you ready?" she asked.

"Yes," Ricky answered, holding out his hands and shrugging his shoulders. "What do I have to do?"

"I have set the Shadow Hopper on auto pilot to land in a fenced-in empty lot a few buildings down the block from the shop."

"Okay, what kind of shop is it?"

"It is a little car repair shop," Poison explained. "I need you to walk down to it and enter the shop. Its open, so act like a customer"

"Right, then what?"

"You're going to ask for a person named Hector Wells."

"Got it, what should I say once I find him?"

"Try and speak with him alone, tell him about yourself, me, and how you got here. I will be close by if he needs proof," Poison concluded.

"Alright, I can do this." Ricky said aloud, trying to calm himself. Poison put her hand on his shoulder.

"I'll be right beside you."

"Okay, I can do this," Ricky repeated. The Shadow Hopper came to a stop. It had made its landing. Poison lead Ricky to the back door. She hit the button and the doors opened slowly. The ramp extended onto the ground and they both walked down it. Poison made sure it was clear first. The empty lot was were the car repair shop kept all the old unrepairable cars. All the mangled cars sat stacked on top of each other, six or seven cars high. The whole lot fenced in with barbed wire lining the top of the ten-foot tall fence. Some nearby trees had also made their mark growing their thin light vines along some parts of the top. As well as growing over the edge to the other side, providing some shade from the sun. It was the perfect place for the Shadow Hopper to hide. No one could see in, even if they were looking. The view from all sides were covered by cars or trees. Both Ricky and Poison had landed right in the middle. At the end of the narrow lot was a gate leading to the sidewalk and street. Poison walked Ricky to it. From above the street looked very busy, lots of people coming and going.

"Use this gate to get out. The repair shop is three buildings down on the right," Poison whispered. They both stood with their backs up against a stack of cars hiding.

"Okay, what about you?"

"I'll be fine, meet you there."

"Okay," Ricky replied, holding a thumbs up. He stepped in front of Poison, who was frozen in place. After passing her, he slowly opened the gate door. "Wait, should I tell him dangerous people are after him?" Ricky said, turning around to ask Poison, but she was gone. "She should be a magician, she disappeared so fast!" he remarked. Ricky slipped out of the gate and onto the sidewalk. The long-locked chain around the gate door provided a big enough gap. The street was busy and the sidewalk was wide and well kept. Parked cars filled almost every parking space on both sides of the street. People were doing their shopping in all the small local shops. Everyone seemed to have some place to go and things to do. Ricky looked up and saw a banner of an upcoming car show. It was a typical main street right down to the light posts and trash cans. All the buildings made mostly of red bricks or brown stone. They sat in a nice row close to one another. Each with its own heavy metal plaque commemorating the year it was built mounted to the front wall to be viewed by everyone. There were lots of parking meters and extra wide cross walks for the handicap. Ricky began to relax a little, but he still felt out of place in his pajamas. He was only a few towns from home after all, maybe he could stop and get some clothes. The people were friendly here, each person said hello in their own way as they passed by Ricky. He slowly walked down the sidewalk, glancing into every store he past. He was making sure nothing was out of place besides him. Ricky saw a clothing store he could pick out some stuff. He reached into his bathrobe pocket, making sure the little bit of cash was still there. It was whatever was left over from when he ordered the pizza for dinner. As soon as he walked in, Ricky was greeted by the shopkeeper.

"Hello there, can I help you find anything?"

"Yes, I seem to have locked myself out and I need some clothes."

"Man, don't you hate it when that happens?" the shopkeeper suggested.

"Yeah!" Ricky answered.

"Sure, I can help you. Right this way." The shopkeeper lead Ricky to a rack of clothes. After about ten minutes, Ricky stepped out onto the street with a fresh pair of clothes. His bathrobe and pajamas rolled up in a white plastic bag. He kept the dark moccasins he used for slippers on, along with a pair of new blue jeans and gray T-shirt. Feeling more comfortable, Ricky made his way down the street to the repair shop. As he walked, Ricky glanced over and saw Poison on the rooftop of one of the buildings across the street. She was pointing to the car repair shop and Ricky looked over. He was only 30-feet from the front door. He could hear power tools going and a low sounding radio playing. Ricky looked back at Poison and she was gone again. Not giving it a second thought, Ricky walked down the sidewalk and into the front door. He pulled open the glass door with a metal frame and a bell rang. Still holding the white plastic bag with his clothes under his arm, Ricky approached the counter.

"Hello there," Ricky said plopping his bag on the tall gray counter. A man stood behind the counter on a computer.

"Hello, can I help you with something?" the man answered.

"I hope so, this is going to sound, odd but I'm looking for someone."

"Alright, I will try to help you out."

"I'm looking for a friend of a friend named Hector Wells," Ricky added. "Does he work here?"

"Hector? Yeah, he's here! Let me page him." Ricky stood there patiently as the man picked up a nearby phone and talked over the loud speaker. "Hector to the front desk, Hector to the front desk!" the man shouted. "So, what's this about, if you don't mind me asking?"

"Oh, well, I found out a good friend of mine died. A few days ago, I learned from his family that he knew Hector, so I decided to look him up."

"Oh, I'm sorry to hear that," the man sympathized.

"Thank you," Ricky continued "I learned Hector worked here in the same state."

"Oh, are you from Washington?"

"Yes, Aberdeen," Ricky replied.

"Really, my mother lives out there," the man said with some surprise.

"Oh, yeah, nice." Before Ricky could say anything else, a door behind the man open. Another man stepped out. He was well fit wearing blue jean overalls and black work boots. He was carrying a red rag, using it to wipe oil off his hands. His black hair was buzzed cut short and he had a goatee. "Are you Hector?"

"Yeah, how are doing?" Hector answered, extending his hand. Ricky reached out and shook his hand.

"Hello, you don't know me, but I think you know a good friend of mine. Michael Eastin."

"Yeah, but I haven't heard from him in a good while."

"Is there a place we can talk in private?" Ricky asked. The man behind the counter went into the back through the same door Hector came out, trying to give them a minute. The man didn't say a word in an effort to be polite. Hector gazed at Ricky with his dark brown eyes, puzzled for a second.

"Sure, this way," Hector answered. Ricky grabbed his white plastic bag from the top of the counter as Hector shows him through a side door. They walked down a hallway and out another door, exiting the back of the repair shop. Hector and Rickey stepped outside into an alleyway in between the buildings. The alley was mostly clean with two large black dumpsters and various trash cans. The alley was just big enough for a dump truck or delivery truck to get in. The two stood at the end of an elevated loading dock for the repair shop. Yellow lines marked the edge, along with two bright yellow half poles protruding from the ground a foot from the loading dock. Rickey looked up at the top of the red brick walls on both side of himself. The sunlight lit up the whole alley and a soft breeze could be felt. Hector turned around to face Ricky. "So, what is going on? Who sent you?" Hector asked impatiently.

"What do you mean? No one sent me. I hate to be the one to tell you this but, Michael is…"

"He's gone, isn't he?" Hector interrupted, putting his head down.

"Yes," Ricky confirmed, putting his hand on Hector's shoulder. "You knew it, too, uh?!"

"I have suspected for a while and then I received this in the mail this morning," Hector answered, pulling out a white envelope from his back pocket. He handed it to Ricky. Not sure what to make of it, Ricky grabbed the folded envelope. Inside was a letter telling Hector he was to turn himself in or he would never see his sister again.

"What's this?" Ricky asked, briefly reading the letter.

"I was given very specific instructions to go to work today and tell my boss that I quit. I would be contacted tonight with further instructions."

"They want you, too?" Ricky said out loud.

"Who?"

"The same ones after me," Ricky said, looking up from the letter.

"Wait, what do you mean?" Hector pleaded.

"I may be able to help." a voice said. Before Ricky could say anything, he looked up. Poison was standing on the roof of the building, looking down at the two of them. Hector looked up.

"What the… Who are you?" Poison jumped down right in front of them. Hector moved back a little in shock.

"My name is Poison and Doctor Eastin saved my life." Hector looked at her curiously. For the moment, he was speechless.

"It's okay, Hector, she is here to help," Ricky implied. "Michael's son sent her to find us." Hector sighed with relief and began to relax a little.

"What are you, some kind of alien?" Hector asked.

"No, I'm half human, half shadow," Poison answered. Hector didn't know what to say, he was still a little shocked. "You two grew up together?" Poison questioned.

"Yes, how did you know that?" Hector answered, rubbing the back of his head and squinting his eyes at her.

"I saw a picture of you two as children in your house."

"You were in my house? Can she help me save my sister?" Hector asked Ricky. Poison turned to Ricky and he handed Poiosn the letter. Poison open it and began to read. Ricky and Hector just stood there in silence while she read. Poison stopped reading and lowered the letter from her eyes.

"We're going to need some help," Poison remarked.

*

Chapter Ten
Past, Present, Future

Silver Shadow and Tyton were taken by the old man's response, surprised at his conformability around them. Most people are afraid at first sight of a shadow. It was as if he knew all about the shadow race. How could he have known? The old man still sat Indian style on the floor with his hands together, praying. His eyes were closed and his head slightly down.

"You know me?" Silver Shadow asked, stepping out of the shadows moving closer to the old man. The old man opened his eyes and stood up. He was very short compared to Silver Shadow. The old man was five-foot five inches tall, thin, bald, and had a wrinkled face. His eyes were blue, clean shaved, with dark colored skin. The old man had an orange colored tattered robe with some signs of age on the sleeves. Little tears here and there all over the front and back. A crimson red colored belt tried tightly around his waist.

"Yes, I am the one you seek. I have waited a long time to meet the Guardian of Shadows."

"Are you Mace Lii?"

"Yes, come sit. Both of you," Mace answered, holding out one of his hands, showing them where to sit. Tyton emerged from the shadow he was hiding in and walked over. Silver Shadow and the old man sat down together on the floor. The room was a bit small and old fashion. It had the traditional Japanese bamboo wooden floor and architecture to go with it. There were no signs of technology or modern conveniences found in a normal house. The three of them sat in a little group around the small table with a incense stick still burning. "You must have so many questions, Guardian."

"Why do you keep referring to me as Guardian?"

"It is the reason you were made, why you came to be. I have seen your future, and I am here to guide you," Mace implied.

"Guide me where?"

"You mustn't concern yourself with where, only the journey. Before your quest is over, you will have to face many obstacles along the way. I must prepare you."

"Did you know my father?"

"Your father, Michael Eastin, was a great man. He may have saved our whole world with you. Yes, I knew him very well. Sad to learn of his death."

"When did you meet my father?" Silver Shadow asked, trying to learn more about his father's past and where Mace fit in.

"He sought me out much like you and your son did," Mace answered. Silver Shadow stopped for a second, Mace Lii knew way more than Silver Shadow thought he did.

"How did you know this is my son?"

"You two are very much the same, the resemblance is undeniable," Mace said with a smile. "The events of your past, your present, and your future remain clear to me." Silver Shadow looked over at Tyton. Tyton was just as surprised as his father. "Long ago Michael sat where you now sit. When he became my student, he called me Master Lii. Much like you, he, too, searched for answers. I began to teach him, and he patiently learned the art of foresight."

"Can you teach me?"

"It is the reason you have come, Guardian." Silver Shadow glanced over at Tyton again, trying to get his impression of Mace. He didn't know what to think. The incense in the center of their little group slowly burned out, leaving the smoke to linger around the top of the room. Before Silver Shadow could say anything else, Mace stood up. "I must rest now, we will start your training first thing in the morning." Mace slowly walked over to another sliding door. Silver Shadow and Tyton watched him as he left. "Make yourselves at home,"

Mace said stepping through the door. Silver Shadow and Tyton just sat there in the center.

"Father, is it true?" Tyton asked.

"Is what true?" Silver Shadow repeated.

"My grandfather could see the future?"

"It would very well explain a lot of things."

"You didn't know?" Tyton inquired.

"I had always felt something, I could never figure it out. Your grandfather worked on many things at once. Almost like he wasn't going to have enough time. He would over work himself," Silver Shadow answered. It was still hard for Silver Shadow to talk about his father. He put his head down. Tyton tried to understand and learn more about his grandfather.

"I'm sorry for asking so many questions."

"It's alright, you should know everything. Sometimes I wish he was still here to see you," Silver Shadow said, looking up again. "One of my biggest regrets is you didn't get the chance to meet him."

"I think we would have had a lot of things in common," Tyton replied.

"The three of us would have done so many things together."

"What do you think Master Lii meant about being your guide?"

"My path may be much different than I had imagined," Silver Shadow remarked.

"You mean like a destiny or something?"

"Yes, exactly right."

"Do you think Master Lii knows your destiny?" Tyton asked, very intrigued by the notion of fate and future.

"Not sure, he did know a lot about my past and your grandfather. It is very possible." Silver Shadow and Tyton continued to talk through the night. Before long the sun began to rise and so did Master Lii. The door slid open and Master Lii walked out.

"Good morning, Guardian," Master Lii said, emerging from the other room. He walked over to the center of the room and sat down slowly next to the small table.

"Good morning, Master Lii," Silver Shadow and Tyton said at the same time. Mace reached down, opening a small panel in the floor. It was a loose floor board with a hidden compartment. Inside were bags of more incense. Mace pulled out one and closed the floor board. He removed what was left of the last incense stick and put the new one in its place. Mace reached under the small table and pulled out a little box of matches.

"Today, we will start by opening your mind," he said, lighting the incense. "I know you don't sleep, but do you dream?"

"Yes, more like flashes. A quick picture or snap shot," Silver Shadow answered.

"Does this confuse you?"

"Yes because I try hard to make sense of it."

"What about you, Tyton?" Master Lii asked. Tyton looked at his father. He was surprised Silver Shadow had flashes like him.

"I dream and have flashes," Tyton went on, "but mine are more like premonitions." Silver Shadow looked over at his son. They really hadn't talked about these things before.

"How come you never told me?" Silver Shadow asked.

"Didn't know what to say and they just sort of started happening."

"Can you decrypt what you see in your visions?" Master Lii requested.

"I see you, Father. Only it's not you," Tyton said, looking at Silver Shadow. Both Master Lii and Silver Shadow took great interest in what Tyton was saying.

"What do you mean?" Silver Shadow asked.

"The shadows I see look like you, but each is different. It is always the same seven, from different places and maybe different lives. I can't tell if they're from my father's past or future. I sometimes feel like they are all searching for the same thing."

"This is most interesting," said Master Lii, rubbing his chin with the tips of his fingers in a circle motion around his mouth. "And how long do your visions last?"

"As long as I remain focused," Tyton replied.

"Very interesting," Master Lii replied, standing up, continuing to rub his face. "I am able to see your father's path but not yours. And if you say your visions last as long as you want them to, hm!"

"What do you think, Master Lii?" Silver Shadow went on. "He is witnessing present live in other dimensions?"

"It is quite possible, it would be the only logical explanation. My teacher told me of such a power and that it could only be held once a lifetime." Master Lii walked back over to the table and sat back down.

"What does this mean?" Tyton asked. Master Lii leaned over the table, looking closer at Tyton, gazing deep into his eyes.

"It means you have a great gift, maybe the most powerful one yet. We will need to unlock it. Only time will tell," Master Lii said with a chuckle, leaning back.

"Where do we begin?" Silver Shadow requested.

"Meditation, a clear mind can always be filled with drive and focus," Master Lii replied. Silver Shadow looked at Tyton, his son seemed ready to learn. This may have been his power trying to reveal itself.

"I am ready," Tyton said aloud.

"First, you must close your eyes and empty your mind. Make your body still and motionless," Master Lii requested, closing his eyes and moving about in his sitting position. Silver Shadow and Tyton followed Master Lii's instruction, doing everything he did. "Listen and feel your heart's every beat," Master Lii whispered. The three of them sat there sitting on the floor in the middle of the room until the incense burned out. Only ash remained, along with the smoke and a bitter smell lingering throughout the room. After a few minutes, Tyton was able to focus and his visions started. He began to see a glimpse of all seven different shadows one by one. Tyton's ghost-like spirit was swimming alongside one shadow deep in a cold dark ocean. The cold water swelled around his body. Then walking next to another through a thick and dense jungle. The dry heat, damp and stuffy. Then Tyton was standing behind a shadow in a high security area of a building. The loud sounds of an alarm pierced his eardrum. After Tyton found himself next to a shadow on the edge of a mountain looking down at the inside of a volcano, he could feel the heat as if he was there. His ghost jumped to another shadow in a dark cave, moving rocks with his mind. With every large boulder being slammed down, he would feel dust raining down on his head from above. In an instant, Tyton was on a glacier in the middle of a frozen wasteland. The last shadow was standing in the middle of a large group. Several robots surround him in what seemed to be a standoff. Tyton's spirit floats just above him, looking on with fear. The robots begin to attack the lonely shadow. Before they could harm him, the shadow's whole body starts to glow. In a blink of an eye, the shadow turns into a big purple dragon. It was absolutely beautiful, with its large wings flapping and yellow glowing eyes. He fights the robots, biting and clawing his way through them. The dragon breathes fire at the robots so hot, most of them melted into small puddles. In a few minutes, the dragon defeats all of his aggressors. Tyton's spirit continues to watch, still floating just above the purple dragon. The dragon stops and looks up right at Tyton's spirit. Their eyes lock for a moment, it was clear the shadow could see Tyton.

"Can you see me?" Those eyes glared at him, looking deep into Tyton's soul. Before the dragon could answer his question, everything went dark. Tyton could no longer see anything and the sound of his father's voice woke and disturbed him from his vision. Silver Shadow's voice was calling to him.

"Tyton, Tyton...," Silver Shadow whispered. Tyton could feel someone shaking him by the shoulders. He opened his eyes to see his father knelt down in front of him. He was holding on to Tyton by his shoulders. "Are you okay?" Silver Shadow asked.

"Yes, what happened?" Tyton answered, shaking his head a bit, trying to escape the trance he was in.

"You were meditating all day, but now we must go."

"Why, what's happening?" Tyton pleaded, looking around the room still a little dazed. Master Lii was standing in the middle of the room in an unusual fight-like stance. His body was very still but ready for anything. It was like he was waiting for something or someone. Master Lii slowly looked at Tyton and Silver Shadow.

"Assassins," Master Lii whispered. Silver Shadow and Tyton stood up together.

"We will protect you!" Sliver Shadow insured.

"Yes, I know. For this is the reason, I call you the Guardian of Life."

"Tyton, be ready for anything," Silver Shadow pointed out.

"Should we use our weapons?" Tyton asked.

"No, we don't want to kill anyone by mistake, and something tells me we will not have enough bullets," Silver Shadow remarked. The two shadows took up positions on either side of Master Lii. Silver Shadow stood in front of Master

The Corrupt Shadows

Lii slightly to the right. Tyton was behind him slightly to the left. The three of them waited and listened. They could hear sounds coming from the roof. Like many people were scurrying across along the top of the building. The sounds were very fain but loud enough for someone who was paying attention. More subtle sounds were coming from the walls around them. It would seem they were surrounded by many assassins. To even Silver Shadow, the sounds of how many were outside made it hard for him to analyze or describe.

"Guardian…" Silver Shadow looked over at Master Lii.

"Yes, Master," Silver Shadow answered.

"They will have swords. Have you studied the ancient samurai? Or how to use a Katana?" Master Lii asked. Silver Shadow glanced over at Tyton. He hadn't studied any Japanese history either.

"No."

"I have a book in my room," Master Lii continued. "Can you learn as fast as I have perceived?" Both Tyton and Silver Shadow shook their heads yes at the same time. Their body language suggested learning in a second will be easy. More sounds began vibrating the floor boards beneath their feet. "We must retrieve the book and head for the temple," Master Lii insisted. He looked back into his room and could see the red book in question. Tyton glanced back and could see the book as well. Using his eyes, Master Lii made a suggestion. Tyton knew what to do. The vibrations became stronger, and before anyone could react, the floor exploded. Fragments of wood from the floor along with dark brown dirt spread widely over half the room. Seconds later the ceiling in two places blew out in front of them. When the dust cleared, nine human figures emerged from the new holes in the structure. They were ninja warriors wearing all black armored-like suits. They lurked in like black mist. It was a silent stand-off with Master Lii, Silver Shadow, and Tyton versus the nine unknown assassins. Each of the nine ninjas were armed with a pair of short swords. One of the pair, a bit longer than the other. Silver Shadow was studying, making a note of which side each ninja wore their swords. Calculating the angles of attack and what hand to isolate when being engaged. He could only see their eyes, so there wasn't much to go on when telling them apart from each other. "Who are you, and why have you come?" Master Lii asked, breaking the silence. One of the ninjas stepped forward.

"Foolish old man, did you think we wouldn't find you?"

"Did you think I was hiding from you?" Master Lii continued. "Who is the foolish one?"

"It makes no difference now. My master wanted you kept alive, but his search for you over the years has exhausted his patience."

"So, you are here to kill me. Are you still willing to follow your master down this path? It will bring you only death."

"You know nothing!" the ninja leader shouted. "I have my honor."

"I know more than you think, young warrior. I have seen things that transcend your understanding," said Master Lii.

"I don't believe in your mind tricks and black magic."

"You will, I only hope it won't be too late."

"Enough, we will kill you and your new friends, old man," the ninja leader announced. Master Lii, Silver Shadow, and Tyton stood ready. With their hands up held out in front of themselves and open fist. With Silver Shadow still standing in front of him, Master Lii quickly reached out and grabbed Silver Shadow's arm. Silver Shadow could see a vision, it was Master Lii's touch. Somehow, he was able to project his thoughts of moments in time before it happens. Silver Shadow could see events that have not yet come to pass. The visions were brief but gave Silver Shadow insight on their current situation. Master Lii let go of Silver Shadow, he glanced back at Master Lii. All the ninjas slowly grasped the handle of their swords. Master Lii nodded his head as if to say what Silver Shadow just saw was real. Silver Shadow's eyes began to glow and he snapped his head back, looking the ninja leader face to face. "What kind of Ancient Samurai are you?"

"A Guardian you have never seen," replied Silver Shadow, looking at the other ninjas like he knew something they didn't. The ninja leader's body language showed a bit of caution. It was all the edge Silver Shadow needed. The lead ninja with others behind him stepped out closer in front of Silver Shadow. Six more ninjas stood behind them, three per side.

"Tyton, go!" Master Lii shouted. The ninja leader reached for his sword and lunched at Silver Shadow. The two ninjas behind him followed. The three ninjas on the right in the back pursued Tyton as he back flipped into the next room. One of the ninjas jumped and use the wall to propel himself through the air at Tyton. The other two ran straight at Tyton, reaching into the side of their shirt for something. Tyton flipped past the doorway and over the bed on the floor. The three ninjas followed him in. Tyton could see the book on the shelf and started to reach for it. He quickly glanced over his shoulder to see the ninjas behind him with their arms cocked back. Tyton touched the book and instantly knew what would come next. "*Ninja stars!*" he thought to himself. They came at him fast, cutting through the air. It almost happened in slow motion. Tyton turned and began to catch each one. After 12 stars were thrown, the ninjas stopped throwing them. The three ninjas looked at one another. Tyton took a second and peered down at his hands, he had caught all the ninja stars.

"What are you?" one of the ninjas asked.

"A shadow you do not want mess with," Tyton replied, dropping all the ninja stars on the floor. The three ninjas drew their swords and jumped into the air. Tyton moved to the right to avoid the first and punched him in the gut. Then he moved to the left, evading the next, close lining the ninja's legs sending him flipping to the floor. The third sword blade swung down the center. Tyton clapped it, catching the blade in his hands. The ninja tried to move it more, but Tyton held it tightly. The ninja continued to struggle as the other two ninjas got up. Tyton snapped his head, looking at the other two. He made two quick kicks to the face of each while still holding the other ninja's blade. Tyton reacted to the one in front of him. The ninja was reaching for his other dagger-sized blade. Before the ninja could, Tyton snapped the sword, breaking it in half. The ninja stopped for a moment, looking at his sword, holding it out in front of himself like he couldn't believe it. Before the ninja could do anything else, Tyton did a backflip kick. The ninja flew off his feet and back into the next room. Silver Shadow and Master Lii stopped fighting the other ninjas for a second, peering down at the fallen ninja. Silver Shadow looked up at Tyton standing in the doorway, holding the book in his hand.

"Who and what are you?" the ninja leader asked.

"We are Shadows," Silver Shadow answered.

"How do you know our fighting style? Who trained you?" the ninja leader continued to question. Tyton threw the book at his father. Silver Shadow caught the dark red hard-covered book in his right hand. Silver Shadow's eyes started to glow more than before. The ninja leader quickly threw a high kick at Silver Shadow. With his left-hand, Silver Shadow blocked the kick almost effortlessly and countered it with two shape punches. One to the rib cage and another to a pressure point on the base of the neck. The ninja leader let out a shout in pain. "You're all dead!" the ninja leader threatened, backing away using his hand to hold the spot on his neck. "Kill them, kill them all!" he shouted. The other two ninjas behind the leader jumped at Silver Shadow, throwing ninja stars while in the air. Silver Shadow deflected all the shape stars flying at him. The ninja leader stood back and watched Silver Shadow. He noticed his fighting style change from the first few minutes they traded kicks and punches. Silver Shadow moved faster, anticipating every attack the ninjas tried. The ninja on the right threw a punch, Silver Shadow ducked and landed two counter blows. In the armpit and the second to the side of the head. The ninja fell to the floor and didn't get back up. The ninja on the left lunged at Silver Shadow, drawing his sword. Trying to slash Silver Shadow, the ninja missed when his target moved. Silver Shadow spun his body with the sword, coming at him backwards and back handed the ninja on the side of his head. The ninja collapsed to the floor. Silver Shadow glanced up, but the ninja leader had vanished. Master Lii had fought off the other three with Tyton's help.

"What's the plan, Master Lii?" Silver Shadow asked, still holding the book in one hand and the other held up in defense mode.

"We must make it to the temple, your swords are there," Master Lii suggested.

"My swords?"

"Quickly now, we must go! Now the ninja assassins know I'm here, they will surely look in the temple for them." The three of them made their way from the now falling down hut into the bamboo garden. Master Lii ran alongside Silver Shadow and Tyton, looking at his garden. Master Lii stopped for a second, trapped in all the memories of tending this garden and watching it grow. He thought about how it reminded him of how beautiful life is. How easy it is to lose sight of the important things life can bring. Also, how quickly life can be lost. Silver Shadow and Tyton ran up the hill and suddenly noticed Master Lii was not running with them. They stopped and looked back to see Master Lii just standing in the middle of the bamboo garden.

"Master, are you okay?" Tyton asked.

"Yes, I'm fine, young shadow. I remember when I started this garden," Master Lii answered.

"It is still going to be here when we get back, Master," Tyton implied.

"We won't return here. At least not for a long time, I have seen it," Master Lii said with a little smile. "The ninja assassins know I'm here now, into safe hiding I will go."

"I'm sorry, Master Lii," Tyton said, putting his hand on Master Lii's shoulder.

"It's okay, it is not your fault. I knew a monk who once told me he was going to spend the rest of his years looking for the strongest bamboo tree. I really did not understand why he would waste so much time doing this. When I started to grow this garden, I realized the irony."

"What irony, Master?"

"All bamboo trees are strong if they are properly cared for," Master Lii pondered. Tyton looked back at his father, still standing on the hill. Silver Shadow shook his head. It was the same kind of irony he had discovered for himself before. "Come now, young shadow, we should go. I have much to teach you still," Master Lii implied. The two of them ran up the hill.

"Which way, Master Lii?" Silver Shadow asked when the two of them reached him. He handed Master Lii the red book. Taking the book with both hands, Master Lii tucked the small book into the front of his robe.

"Let's use this side path, it's faster," Master Lii said, pointing to a dirt path covered by thick tree covers. The path was very narrow and ran alongside the steep hill.

"Okay, I'll take point. Tyton, watch our backs," Silver Shadow ordered.

"I got it," Tyton replied. The three of them quickly ran down the narrow path. Before long they could see the lights from the staircase leading to the temple. Keeping an eye out for more assassins, they made their way up to the top of the steps. Master Lii cut in front of Sliver Shadow and pushed open both the tall golden temple doors. Tyton stayed outside for a moment. He continued to keep his eyes out for the ninjas while his father went in with Master Lii. Silver Shadow followed closely as Master Lii lead him into the temple.

"I don't see any assassins," Tyton said, catching up to his father and Master Lii.

"They will be here soon if they are not watching us already," Master Lii replied.

"Master, tell me more about these swords?" Silver Shadow inquired.

"They are not just swords. They were crafted for the Guardian of Life, for you, my dear shadow. We have kept them safe here, hidden in this temple for countless generations."

"Master, what do you mean by we?"

"Other Masters before me, of course," Master Lii answered as he walked through the temple. He led the two shadows down the large main hall. They reached the center room. There were thousands of candles stacked on tables in a square along every edge of the walls. The red painted walls with light brown rugs made the room very peaceful. Enormous circular gold colored wooden pillars stood at every corner on the perimeter of the room. They stood tall, holding an even higher ceiling, making the room seem large and bright. The light from the candles reflected off the gold paint.

"Other masters?" Silver Shadow questioned

"Yes, these swords were crafted more than 500 years ago. The Masters are part of an ancient order."

"What is the order's purpose?"

"Its purpose is to wait for you. Safe guard the weapons for the Guardian of Life and become chronicler," Master Lii continued. "We have waited a long time for you to arrive." He stopped in the center of the sanctuary. Silver Shadow looked over at Tyton. His son was mesmerized by the story and captivated at the same time. The truth about the shadow race and their destiny may have been more than anyone had thought. Silver Shadow glanced back at Master Lii. He was knelt down on the floor, removing a wooden panel. Hidden beneath the panel was a very old-looking silver metal box.

"Here, guardian, you will need this," Master Lii implied as he stood back from the hole in the floor. Silver Shadow walked over and got on his knees. He carefully reached his entire arm down into the hole. His fingers felt around and found a handle on the top of the box. Tyton looked on with anticipation, wondering what these swords would look like. Silver Shadow pull the long silver metal box from the hole and placed it on the floor.

"Stop, you're not the Guardian of Life!" The three of them looked back. The ninja leader stood at the sanctuary entrance. Behind him stood ten more ninjas, waiting for the order to strike. "My master is the one true Guardian!" the ninja leader continued to shout.

"You mean he is the taker of life," Master Lii replied.

"It makes no difference!"

"But it does. After all you have witnessed your master do, you really think the swords belong to him?"

"It's not up to me, I was sent to find and obtain the ancient swords. That's what I intend to do. Kill them!" the ninja leader commanded. All the ninjas began to run and jump toward the silver metal box. Silver Shadow, Tyton, and Master Lii form a line between the assassins and the swords. Master Lii stood closer to the box, becoming the last line of defense.

"Guardian," Master Lii called out. Silver Shadow quickly glanced back at Master Lii. He could see a serious look on his face. It wasn't anger but determination, like Master Lii was mission driven. He stood there with his hands up in a fighting stance, ready for combat.

"Yes, Master Lii?" Silver Shadow answered.

"You must make breaking blows to stop them or they will continue to fight."

"But Master…"

"Many more will come. You will have to fight a different way. These assassins are much more devoted than anyone you have fought before now."

"How?"

"Like this," Master Lii replied, reaching out and grabbing Silver Shadow's arm. With Master Lii's touch, Silver Shadow had learned a new style of fighting. Master Lii channeled knowledge to him at will, like plugging a light into an outlet. Master Lii let go of Silver Shadow's arm and faced the ninjas. Using the new and deadly technique, Silver Shadow began defending. Tyton fought beside his father, learning by watching Silver Shadow's form. As each traded punch for punch, the shadows and Master Lii were breaking bones. The ninjas all fell one by one, some remain on the floor. Master Lii fought hard, keeping the ninja back from the silver box. The rest of the assassins were jumping and flipping around the three of them. During the fight, Master Lii lost track of the ninja leader. Before anyone realized the distraction they had let unfold, the ninja leader had the silver box open and the two swords in his hands. Suddenly, all the ninjas stopped fighting at once. Master Lii looked back and could see the ninja leader standing there with the swords.

"You have made a mistake, young assassin," Master Lii implied.

"These belong to my master," the ninja leader suggested, holding the swords up close to his face. He held them out, looking down at the shiny silver sword sheath and the light blue cloth wrapped handles with pearl white ends. The silver sword sheath was so clean, Master Lii could see his refection. The Samurai sword set were the best and oldest swords on earth. One long traditional katana and matching short sword. Silver Shadow and Tyton could only watch helplessly. The battle had been lost. Silver Shadow knew he couldn't make a move without losing the swords all together. He also noticed Master Lii was very calm for something so serious. Silver Shadow could only think of one reason why. The remaining ninjas began to make a line behind the leader. Some still laying on the floor with wounds too severe to stand. Silver Shadow put his hands down, as did Master Lii.

"Well, what are you waiting for?" Silver Shadow instigated. The ninja leader quickly peered up from admiring the swords.

"Foolish old man!" the leader shouted on. "You fell into my trap. You and your followers lead me right to the swords. You should have just let me have them."

"Did I fall for your trap?" Master Lii replied.

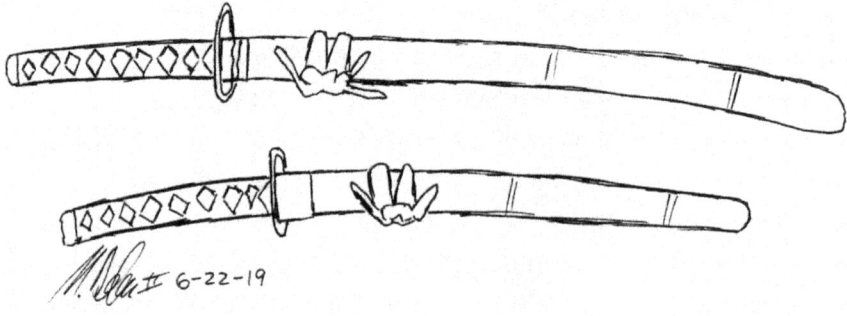

The Samurai sword set were the best and oldest swords on earth. One long traditional katana and matching short sword.

"Fool! Of course, you did!" the ninja leader argued, finally pulling his mask from his face. Silver Shadow could tell by the ninja leader's facial expressions he was a little thrown off by Master Lii's calm demeanor. He seemed so young with no facial hair and shaved head.

"Have you forgotten, I can see the future?" Master Lii implied, putting his hands by his side and letting his guard down.

"I will waste no time presenting my master with what he seeks," the ninja leader explained.

"Why don't you finish what you've started?" Silver Shadow suggested, walking forward past Master Lii. "I'll make it easy for you." Silver Shadow moved in front of the ninja leader and knelt down on one knee. "Use them on me. I shall be your first kill with the ancient swords." Tyton watched, hoping not to be a whiteness to his father's death. Master Lii did nothing but wait. He watched with curiosity, wondering if Silver Shadow knew the truth to the legend.

"Don't tempt me!" the ninja leader yelled, grasping the handle of the sword."

"Just imagine the reward you will receive when you bring my head to your master."

"Your death will bring honor to my master," the ninja leader confessed. He held out the long sword and slowly gripped the handle tightly. The ninja leader began to pull. "What the…" he uttered. The sword would not emerge from the silver sheath. "Why won't this sword come out!" the ninja leader yelled out, pulling on the handle of the sword, like a rip cord from a lawn mower.

"Who's the fool now," Master Lii continued to gloat. "You see, the sword can only be wielded by the Guardian of Life."

"I will be the first," the ninja leader expressed, looking at the handle, trying so desperately to fix the problem. There was nothing he could see preventing the sword from being removed.

"No, you will not be the first," Silver Shadow said, standing up. His eyes were glowing. The ninja leader glanced up with fear on his face. Silver Shadow clenched the sword in one hand and pushed the ninja leader with the other. A flash of light came from Silver Shadow's hand and sent the ninja leader flying across the floor through the line on ninjas. Silver Shadow grasped the handle of the sword and pulled it from the sheath. The blade was glowing the same color as Silver Shadow's eyes. It was as if the blade was on fire, low burning with no smoke.

"The Guardian of Life has come," Master Lii announced loudly, holding his hands up. Silver Shadow looked around the room and all the ninjas were bowing down. The ninja leader watched from the floor, laying on his back, still holding his chest. The prophecy was true and there was nothing he could do.

"Stand up, he's no Guardian!" the ninja leader screamed as he quickly got back on his feet. "How can we believe you, old man!?" he snapped.

"If you knew the legend as well as I do, this question you would not ask," Master Lii replied, putting his hands together in a praying-like fashion. He slowly tilted his head, bowing at Silver Shadow. Seeing no reason to defend himself, Silver Shadow put the glowing blade back into its sheath. Master Lii reached into his robes and pulled out a long black cloth belt. He held it out in front of himself. It was neatly folded and wrapped with two silver metal clips. Before anyone understood what was going on, two random ninjas stood up and ran over to Master Lii. They both bowed down in front of him like they were waiting for something. One of the ninjas held out both hands while still bowing. Master Lii placed the black cloth belt in the ninja's hands. The two ninjas quickly stood up and walked slowly over to Silver Shadow. Now they were both bowing down in front of Silver Shadow. Not sure what to think, Silver Shadow looked up at Master Lii.

"They want to perform the sword presentation and outfit you with the belt," Master Lii implied.

"What do you mean?" Silver Shadow asked.

"It is the highest honor one can perform, especially for the Guardian of Life. They bow for your respect and your forgiveness."

"You may proceed," Silver Shadow said, looking down at the ninjas. He held the swords out and his arms up as the two ninjas stood up. They both began to wrap Silver Shadow with the belt around his waist, making places for the twin swords to slid into. Tyton stood by and watched as his father was being honored by the ninja, who fought against him. He looked over and saw the ninja leader throwing two ninja stars at his father.

"Watch out, Father!" Tyton yelled. Silver Shadow and Master Lii flinched, glancing over. Before the stars reached Silver Shadow, three ninjas jumped up from bowing. They quickly drew their swords and swatted away the projectiles like common house flies. They stood between the ninja leader and Silver Shadow protecting him, swords still drawn. They stood firm, like they were waiting for Silver Shadow to give the word.

"You have made allies here today, Guardian," Master Lii suggested as Silver Shadow held still. He gave Master Lii this look like, really?

"My master will hear about this!" the ninja leader confessed. The ninja leader ran away, making his escape down the hall and outside the temple. The tree ninjas looked back at Silver Shadow.

"Let him go, he will meet his own fate," Silver Shadow said. The three ninjas put their sword away. Tyton ran over.

"Father," Tyton said. Silver Shadow turned to him. The two ninjas were done with the belt. Silver Shadow took the swords and place them into their place. The belt was tied perfectly and they fit on his left hip. "What do we do now?" Tyton asked.

"We should go," Master Lii continued. "I will come with you, there is much to do."

"What about all of them?" Tyton said, pointing to all the ninjas still bowing to Silver Shadow.

"You're right. Master, but where will they go now?" Silver Shadow asked.

"They abandon their order; by the looks of things, they have sworn loyalty to you," Master Lii implied. Silver Shadow stopped for a second, he walked over to the ninja group.

"Stand," Silver Shadow commanded. The entire group of ninjas stood up at the same time like a small army. "You have abandoned your order. So, today, we will start a new order. The order of Guardians. This temple has stood here for over 500 years, and it will continue to stand for another 500," Silver Shadow announced to the group. All the ninjas looked at one another. "I need two leaders to step forward." Every member in the group moved, forming a circle with only two ninjas standing in the middle. "You two come forward," Silver Shadow asked, pointing to them. The two ninjas slowly walk up to Silver Shadow and bowed. "My friends, I need your help to build our new order," he continued, whispering to them. "Protect this temple, recruit new members, and wait for my return. Master Lii and I will keep in contact and send the necessary supplies." Without a word, the two ninjas shook their heads yes and bowed to Silver Shadow as they stepped back.

Chapter Eleven
Broken Deals

It would seem the Shadow Runners will be getting some help from the outside world. This list of human names has started a new chapter for the shadow group. There's also the matter of the new ninja order Silver Shadow has started with the help of Master Lii. Will this order of Guardians play a significant role in the battles to come? Is this what Michael Eastin would have wanted for his son or had for seen? Silver Shadow finds himself daydreaming in the cockpit of SGD with the autopilot lit up. The aircraft on its journey home. There are still many questions on Silver Shadow's mind. To what end, where will these new bread crumbs lead. Doctor Eastin had obviously known more about Silver Shadow's true future than he wanted to say. This may have been the destiny Master Lii had spoken of. Silver Shadow was in a fragile state of mind, still trying so very hard to come up with answers. Before he could reach a conclusion, Silver Shadow felt a hand on his shoulder. It was Master Lii with a concerned look on his face.

"Master Lii?" Silver Shadow quickly said, looking up at him.

"Sometimes to be more, one must overcome," Master Lii implied. "You will soon have the answers you seek."

"You can channel my thoughts as well?"

"Yes, but it only works with you, guardian." Silver Shadow looked back at the aircraft control panel and saw a light blinking. A live message was coming through from the Shadow Hopper. It was Poison.

"Hopper to SGD, come in SGD," Poison's voice said. Silver Shadow reached over, hitting a button to open the channel link.

"Go for SGD, this is Silver Shadow."

"Hello, my love," Poison softly answered. "I have found two people from the list, Ricky Bartos and Hector Wells."

"Good, are you safe?" Silver Shadow replied with concern.

"Yes, we are safe."

"How long before you reach The Shadow Dome?"

"Unsure, we have a situation," Poison reported.

"Will you need help for this situation?"

"Yes but not yet. I will have to do some recon before making any kind of move."

"Copy, but be careful, please!"

"Yes, I will, you, too. Poison, out!" Silver Shadow disconnected and looked back over his shoulder. Master Lii was still standing there right behind him.

"Things will work out fine," Master Lii assured Silver Shadow.

"Somehow I believe you."

"There is someone we must go see first."

"Where?" Silver Shadow asked.

"New York, a man named Andrew Bouwers," Master Lii remarked. Silver Shadow made a point to remember every name from the list and that name rang a bell. It soon became clear Master Lii might know almost everyone on the list as if he had read it himself. It is also possible Master Lii had seen the list from Silver Shadow's own memory. Only time could tell more of this story and Master Lii's true role in the shadow's lives. Silver Shadow, Tyton, and Master Lii traveled to New York to find another name from the list while Poison helps Hector find his sister. The Shadow Hopper hovers high in the clouds out of sight. Poison looks over the letter Hector received to discover a clue to where they might keep his sister. Hector and Ricky both sat there, hoping she might be able to help.

"I read this over and over. What were you supposed to do, just go home?" Poison asked.

"I guess so," Hector replied.

"It doesn't make any sense."

"I don't know what to tell you. What doesn't make sense?"

"They don't say how or when you would be contacted."

"Is there a way to see who they are?" Ricky interjected.

"Maybe," Poison answered. She walked over to one of the computers and started accessing the SF (*shadow finder*) system Tyton had set up before the team left The Shadow Dome.

"What are you doing?" Ricky asked.

"Linking up with SD. I'm beginning to think this is all connected. I don't think they were planning on contacting Hector at all. They knew I was going to come for him, but how did they know about me? When I took that guard down before we escaped from your house, I thought I'd seen the gear he was wearing before."

"Wait, didn't you leave some kind of device behind?" Ricky excitedly announced. Hector was sitting there in silence, a bit confused about what they were discussing.

"Yes, and I am checking the SF (*shadow finder*) and RSDC (*remote self-destructing camera*) memory banks to see if anything was recorded."

"Right, I knew that," Ricky said, stepping closer to look over Poison's shoulder. In a few seconds, Poison had the list of data logs from SD and a video feed.

"Got it," Poison said, touching and highlighting the newest video entry.

"How long is the video?" Ricky asked. Before Poison could answer, Hector stood up from his seat. He made his way over and peered at the computer screen.

"Five in half minutes."

"That's it!" Hector blurted out.

"If it lasted any longer, some might be able to back trace the signal," Poison explained. The three of them huddle around the small computer screen as Poison taps the play icon with her finger. The video picture was a little fuzzy but becomes clearer as it played. The inside view of the house was good. All the rooms could be seen, except one and the upstairs. They could make out movement at the front door through the one little window. Then the front door flies open, breaking parts of the wooden door frame and three men storm in. The three men quickly search the house and a fourth man runs up the stairs.

The whole team was wearing all black tactical gear and carrying compacted machine guns. For three and a half minutes of the video, the group goes from room to room, searching both floors. Then the four men gather in the living room like they were waiting for something.

"What are they doing?" Hector asked.

"Not sure," Poison answered. Before she could offer a theory, she saw him. The leader of the group walked in the front door. The four men snapped to attention and saluted him as he made his way into the house. "I knew it, somehow I knew it!"

"Knew what?" Hector questioned. Poison stopped the video, so the leader's face could be seen clearly.

"That guy is Terry Winddel, my ex-boyfriend," Poison said, pointing to the leader of the team. Ricky and Hector both look surprised as they took a precautionary step back. They could see she was a little upset. They are guys, and they also know the one thing you never talk to a woman about is their ex-boyfriends. Between the two of them, they both shared a look. Ricky and Hector didn't have a whole lot of experience with women in their lives. They just knew break ups were either very bad or very good. There is no such thing as a good or even neutral break up. Poison put her head down as Ricky and Hector stood there. They looked at one another, wondering what to do or say. "He took my life away!" Poison cried out.

"It will get better," Hector stated, stepping forward and putting his hand on her back. He glanced back and Ricky had a panicked look on his face, shrugging his shoulders. Hector continued to console Poison, but she was filled with mixed feelings.

"I have to track him," Poison remarked. She snapped back to the computer screen and hit play to watch the rest of the video. Ricky and Hector found themselves clued to the video again. Tarry Winddel moved into the middle of the living room and looks around. He then turns to the men still standing at attention and gives them an order. The men quickly run out the front door. Poison watches and studies Winddel's every move. He begins go through the house, starting with the computer on the desk in the living room. The men come back into the house, escorting what looks like a young female shadow at gun point. "What the!" Poison whispered.

"What? What happened?" Ricky asked. Before Poison could answer, the video ended.

"I thought that was a shadow," Poison answered, scrabbling to rewind the last few seconds of the video.

"Wait, who was that?" Hector questioned.

"I don't know, hold on," Poison answered as she tried to rewind the video a few seconds. She stopped the images as the young unknown female shadow walked in through the front door. "I have no idea who that is, but we better find out," Poison said out loud. Rickey and Hector just stood there, puzzled. Poison hit a small icon on the screen that looked like a microphone. "SD, come in."

"Yes, Poison."

"I need you to save this video file as Priority One and capture the still shots I have made."

"Confirm, file saved."

"I also need you to track these targets from the location using terrific cameras and any other surveillance in the area."

"Confirm, tracking," the Shadow Dome replied. Suddenly, the computer screen next to Poison turned on and images of street corners and stop lights started popping up quickly. Hector sat down in front of the screen as Ricky stood behind him. Poison glanced over as she saved some more images from the video.

"Subjects located."

"Give me the coordinates with longitude and latitude," Poison ordered. A bell-like chimed rang out and the three of them peered over at the other large screen on the wall. A mini map was displayed with a red blinking light pinging the new location. Without saying a word, Poison got up from her chair and proceed up the latter to the cockpit. Hector got up from his seat.

"What does this mean?" Hector asked Ricky, looking for some words of hope or encouragement.

"I think she has track them down," Ricky replied with uncertainty on his face.

"Did she find my sister?"

"I think she found more than that."

"Then what?" Hector said. It became clear he was starting to panic a little, waving his hands around in the air.

"The people who may have taken her," Ricky suggested.

"What do we do now?"

"Let her handle it, she's good at what she does. Trust me on that," Ricky said, trying to calm Hector down. "Here, let's sit down over there and relax a little," Ricky continued as he walked Hector over to the rest of the seats toward the back of the Shadow Hopper.

"I can't just sit here!" Hector shouted. The Shadow Hopper stared moving before Ricky could answer. Poison came climbing down the ladder.

"I'm going to need your guys help," Poison requested. "Think you two can deal with this."

"Yes, I'll do anything," Hector replied, standing up.

"What do you need us to do?" Ricky asked.

"We are going to do some recon until the rest of the team can back us up."

"Wait, you mean there are more like you?" Hector questioned, sitting back down and rubbing his head. As day becomes night, the Shadow Hopper soars through the air to its new destination. Meanwhile, the SGD aircraft is flying to another location in New York City. Silver Shadow flies the SGD aircraft and feels a hand on his shoulder. It's Master Lii standing behind him.

"There," Master Lii instructed, pointing to the 3D (*three-dimensional*) mini map lit up in the center of the pilot controls. Silver Shadow glanced down at where Master Lii was pointing. Tyton sat next to his father while Master Lii stood in the middle of them. He peered out the window and could see a large apartment building.

"Tyton, you ready?" Silver Shadow asked.

"Yes, ready to take the controls."

"Okay, remember, keep us level, Master Lii and I shouldn't take long."

"Copy that," Tyton confirmed. Master Lii walked out of the cockpit and Silver Shadow followed. The aircraft hovered near a fire escape completely invisible. Silver Shadow and Master Lii made their way to the side door of the aircraft. On the way to the door, Silver Shadow grabbed a com link device and placed it on the side of his neck.

"Tyton, do you read me?"

"Yes, Father, I can hear you loud and clear."

"Good, stay alert out there," Silver Shadow suggested as him and Master

Lii walked from the hovering aircraft to the fire escape. It was starting to get dark as the sun began to set.

"This way," Master Lii whispered. He walked up a few levels and Silver Shadow followed with caution. He kept his head on a swivel, glancing everywhere to make sure no one saw them. As they went up the fire escape, Silver Shadow couldn't help but notice the apartments they past were kind of upscale. Each window expensive looking and well maintained. The things inside each unit high priced.

"This one," Master Lii said, pointing to the window above. The two of them climbed up to what looked like the 13th floor. If Silver Shadow had counted right. "He is in there alone, for now."

"Andrew Bouwers?" Silver Shadow asked.

"Yes," Master Lii answered.

"Is he dangerous?"

"Only to himself, and no, he is not armed." Master Lii took the question right out of Silver Shadow's mouth before he could ask it. He always seemed to be one step ahead of everyone around.

"How do we talk to him?"

"Sometimes to be built up, one must start from the very bottom. We must offer our help and act quickly," Master Lii replied. Silver Shadow stepped up close to the window to hear. There were no sounds coming from the room. He placed his hands on the glass and pushed a little to make the window slide up. With a small space now at the bottom, Silver Shadow stuck his fingers in and lifted the window up slowly. Silver Shadow entered first, followed by Master Lii. The room they stood in was big and dark with multicolored hardwood flooring. They walked softly across the room. In the middle of the room were two slim white colored support beams that matched the white walls. The room was empty with no furniture of any kind. There were also half-drunk beer bottles everywhere. Around the beams on the floor and plied in two corners. Master Lii stood in the middle of the room like he was waiting for something. Silver Shadow peered around to see a hallway in the back of the room. It must have led to the rest of the apartment bedrooms, maybe a bathroom. There was a small kitchen in the far corner of the room and the main exit door leading to the outside hallway nearby. Light was coming from the peep hole and under the door. The door was locked up with the chain in place. "*Someone must be home,*" Silver Shadow thought to himself. He slowly walked over to the L-shaped kitchen counter covered with more beer bottles. Suddenly, Silver Shadow saw a man stumble into the room from the back hallway. The man fell into the room, knocking over more empty beer bottles, making a lot of noise, breaking the silence. Silver Shadow stood fast, ready for anything. The man was laughing at himself. Master Lii continued to stand clam and still with his hands held behind his back in the middle of the room.

"Andrew Bouwers, it is time," Master Lii spoke aloud. The man looked up from the floor. He stopped for a minute.

"Here to collect, I don't have it, it's all gone," the man said. He began to laugh again, drinking the half-finished beer in his hand. He missed his mouth as he laughed, spilling it all down his shirt.

"We are only here to collect you before it's too late." The man started to pick himself up off the floor.

"What?" the man said, finally standing on his feet. The man had a light blue stripped tie with white collared shirt and dark navy-blue dress pants. He had nothing on his feet and a flesh yellow vomit stain down the front of his clothes. The large bottle of alcohol hung from his left hand. "Who are you?"

"I am Mace Lii, are you Andrew Bouwers?"

"Yeah, what's it to you?" the man slurred, pointing his finger at Master Lii.

"You must come with us," Master Lii repeated, pointing to Silver Shadow still standing in the corner. Andrew turned to see who Master Lii was pointing at.

"What the… Who is that?" Andrew asked, frightened and falling to the floor again. Silver Shadow ran over and helped Andrew off the floor.

"We are here to help you," Silver Shadow whispered. Andrew kept staring at him, unsure what to make of Silver Shadow. Andrew had blue eyes with light blond hair cut short. They both helped Andrew off the floor, so he could stand on his own.

"Help, you mean the Russians didn't send you for the money?"

"No, we are here to get you out of trouble, so you can help us," Master Lii explained. Then there were three big bangs on the door to the apartment.

"Open up, Bouwers, we know you're in there!" a voice shouted from behind the door. Silver Shadow could tell the voice had a Russian accent. Without words Silver Shadow and Master Lii looked at each other and knew what to do. Master Lii began to help Andrew to the hall leading to the back of the apartment. Silver Shadow stood up and hid beside the door the Russians were banging on. He could see movement in the light coming from under the door. It sounded like there was more than one man on the other side. They banged some more. "Bouwers, you better open the door, or we're going to kick it down!" the voice continued to shout. Silver Shadow could hear another neighbor down the hall open their door to see what all the yelling was about. "Hey, mind your own business, or you'll be next!" the voice threatened. The neighbor quickly slammed their door.

"Tyton, prepare for pick up," Silver Shadow whispered into his com link.

"Copy that, in rout," Tyton replied. Silver Shadow could hear the men talking amongst themselves. Without warning the door was kicked so hard that it came off the hinges, sending it flying into the apartment. Four large men came rushing in and quickly started searching the apartment. Silver Shadow grabbed the last man in from behind. One quick blow to the back of the neck knocked him out. The man fell, making a loud thud on the wooden floor. The other three men turned around to see one of their friends down and Silver Shadow standing over his body. The only thing they could see was Silver Shadow's eyes in the darkness.

"What the…!?" the ring leader yelled. Before anyone could say anything else, Silver Shadow lunged at them. He jumped at the middle two guys, high kicking them in the face. The two men fell back unconscious, landing at the ring leader's feet. The man just stood there for a second. Everything happened so fast. Before the man could react, Silver Shadow grabbed him with an arm bar pin, slamming his face onto the nearby kitchen counter. The empty beer bottles were pushed to the floor in the struggle. The bottles made so much noise. "Who are you, what are you doing here?"

"No one you want to mess with!"

"Bouwers can't pay us back, but he can hire bodyguards!?" the man concluded.

"Not a bodyguard, friend. Don't make the mistake of looking for him again," Silver Shadow said.

"Okay, okay, he just better not go gambling at any of our places again!" the man said in pain.

"Fair enough," Silver Shadow answered as he slid the man across the counter. He threw the man to the floor and delivered a knockout punch to the face. Silver Shadow saw Master Lii and Andrew out of the corner of his eye, peering into the room from the back hall. "Tyton, are you in position?"

"Yes, ready and waiting."

"Come on, let go," Silver Shadow requested, waving to the two of them. Master Lii helped Andrew with his arm over his shoulder. Andrew was so intoxicated, he could barely walk on his own. Silver Shadow opened the window they came in from and looked out. SGD and Tyton were hovering there, waiting for them. When Master Lii and Andrew reached the window, Silver Shadow help them board the aircraft. "Tyton, we're clear."

"Copy, dusting off," Tyton replied. Master Lii helped Andrew sit down in one of the seats.

"Where are we going?" Andrew asked Master Lii.

"We will need your help to find a safer place for those who want to help us," Master Lii suggested.

"I don't know what you're talking about," Andrew admitted.

"You will, in time you will help many others like you to find their way."

"What…?" Andrew had a look on his face of complete confusion.

"Rest now, your mind must become clear before you can understand," Master Lii said, gently pushing Andrew back in his seat. Silver Shadow just stood there listening.

"Master, what do we do now?"

"We wait, for now we must go and help." At the time, Silver Shadow didn't understand what Master Lii meant, but he was always right. The shadows don't know it yet, but Master Lii's power of foresight will be a tremendous asset to their world. Meanwhile, Poison tracks the man from her past with extreme prejudice, no matter the cost. After seeing a new young female shadow on the video capture at Ricky Bartos's house, Poison has more questions. *"What is this shadow capable of? Where did she come from? Was she somehow involved with the Trigger program?"* Poison thought to herself. She sits in the cockpit alone, thinking the worst possible scenarios. While the Shadow Hopper's auto pilot flies them to a secluded location. An alarm sounds, interrupting Poison's thoughts. She glances up at the mini map, the SH (*shadow hopper*) has reached the destination.

"Poison to SD, come in."

"Yes, Poison, I receive you."

"Can you use the SH's long-range scanners and tell me where we are. Something about this place feels familiar," Poison requested as she looked out the window. The aircraft was hovering over an ice-covered frozen lake. Before she could do anything, Poison started having flash backs. They were very strong and she could not control them.

"Poison, Poison, are you okay?" Ricky asked, standing over her. Poison found herself on the floor with Ricky and Hector standing over her. She must have blacked out, something she hasn't done in a long time.

"I'm fine," Poison answered.

"Are you sure, you gave us a little bit of a scare," Ricky admitted.

"What happened?" Poison asked, getting up from the floor and rubbing her head.

"We were downstairs and heard a bang. When I came up, I found you on the floor," Ricky explained.

"We wanted to make sure you were okay," Hector added.

"I have been here before," Poison implied.

"Where is here?" Hector asked, looking out the window. "There's nothing for miles."

"Trust me, there is something here!" Poison answered.

"So, what do we do?" Ricky questioned.

"Ricky, I'm going to need you to fly the Shadow Hopper for me."

"Right, okay!" Ricky said with excitement.

"Hector, you're riding shotgun. Sit here and help me once I'm in the facility," Poison ordered, showing Hector the co-pilot seat.

"Will do."

"Wait, you're going in alone?" Ricky questioned.

"Yes, the rest of the team will be here soon. I can't wait," Poison confessed.

"I don't think that's a good idea," Ricky remarked.

"It's okay, I'll have you two watching my back from here," Poison insured.

"SD, are you still with me?"

"Yes, Poison, I am here," the Shadow Dome replied.

"Ping my location to Silver Shadow."

"Confirm." Before Ricky could convince Poison to stay, she walked straight down the ladder and out of the cockpit to the back of the aircraft. Poison hit the button for the deploy door and grabbed her sniper rifle from the weapons locker. She walked to the end of the ramp and looked down at the frozen tundra. Poison checked her ammo and put a few extra clips on her belt. She placed the com link to the SH on her neck.

"Ricky, can you hear me?" Poison asked, speaking into the com link.

"Yes, I'm receiving you. I still think this is a bad idea," Ricky answered. Without defending her actions, Poison leapt from the end of the ramp, free falling to the ground. After seven seconds and 800-feet, Poison landed on the ground. She looked up into the cold air and could just barely make out the Shadow Hopper's shape. The thick white clouds provided cover and limited visibly. Poison knelt down on one knee and used her sniper rifle to look at her surroundings. Peering through the scope, she could see a small amount of smoke coming from the ground in the distance. Everything was covered in snow and ice. The smoke was a clue that she was close. Following her instincts, Poison began walking in the direction of the gray colored smoke. Holding her sniper rifle tightly, she kept her guard up. The cold wind was blowing almost nonstop. As she got closer, Poison noticed there were no tracks of any kind. *"How did they get here? There should at least be deep impressions of a vehicle or something,"* Poison thought to herself. After a few more steps, Poison reached the source of the smoke. She found a white pipe sticking out of the ground.

"Ricky, come in," Poison said into her com link, staring at the pipe.

"Yes, are you okay?" Ricky answered.

"I'm fine, have SD check these coordinates, I need a way in. There's no door or anything here."

"Okay, hold a sec. SD says thermal scans indicate you're standing right on it," Ricky implied. Poison stopped for a second and closed her eyes. Suddenly, she heard a sound, like cracking. It was the ice under her feet. Poison quickly glanced down, but before she could act, the ice collapsed, sending Poison spiraling down a large dark air shaft. After sliding down a long shaft, she hit the bottom. A little dazed and confused, trying to stand up, Poison found herself in an old, dark, metal room. Then a sharp pain on the back of her neck. Someone or something hit her from behind. She went in and out of consciousness, laying helpless on the cold metal floor. Flashes of what was happening around was all she could see with her eyes. Something was there with her in the darkness. Poison could see her rifle lying next to her. She tried to reach for it, pulling herself across the floor. Before her fingers could grasp it, a mechanical arm emerged from the darkness. It grabbed the sniper rifle and pulled it back into the darkness. Poison could hear a cracking sound and then the rifle fell back into the light, broken in half. It was cast out in front of Poison like a bone from a big, mean dog. Poison gathered her strength and started to pick herself up from the floor again. Before she could get up, Poison was hit in the face. She fell hard onto her back and black out completely.

"Hello again," a voice said. Poison woke up and saw Tarry Winddel standing in front of her.

"You!" Poison screamed, trying to grab him. "What have you done?!" she demanded. Poison was pinned, she couldn't move.

"Finally getting rid of you for good. Where's your friend, he's not here to save you now?" Tarry antagonized. He was daring her to try and escape. Tarry was standing in front of Poison on some kind of cat walk with two big robots standing behind him.

"Where are we?" Poison questioned.

"You don't remember this place? Sad, this is where we meet for the first time. This old abandoned missile silo was a great base once. But we've move on since then, on to bigger and better things, I guess. I just happen to get lucky. One more missile left," Tarry boasted, turning his back to Poison. She quickly looked around, her body was suspended in the air. She was chained to a very large missile measuring about three stories tall and 15-feet in diameter. The whole place was dark with little pockets of light scattered throughout the tall room. The light on Poison was coming from the two robots' shoulders. They stood there, ready for her to try and escape.

"How are going to lunch this missile? Doesn't look like there's any power in this facility."

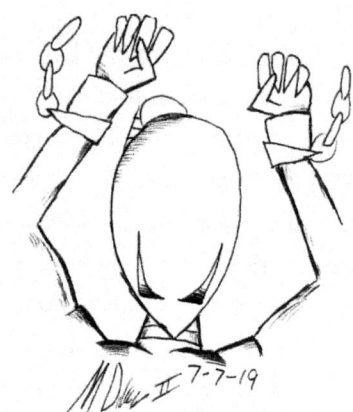

She quickly looked around, her body was suspended in the air.

"Oh, yes, that's right, you haven't met my new friend," Tarry answered, looking back at her over his shoulder. "Bring her in, it's time," Tarry ordered one of the robots, waving his hand. The robot on the right turned around and walked down the tunnel behind them. "You Shadows are hard to control. So, I have upgraded my team."

"My friends will come for me," Poison suggested.

"Oh, I hope they do. Just in time to see the end of you and your kind." Poison saw movement coming from the tunnel over Tarry's shoulder as he turned back around to face her. The robot was dragging someone small by the hand. The two of them walked into the light and Poison saw her. The young female shadow from the video. "When you and your team are gone, we will make more Shadows we can control."

"Who's she?"

"I introduce Sa-Rose, my little power bug," Tarry sarcastically admitted with a laugh.

"Where the…?" Poison began to question.

"What, you didn't think you were the only assassin in the Trigger program?" Tarry said before Poison could get a word in. "You did! Oh, there were hundreds. Two of them escaped with your team's help. We've been trying to track you guys for months. I knew a way to lure you out, and it worked," Tarry confessed, mocking Poison.

"They're just using you, Sa-Rose!" Poison shouted at the little shadow. She looked like a child in size with an oval-shaped head. At the top of her head were metal thick string-like hairs. Sa-Rose's body had a gray undertone color. Her and Poison had very similar features. Tarry turned and peered at Sa-Rose's blue glowing eyes in the darkness.

"She won't help you," Tarry suggested as Sa-Rose glanced up at him. He put his arm around her shoulder. "It's time," he whispered to her. Sa-Rose took a step forward and she held her hands out. Her eyes started to glow brighter blue along with her finger tips as well. The whole facility began to light up. Poison looked to her right and there was a gray concrete control room with a rectangle window. All the machines, hallways, and tunnels lit up. One by one, the lights in the entire building were humming. Poison could hear a countdown coming from the control room. The missile she was chained to started warming up, preparing itself. Sa-Rose stopped glowing and put her hands down by her sides. She turned around and walk over to Tarry. He put his arm around her again like she was his daughter. Poison struggled to break free.

"Why are you doing this?"

"This missile is set to hit the Edwards stadium in Berkeley, California where a sold-out crowd watches the championship game. It will take 73 minutes for impact. It will be one of the largest attacks the world has seen. People will be looking for someone to blame. When they find your body amongst the rubble, I'm guessing they will blame the shadows," Tarry bragged.

"When I get free, I will find you."

"You're too late, I will kill your whole team, starting with you," Tarry stated, laughing as he turned around and walked away with his arm round Sa-Rose. The two robots followed behind him down the hall. His intimidating laugh echoed through the hallway off the dense walls. Poison struggled to get free, it was no use. Her arms were chained up over her head. Her ankles were chained tightly, leaving her no room to move. Poison could still hear the countdown coming from the computer in the control booth. Yellow warning lights were flashing and the silo doors above the missile began to open. Poison glanced down and could see smoke coming from the bottom. Launch arms detached from the sides of the missile. Poison could feel the vibration of the missile in her bones. Helplessness sank in and fear ran through her heart. Poison's emotions took control *"I don't want to die like this!"* she thought to herself. Poison didn't know what to do as the vibrations grew stronger. She thought of those innocent people on the other end. *"Why do other people always get hurt because of my mistakes?"* she thought to herself. *"I should have waited for the others."* Before long the red lights started flashing red instead of yellow. Warning alarms rang through the whole facility. Poison felt the missile moving and her heart jumped. She looked down to see the ground slowly disappear. Poison and the missile sailed high above the clouds. She was so terrified, filled with anxiety. The air was rushing past her helpless body and it started to get cold. *"I can't give up, I have to fight,"* she thought. Poison began to clear her mind and focus. *"It always just came out, I was never able to control when."* Poison focused even harder, then she could feel it. It was the mysterious pink fluid that seems to course through her blood, it was like potent acid. The pink liquid formed on her finger tips. Poison glanced up at her hands, *"There's not a lot, but it might do the trick."* With her hands pined, Poison flicked her wrists as hard as she could. The pink liquid splashed down the side of the missile to her ankle chains. The chains dissolved slowly and Poison could feel her legs coming free. Poison broke the deteriorating chains and turned her body around. Using more pink liquid, she spread some on the chains around her hands. *"No one will die today!"* she thought. After getting one hand free, Poison looked down and saw she was flying over water. *"This is a good place."* She hit the side of the missile as hard as she could over and over. Her right hand filled with pink liquid, she punched a hole in the paneling. Poison pounded the missile like she was beating a steel drum. Soon she could see exposed wires and circuitry. Poison opened her hand inside, letting the pink liquid soak all the parts. Everything she did wasn't making this missile go down any faster. She quickly peered down. *"It will reach land soon!"* Poison could see land in the distance. She looked back at the large triangle-shaped fins on the bottom of the missile. *"This should slow it down,"* she thought as Poison shook her hand in the air. Large drops of the pink liquid splashed down near one of the fins. The acid burned its way through, causing pieces of the missile to break off. Poison splashed more toward the bottom of the missile. *"It's working."* The missile was splitting up into many pieces with all the fragments falling in every direction. Poison peered down. *"It's still over water, no one should get hurt from it."* The missile was falling, quickly losing altitude. Poison decided she would jump before the rest of the missile she was on hit the water. Poison tracked the surface of the water as she got closer. As she prepared to jump, she looked down and realized her left hand was still chained to the missile. *"Oh no!"* she thought in a panic. Poison quickly splashed the pink liquid near her hand. It was too late, the missile she rode like a bull fighter hit the water hard. A big splash in the open sea followed by many others pieces. Poison fought hard to get her hand free as the large middle half of the missile slowly sank. The pink liquid round her hand didn't have a chance to work. It quickly dissolved as the water surrounded everything. Poison's body was caught being pulled down with the submerging missile. *"No, no!"* she shouted to herself. There was nothing she could do, and no one would know where to even find her. Poison looked around as she sank, other pieces of the missile slowly sank around her as well. There would be no trace of the crashed missile from the air. Poison continued to fight, she wasn't giving up. She held her breath for as long as she could. She started to lose hope after seeing everything getting dark around her. Poison could not see the surface and the light anymore. It was becoming colder and the pressure was building up on her body. She hoped the missile would hit something and stop. It seemed to sink forever, like the ocean floor would never be found. Poison was all alone and no one would hear her. It was scary silence and unbearable. Nothing but the sound of her own heartbeat. Poison became slower as did her heart, her air was gone and she started to choke. She was going to drown and this was her end. *"At least I stopped the missile,"* she thought, holding on to one of the only good things she had done in her last moments. She had saved many, but who would save her? Poison could see a light, *"This must be the light everyone talks about when they die."* It wasn't, she was still alive. The light was in the water with her. Then she recognized the light, it was the Silver Shadow's eyes glowing in the deep darkness. He swam down to save her. *"I've got you, my love."* Poison could hear him in her head. Silver Shadow quickly grabbed the chain holding her hand. With one pull, he broke it and grabbed her body. *"Hang on,"* he said to her. Silver Shadow wrapped his arm around her chest and swam up to the surface. Poison couldn't move to help swim, her body was so drained. She was beginning to see the light again. Just before they reached the surface, Silver Shadow started swimming faster and faster. The two of them flew out of the water, jumping in the air like dolphins landing on the edge of the SGD aircraft ramp. Master Lii stood there waiting for them. Silver Shadow held Poison in his arms and carefully laid her down on the ramp while the aircraft hovered there.

"Are you okay?" Silver Shadow impatiently asked. Poison took many deep breaths and opened her eyes to see him knelt down over her.

"Thank you, my love," Poison answered.

"Well, is she okay?" a voice said over the com system. Silver Shadow looked over his shoulder. The Shadow Hopper was hovering behind SGD with Ricky and Hector in the window of the cockpit.

"She's okay," Silver Shadow answered over his com link. Master Lii smiled and they could hear the sounds of everyone celebrating over the shared intercom system. Silver Shadow put his hands under her body as Poison took more deep breaths. She was happy to be alive and being held close. She peered at Silver Shadow like it was the first time she had seen him. Poison had to rest and regain her strength. Silver Shadow picked Poison up and carried her into the SGD aircraft with Master Lii leading the way. The ramp closed behind them and the two aircrafts flew to a higher altitude. Silver Shadow gently placed Poison in one of the empty seats. Master Lii sat beside her, trying to get a read on how she was doing. Before words could be exchanged, Tyton came running from the cockpit. He rushed to his mother and hugged her tightly. Poison let out a yelp in pain, but she was glad to see him.

"Are you okay, Mother?!" Tyton asked very concerned.

"I am now," Poison said, glancing over at Silver Shadow. He was knelt down beside her. Tyton let go of his mother and she found herself with all three of them sitting in front of her. Waiting to hear what happened.

"Poison, my love, who did this?" Silver Shadow asked.

"Tarry Winddel," Poison answered. Silver Shadow immediately stood up, his eyes started to glow. He balled his hands into clenched fists. Silver Shadow turned around and started walking to the cockpit. It became very clear Sliver Shadow was more than angry.

"Who is Tarry Winddel, Mother?" Tyton quickly asked.

"Someone I should have killed the first time we met," Silver Shadow interjected.

"Maybe, but there's something else," Poison announced. Silver Shadow stopped in his tracks, he turned back around. "He has another Shadow with him." Silver Shadow's eyes and hands stopped glowing, his vengeance would have to wait. He slowly walked back to the group.

"What do you mean?" Tyton inquired.

"She means many more Shadows will have to be saved before this war begins," Master Lii interrupted. Silver Shadow sat down, trying to understand how this weasel of a man got his hands on another Shadow.

"Master, can you see the other Shadows or maybe guide us to them?" Silver Shadow asked.

"I cannot, but this Shadow Poison has met will be a great help in finding the rest," Master Lii replied. "You must first face a hard truth, and it will not be easy to overcome," Master Lii implied, talking to Poison. She looked at him, Poison had no idea what this truth could be. She had already lost so much, and this time almost her life.

"What was the shadow like, Mother?" Tyton asked.

"She was young," Poison answered.

"She?" Tyton and Silver Shadow said at the same time.

"Yes, she, and her power was like nothing we have seen before," Poison continued.

"What is her ability?" Tyton asked.

"She was somehow able to use energy to give things power. She singlehandedly made an abandoned missile silo turn on like it was new. All the computers and lights turned on in seconds," Poison admitted.

"She sounds very powerful," Tyton said.

"He called her Sa-Rose," Poison confessed. Poison looked up and saw someone sitting in one of the front seats. After all the conversation about her near-death experience, she wasn't really paying attention to everything. "Who's that in the front?" Poison asked. Everyone glanced up.

"His name is Andrew Bouwers, and he is going to help us," Silver Shadow pointed out. Poison sat up in her seat, she could see him moving around. Andrew was starting to wake up from his hangover.

"Oh, my head," Andrew moaned out loud, holding his face. Silver Shadow stood up and made his way up to the front along with Tyton. Poison tried to stand, but her body was too weak. Master Lii helped Poison sit back and sat next to her.

"You must rest now, heal," Master Lii insisted.

"Yeah, you're right," Poison said, reclining back in her chair. "I just wish I knew everything about Tarry's plain."

"There is more to life than having all the answers. Some stories cannot be written, they must unfold in order for you to understand."

"Right, but how can we be prepared?"

"With rest and patience."

"Okay, I'll try," Poison commented, relaxing in her seat. Master Lii sat back as well. "So, you are Mace Lii, uh?"

"Yes, but we will get better acquainted after you rest," Master Lii answered, closing his eyes. Silver Shadow and Tyton were in the front of the aircraft talking to Andrew.

"Are you good now?" Silver Shadow asked.

"A little, what is going on and where am I?" Andrew questioned, still out of it. Silver Shadow and Tyton stood in front of him. "Wait, there are two of you?" he said, finally looking up at them. Andrew's eyes were wide open.

"We are called Shadows. I am Silver Shadow and this is my son, Tyton. You are aboard our aircraft," Silver Shadow explained.

"Okay, this isn't a dream, is it?" Andrew politely asked, rubbing his head and eyes.

"No, we are real. For right now, we need you to relax, we will be at our headquarters soon," Tyton replied.

"Headquarters?"

"Yes, it's where my team and I live," Silver Shadow answered. In the background, a low-sounding alarm chimed. Tyton glanced out the closest window. The two aircrafts had arrived at the Shadow Dome. SGD was changing into submarine mode. Then the two aircrafts dropped in the water and began to submerge. Silver Shadow and Tyton gathered their things, getting ready to disembark once they reached the hanger. SGD flouted inside the pressurized hanger first. The Shadow Hopper still carrying Ricky and Hector waited. The hanger wasn't big enough to fit both aircrafts at the same time. The hanger doors closed after SGD entered. The team with Master Lii and Andrew exited SGD and made their way to the laboratory. Silver Shadow helped Poison, she was still a little weak.

"This place is crazy!" Andrew admitted, looking up and around the hanger.

"Andrew, this way," Tyton said, trying to guide him into the lab. As they walked in, CD and Cyber Ball were standing there, going over something on the main screen. They both peered over.

"Holy…there are more!"

"CD, Cyber Ball, we have guests. Ready the two rooms for them," Silver Shadow requested, assisting Poison onto a nearby hover gurney.

"Okay, we're on it," CD answered for the both of them, holding a thumbs up. They ran from the laboratory into the hallway leading to the living quarters. Silver Shadow tapped a small button on the side of the gurney.

"Rest now, my love," he whispered to Poison.

"I will," Poison answered back as she laid down and the gurney hovered away. It carried her out of the lab and down the hallway to her room. Silver Shadow turned around and closed the door to the hanger. The elevator came up and Ton stepped out with Liset by his side.

"SD, send SGD down to the vehicle room and let the Shadow Hopper in. We have more friends waiting to come in."

"Confirm, Silver Shadow," SD replied. Silver Shadow glanced back to see Master Lii, Tyton, Andrew, Ton, and Liset standing in a small group. Silver Shadow walked over.

"Master Lii, this is…"

"Ton and Liset, yes, I know. Where is Jean?" Master Lii interrupted. Ton and Liset were surprised he knew their names. CD and Cyber Ball came back walking in from the hall.

"Yes, of course, you know them," Silver Shadow suggested.

"Those two are CD and Cyber Ball," Master Lii said, pointing to the two of them as they joined the group. The team was caught off guard.

"Okay, team, take our friends down to the conference room so I can make all the introductions," Silver Shadow announced. Everyone started to move toward the elevator with Tyton leading the way. Silver Shadow could hear the hanger finish draining the water. He walked back over to the door. When it was done, he entered in to greet Ricky and Hector. They stepped out of the Shadow Hopper and saw Silver Shadow standing there. They moved slowly with their eyes wide.

"I am Silver Shadow, Doctor Michael Eastin's son," Silver Shadow said, extending his hand.

"It's good to meet you," Ricky said, shaking Silver Shadow's hand.

"Yes, me, too," Hector implied.

"Come with me and you guys can meet the others," Silver Shadow suggested, leading them into the laboratory. They crossed the lab, walking over to the elevator. Ricky and Hector were looking around, impressed by what they saw. The three of them went down to the conference room where everyone was waiting, except Poison.

"Okay, everyone, can I have your attention?" Silver Shadow requested from the large group. Everyone got quiet and took their seats. The room was divided, Shadow's on one side of the table, humans on the other. "I want to first welcome you to the Shadow Dome, our home. I know all of you have lots of questions, and we will answer them all. But for now, we need to come together. There is a war coming, so we must prepare for it."

"How?" Hector asked, raising his hand.

"We have to set up a safe place for our operations and establish a network."

"Wait," Andrew shouted, standing up, "I know of the perfect place!"

Chapter Twelve
Shadow Corporation

It would seem the Shadow Runners have become what Doctor Eastin always envisioned. For the Silver Shadow to evolve into something much bigger than himself. To feel love, to be loved, to have someone close to him depending on his every decision, and to become a light for humanity in an age of darkness.

"We have a plan now and maybe a place to go," Silver Shadow said out loud, standing in his father's grave room. He would find himself in the room, talking to his father like he was there. Silver Shadow could feel him watching over him, maybe one day he would answer. Silver Shadow was slowly pacing back and forth in the small room. "I almost lost Poison today, I was so scared. When I found out who tried to kill her, I became so angry. I have never felt so angry before. It was the same anger I felt the day you died. I wanted to find that weasel of a man and end his life," Silver Shadow admitted, putting his head down. He was holding his hands out in front of himself, slowly clenching his fists tightly. Silver Shadow feels someone behind put their hand on his back. Silver Shadow quickly released his fingers, opening his hands. It was Master Lii. "Master," Silver Shadow said surprised. No one was able to sneak up on him before.

"He is here," he said, taking a deep breath. "I can feel him, may I come in?" Master Lii requested. Silver Shadow was kind of blocking the doorway.

"Yes, yes, of course," Silver Shadow answered, stepping aside.

"You talk to him often, don't you?"

"Yes, almost every day."

"Does it help?" Master Lii asked.

"Yes, I find myself at peace in here," Silver Shadow suggested. "The pain never really goes away, just an emptiness."

"I'm afraid everyone goes through this, you must find a way to move on. I know that's what your father would have wanted for you. I can feel your anger, you must let it go."

"How? I wanted to kill the man who tried to hurt Poison!" Silver Shadow scowled.

"You don't have to kill, and you can't save everyone. You must find the balance between the two. Those filled with anger or hate may find themselves fighting an internal battle," Master Lii advised.

"I am not sure I can do that," Silver Shadow confessed.

"You will, those who go out of their way to do harm to others will meet their own fate," Master Lii didn't have to say anything else. Silver Shadow knew he may have to cross that line. There is a big difference between revenge and justice. CD and Cyber Ball walked up to the doorway.

"Silver Shadow, we are ready to go," Cyber Ball interrupted.

"Okay, let's go," Silver Shadow answered, turning to the two of them. "Master Lii, will you be okay here?"

"Yes, my old friend, and I have a lot to discuss," Master Lii said, looking at the grave cover. He put his hand softly on the front of it. Silver Shadow left the room; he walked down the hallway with CD and Cyber Ball. The three of them made their way around the corner into the laboratory. Andrew stood on the other side of the room next to the hanger door. Ricky and Hector were seating at one of the lab tables. Ton lingered near the elevator. He was leaning against the wall with his arms folded across his chest, peering at everyone in the room.

"You two go ahead and start up SGD, I will be there in a minute," Silver Shadow ordered.

"Okay," said Cyber Ball as he and CD continued walking over to the hanger door. Silver Shadow walked over to Ricky and Hector. He could see Hector was still a little on edge, his sister was still missing. Hector was moving in his chair like he couldn't sit still. It would seem Ricky was trying to comfort him.

"I know your sister is out there and I will find her," Silver Shadow stated.

"You know, I feel more helpless than anything. There's got to be something I can do here," Hector replied.

"Yeah, something we can do!" Ricky interjected.

"Well, we could use each of your skills, it is no coincidence my father brought us together. Downstairs, we have a vehicle mechanical room where you can apply your knowledge."

"If I throw myself into something, it will take my mind off everything," Hector confessed.

"I just want to help in any way I can," Ricky admitted.

"Ton will show you the way," Silver Shadow said, pointing to the elevator. Hector and Ricky glanced over; they could see Ton still leaning against the wall next to the elevator. Ton reaches over and hits a button and the elevator doors open. Ricky and Hector trade looks at one another and made their way over. Silver Shadow watched as the three of them boarded the elevator. Silver Shadow turns, grabbing his weapon with extra clips off one of the tables, and walks into the hanger boarding SGD aircraft. "Okay, SGD, let's go," he said, walking through the aircraft to the cockpit.

"Affirmative, Silver Shadow." The hanger began to fill with water and SGD floated through the ocean to the surface. As the aircraft took off, Silver Shadow stowed his M4 rifle and placed SGD on auto pilot. He made his way to the back. CD and Cyber Ball talked among themselves while Andrew sat in silence alone.

"Andrew, show me where we are going," Silver Shadow suggested, waving him over. Andrew jumped up from his seat and walked over to where Silver Shadow was standing. The two of them sat down at the small meeting table near the front of the aircraft. Silver Shadow started hitting some icons on the top of the table, bringing up 3D map with GPS navigation.

"Where are we?" Andrew asked.

"We are here," Silver Shadow said, pointing to a blue blinking triangle.

"Okay, the building is here in the city on this small city block. All the buildings around it are abandoned, too."

"It looks good on the map, we will have to check it out once we get there."

"Okay, how long will it take to get there?" Andrew asked.

"Sixty-three minutes. When we arrive, you will stay aboard SGD while my team and I do recon," Silver Shadow suggested as he sat back in the chair.

"Oh, okay," answered Andrew with a sigh of relief. For a second, he traded looks with Silver Shadow as they sat there in silence. Then came one of the obvious questions no one had asked Andrew yet.

"How did you know Doctor Eastin?"

"I brokered the deal to help him purchase the property for his first laboratory."

"You mean the one he was killed in?" Silver Shadow uttered.

"I'm sorry," Andrew confessed. He could tell this was a sensitive subject for him. "I didn't mean…"

"I think they may have followed the paper trail to the sale of the property," Silver Shadow said, putting his head down.

"They couldn't have, I used shell companies to make the deal. I even concealed mine and his identity just like Eastin wanted," Andrew admitted.

"Then how did they find us?"

"I don't know, I did everything Eastin told me to. Only the three of us knew about the project."

"The three of you?" Silver shadow asked.

"Yeah, Michael Eastin, Nona Winthorp the architect, and myself."

"Someone made a mistake?"

"It had to be one of the construction works. They weren't told what they were building, but it would not be hard for them to figure it out. Anyone could have easily asked a few questions about the project and got suspicious."

"I know."

"Look, I'm sorry about what happened to him, but I'm here now and I will help in any way possible. He was a good friend to me."

"He was more than a friend to me," Silver Shadow claimed, looking up, "He was my father, and if you're his friend, you will help me build his legacy. We owe him that."

"You're right, his legacy will live on," Andrew vowed, sitting up straight in his seat. For a while, Andrew and Silver Shadow talked. They got to know each other a little better. Each learning how they were connected to Eastin. A soft tone rang out and SGD interrupted.

"Silver Shadow, we will arrive at the location in seven minutes," SGD confirmed.

"Copy that, SGD. Alright, boys, gear up equipment check in three," Silver Shadow ordered, peering down the aisle at CD and Cyber Ball. They both glanced up and shook their heads yes. The two of them proceeded to their weapon lockers in the back of the aircraft. Silver Shadow turned back to Andrew, he had this look on his face. It was a look of admiration, then it dawned on him. Andrew realized Eastin's life work was unfolding in front of him. He was going to play a larger part in the future of the Shadows.

"Stay here," Silver Shadow said.

"Can I help from here?" Andrew questioned.

"You can watch our backs from this station, SGD, bring up onboard external cameras."

"Affirmative, Silver Shadow," SGD answered. The surface of the table where Andrew sat lit up. Live images appeared, showing everything around the bottom of the aircraft.

"Okay, there are four cameras. You can touch any image to use and control each one," Silver Shadow instructed.

"Alright, I got it," Andrew said.

"If you see anything, you can talk to me through SGD's communication link."

"Right, be careful and good luck." Silver Shadow shook his head and walked to his weapon locker in the cockpit. Andrew pulled himself closer to the table. He looked over all the images to see which one would be the best to use. CD and Cyber Ball were ready for action. Silver Shadow approached them as they stood at the backdrop door.

"We will recon the area and make sure it is safe. Then we set a perimeter and find out what we have to work with."

"Got it," Cyber Ball said.

"Any people in the area?" CD asked.

"Unknown, that's why we are here," Silver Shadow answered, opening the drop door.

"Rules?" CD asked.

"The same, stay invisible, remain secret, and preserve all life," Silver Shadow ordered.

"Understood, commander," CD answered.

"Agreed," Cyber Ball replied. Silver Shadow checked his black M4, looking through the sights and turning on the flashlight. He slung it onto his back and attached his ammo belt. Cyber Ball and CD stood ready in a line at the drop door. Silver Shadow put on his map bracelet and attached the com link device to the side of his head. He joined the end of the line.

"SGD, do you read me?" Silver Shadow asked, testing the com link device.

"Affirmative," SGD answered.

"Andrew, can you hear me as well?"

"Yes, yes, I can," Andrew replied.

"Good, SGD, lower altitude and locate safe drop point," Silver Shadow commanded.

"Affirmative, Silver Shadow."

"Once we deploy, stay on station with pattern Sierra Delta."

"Sierra Delta flight pattern, confirmed," SGD repeated. The three Shadows patiently waited at the drop door as the aircraft started its decent. SGD sailed above a few old buildings and stop, hovering over an alleyway leading to a street corner. CD, Cyber Ball, and Silver Shadow saw the red light turn green. The drop door ramp extended and the three Shadows jumped from the edge. Falling through the night time air in unison from 600-feet. They floated into the alley between the buildings to the ground. Landing on their feet, they quickly spread out on the ground with weapons drawn. For a few minutes silence, as they checked everywhere remaining unseen, CD stood fast with an orange glowing disk in hand. Cyber Ball already engaged two bomb balls into the air, they hovered around him like little pets. Silver Shadow was pointing his M4 in every direction. He glanced over at CD.

"We're clear," CD said, breaking the silence.

"Let's move, on me," Silver Shadow whispered, waving his hand to CD and Cyber Ball to follow. CD fell into line behind Silver Shadow as Cyber Ball followed behind him. The three Shadows made their way through the darkness along the side one of the buildings to the street corner. Stopping at the end, they continued to observe their surroundings. Only one street light illuminating the sidewalk corner. It was quiet with no signs of street traffic or even a parked car. These five city blocks seem to be abandoned with a lot of old run-down buildings. Silver Shadow knew looks can always be deceiving.

"SGD, run thermal scan, five block radius. Tell me how many people in the vicinity," Silver Shadow said, speaking into the com link.

"Scanning…my sensors detect many small heat signatures. Only one big enough to be human," SGD replied.

"Show me," Silver Shadow requested. He hit the button on his bracelet and the mini 3D map projected up high just above the three Shadows' heads. The blue light brightened up some of the dark alley.

"Affirmative, sending location." A small red and orange blip appeared on the blue 3D map. Silver Shadow took a second to memorize the building and everything around it.

"Wait, Silver Shadow, that's the building I was talking about," Andrew interrupted. He was looking at the same thermal images on the screens; he was sitting in front of on the aircraft.

"Copy, Andrew, we will check it out," Silver Shadow answered, turning off the 3D mini map. He glanced back at CD and Cyber Ball. "Cyber Ball, go high, CD, with me," Silver Shadow ordered.

"I'm on it," Cyber Ball answered. He peered over at CD, "Hey, bro, little help!?"

"I got you," CD replied, pulling three small purple oval-shaped disks from the side of his leg. With a flick of CD's wrist upwards, the three disks sailed through the air. They landed in the wall of the build next to them, one after the other. The disks stuck out of the wall in a diagonal elevated line-like steps.

"Use the rooftops and cover our movements," Silver Shadow commanded.

"You got it," Cyber Ball said. He quickly turned around and used the disks as stepping points. Cyber Ball leaped from the ground and onto each disk up to the roof. CD stood there looking up, making sure Cyber Ball made it up. He glanced back over his shoulder at Silver Shadow.

"Nice work," Silver Shadow admitted, "Let's move!" The two Shadows darted out of the alley through the light and across the street. They ran fast down the sidewalks and through more alleys. CD would peer up every few minutes, making sure Cyber Ball was still with them. He could see Cyber Ball jumping from rooftop to rooftop from the alleyways below. "Hold up!" Silver Shadow whispered, holding his hand up in a fist. CD stopped behind and took up a position to watch Silver Shadow's back. The two of them were in the other alleyway cross the street of what looked like an old run down office building. CD peered up and could see Cyber Ball peeking down at them from the roof. "Cyber Ball, come in."

"I read you, Silver Shadow," Cyber Ball answered.

"We are heading for the building across the street from our current position. Stay close, target point is on the seventh floor," Silver Shadow instructed.

"Copy, shadowing."

"Alright, CD, on me." CD shook his head yes, looking at the burnt and rotted out open doors. The air was thick, the smell of mold and mildew was familiar. The two Shadows ran across the street and into the doorway, like a pair of wolves in the lush forest. They entered the front of the building and found themselves in an old lobby. The main lobby was way past its prime. It looked like a hotel lobby with a decaying front check in desk. Wrecked furniture missing their cushioning littered the waiting area. The floor was covered with all kinds of loose papers, old magazines, and brochures. There were small piles of garbage and trash in different spots. Everything in the room was covered in five years of dust and black mold. CD looked over at Silver Shadow, he was pointing to a doorway at the far side of the lobby. The doorway was next to a pair of elevators. CD shook his head as the two Shadows walked over slowly. Silver Shadow could hear a faint sound coming from beyond the doorway. As they got closer, CD could hear it, too. He pulled another larger yellow disk from his back. Standing on either side of the doorway, CD peered at Silver Shadow waiting. He shook his head and CD ran into the open doorway, followed by Silver Shadow. They were standing in an old square spiral gray concrete staircase. Water was dripping from one of the higher floors down the center of the staircase. CD glanced up from the middle and could see so many stairs. He looked back at Silver Shadow and shrugged his shoulders. Silver Shadow lowered his weapon a little.

"Just water," CD whispered.

The Corrupt Shadows

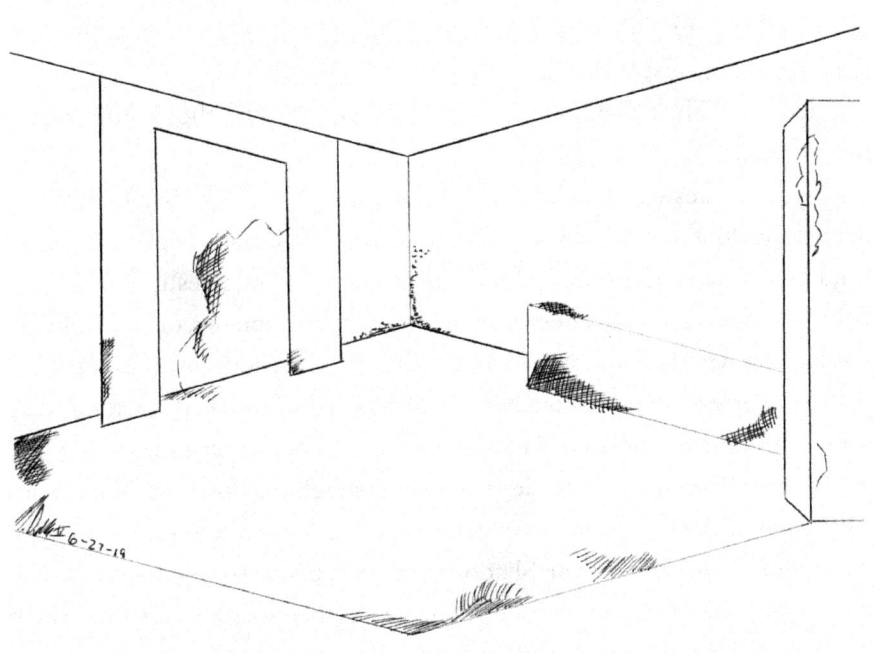

Everything in the room was covered in five years of dust and black mold.

"Take point, find the seventh floor."

"On it," CD replied, going slowly up the stairs.

"Cyber Ball, come in," Silver Shadow called into the com link.

"I'm here," Cyber Ball answered.

"We are headed up. There is a fire escape on the side, meet us on seven."

"Copy, already on my way," Cyber Ball replied. Silver Shadow followed CD up the stairwell, keeping a little distance covering his back. Before long the two Shadows reached the seventh floor. CD stood ready three-feet in front of the metal door. The emergency fire doors seem to be the only things in the whole building not falling apart. Silver Shadow slowly moved beside the door with his back against the wall.

"Ready?" Silver Shadow whispered to CD, grasping the slightly rusted door handle.

"Yes," CD answered, holding two disks in his hands. Silver Shadow quickly opened the door and CD silently darted in. Silver Shadow checked the stairwell one last time and followed CD. They found themselves in a small hall with very little light. This floor seemed warmer than the rest of the building. The hallway had three doors leading to other smaller rooms. At the end of the hall was a large conference-like room. CD checked all the small rooms as they moved through the hallway. Each time looking at Silver Shadow, giving him the all clear. They silently made their way through the corridor. The rooms were empty with only the moonlight glaring in from the windows. CD stopped at the end of the hall, Silver Shadow glanced up and stopped as well. CD peered into the large conference room. Using hand signs, CD told Silver Shadow he could see someone. Pointing to his eyes and holding out one finger, CD put the two disks in his hands back onto his body and crept into the room. Silver Shadow followed, staying in the shadows. After entering the room, the two Shadows observed a homeless man sitting on the floor in the corner. Three or four pieces of cardboard lay underneath him. His head was down and his arms wrapped around his knees. He was rocking back and forth, trying to stay warm. Next to him was a low burning mini propane camping grill. A handful of mini green propane tanks were scattered across the floor. Three big, black garbage bags sat on the other side of the man. He was unarmed, Silver Shadow slung his M4 onto his back. The homeless man looked up.

"Is someone there?" he asked, peering into the darkness. He was a dark-skinned man with a thick, black full raggedy-looking beard. His short black hair shaped like a mini afro puff with a thinning bald spot in the front. The man's face was narrow with light colored, dry, cracked, chapped lips. There was some sadness in his brown eyes. Silver Shadow stepped out into the moon light. "What the...!" the man started to say. He quickly sprung up and ran over to the nearby window leading to the fire escape. Keeping his eyes on Silver Shadow, he opened the window. Before he could climb out, Cyber Ball jumped down in front of the window, blocking the man from exiting the building. "What the, another one!" the man screamed, backing up with his hands up. CD stepped forward and revealed himself. "Oh, man, I'm not going down without a fight," the man said, taking up a fighting stance.

"We are not here to hurt you," Silver Shadow suggested, holding out his hands. With his weapon on his back and his hands empty, Silver Shadow was trying to appear non-aggressive. He is well aware of the dangers when you corner a threatened animal, it becomes agitated.

"I knew one day someone would come, you special forces guys are way more advanced than I thought you'd be. I tried to stay off the grid, but you guys still found me!" the man said, still being defensive. CD and Cyber Ball held their position to avoid provoking the man who seem to already be on edge.

"We are not who you think we are," Silver Shadow clammed.

"Yeah, well then, who are you guys?" the man asked.

"Behind me is CD," Silver Shadow went on. "The one at the window is Cyber Ball, and I am Silver Shadow."

"Nah, man, whatever you're sellin', I ain't buying. Who sent you?"

"No one sent us, we are here, like you to seek refuge." The man took a brave step closer to Silver Shadow.

"What kind of Tec are ya wearing," the man asked, turning his head sideways, "I've only seen one thing like this before, and it still doesn't even come close to being as advanced as what you have."

"May I ask, what is your name?"

"My name is Cedrick Cing. That's Cing with a C!"

"Nice to meet you, Mr. Cing with a C," Silver Shadow said, holding out his hand to greet. Cedrick peered down at Silver Shadow's extended hand. He quickly looked over at CD, then Cyber Ball to make sure this wasn't some kind of trick.

"Yeah, nice to meet you, too, bro," Cedrick said, shaking Silver Shadow's hand. "So, what are you guys exactly?" Cedrick asked as they continued to shake hands. He noticed Silver Shadow's hand was not like a human's.

"We are called Shadows."

"You guys from space or something?" Cedrick questioned, letting go.

"No, we have lived alongside man kind in secret for some time," Silver Shadow remarked.

"Oh, yeah," Cedrick said, backing up from Silver Shadow. He was still a little on edge, unsure as to the Shadows' intention. Reading his body language, Silver Shadow sat down on the floor where he stood.

"CD, Cyber Ball, check the rest of the buildings. Report back here once you're done."

"Understood," CD answered. Cedrick watched as CD faded back into the shadows and Cyber Ball disappeared from the window.

"Cedrick," Silver Shadow called out, trying to get his attention. Cedrick kind of jumped a little. "You said before you have seen something like us before."

"Well, yeah."

"What did you used to do, if you do not mind me asking?"

"I used to be a military intelligence officer."

"For what branch?" Silver Shadow inquired. Cedrick began to relax a bit and sat down in front of Silver Shadow.

"All of them. My job was to recruit, train, and assign task for field operatives," Cedrick explained.

"What happened, now what do you do?"

"Oh, you mean how did I end up here, right?" Cedrick asked, getting up from the floor. "How did you end up some bum living out of an empty, nasty, mod covered building?" He was beginning to raise his voice as he turned his back to Silver Shadow.

"I did not mean to offend you, Cedrick."

"No, but you have, bro." Cedrick put both of his hands on the wall, leaning against it with his head down. "How did I end up here?" he whispered to himself.

"Cedrick, do you have anyone, a family?" Silver Shadow asked.

"Yes," Cedrick answered with tears in his eyes. "You know, I made the military my whole life. I lost so many good operatives, too many, man. Then one day it was gone, along with all the people I cared about."

"I am sorry, but it is not too late," Silver Shadow suggested.

"I think it is, bro. I've been gone for so long, I don't know how to go back!" Cedrick shouted, turning around with tears rolling down his face. "My wife and I split, my rebellious daughter won't talk to me, and my son is in college. He can't be held back by my burdens."

"Cedrick, things will change, help us."

"Help you do what, man, take over the world. I mean, what can I do? I'm nobody," Cedrick shouted.

"You were a soldier. There is a war coming and we will need your help. My father died defending me and my kind. More will die if the Shadows stand by and do nothing."

"I can't, I've already lost so much," Cedrick confessed.

"Then let me help you up. You are not broken, just lost. I know, I was there in that place for a while. When my father died, I was lost, too. Then someone reminded me why Doctor Eastin died. It was so I could live."

"Wait, Doctor Michael Eastin?"

"Yes, he was my father. Did you know him?"

"Only by reputation and his work. He was a legend, everyone knew what he tried to do."

"Then you know what I am fighting to protect?" Silver Shadow remarked, standing up.

"Yes, yes, I do! Are you his creation?" Cedrick asked, moving closer to Silver Shadow. "Wow, he did it, he really did it. Most people only dreamed of working with him. He set the bar for advanced biotechnology."

"Will you help us stop those who would use my father's creation to make an army?"

"I've seen what the government is capable of," Cedrick held out his hand. "I'm in!" Cedrick remarked, wiping the tears from his face.

"Good," Silver Shadow answered, shaking Cedrick's hand once again.

"Silver Shadow," CD interrupted, emerging from the shadows.

"Wow, you guys are really sneaky!" Cedrick commented a little caught off guard. "You got to show me how you do that." Silver Shadow glanced over his shoulder.

"We've checked the surrounding buildings. All clear."

"Sounds right, aren't many people come around here. Part of the reason why I was able to hide for so long," Cedrick added.

"How long have you been living here?" Silver Shadow, asked looking around.

"Let's see…" Cedrick tilled his head back, peering up at the ceiling. He started counting his fingers and whispering to himself. CD and Silver Shadow just stared at him for a moment. Then Cedrick just stopped like he was frozen. His head came down and he looked Silver Shadow in the eyes. "It, it's…"

"What's wrong?" Silver Shadow asked.

"It's been almost ten years," Cedrick answered with a shaky voice. There was pain in his eyes. His face almost went blank and his mouth hung open like his jaw was broken. "I've been hiding here for so long," Cedrick repeated in disbelief. CD and Silver Shadow were in a bit of shock. Cedrick was alone, living on the streets for such a long time.

"It's okay now," Silver Shadow said, putting his hand on Cedrick's shoulder. "We can help, and maybe you are going to help us."

"What do I do now?" Cedrick asked, still holding his hands out in front of himself, fingers fully extended.

"I think it is time for you to start a new chapter in your life," Silver Shadow said, leading Cedrick to the door. The three of them started to leave the room, making their way to the door and stairway.

"Wait!" Cedrick shouted, stopping in his footsteps. He ran back to the corner of the room where the big black garbage bags still sat. Cedrick began frantically rummaging through them in search of something. Silver Shadow and CD stopped for a second and waited.

"Go on ahead, have SGD meet us on the roof," Silver Shadow said, turning to CD.

"You got it," CD answered. CD took off through the hallway and into the stairwell. Silver Shadow turned to see Cedrick still searching.

"I got it!" Cedrick declared, holding something up. His body was draped over all three full garbage bags. It would appear the bags had all Cedrick's belongs, or what was left. He was holding an old-looking cell phone.

"A cell phone?" Silver Shadow inquired. Cedrick jumped up from the floor and quickly walked over.

"Yeah," Cedrick answered, rubbing the phone on his shirt like an apple. "It's a little dirty, but it still works. The charger broke a while ago, so I only turn it on when I need it."

"What is on it?"

"My life, man, I mean everything I lost and everything I will need to start fresh."

"We should go, there is someone I want you to meet. He will help you like he has helped me." Silver Shadow and Cedrick made their way to the roof. SGD was already waiting in cloak mode with the hovering stairs deployed. The night time air swirled around them as the two exited the building.

"What's that, bro, your space ship?"

"My stealth aircraft."

"Oh, right, what was I thinking," Cedrick sarcastically went on, "Can't just walk everywhere."

"Are you ready to embark on a new adventure?" Silver Shadow asked, climbing the first step.

"I got nothing else to do," Cedrick replied, follow Silver Shadow's lead. The two entered SGD where it became quiet.

"Make yourself comfortable," Silver Shadow remarked, showing Cedrick a seat. CD and Cyber Ball were already in their seats next to each other. Andrew was still sitting up toward the front of the aircraft at the computer. They all watched as Silver Shadow and Cedrick came on board. Feeling like everyone was looking at him, Cedrick slowly sat down in one of the back seats. Silver Shadow walked through the aircraft over to Andrew. They started talking among themselves. The aircraft sailed to a higher altitude. Cedrick was still unclear as to where they were taking him. He sat back in his chair, slouching a little to hide from everyone's view. His eyes became heavy; before long Andrew came and sat down in the chair across the aisle from him. Cedrick snapped out of it.

"Hey, my name is Andrew Bouwers," Andrew said with his hand extended to shake.

"Cedrick Cing with a C," Cedrick answered, extending his hand and shaking.

"Good to meet you. So, it was you hiding in that old building."

"No, I was living there."

"Oh, yes, of course. Sorry to hear that," Andrew expressed.

"Yo, let me ask you a question?" Cedrick went on, leaning closer to Andrew. "What's the deal with these guys? Are they aliens or something?"

"No, I mean, not really. If I had to classify them, I would say they are super humans."

"What do you mean?" Cedrick inquired.

"Well, Silver Shadow was made in a laboratory," Andrew suggested.

"By Doctor Eastin?"

"Yeah, that's right, you know Eastin?" Andrew asked a little surprised.

"No, only by reputation."

"From where, what did you use to do for a living?"

"Military Intelligence, I was a training officer."

"Well, you are going to fit right in then," Andrew confessed, leaning back in his seat.

"What do you mean? Where are we going?" Cedrick questioned.

"We are going to The Shadow Dome, their headquarters. You'll see."

"It's off the hook, huh?"

"Oh, yeah, it's like nothing you've ever seen before."

"I've seen a lot though."

"I bet. Take everything you've seen and roll it all into one, and this place will surpass it times ten," Andrew bragged.

"Word," Cedrick replied, leaning back. "I guess I will be starting a new chapter in my life," Cedrick whispered to himself, closing his eyes. He dozed off, thinking about his family. Cedrick was woken up abruptly when Silver Shadow exited the cockpit and quickly made his way to the back of the aircraft.

"CD, Cyber Ball, on me!" Silver Shadow ordered. CD and Cyber Ball immediately jumped from their seats. Cedrick and Andrew watched as the three Shadows lined up at the back-drop door. Silver Shadow hit the red button on the side and the drop door open, extending the deploy ramp.

"What's going on?" Andrew blurted out. Silver Shadow turned around as the air from outside rushed in.

"Someone needs help." Without another word, the three Shadows leap from the end of the ramp, disappearing into the darkness. Andrew got up from his seat and ran down the aisle toward the front of the aircraft. Cedrick quickly followed him. Andrew sat down in front of the table with all the screens he used earlier.

"Did they just…?" Cedrick shouted, pointing to the open doors.

"Yeah, I told you, super humans."

"Holy…!"

"SGD, what's going on?" Andrew asked.

"I spotted a civilian car trapped under a fallen electrical pole. Silver Shadow has decided to aide the person trapped inside," SGD replied.

"What the? This plane can talk?" Cedrick implied.

"Yes, Cedrick," Andrew answered a little annoyed. "Can you bring it up on the screen?"

"Affirmative, Andrew." The surface of the table lit up and three different images from SGD's surveillance system appeared. Andrew and Cedrick could see the car in question. There was a little green four-door car waged under a fallen telephone pole. Live wires were draped over all sides of the car, making it impossible for anyone to get out or in. The wires were sparking, making them look like they were jumping around on the ground. There was minor damage to the front of the car. The driver must have lost control and hit the pole head on. It also looked like gas was leaking from the car as well.

"How long before emergency rescue gets there?" Andrew pleaded.

"There is no response team in route. It is likely this crash has just taken place. I have already notified the local authorities."

"That's why he was in such a rush," Andrew implied.

"What are they going to do?" Cedrick asked.

"What they seem to do best, help people." They both watch the screens like two kids staying up late to view their favorite movie. Suddenly, they saw a flash of light.

"What was that?"

"I think it was one of CD's disks," Andrew answered, squinting at the screen.

Michael Dunkley, Jr.

"I spotted a civilian car trapped under a fallen electrical pole. Silver Shadow has decided to aide the person trapped inside," SGD replied.

The live wires stopped sparking and fell to the ground, cut along the top of the car driver side door in a straight line. Then the pole itself began to roll off the top of the car roof. It was too dark, they couldn't see who was moving it.

"The people inside can't even see them moving the pole I bet," Cedrick announced.

"Probably not, but this is how they work, in secret."

"Really!"

"Yeah, just think back to all those stories you've heard in the last few years."

"What stories, bro?"

"The unexplained ones people talk about, how they survived when they should have been dead."

"Name one," Cedrick questioned in disbelief. Andrew starts to think for a second.

"Okay, I remember one. Two years ago, I saw an interview on TV about a trucker falling asleep at the wheel because he works way too hard. He wakes up and finds himself still in the cab of his 18-wheeler hanging off the side of a bridge."

"Yeah, so!"

"So, the truck falls off the bridge and he ends up magically on the street and he doesn't know how he got there."

"Nah, bro, there's no way."

"I think our friend had something to do with it," Andrew suggested. "That's how he works, saving people without them even knowing." Andrew looked at Cedrick. Andrew could tell he was really thinking about it. Cedrick had kind of a blank expression on his face. "Wait, look!" Andrew blurted out, snapping his attention back to the screens. The pole and all the dangerous live wires were finally off the car. The driver door slowly opens and a woman stumbled out. She looked a little afraid and kept glancing around. The woman was well dressed and had a cut on her forehead. A small amount of blood on the side of her face.

"What's she saying, I can't hear her?" Cedrick suggested.

"There's no sound, but I bet she is looking to thank who ever saved her," Andrew replied. The woman turned in a full circle, peering in every direction.

"Maybe, you think she knows?"

"Most people are not stupid, the pole didn't move itself," Andrew implied, continuing to watch the woman. After searching the darkness and rubbing her head a few times, the woman attempted to get some things out from the car. Suddenly, she jumped back.

"Yo, what is she doing now?" Cedrick asked, turning his head sideways curiously.

"Not sure," Andrew said, eyes glued to the screens. The woman started backing up from the car. Before long it started to catch fire. The fuel puddle finally spread, reaching the live wires still on the ground. The car was now covered in flames and red lights could be seen in the distance. The firetrucks would soon arrive. Andrew and Cedrick jump when a voice interrupted the silence.

"SGD, evac on my location," Silver Shadow ordered.

"Affirmative, Silver Shadow," SGD replied. The aircraft took evasive action and met the three Shadows on a nearby rooftop. The ramp opened and Silver Shadow jumped in. CD and Cyber Ball followed.

"So, is this what you do, save people?" Cedrick questioned, standing up and greeting Silver Shadow in the middle of the aisle.

"All the time," Silver Shadow answered.

"I'm all in, bro."

Chapter Thirteen
Justified Means

The team has come a long way and continues to grow. With every new day brings more allies to help. The few human members have shown they can be trusted so far. There are, however, two matters that have not been addressed. After four long days, Silver Shadow has finally tracked down Hector's sister and her location. He stands ready in the shadows at an old shipping warehouse down by the docks. M4 rifle on his back with a silencer for a stealth mission. From the outside, it seems to be busy with shipping containers being moved by dock workers. *"It will be easy to slip in unnoticed but hard to find the girl,"* Silver Shadow thought to himself. He placed the com link on the base of his neck.

"Check, check!"

"Copy, I can hear you," Poison answered on the other end. She was set up with her sniper rifle in the highest place she could find overlooking the entire area. Back at full strength, she was ready for a little payback on those who would pray on the innocent.

"SGD, there are a lot of robots guarding this place. Scan the structures for heat signatures," Silver Shadow ordered SGD, hovering high in the clouds above.

"Affirmative, scanning… There are two groups of people in the southwest corner of the second warehouse. One group is large and the other is small."

"Copy, SGD, maintain observation mode and be ready for a quick dust off at one of the three pick up points," Silver Shadow commanded.

"Affirmative, Silver Shadow," SGD replied.

"What are you thinking?" Poison asked, listening.

"Not sure, guards and prisoners?" Silver Shadow suggested.

"Maybe, better move quickly. A bunch of trucks just showed up at the front gates," Poison said, peering through her sniper's scope.

"Who are they?"

"Not sure, more guys with guns." Without warning Silver Shadow darted from his hiding place and across a large open area into the first warehouse.

"Cover me."

"Don't worry, I got you covered." Silver Shadow may know what is happening here. They may have found an underground human trafficking operation. The men outside, just arriving, may be buyers. Silver Shadow stopped beside a few stacks of boxes. He will have to cross this warehouse to get to the second.

"On my right, catwalk," Silver Shadow whispered.

"I see him." Poison makes one precise head shot. The heavy silencer on her rifle makes the shot completely unseen or heard. The hollow point round hits its mark. The robot guard staggers forward and over the rail to the ground blow. "He's down."

"Thanks," Silver Shadow answers. He moves around the boxes and sees another robot guard standing over the body. Before he could react, Silver Shadow runs full speed. The robot turns around in time to see Silver Shadow sliding across the floor; he sweeps both legs, knocking the robot backward. While on the ground, Silver Shadow delivers a dropping heel kick to the robot's head, caving it in. The robot sparks and stops moving. "That was too close."

"Yeah, now watch yourself. There are a few just outside the door," Poison implied.

"Can you take them out?"

"Yeah, with your help!"

"How many?"

"I count five."

"Right, how many can you hit?" Silver Shadow asked, moving closer to the big doorway leading out. The second warehouse was on the other side of the small group of robot guards.

"Three before they realize it."

"Copy, I will take the back two, you take the three in the front?"

"Got them, go!" Poison said, taking her shots. Silver Shadow emerged from the doorway far enough, M4 in hand, making two quick head shots on the guards. All the robots dropped, hitting the ground at almost the same time. Their timed attack was flawless. With this take down done, Silver Shadow slung his M4 onto his back and quickly ran into the second warehouse. The building was full with tall stacks of wooden boxes and crates. Silver Shadow jumped and flipped up one of the tall stacks, trying to get as high as he could. *"I will be able to see more from up here,"* he thought to himself. At the top was a catwalk. Silver Shadow jumped from the stack he was on to the rail of the catwalk. Once on he hopped over the rail, landing onto the catwalk, Silver Shadow could see the catwalk traced the outer edge of the warehouse. Moving slow and in the shadows, he peered down at the southwest corner. He could see a small clearing where the rows of boxes ended. There was a large cage with bars like a prison. Silver Shadow couldn't see who or what was inside. In the only light were two men sitting in chairs, playing cards at a small brown wooden table. Their weapons lay on their laps, rifles of some kind.

"I am in, two armed guards and possible hostages," Silver Shadow whispered into his com link.

"Copy, what do you need?" Poison replied.

"Clear a path to one of those large trucks outside. Marking a pick-up point on the map," Silver Shadow requested, using his mini map bracelet. Poison's bracelet on her wrist began to glow blue. Taking her left hand off her rifle, she opens the 3D image. A new location had been added, it blinked in blue.

"I'm going to need time," Poison answered, looking at the mini map.

"How much?"

"Twelve minutes."

"Copy, time starts now," Silver Shadow suggested, starting a timer.

"I'm moving, stay safe," Poison remarked, glancing at the countdown that was now on her bracelet as well. She quickly got up, folding the sniper rifle legs down, and ran east on top of the metal containers she was set up on. "SGD, on the move. Can you disable five vehicles using an electronically disruption? Two west and three south of primary location."

"Affirmative, Poison," SGD complied. Poison continued to move until she had a direct line of sight of the two eighteen wheelers. They were parked southeast behind the first warehouse. One robot guard stood in front of both. Poison took one head shot.

"Six minutes."

"Acknowledged," Silver Shadow replied. He moved around the catwalk over head of the two men. Using his M4, Silver Shadow shoots out the light hanging over the two men. He quickly jumps over the rail of the catwalk and down behind both men. They immediately stood up from their wooden chairs and struggle to see in the darkness.

"What's that?" one of the men yell, pointing to Silver Shadow's red glowing eyes. Before the men could move a muscle, Silver Shadow knocks out one, using the back of his M4. He then jumps over the small card table and kicks the other men in the chest, sending him flying over his chair into a wooden box.

"The men are down, moving hostages."

"Copy, three minutes," Poison confirmed. Silver Shadow steps up to the door of the large cage. Peering inside he counts 16 young human girls. They couldn't have been any more than 17 or 18-years-old. He could sense their fear as they moved back from the cage door and shivered. The door had a big padlock. Silver Shadow grabbed the lock and twisted it off, breaking part of the door along with the lock. He opened the door and took two large steps backward.

"I am not here to hurt you. Do not be afraid," Silver Shadow whispered. He held out his hand. "Come, I will take you all home now." All the girls were dirty and still wearing the clothes they were taken in. There were a few buckets in the corner and old wrappers on the floor from the little bit of food they were given. All the girls were bare footed as well. Silver Shadow felt sadness, *"How can people do this to the innocent?"* he thought to himself. He noticed one girl laying on the floor. Silver Shadow stepped inside, moving through the group of girls and knelt down. He quickly checked for a pulse, it was weak. "We have one in need of care."

"Copy, one minute."

"Check, 16 in total, on the move." Silver Shadow picked the girl up off the floor. Her body was limp almost lifeless, and her skin was cold. He walked to the door, "Come, time to go home." All the girls started to follow him. Silver Shadow led them down one aisle between the boxes. There was a door on the south wall. When they reached the door, Silver Shadow saw another padlock with chain. His eyes began to glow and he kicked the door as hard as he could, still holding the girl in his arms. The door flew off its hinges and fell to the ground. Poison had backed the truck up right to the door. Silver Shadow stepped out, looking to the left. Poison hopped from the cab of the truck.

"They're so young," Poison exclaimed, opening the truck trailer doors.

"Yes, too young," Silver Shadow replied.

"Come on, girls, climb in, we're going to get you out of here," Poison said, helping each girl into the back of the empty cargo trailer. After the last girl was safely on, Silver Shadow carefully laid the girl in his arms down. Another girl helped him get her in.

"Do you know what this girl's name is?" Silver Shadow softly asked. She just gazed at his for a second. Poison and Silver Shadow traded looks.

"I think she said her name was Maddie Wells," the young girl whispered. It was her, Hector's sister. Silver Shadow stopped, he put his head down. He was filled with sadness. *"What could she have done to deserve this?"* he asked himself. Silver Shadow felt a hand on his shoulder, it was Poison.

"I know what you're feeling inside, but this is not the time or place. We have to get them safe first."

"I'm going to close this now, do not be afraid anymore," Silver Shadow suggested to the girls. He closed the trailer doors. "You're right, let's get them safe. Drive, I will provide cover."

"Okay," Poison answered. She ran to the cab of the truck, climb in, and put it in gear. Silver Shadow pulled his M4 from his back. There was no more sadness, only rage. His eyes began to glow as he jumped to the top of the trailer. As Poison started to drive, Silver Shadow remained on top, riding the tractor trailer like a giant surf board.

"SGD, go flight pattern Zulu, cleared hot."

"Affirmative, Silver Shadow," SGD replied. Seeing no other way, Poison drove past the buyers.

"I've got no choice, guys and guns contact, left!" Poison yelled into the com link.

"I will cover us, SGD is our air," Silver Shadow assured her. He knelt down and hit every target twice. Bullets and gunfire filled the once quite nighttime air. The men and robot guards dropped like flies one by one. SGD fired short range air to ground missiles destroying any vehicles nearby.

"Contacted front!" Silver Shadow glanced up and saw two bulletproof black SUVs blocking the only exit along the edge of the docks. No place to go but through, water on one side, army of bad guys on the other.

"On it, SGD, take out the blockade."

"Affirmative, removing threat." More robot guards lined up behind the SUVs and open fire on the cab of the truck. Poison ducked down below the dashboard. Silver Shadow watched as SGD lunched two rockets. The SUVs were hit with a direct impact, sending one of the them flipping backward into the water. Poison peered over the wheel when she heard the explosions. It was clear and she drove through the open side. Silver Shadow quickly hit the few robots not destroyed in the blast.

"We are clear, are you okay down there?"

"Yes, where to?" Poison answered.

"Nearest hospital," Silver Shadow instructed. He sat down and reloaded his weapon still on top of the trailer. *The girls are now free, but how many are still out there? Suffering in the same conditions,* Silver Shadow thought. It would seem The Shadow Runners were just in time for these girls. This might be one isolated incident, a private party trying to bite off more than they can chew. Or this could be one small piece to a larger on-going problem. The team might have to face this kind of evil again and strike at the root's source. Tyton sits in the laboratory, anxiously awaiting his parent's return. Before they left, his father told him to be ready. He was very vague about the next assignment. His father mentioned something about doing some Recon. The sound of the pressurized hanger removing water from its chamber got Tyton's attention. He stood up right away. In the background, the sound of the elevator pinged, Hector, Cedrick, Ricky, Andrew, and Master Lii came pouring out into the lab. The hanger door opened and everyone stopped to look, they all stood there almost frozen in place. Poison walked through, first carrying her sniper rifle and Silver Shadow's unmistakable M4. Silver Shadow followed, carrying Maddie in his arms, she was wrapped up in a dark gray wool blanket. Hector ran over as Silver Shadow put her down into a nearby chair. Maddie opened her eyes to see her brother standing over her.

"Hey, you," he whispered softly; he knelt down beside her. His eyes filled with tears, it was as if a large heavy weight had been lifted. She embraced him, wrapping her little arms around Hector's neck. He peered over Maddie's shoulder at Silver Shadow. "Thank you." Silver Shadow gave Hector a thumbs up. Everyone in the room was speechless as they watched the reunion. It was a true testament of what this team of Shadows were willing to do to protect life.

"I know it's been hard for everyone to adjust," Silver Shadow started to say, addressing the group, "I am sorry about your lives being turned upside down. The Shadow Dome is not really designed for human living."

"So, what will we do?" Ricky asked.

"We have found a place, and I have a plan to make sure you will be safe. It is going to take a while for us to set everything up and I will need your help to prepare it. My father brought us all together for a reason, and I believe in his dream. I think everyone here does, too."

"Yo, Silver Shadow, I'm with you, bro," Cedrick implied, tapping his fist to his chest.

"I think I can speak for everyone here when I say what you did for Maddie was remarkable," Andrew suggested. Everyone shook their heads in agreement.

"Thank you, but there is still a lot of work to do. SD has the plans and assignments for each of you. Rest assured there will be room for all of your families as well," Silver Shadow replied. Everyone broke up into pairs to start their work. Hector remained behind as everyone got into the elevator. Master Lii stood close by behind Hector, Tyton lingered near the hanger door.

"I'm going to put these away," Poison said to Silver Shadow, still holding the weapons.

"Okay, then get some rest."

"I will, honey," Poison answered, giving Silver Shadow a quick hug and walking away toward the weapons room. Silver Shadow turned his attention back to Hector and Maddie.

"Take her to the first room, so she can rest. She is still a little dehydrated."

"Okay, thank so much, Silver Shadow," Hector replied.

"It is no problem," Silver Shadow said as he watched Hector carry Maddie to the hallway. Silver Shadow felt a hand on his shoulder, it was Master Lii.

"Good thing you have done, more good things you will do. Your father is proud of what you have become."

"Will it be enough?" Silver Shadow questioned.

"All long journeys begin with a single step. The path of true good is often the hardest path," Master Lii responded.

"I miss him," Silver Shadow admitted, putting his head down.

"In time you will learn death is a part of life. Go now, many things to do, Tyton waits. When you return, come see me, must train you mind," Master Lii said, walking away.

"Yes, Master." Silver Shadow looked up and saw Tyton standing near the hanger door.

"You will see your father again," Master Lii uttered. Silver Shadow stopped as he walked over to Tyton, he turned around. Master Lii was already gone.

"Father, is everything okay?" Tyton asked.

"Yes, come, we should get going," Silver Shadow answered as the two Shadows went into the open hanger door. Silver Shadow had a feeling there was something Master Lii was not telling him. Whatever it was would have to wait for now. Silver Shadow and Tyton now travel to the prison. In hopes to find Dark Shadow or pick up a trail to follow. The SGD aircraft sails flying low over the prison complex, carrying Tyton and Silver Shadow. They do not know it yet, but the Shadow Runners are too late. Dark Shadow has made his escape. Molric and what is left of his team are already making their way back to the BIO-TEC Otilum facility.

"Drop us just outside the main gates," Silver Shadow requested.

"Affirmative," replied SGD.

"Father, what are we doing here?" Tyton asked.

"Recon, son!"

"Are we going in as well?"

"Yes, so get ready." Suddenly, an alarm started going off inside the aircraft.

"Four helicopters are incoming," SGD warned.

"Copy, SGD, go stealth!" The aircraft hovered to a lower altitude and turned invisible to avoid detection. The helicopters past overhead, moving toward the prison.

"Something has happened. Drop us here," Silver Shadow said, looking at Tyton. "You ready?"

"Yes!" Tyton answered confidently. The two of them ran out of the already open back ramp. They both jumped one after the other. The ramp quickly closed as they landed. The two shadows ran as fast as they could, trying to reach a good vantage point. Their objective was to maintain a line of sight with the prison. They were on the other side of a small hill about 70 yards away. When they reached the top of the hill, Silver Shadow and Tyton laid down, so they were not seen by the still hovering helicopters. Three of the choppers formed a triangle over the courtyard. All three back doors opened and six highly advanced robots jumped from each. They dispersed after landing in two by two formation. It was clear they were securing the area. The three choppers landed ten-feet from the main gates. The fourth chopper stayed hovering with gunners on each side. Three human men exited one of the landed helicopters, two guards and one commander. They walked inside for a few minutes. When they came out, Molric followed. The rest of Max Force came out shortly after. Each member was being assisted by one of the advance robot teams. They looked like they had just been in an intense battle. Silver Shadow is willing to bet it has something to do with his brother. Within five minutes, everyone was gone. After the dust settled, Silver Shadow and Tyton began to make their way down the hill.

"Now is our chance," Silver Shadow whispered. The two shadows moved in the moon light down the hill. The whole complex had a primitive look to it. Much like a tomb or an Egyptian pyramid. Everything was stone made, the only modern technology were the lights. They were hanging from the ceiling and not all of them even worked. After entering the main doors, Silver Shadow noticed body parts from robots lay spread down the entire narrow hallway. At the end of the hall was a cell with broken and bent bars. The bars were bent outward, like someone broke out. Silver Shadow had some idea who it was. He stood still in front of the cell, he touched the bars. Silver Shadow could feel what his brother felt: anger, rage, frustration. They are physically connected, closer than twins, and more opposite than night and day. He stepped back, there was one thing he didn't feel. Something he had expected to feel from his brother. Dark Shadow at no time felt fear or trapped. It was like he wanted to be there, in that cell. Like he wanted to be captured. Tyton had been watching his father this whole time. Silver Shadow turned around, looking him right in his eyes. Tyton could feel it, too, zoning out like a daydream of what was and what could have been. They both snapped out of it and continued their investigation. Looking around some more, they discovered there were scorch marks on the walls. Silver Shadow glanced back at Tyton.

"I guess we missed the party," Silver Shadow commented.

"What do you think happened here?" Tyton asked.

"Something very big happened. It was Dark Shadow, I have seen these burn marks before."

"Is he still here?" Silver Shadow was now hunched over, examining things more closely. He put his hand on one of the burn marks.

"It is still warm, he is not in here with us. I can…" Silver Shadow paused for a moment. Tyton was peering around and heard his words stop. Tyton snapped his head back, putting Silver Shadow in his sight line again.

"What?" Tyton impatiently asked.

"I can still feel him. He is close, our connection is not as strong. I fear his anger has consumed him."

"I know, I can feel him, too," Tyton admitted. He began looking around vigorously, making sure Dark Shadow wasn't lurking in the shadows. A large puddle caught Tyton's eye. Inflamed with curiosity, he walked over to it.

"Father, look at this." Silver Shadow glanced over to see Tyton on one knee next to a blood trail. Silver Shadow walked over to examine it, to him it was a clue to what took place here. "Looks like blood. What do you make of it?" Tyton remarked.

"There are two colors, the red is definitely blood. The other appears to be hydraulic mechanical fluid of some kind," Silver Shadow answered, touching the stain.

"I've seen it come out of Skade's mechanical snake tail."

"You're right." Silver Shadow started looking around for more clues. There were some distinct indications Dark Shadow started in the cell and broke free. "We better go before we over stay our welcome," Sliver Shadow indicated. Tyton shook his head yes. They both took off into the shadows, darting through the hallway like they were floating. When they reached the exit, Silver Shadow noticed glass footprints in the sand leading away from the complex. A path of foot prints he hadn't noticed on the way in. The amount of heat it would require to make the surface of the sand turn to glass is extreme. Silver Shadow had an idea who these footprints belong to. The two of them had come down the hill from another direction. He should have seen this. Silver Shadow stopped and remained frozen in the middle of the doorway.

"Father, what is it?" Tyton whispered, wondering why his father hesitated.

"Follow me," Silver Shadow said, waving his hand in the direction he wanted them to go. Dark Shadow's body admits so much heat, these glass tracks were more than likely his. Every step he took on the sand left glass footprints behind. It was almost too easy to follow, but maybe that was the point.

"Wait!" Silver Shadow shouted, holding his arm up with his hand closed. Tyton stopped when he almost walked into Silver Shadow's arm. The two of them were now over the hill and about 30 yards from the complex. At the same time, they both glanced back over their shoulders to find Dark Shadow raising from the sand beneath their feet. He came up just behind Tyton. Like a reflex, Tyton preformed two back flips, landing behind his father. Dark Shadow rose from the sand slowly like a draw bridge rising for boats to pass. His arms folded across his chest with closed hands. Dark Shadow's eyes glowed and his head was down until he spoke.

"The little one is fast. He is also not so little anymore," Dark Shadow remarked, finally emerged fully from the ground.

"His name is Tyton and he is the first of his kind," Silver Shadow answered.

"So, he's what all the fuss is about. You know they want to imprison him. They want to clone him and make an entire army. Like they tried to do with me," Dark Shadow implied.

"Is that the reason why you're so angry?"

"The human race doesn't deserve to live. They don't care about what they have. Humans should be made to suffer like I had to!" Dark Shadow snarled, clenching his fist tighter. After hearing that, Silver Shadow realized it was clear he wasn't going to be able to change his mind. It would be a slow process, but at this point, all Dark Shadow knew was pain. It was the series of actions that lead to Dark Shadow's core ideals. His very principles couldn't have been further from the truth.

"Come with us. I can help you."

"You think you can help me? Don't be ridiculous! My only quest is to find the ones responsible for my pain! They will be made to suffer, like I did!"

"Then what, what if you catch up with them? Nothing you do to those responsible for your imprisonment will make it better. That pain you feel every single moment will still be there, eating at you. Killing them won't make the pain stop," Silver Shadow replied.

"Maybe not! But it will make me feel better!" Dark Shadow insisted.

"And when it is over, then what!?" Tyton said, peering from behind his father. Dark Shadow just stood there, he didn't have an answer. "You don't seem to have it put together very well. Let us help you." Dark Shadow turned around.

"I can't," Dark Shadow said with his back to them. It would seem like he was thinking it over, considering all the possibilities. His hate and pain had already consumed him, fueling his private war with the human race. At the same time, it made Dark Shadow sad. Even young Tyton could feel what he was going through. "There is still something I have to do, or all this will have been for nothing!" Without warning the sand surrounding Dark Shadow began to circle around him, creating a mini tornado cyclone. Before Silver Shadow and Tyton could do anything, Dark Shadow disappeared. The sand began to settle and he was gone without a trace. Silver Shadow could see there was a side of Dark Shadow that wanted help. A part of him with some good left, a conflict second guessing every action. They were more alike than they both could see. There is still some good left. As long as that hope was there, Silver Shadow could not give up. His brother's path may not lead to the side of good. But his destiny is far greater than either of them would realize.

"Father, he disappeared!" Tyton remarked.

"Yes, but I think I know where he is going. SGD, we're ready for dust off!" Silver Shadow said into his com link.

"Affirmative, Silver Shadow!" The aircraft picked up the two shadows in seconds and they traveled back to The Shadow Dome. As soon as the aircraft began to climb altitude, the sand where they stood started to move. Dark Shadow emerged from the ground again. With his body beneath the sand and his head above the surface like a mushroom. He watched the aircraft. He had only been hiding until Silver Shadow and Tyton left. He climbed out of a hole, then it closed up as soon as he stepped to sold ground. He stood there watching as the aircraft flew away out of sight. Dark Shadow had discovered BIO-TEC's biggest secret. There was no way he was going to let it go, he had to act. The answer lays in the lower levels of the new Otilum weapons research laboratory. It was the very place Molric and his battered team was heading right now. Molric sat in the helicopter going over the reasons why his team failed to stop Dark Shadow. Then the real question popped into his head like a thought bubble. They were clearly out matched, it may have been a set up. It would have taken an army of shadows with exceptional skills to stop Dark Shadow. After all, they made him. *"BIO-TEC clearly would have known how powerful he was!"* Molric thought. Then a much more frightening thought occurred to him. *"Was his team now in danger?"* It was too alarming to remain unanswered. He was in the back of the helicopter among a team of robots. They lined the whole helicopter sitting motionless, weapons in hand. Two of his team members were aboard, Carben Arms and Cotolek. Molric got up from his seat, walking past the robots to talk to the pilot.

"Where are we headed?" Molric asked.

"I have orders to bring Max Force to the Otilum facility for repairs," the man answered.

"Copy that!" He made his way back to his seat, and within a few minutes, the helicopters were landing. As the team entered the gates, another smaller chopper landed. Molric recognized it before anyone stepped out. It was Sundice's personal transport. What was he doing here? The team gathered in the living quarters where repairs would begin. Every member laid on their assigned bunk. Little rolling repair bots started hooking themselves to each bunk. One began repairing Skade's tail, another removed Carben Arms' hands and replacing them with new stronger fingers. Both Soufaul and Rojet needed work done on their chest. As they laid there, little hovering robots started reassembling anything in need of repair. Every repair robot was small, about the size of a football. There seemed to be all kinds. They all moved like insects flying, hovering, and climbing on each member, needing repairs. Alongside each bed was a small screen with a timer of how long it would take to finish repairs, along with technical specifications. Molric glanced around the room, Cotolek stood beside him. The two of them just need rest. The two longest repair times were Rojet at 25 minutes, and Skade at 23 minutes.

"What do we do now, commander?" Cotolek asked.

"Get some rest, I need everyone at 100 percent ASAP!" he responded.

"Yes, sir!" Molric was the only one who couldn't sleep. With Sundice here in the building, he didn't know what to expect. Molric walked through the large meeting area and into his room. He sat up and positioned himself on the end of his bunk. The more he fought to stay awake, the more tired he became. Molric is only half human and still needs to sleep. He began to lay back, interlocking his fingers together behind his head. His eyes started closing like a candle burning its last bit of wick, being overwhelmed by hot wax. He woke up to the sounds of his team talking amongst themselves. Molric snapped to getting up and walked out to the center of the meeting area. Everyone was at the briefing table, except Rojet. Molric fell asleep even after trying to stay awake.

"Attention on deck!" The team jumped to their feet and stood at attention, saluting Molric.

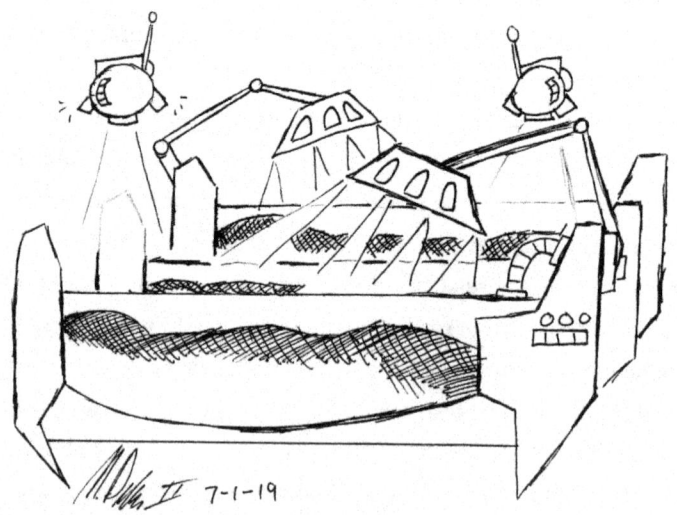

Alongside each bed was a small screen with a timer of how long it would take to finish repairs, along with technical specifications.

"How is everyone feeling?" Molric asked. They all answered at the same time.

"Just fine, sir!" the team shouted.

"Alright, as you were." As everyone went back to the table, Molric pulled Cotolek aside. "Any orders from Sundice?" he whispered.

"Nothing yet, sir," he replied. *"What's next?"* Molric thought to himself. *"Why hasn't Sundice given Max Force any orders yet?"* His questions, concerns would be answered and fulfilled in a matter of minutes. The whole team stopped when sounds of the elevator coming down started. Molric stepped toward the door with the team behind him. The elevator was coming to their floor and only Sundice and the major of the facility had the key. Molric glanced back at the team still sitting there. With his hand movements, he gave the sign to take cover. The team dispersed like mice running from the sound. Molric faced the doors alone, waiting for them to open. The large elevator finally came to a stop, opened, and out came Sundice. The doors closed and the elevator went down to another level.

"Hello, commander," Sundice said with a sinister smirk on his face.

"Sir, my team is almost fully repaired. We will be back on our feet within the hour."

"Good," Sundice replied, "But do you recall our previous conversation? I remember distinctly saying this assignment was your last chance," Sundice indicated.

"I remember. We also fought and learned more about a new enemy," Molric replied. "This wasn't much of an assignment, you offered us no intel at all."

"True, but we knew about Dark Shadow. Our lab cloned him from the first shadow. This was just a test, and your team failed again," Sundice accused. Molric had a bad feeling Dark Shadow was right. He plans to replace Max Force. Sundice turned around and began walking back to the elevator. The whole room was very quiet, only the sound of Sundice's shoes could be heard. The elevator came up and opened just before Sundice reach the doors. Molric was left standing there alone in the center of the room, clueless to what would happen next. The rest of the team hidden throughout the room watched. "You and your team are of no further use to me. I will no longer require your services!" Then the largest shadow Molric had ever seen climbed out of the elevator. "For more than obvious reasons, I can't allow Max Force to live," Sundice continued.

"You lied to us. There are no words to descript your betrayal!" Molric shouted, vigorously pointing his finger at Sundice.

"I owe no one an explanation for my actions. This is my shadow killer, Rowtila. Good-bye, Commander!" Sundice said, getting onto the elevator. When the doors closed, the whole team came out from hiding. This was the team's problem now. Standing before them was Rowtila, paused still like a statue. Rowtila was very big, biggest they had ever seen before. There would be no stopping him in a fight. He was 15-feet tall and at least 1,500 pounds. His head was shaped like a round tear drop with three points instead of just one at the top. Molric glanced back, the team was ready. Rowtila started walking toward them, then two more arms unfolded from his back. *"This could be the end,"* Molric thought.

"Stand ready, Max Force! If this is our last day together, we will not go without a fight!" Molric cried out. With those arms, Rowtila would surly destroy them all. Max Force was still one shadow team member short, they would have to fight hard. Rowtila's walking became running. Carben Arms jumped forward, Skade slithered to the right, and Soufual ran to the left. The three of them attacked at the same time. Two of Rowtila's hands tried to grabbed Carben Arms. The hands were pushing down on Carben. He fought to stop the giant hands from crushing him like a pancake. Soufual sprayed flash fire at the left hand. The hand opened flat to stop the flames. Skade used his hook and tail to claw at the right hand. Molric ran at Carben Arms. "Carben, hold still!" Molric yelled as he ran up Carben Arm's back and leaped at Rowtila's head. Molric's jump kick was meant to throw Rowtila off guard. Before Molric could make contact, Rowtila head butted Molric, nearly breaking his leg. Molric's body bounced off Rowtila's head and plunked against the wall. He was out cold as his body twitched like he was having a seizure. Rowtila's left hand stopped blocking the fire and quickly turned into a fist. Rowtila punched Soufual fast across the room like a jack hammer. Rowtila's right hand snagged Skade's tail. He dragged Skade to the left hand and both hands started to pull him apart. Skade was ripped in half, his body was thrown to the ground like two busted garbage bags spilling unknown liquids all over the floor. Carben Arms was starting to be overwhelmed.

Rowtila was way too powerful. All Carben's arms started to buckle under the pressure. The hands crushed Carben Arms, and when the hands opened again, Carben lay on the floor. His torso was the only thing still intact. Only Cotolek and Nethal were left, they both looked at each other. They would have to combine their attack if they were going to survive this. Cotolek could see a small weakness. Rowtila was strong but a little slow, this would be their only chance.

"We have to trap him," Cotolek suggested.

"How?" Nethal questioned.

"Follow my lead." Rowtila was already getting closer to them. Cotolek ran for one of the small rooms, Nethal followed running right behind him. Once they were in the room, they would have just one chance.

"What are we doing? Now we're trapped!"

"I noticed Rowtila has a wide stance. When he gets in here, we will run and slide across the floor."

"Ok, got it!" Nethal replied. Before long Rowtila was coming into the doorway. His big body hardly making it through what seemed to be a pin hole to him. Rowtila was trying to grab the two of them. His effort appeared more like a hungry bear's paw in a small bee hive.

"Wait for it, wait for it!" Cotolek repeated as Rowtila completely entered the room. "Now, go!" he yelled. Nethal and Cotolek ran like two groundhogs at Rowtila's legs. Rowtila anticipated their movements and spread all his arms out like a huge spider trying to stop them. He attempted to grab the two as they ran under him. They ran and slid under Rowtila across the floor between his legs. Nethal slid on his stomach like a penguin on the ice. Cotolek trailed behind and he was the last one out the door. After passing the doorway, Cotolek scurried to the door switch. He closed it and lock Rowtila in the room.

"Will that room hold him?" Nethal enquired.

"For the moment, he is contained," Cotolek answered.

"Let's get the others out."

"Right!" Cotolek replied, giving him the thumbs up. Without warning they heard deep growling behind them. They both glanced back at the room Rowtila was trapped in. The whole wall busted down and Rowtila swung at Cotolek. As he ducked, Rowtila's swing missed and hit Nethal in the chest. Nethal's body flew to the other side of the living quarters. Cotolek ran, jumping down, and rolled behind the table. He carefully peered over and saw Nethal's body on the floor. The elevator doors had been damaged by his body. He was going to run for it; without a weapon, he would never stand a chance. Cotolek jumped over the table and Rowtila was waiting for him. Rowtila grabbed Cotolek before his feet hit the floor again. Rowtila started to crash Cotolek's body like a grape.

"Hey, let go of him!" a voice yelled. It was Molric, he was up and ready to finish this fight. Rowtila snapped his head around, but Cotolek was already dead. Rowtila threw his lifeless body at Molric's toes. "It ain't over yet!" Molric didn't stand a chance against Rowtila, but he needed a way out. As he quickly thought of an idea, he had a plan. There may be a way to kill two birds with one stone. He would have to switch places with Rowtila. He was blocking the elevator doors. Molric approached and Rowtila started throwing punches, using all four arms. Molric blocked each one, the power of his swings almost knocked Molric over with each impacted. He stood his ground, relying on all his military training. Rowtila, with a right high punch, Molric, with the block and a counter low kick. Then came a left-hand punch, Molric ducked out of the way. Rowtila's fist hit the floor and Molric grabbed his wrist. Molric pulled it hard while he moved, going under Rowtila. This flipped Rowtila off his feet and onto his back. Wasting no time, Molric bolted to the elevator doors. Rowtila got up and charged head on at Molric. Just before Rowtila hit him, Molric leaped out of the way. Rowtila flew through the elevator doors and down the empty shaft. As he fell, Rowtila's leg brushed along Molric, sending him over the edge as well. They both free fell down the dark elevator shaft. Molric saved himself by getting a hold of the elevator cable. Rowtila wasn't so lucky. Molric dangled there for a moment to catch his breath. Looking down he noticed he only fell about ten or so meters. The shaft was very dark and there were two lights. One bright white light above him, emulating from the room he fell from. Another green light just one floor below. Molric quickly glanced around for that shadow hunter. Rowtila was no were in sight, a bit of relieve filled Molric. He hung there, gathering his strength; he was going to need it for the climb up. Before he could start his climb for freedom, curiosity got the better of him. *"What was on this other lower level? Was there any truth to what Dark Shadow had said?"* Molric began swinging lower on the wire until he reached one level under the living quarters. He pulled himself to a small ledge and forced the elevator doors open. The outside of the doors had SUB A written on it in yellow. The green light was coming from inside. Molric pulled himself in and left the doors open. The very large room was divided into three sections with these long tube-like life pods. They line almost every wall on both sides. There must have been 70 or 80 pods. The pods were hooked up to big tubes running along the bottom of the walls. These large core gated tubes lead to these two big machines. In front of Molric were two main computer consoles. Approaching the consoles, he could see the displays for all the pods. He glanced up to the first pod, there was something moving under the dark colored glass. They must have been unborn shadows. It would explain why there is such low-level lighting. Sundice was making his own army of shadows. Dark Shadow was right his team was obsolete. Then it hit him, that was the test. If the Max Force team couldn't defeat Dark Shadow, Sundice would make some shadows that could. *"He wants to kill the first shadow, the one who started it all, The Silver Shadow!"* Molric thought to himself. Before Molric could do anything, he heard the sounds of ropes and robot guards coming down the elevator shaft. He had stayed too long and didn't learn enough, time to go. He turned and sprinted to the already open doors. Molric stuck his head out and peered up. Three robot guards were repelling down the dark shaft. The base was on alert, a red light at the top of the shaft was blinking. One of the ropes dangled in front of Molric. Before he could grab it, the guard on the rope had reached the doors. Molric jumped on the rope hanging on to the guard. He stopped the guard from pulling his MP5 from his back. Molric grabbed the pistol on the guard's leg and wrapped his leg around the rope. Molric shot him in the face, grabbing the rope. The robot's body fell from the rope down the shaft. The other two guards higher up open fire on Molric. He swung back through the elevator doors to avoid the bullets into the green room again. When the guards stop to reload, Molric stepped to the very small edge and shot the ropes holding them. He shot their bodies as they fell two rounds each. One was able to clench the ledge before falling, he grasped the edge at Molric's feet. Molric looked down, the guard began to point his weapon at him. Molric grabbed the MP5 from his hand. Molric swung the weapon onto his back. Then he pulled the robot's body up and shot it twice more in the head. The pistol was empty, Molric tossed it to the floor. He turned the robot over and proceed to remove all the ammo for the MP5 along with another pistol. It was going to be a hard fight to get clear of this facility. There was no doubt in his mind more robots would be waiting for him on the upper floors. It will be the fight of his life. Sundice cannot afford to let Molric escape alive. The Max Force team has too much knowledge of Sundice and his whole operation. Preparing himself he reloaded the MP5 and placed it on the back. Molric's belt was full with extra ammo clips for both weapons. He crept over to the elevator doors and quickly looked up. Seeing nothing he clenched the rope and started climbing up, his weapon hanging from his back and the pistol tucked behind in his belt. It was very quiet, too quiet. Molric made it up to the ledge of the top floor just outside the closed elevator doors. Still hanging onto the rope. he slowly pried the doors open ever so slightly. He could barely see into the large hall where 20 or 30 robots had assembled. Five feet from the door stood the Major, waiting.

"Come out, commander Molric," Major Docard said. He knew Molric was on the other side. His options were limited, this is the only way out. Molric pushed the doors open more and stepped out, gun first. The entire army of robot guards behind Docard pointed their weapons. They all stood, ready to shoot Molric on command. The sound of them all pointing weapons at the same time was stifling. Molric didn't back down, he had the cross hairs on Docard's head. "Drop your weapons!" Docard yelled as Molric slowly came walking out.

"Why was my team killed?" Molric questioned.

"The why is easy. You and your team are being replaced. I have orders to kill the Max Force. Surrender now and we will make sure you die a soldiers' death." Molric started to lower his weapons. He quickly glanced around the hall. There was a door on his left. His instincts said things were going to get real ugly, real fast.

"Then so be it," Molric said, walking toward Docard. He started to give his weapon to the Major. Just as Docard reached for it, Molric pulled back and grabbed Docard's wrist. Molric round housed him across his face. He grabbed Major Docard before his body fell to the floor. The robots started shooting, and Molric use Docard as a human shield. He hustled over to the door and bust through it, falling to the floor. The first line of robots ran at the door, firing. Molric let them get close and dropped them with a wave of automatic gun fire. One of the bodies fell within inches of the door. Molric squatted down, pulling it in by the arm, dragging it along the tiled floor still under gun fire. After getting it inside the small hallway, Molric was now stuck in, he rolled the mechanical body over. He found three grenades he could use. Molric stood up and leaned against the wall and rapidly reloaded. He pulled a pin and threw one of the grenades down the hall. It rolled to the feet of the second line of guards. It blew up and the blast filled the hall with smoke. Molric aimed out from the doorway and began taking down as many as he could with each clip. After the smoke cleared, there were only a few left. Molric threw another grenade and came running out scooping another MP5 from the floor. He picked it up from one of the many robot guard bodies lying there. Molric ran straight for the main entrance, shooting both weapons at the remaining guards. Into the smoke and out the other side. Molric hopped over the guard desk and past the metal detector station. A robot guard was standing in front of the big black glass windows. Molric charged toward him, shooting at his head. The bullets pummeled the robot's face and the glass behind him started to break. As the guard fell, Molric ran up his body, jumping through the glass. He hit the ground and rolled, letting go of the weapons. The armored truck was still parked in front of the building. The last hand full of robot guards tracked his movements and continued to shoot. Molric ran, ducking behind the armored truck, he made his way to the driver's side. The guards moved outside and the armored truck turned into a bullet magnet. Molric quickly hotwired it and pealed out in a half circle, hitting as many robots as he could in the rotation. He could never give up, but for now, he would have to disappear.

Chapter 14

Chapter Fourteen
Reveling Secrets

The Shadow Dome is quiet, with Poison anxiously awaiting Silver Shadow and Tyton's arrival. She sits in the middle of the large laboratory, going over all the Intel on these new BIO-TEC locations. Poison sifted through the images one by one. With all the information they have gathered, the next mission may be the most difficult. CD and Cyber Ball were training together, disks verses bombs. Those two were like brothers, like two pees in a pod. The room they train in is narrow with matching floor and walls. The bright white color makes it hard to tell where the floor ends and the walls begin. Cyber Ball stands on one end of the room, CD on the other. Cyber Ball would launch a bomb and CD would throw a disk, cutting it in half. The two are equal, each with their own method of hitting a target. Ton was working out in the custom gym he set up in his room. He was becoming stronger and stronger every day. Ton is more of the strong and silent type. He is that way for a reason. The reason is unknown to the others. The sisters, Liset and Jean, were in their room down the hall, challenging each other. It's more like playing a game, to see who's better with their power.

"Okay, I'm sitting over here. You have to get to me and I'm going to try and stop you," Liset explained.

"That ain't hard at all!" Jean insisted.

"Well, I can use anything in the room and you can't move in smoke mode."

"Oh, you know what!"

"Go!" Liset shouted. Jean decided to run straight for Liset, she was about 20-feet away. After Jean's third step, things all around the room started sliding toward her. A chair, a table, even a stool. As the chair slid at Jean, she jumped over it. She let the stool pass through her, but she didn't move any closer to Liset. The small table hovered toward Jean, she quickly ran and slid across the floor under it. Liset was learning to control her powers. Liset started to lose her focus when she could hear someone else's thoughts. It was like a faint whisper in the back of her mind. As Jean continued trying to make her way to Liset, the voice got loader. Liset glanced up at the door way, it was Ton. He was just standing there, staring hard at Liset. Before she realized it, Jean's hand was on her shoulder.

"You can play your mind games all you want. I'm always going to be faster," Jean gloated. Liset was kind of in a trance, embarrassed almost. She peered back at the doorway and Ton was gone.

"Whatever, I was distracted. We'll redo in a minute," Liset said, getting up. She ran over to the doorway to see if Ton was still there. He was already down the hall, rounding the corner. "Hey, wait!" Liset said, speaking up and running down the hallway. She confronted him on the spot. "Were you watching us?" she asked, catching up to him and grabbing his arm, forcing him to stop walking. She made him spin around and face her.

"Maybe," Ton answered with his deep voice. Ton was never a conversationalist, spitting out those one-word answers for things that may be more complicated than they seemed. There she was, standing in front of him, wanting more from him than just one word. Her frustration was valid and could be read from her attitude. Something she would show others, no matter how hard she tried suppressing it. Her attitude was never absent, it kept everyone at a safe distance for her.

"What's your deal?" Liset questioned. Ton turned back around and started walking away from her. Liset, being persistent, followed him into the conference room. "So!" she said, putting her hands on her hips. She was waiting for an answer. She thought it was going to be just that easy with Ton. He turned to her.

"I'm glad to see you're embracing your power."

"Aye, papi! I don't get you. You're always the first to help me. You're always staring at me. You're always protecting me, and now you're giving me the silent treatment. Will you talk to me? Tell me what's going on with you." She was becoming a little discouraged. She was on the verge of giving up on him. Liset used her power to hit the button on the wall behind her. The table and seats rose from the floor. She sat down at the table. "Talk to me." Walking toward the elevator, Ton stopped. He stood there and did a half turn, focused on the table and chairs coming out of the floor. Underneath it all, he was a big, soft, caring teddy bear. He thought about it for a second. *"Is it time to show her my other side? Is she ready to see?"* Ton thought to himself. *"Will she accept my true feelings no matter what they are?"* Those were the questions running through his mind. He walked back over to the table. Ton sat beside her.

"I want to tell you something, but I'm not sure you're ready to hear it yet," Ton explained.

"What, you're afraid to tell me?"

"Not afraid, hesitant, maybe a little anxious."

"Tell me, you can talk to me," Liset insisted, putting her hand on his shoulder. It would appear she had a gentle side or was it just curiosity in disguise?

"From the moment I laid my eyes on you, I felt something. I know in my very being it is real, because I never felt this way before." Ton sat there, confiding in Liset, spilling out his feelings. His hands propped flat on the table. Liset's hand gently moved over to his, her small fingers embraced his hand.

"I heard your thoughts, you shouldn't be afraid to tell me how you feel."

"You could hear what I was thinking?"

"A little, only when the feelings are strong."

"I didn't want to say anything until I knew if you felt the same. I was more afraid of what you might think."

"I could never be afraid of you." Liset leaned closer and hugged on Ton's arm. Her hold was tight but loving. Ton realized she had fully let go of her old life. All those disappointments and past failed relationships filled with men who didn't really appreciate her. The high hopes of a perfect fit and heart breaks of another gone from what seemed to be an empty life. Her shell like an important egg, fragile and maintaining life with the right conditions. Liset knew this would be different. She will learn a shadow's love can be felt on a much deeper level.

"That is my secret, my affection. I offer all that I am to you," Ton said as he embraced her.

"I will make room in my life for only you, and I look forward to all the love we will share." Ton was overcome with joy, she, too, had the same feelings. The both of them sat there at the table alone. Ton's most well-kept secret had been revealed. In the laboratory, Poison continues to wait for Silver Shadow and Tyton's return. She is also expecting a transmission from Lacey Carson from her most recent assignment with more Intel to share. Lacey was able to compile some information about BIO-TEC's new labs. The hanger to Poison's left started making sounds. The aircraft had come back, and it wasn't long before the hanger door open. Tyton and Silver Shadow came out with some recon photos. Tyton ran in and gave his mother a hug. Silver Shadow followed.

"I'm back, Mother," he broadcasted.

"I can see. Did you honor your father's instruction?" Poison asked.

"Yes, and I also met Dark Shadow."

"Okay, well, there is still some things you have to learn. Why don't you go to your room and complete all your new training?"

"Okay, Mother," Tyton replied less than happy. He ran off to his room. Poison was a little worried about their encounter with Dark Shadow. She glanced over and Silver Shadow was already at the computer downloading the recon photos. She walked over and hugged him from behind.

"How did he do?" Poison questioned.

"Tyton did great, he's a natural," Silver Shadow replied.

"Your brother try to hurt him?"

"No, but I think I know what he is after. I do not think he is all bad. I think he was just treated badly."

"Well, he has been destructive so far," Poison remarked.

"In his mind, the ends justify the means. I may be able to get him to join us."

"Just be careful; in the end, he might just destroy you both to get what he wants."

"I know. He is filled with so much hate. I must show him the good side of life. He has to see it with his own eyes," Silver Shadow insisted. Poison let go of him and headed for the elevator.

"I have to go to the control room. Lacey will be checking in soon. After, I'll gather the team for a meeting," Poison replied, changing the subject.

"Okay, good, I should be done with the pictures by then," Silver Shadow answered. The elevator doors open for Poison. Before she got in, CD and Cyber Ball came darting out, running from the elevator right toward Silver Shadow. Their demeanor suggested they had discovered something extraordinary.

"Silver Shadow, you're never going to believe what we found!" Cyber Ball shouted. Silver Shadow stopped what he was doing.

"SD, finish editing recon file."

"Confirm, Silver Shadow. Estimated task time, seven minutes," replied The Shadow Dome.

"Okay, boys, what did you discover?" Silver Shadow said. turning his attention to the both of them. They both stood at a different computer panel. Each brought up separate key discoveries, together the research would answer questions. Silver Shadow propped himself in the middle behind them.

"I found some foot notes from three separate scientists," Cyber Bell explained.

"Anyone we know?" Silver Shadow asked.

"Yes, the scientists your father work with. From the looks of it, they are all still working on the Silver project. Each scientist, same big project, but different applications."

"Meaning what?"

"Their notes seem to be the way they pass messages to each other. It's what makes me think they're not in the same facility. Their notes are posted almost like a blog. Look at this, all the scientists have code named projects in progress. Doctor Junior Northberg working on a project code named Shift. Doctor Duncan Wester is experimenting on a project called Blue. Doctor George Southland doesn't have a project name yet," Cyber Ball concluded.

"Does it say what Southland is working on?"

"No, there is just a file name with letters. The letters are: G-B.R.B.T.S."

"Any idea what that means?" Silver Shadow asked.

"Unsure, it could be anything," Cyber Ball replied.

"At some point, we are going to figure out what those letters mean," Silver Shadow directed.

"Okay, while he was making a discovery, I tracked the location of the disk," CD butted in.

"Alright, where is it?" Silver Shadow asked.

"I know where it is, but the level it's on is a different story," CD replied.

"We have to get a look at the building from the air, but it will not be much to go on. Tyton and I can do some recon."

"Well, the sub-floor the disk is on is so deep, our sensors aren't able to take a thermal snap shot."

"It means we'll be going in blind."

"Silver Shadow," the Shadow Dome interrupted.

"Yes, SD?" Silver Shadow answered.

"Recon images are complete." Silver Shadow peered at CD and Cyber Ball.

"Get the team together." Silver Shadow went into the elevator, he thought about some things. There was so much on his mind. All those scientists worked with his father in the past. He may have encountered some of them before himself. Dark Shadow knew something as well. There may be some truth to his accusations. If the Shadow Runners go to the Otilum facility, they may face an army of shadows with unknown powers and strengths. All these thoughts unraveled in his mind like a ball of yarn on the ride to the conference room. The many theories are not what troubled him, it was the answers and truth. The team began assembling at the table. Silver Shadow was already setting up the main screen. He sorted the photos on the surface of the table. Ton and Liset strolled in the room, holding hands. Liset glanced at Jean, who was at the table.

"Don't say a word," Liset snarled.

"You know what…" Jean snapped. She waved her hand like she didn't care what Liset did. Jean had her wall up, trying to pretend she wasn't important. The truth is Jean cared and watched over Liset like a big sister. That aspect of their relationship would never change. In the past, Jean would be there to pick up the pieces from Liset's broken heart. Every one of Liset's relationships started this way. All ended badly, and Jean would be there. The shoulder to cry on and the one person who would boost Liset back up. Each time Jean would lose a small part of herself, standing by watching and feeling the pain Liset felt. This time feels a little different than all the rest. The meeting was starting. Silver Shadow stood at the head of the table, everyone was seated.

"As I stand here and look at all your faces, I'm reminded of all the reasons why we are here. So far BIO-TEC has robbed some of us the chance to live a long and happy life. The time has come to repay them for all the kindness they have shown us. Right here and now, we put an end to their misdeeds. We won't do it for us, that is not enough. We will do it for all the innocent people they have hurt and for all those they intend to harm. Since my fathers' death, you all have been my only family. This team is a part of me, just as I am a part of everyone. This mission is going to be the hardest, and we are going to be in harm's way. If any shadow doesn't want to be put at risk, speak now." Everyone peered around the table at each other.

"Silver Shadow, I think I can speak for everyone at this table when I say we're with you to the end. Without you we wouldn't have made it this far. BIO-TEC has affected each of us, some more than others. We all want the chance to hit them where it hurts," Poison announced. The entire team seemed to agree. In that very instant, Silver Shadow understood his family was with him.

"I had nothing and was a prisoner until you came along. I'm going to make sure they never take away someone's life, or I'm going to die trying," said Jean.

"Thank you all, we are going to begin take BIO-TEC apart. This operation will be the first of many. We have to gather as much intel as possible. If there is a laboratory, we will have to destroy it," Silver Shadow started to explain. He brought up images on the main screen.

"How do we get in?" Cyber Ball asked.

"SGD will fly us in low under the radar. We will land at the drop point here." A small spot on the map was blinking. "After landing we will have to make our way to the building through the desert." The team was looking at the map on the screen. The images were also displayed in front of each member on the surface of the table.

"There is one small problem. The building is almost a mile from the DP," CD directed.

"Yes, but a necessary precaution. If you look closely, you will see these small sand mounds."

"Yeah, what are they?" Cyber Ball questioned.

"Unsure, but the mounds are spread out all over in key places around the outer perimeter. We are not able to get a closer look at them. My guess is they are underground gun turrets."

"Okay, so, how are we going to get past those things?" Jean chimed in.

"I have developed a number of new weapons designed just for this purpose. After making it through the building's defenses, we'll face a large robot army. If the alarm hasn't been tripped by this time, we should be able to use sniper rifles. Once inside, Jean, I want you to smoke yourself up to the control center."

"Okay, what do you want me to do up there?" Jean asked.

"You will shut down their communication uplink controls." She shook her head okay. "CD and Cyber Ball, I want you two to say outside to cover our escape and keep out of sight."

"We got it," CD said, answering for the both of them.

"Ton and Liset, you two go down to the second sub-level. Thermal snap shots show a small floor with rooms attached. It suggests it is a living area of some kind. Poison, Tyton and I will secure the other levels." Ton and Liset, still holding hands, tighten their grip and glanced at each other.

"Right," Ton replied.

"Find out what you can about the occupants inhabiting that space. Also, based on our encounter with my twin, I have reason to believe there are more shadows in this complex." Everyone was a bit taken and upset by this news.

"How many are there?" Tyton enquired.

"Unknown," Silver Shadow answered.

"If there are more, how come we haven't seen any?" Liset interjected.

"Unsure, they could still be in the testing growth," Silver Shadow suggested.

"What do we do if we come across one?" Ton said, speaking up.

"Use discretion, there is no telling what they will be capable of. Remember, when a shadow is made or born, they are like social sponges. Anything they learn, see, or experience will in all likelihood determine who they will become. Their gifts and powers will come naturally," Silver Shadow explained.

"Father, what about me?" Tyton asked, raising his hand.

"You will stay with your mother and I, okay?"

"Yes!" Tyton replied.

"Any more questions?" Silver Shadow persisted. The team remained silent, everyone had a job to do. The question on everyone's mind, the one question no one would ask. Would this be their last mission together? Will everyone come back to sit at this table again? "Gear up," Silver Shadow ordered. One by one, each member began making their way to the weapons room. CD and Cyber Ball were getting their weapons from hidden lockers in the wall. Silver Shadow was handing out a small device. Cyber Ball was loading his bombs into the cylinders on his chest. CD was loading disks into every place he could fit them on his body.

"Here, you guys," Silver Shadow said, handing them their device.

"Something new?" Cyber Ball remarked.

"I call them Shadow Shields."

"What does it do?" CD asked, playing with it in his hands, looking at every part of it. He was like a little kid with a new toy again.

"This is almost designed for you two especially." Cyber Ball and CD snapped, stopping what they were doing immediately. Silver Shadow had gotten their attention. "When you're being shot at, hit this device and a shield will project itself in front of you."

"Sounds excellent," Cyber Ball claimed.

"We will both put it to good use," CD implied. Tyton approached Silver Shadow. He was still standing there next to CD and Cyber Ball.

"Father, I'm ready." Silver Shadow turned around to him.

"Okay, son, I have something special for you," Silver Shadow answered. The two of them walked over to the design table in the corner of the weapons room. He picked up a backpack with a set of strong looking arms attached.

"Let's see if it fits."

"What is it?" Tyton asked as his father help him put it on.

"They're called Shadow Arms. Here, let me show you how they work. Strap it to your back and pull this little antenna up. Then place the insight module somewhere on your head or neck," Silver Shadow said, showing him where to place it.

"This is perfect for me," Tyton said, activating the arms. The arms started moving around. "How do they work exactly?" he asked, still a little unsure.

"The insight module is linked to your brain waves. All you have to do is change your perception and treat them like your own hands. The backpack is also holding two pistols and plenty of ammo."

"So, these arms will watch my back," Tyton replied.

"Right, they will also be able to help you lift, pull, and climb places that would prove difficult on your own," Silver Shadow recommended.

"With these Shadow Arms, I'm ready for action," Tyton boasted. Silver Shadow could feel someone behind him, he peered over his shoulder. It was Master Lii standing at the doorway.

"Okay, Tyton, you go get ready. I will meet you on SGD."

"Okay," Tyton replied. Silver Shadow walked over to Master Lii. He had a look of concern on his face.

"Is everything okay, Master Lii?" Silver Shadow blurted out.

"Yes, Guardian, I was hoping you would come sit with me before you go."

"Yes, of course, Master." The two of them began to walk slowly as Silver Shadow grabbed his gear.

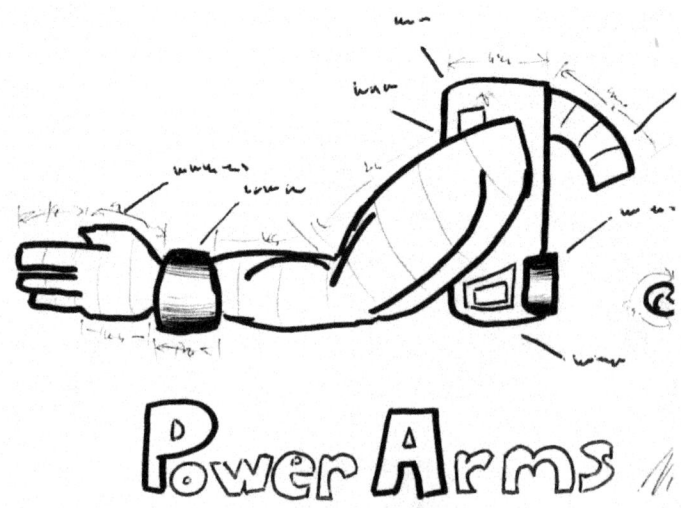

"With these Shadow Arms, I'm ready for action," Tyton boasted.

"It is still early and everyone else is asleep. The people here trust you; in time more people from the outside world will as well."

"Do you think so?"

"Yes, I have seen it," Master Lii insisted as they walked back into the conference room. They both sat down in the closest chairs. "Before you can move forward, you must let go of this sadness."

"How, I try to bury it deep inside, but it always seems to resurface," Silver Shadow confessed, putting his head down.

"You must start meditation. Your mind is different than anyone else, always going. You never sleep, but your body needs stillness. You must remember one cannot change the past, only safe guard the future." Silver Shadow glanced up.

"My father would not want me to dwell on his absence. He would want me to move forward."

"Yes, that is what he wants. Keep your mind clear, only then will your path lead to the true goal," Master Lii advised.

"Thank you, Master Lii."

"Good luck, Guardian of Life, keep our team safe."

"I will, Master," Silver Shadow answered as he stood and bowed. Master Lii bowed back and Silver Shadow made his way to the hanger. The rest of the Shadow Runners boarded the aircraft. CD was loaded up with his disks. Cyber Ball filled with his bombs and a pair of twin rackets. Ton carried his M249 with six boxes of belt fed ammo. Poison was equipped with a 50. Cal. BarrettM82A1 sniper rifle with suppresser. She also had a G18 automatic pistol strapped to her leg for back-up. Both Jean and Liset were armed with P90s set up with night vision scopes, red dot laser sight, and silencer. Tyton was also packing, with his mini Uzi. It also came with silencer, extended clip, and extended stock for control. His two Shadow Arms carried a twin pair of Desert Eagle pistols. Silver Shadow was armed with his classic black M4 with green camouflage markings. His vest carried all the nursery tools, like silencer and extra clips. All the members were on board and seated. The aircraft started its launch sequence. Everyone was armed to the teeth and ready to drop in on the Otilum fortress. The Shadow Runners have now declared war, a fight they will see through to the end.

Chapter Fifteen
A Father's Legacy

The team is gathered in the SGD aircraft. Everyone a little on edge as the tension begins to mount. This team is the best there is and now at full strength. With Silver Shadow's advance training, they will be able to face anything. This mission will truly test each member of this team to the limit. Only 23 minutes until the Shadow Runners land and hit the ground. Ton sits alongside his new love. Liset huddled up close to him. Jean sits on the other side of the aisle. She glances at Ton. Feeling her eyes, he peers back. Using her finger, Jean tells Ton to come over there. Ton looks down at Liset and she shrugs her shoulders. He gets up, crosses the aisle, and sits down beside Jean.

"So, you and my girl hooked up?" Jean states.

"Yes, I told her how I truly felt about her," Ton replied.

"That's good, but don't mistreat her. Cause I don't care how big you can get or how strong you think you are. If you hurt her, I'm going to hurt you, got it!"

"Yes, I will only treat her the way I would want to be treated. I care more for her then I care for myself," Ton answered.

"Well, that's good, but many have said that before! Just keep in mind I'll be watching. Now go on back over there, she's waitin' on you," Jean concluded, waving her hand for him to go away. Her hand motion was like she was a little annoyed with the two of them. Ton removed himself from Jean's side and went back over to his seat. He cuddled up next to Liset, putting his arm around her. They both quickly glanced over at Jean; she turned away, making herself more comfortable in her seat, rolling her eyes.

"What did she say?" Liset questioned, looking up at him.

"I think she gave me the big sister talk," Ton remarked. Liset had been through this before with her.

"Don't take whatever she said the wrong way."

"I won't, I know she has your best interest in mind," Ton replied.

"Yeah, I guess she's always had my back, even when I was too caught up in my own drama." The bond between these two women was more than just sisterhood. Sometimes they would have their disagreements, but in the end, they never stop caring about one another. Every argument gave each party a chance to clear the air. Saying those things they had been holding onto. This was the glue that held their friendship, their sisterhood together. Silver Shadow came out of the cockpit, walking down the aisle in front of the whole team.

"It's time," he said. The team could feel the aircraft slowing down and lowering its altitude. The whole team stood and lined up at the back. "Let's stick together and I want everyone to be safe," Silver Shadow declared. The ramp started to lower and the sand from the ground swirled around the aircraft. Inches from the ground, the team deployed from the cloaked aircraft like they were appearing from thin air. Cyber Ball and CD were the first to hit the ground. They both secured the area in a half circle. Followed by Liset, Jean, then Ton, and Poison. Tyton followed her and Silver Shadow was last. The aircraft did not stop moving and took off, leaving a trail of dust floating around the team. So far, so good, for now the Shadow Runners were undetected. "Let's go, stay low!" Silver Shadow whispered, waving his hand for the team to move forward. Ton, Liset, and Jean ran in one small group. Silver Shadow, Tyton, and Poison ran in another. CD ran on the right side, Cyber Ball on the left. In the darkness, they could just make out the building. The full moon was their guide as they ran across the sand. "CD, Cyber Ball take point!" Silver Shadow commanded. The two of them ran faster than the rest, leading the whole group of shadows. The team was getting closer to the complex. CD stopped and the ground in front of him started to shake. A circle-shaped six barreled mini cannon emerged from the sand under his feet. It aimed right at CD, the base was on alert. Heavy machine gun rounds began firing from the complex lighting up the night. CD quickly put up his shadow shield. The rest of the team took cover along a small trench like hill. Cyber Ball released a bomb ball and slapped it at the back of the gun turret before it could begin shooting. It blew up in front of CD, sending him flying backward. Cyber Ball ran over to make sure CD was okay.

"Thanks, brother, I was almost a goner!"

"No problem," Cyber Ball replied, grabbing CD's hand picking him up from the ground. CD stood up and glanced over Cyber Ball's shoulder.

"You ready for more of those things?" CD asked, pointing at what was behind him. Cyber Ball turned around to see more machine gun turrets revealing themselves from the sand with their barrels beginning to spin and fire.

"I bet I blow up more than you do!"

"You're on!" CD yelled, accepting his challenge. Cyber Ball looked back at Silver Shadow.

"Stay close behind us. We'll cover you," Cyber Ball suggested. Silver Shadow shook his head okay. CD and Cyber Ball put up their shadow shields at the same time. The rest of the team got behind them as the two ran toward the guns. Bullets were sailing all around hitting the shields. CD was throwing his disks sideways around his large contact lens-shaped shield. Cyber Ball was bouncing his bombs off CD's shield trying the get more than him. The team was beginning to be pushed back a little, losing ground. Tyton noticed the sand behind them starting to move.

"Father!" he yelled. Silver Shadow turned around and saw these little beetle-like bots flying out of the ground a dozen at a time. Once free of the sand, they took flight toward the team's flank. More and more were popping out of the sand. It would seem the beetle-like bots were bombs with only one purpose. They would try to get close to their target and self-destruct. Silver Shadow, Poison, Tyton, Ton, Liset, and Jean were doing their very best to stop these bomber-beetles from over running the team's position. CD and Cyber Ball continued to stop the mini guns from decimating the shadows. The last mini gun turret was bigger than the rest. The team was now gaining ground and about 20 yards away from the building. A spot light from the building was on them, highlighting the team in the darkness. It would only be moments before The Shadow Runner team is consumed, Silver Shadow had to do something.

Michael G. Dunkley Jr.

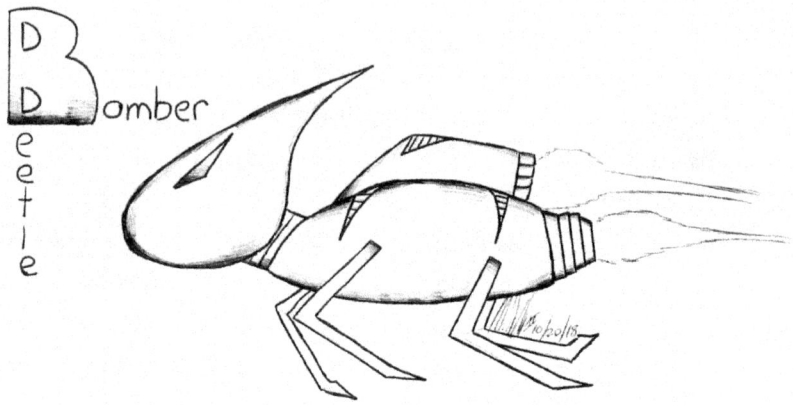

They would try to get close to their target and self-destruct.

"Cover me!" he yelled. Silver Shadow swung his weapon onto his back. He held his arms out and clapped his hands together. Silver Shadow's eyes began to glow along with his hands. He ran toward the gun turret and dove into the sand. Before CD and Cyber Ball knew it, Silver Shadow was standing on the other side of the last big gun turret. He slowly emerged from the sand and pulled a small C4 charge from his belt. Silver Shadow ran at the gun turret and place the bomb at the bottom. He jumped over it as the charge blew up, destroying the gun turret. Silver Shadow landed right in front of the whole team. CD and Cyber Ball lowered their shields and turned their attention to the bomber-beetles still at their backs. The whole team kept back pedaling toward the building. Silver Shadow ran to the front doors of the building, but the base was locked down. The black colored glass could be broken. There were also some signs it had been replaced recently. By now thousands of beetles had been trying to overrun the team. Blowing up in small waves as the team shot them before getting close enough. Ton stood in between the team and the beetles keeping them at bay with his light machine gun. "Ton!" Silver Shadow shouted.

"Yes, sir!" Ton answered.

"I need a hole!" Silver Shadow ran over and took Ton's position, maintaining fire on the bomber-beetles with his M4. Ton's eyes started to glow.

He put his weapon down and removed his size bracelet. Ton instantly became big. Using his huge fists, he smashed the black glass, creating a hole so big, Ton could see both first and second floors. Robot guards jumped down from the top floor through the hole at Ton in an effort to stop him. They were no match for Ton's size. He crushed their mechanical bodies like a hammer on cold French fries. Silver Shadow glanced back at Ton. "Lift me up!" he suggested.

"Here!" Ton said, holding his large hand out flat. Silver Shadow stopped shooting and ran at his hand. He leaped from the ground onto Ton's hand and into the hole. Silver Shadow slid across the floor toward some computer control panels like a baseball player sliding into second base. There were still two robot guards standing at the consoles. Silver Shadow dropped his weapon as one turned around. With his eyes still glowing, the robot threw a punch. Silver Shadow stopped his punch and planted his foot into the robot's chest, sending it flying across the room. The last guard turned around too late. Silver Shadow was already performing a low sweep, knocking the robot on its back. Then he ended it with one deadly punch to the robot guard's head. Silver Shadow used so much force, he had punched through the robot's head and into the floor. He quickly pulled an E.M.P. mine from his belt and threw it at the computers. Then he ran, scooping his weapon up and jumped from the hole as the mine went off. The bomber-beetles stopped rushing the team almost instantly, dropping to the ground in mid-flight. The wave of beetles had finally subsided and the team had a brief moment to breath.

"Everyone in!" Silver Shadow insisted. Ton put back on his bracelet and returned to normal size. Picking up his weapon from the ground, he led the team inside. The Shadow Runners entered the large white hallway, it was clear. "Ammo check!" CD looked at Cyber Ball, he shook his head.

"We're good!" CD said, answering for the both of them. Poison was securing her sniper rifle to her back. She pulled the fully auto G18 from her leg.

"Ready to go!" Poison replied.

"I'm good, too," Tyton said, standing next to his mother.

"Four boxes left," Ton stated.

"We have four clips each," Jean answered, handing Liset one of her clips to make them even.

"Alright, let's move," Silver Shadow said. The team briskly jogged down the hall toward the elevator. The hallway had some noticeable damage. There were light gray stains on the floor and bullet holes littered the walls. The smell of gun powder suggested a fire fight had taken place recently. Jean turned to the only other door in the hallway. It led to a small hallway and a short staircase up the control room. She stood there for a second, holding the door handle. Silver Shadow glanced back at her and shook his head. Jean turned the door knob and pushed the door open. She quickly ran in and up the stairs. The team stood at the large elevator doors. Tyton hit the button and it didn't light up. The power must have been off. "Ton, would you mind?" Silver Shadow asked, pointing to the elevator doors. Ton swung his weapon to his back. His eyes and hands started to glow. He stepped up to the center of the doors. He placed his hands near the crack in the center. His fingers punctured the first layer of the six-inch thick cast iron shiny doors. He slowly pulled the doors open, sparks began to fly from the edges. Ton got them open and stood between them. The doors kept trying to close, he was pinned. Ton pushed them open as far as he could. Then Ton bent both doors, folding them like a cardboard box. The doors folded off the track and buckled into the floor. A heavy amount of warm steam blew from Ton's vents under his chin. His eyes and hands stopped glowing.

"That was hot!" Liset remarked. The team gathered in a circle in front of the open doors.

"Be prepared for anything!" Silver Shadow whispered. He looked down the dark elevator shaft. Silver Shadow glanced back and gave the okay. One by one, each team member slid down the elevator cable. Silver Shadow, Poison, and Tyton embarked first. Jean came down from the control room and rejoined the team. CD and Cyber Ball stood back so the rest could follow. They took positions on each side of the bent elevator doors. Jean turned into smoke and floated down alongside Tyton.

"Liset, get on," Ton insisted, standing in front of her, holding onto the cable with his weapon hooked to his chest.

"What, on your back?!" Liset asked.

"Yes, I'll take you down." Liset shrugged her shoulders and used the strap on her weapon to place it over her head. Then she used the boxes of ammo on

Ton's belt to climb onto his back. He swung into the shaft and confidently lowered the both of them. The shaft was warm and a little dark. Looking down Liset could see the top of Tyton's head slowly disappear into the darkness. Ton stopped at the first door he had seen as the first group kept going down. A slight lonely feeling came over Liset, but she felt safe as long as Ton was by her side. He is like her little protector now, even if there was nothing little about him. They hung inches from the sub-level one door.

"Okay, push the door open," Ton whispered, swinging toward the small ledge. Liset used her foot each time Ton swung.

"Wait!" Liset blurted out.

"What?"

"There is someone waiting for us on the other side, I can feel them."

"Who is it?" Ton asked.

"I don't know, there are no thoughts. Just a lot of energy," Liset explained.

"It might be another shadow. This might be our only chance to show it we are peaceful," Ton replied.

"Okay, but let me go first." Ton swung Liset to the ledge; once on she pushed the doors open all the way. The doors looked new with some clear blue protective tape on the inside. Liset climbed through and walked in with caution, unsure of what she may encounter. It was a big room with a meeting table in the center of it. She stood in what used to be The Max Force's living quarters. There were some obvious signs of damage around the room here as well. Different colored stains marked small areas on the floor. Ton swung himself in and stayed perched in the elevator door way. Liset made her way to the other side of the room. She peered back at Ton.

"Rowtila..." she whispered to herself. "Watch out!" Liset screamed. Before Ton could react, a large hand reached down from over Ton's head. It grabbed Ton's helpless body like a candy bar from a store shelf. The hand's grip tightened around Ton as he started shooting wildly. Ton was being whipped all over the place like a rag doll. The giant hand finally let Ton go, sending him through a wall into another small room. A giant four-armed beast emerged from the shadows, hiding on one side above the elevator doors. Liset took a few steps back as this large shadow stood before her. It did not speak, but she could hear its thoughts. Its name was Rowtila, and his only purpose seemed to be death. He didn't have a normal thought process, just flashes of experiences. Memories of past events that could not be known by others. Rowtila began making suspicious movements, much like a bull getting ready to charge. With Ton down and no way to get in Rowtila's head, Liset found herself in a dangerous situation. Rowtila started running full speed at her. Liset pulled and pointed her P90 at him. Before she could pull the trigger, she heard a sound coming from the other small room. Ton came barreling out from the room he was thrown into. Rowtila was within six-feet of Liset. Ton pulled the size bracelet from his wrist and dove at Rowtila, intercepting him before he reached Liset. The two of them rolled across the floor like two large bears fighting over a scrap of meat. Rowtila's four arms wrapped around Ton like a spider. Ton head butted Rowtila, making him let go. Ton quickly got back on his feet. Rowtila regained his balance, trying to recover from the head blow. The two foes squared off like two opposing football players on the line. In comparison Rowtila was bigger and had more arms, but Ton had more skills. Rowtila made the first bold move. He threw a high and low punch at the same time, using both left hands. Ton caught both hands and turned, putting his back to Rowtila. Using his back, Ton flipped Rowtila over himself and into a wall. Rowtila fell through the wall and into another small room. In a matter of seconds, Rowtila came flying from the rubble, galloping on all fours like a horse toward Ton. Resetting his stance, Ton grappled Rowtila as he charged. Ton stopped Rowtila in his tracks. With one knee to the head and a killer sweep to Rowtila's legs, Ton flopped Rowtila over on his back like a butcher flipping a large piece of beef at the meat packing plant. Before Rowtila could counter, Ton finished him with one strong blow to the head. Rowtila was out cold, Ton glanced at Liset.

"Is he dead?" Liset asked.

"No, just unconscious!" Ton replied. "For now!"

"That was too close, what do we do with him?"

"For now, we just leave him there. He'll be out for an hour or two," Ton answered. He walked over and picked up his bracelet. Ton returned it to his wrist. "Did you get anything from his thoughts?"

"Just little fragments." Liset began looking around the room. Ton walked over and knelt down next to one of the many stains on the floor. Before he could say anything, "I think he killed the Max Force team!" she blurted out.

"Okay, maybe you're right, but where are all the bodies?" Before anymore words could be said, they both heard a loud scream. It was Tyton, Liset suddenly had this feeling that something had gone very wrong. Ton and Liset ran to the still open elevator shaft. They looked down into the darkness. Ton glanced at Liset, he didn't have to say anything. As he reached out to grab the elevator cable, she jumped onto his back again.

"What about him?" Liset quickly asked, pointing to Rowtila's lifeless body sprawled out on the floor like an outdoor rug.

"If we have time, we'll come back for him. This is more important!" Ton answered, clenching the cable. The two of them started sliding down the cable as fast as they could like a zip line. They past two more levels before hitting the bottom. The elevator doors were already open and a bright white light coming from inside. Ton and Liset stayed in the shaft, peering in to assess the danger. There was a small hallway with many closed doors. Jean floated down the shaft from another floor and formed behind them. Ton glanced over his shoulder.

"Jean, cover us," he whispered. Ton stepped in first, he had left his gun up on the other floor. He still had his strength. Liset followed closely, nervously pointing her weapon every which way. Last was Jean covering their backs. The three of them carefully walked in a few feet. Ton continued looking around the area.

"This must be the laboratory level," Ton insisted. The three of them stood in the middle of four rooms marked "Lab." In front of them was a large door leading to another hallway. The door was closed, but they could hear gun fire coming from the other side. Liset grabbed Ton's shoulder.

"They're trapped, can you get us through?" Liset asked.

"Yeah, hold on! Jean, see if you can get through and help while I take down this door," Ton replied.

"Good idea, my baby is in trouble and I ain't waiting for you two!" Jean answered. She snapped into smoke mode and floated beneath the door along the floor, leaving her weapon behind.

"Stand back," Ton said as his hands, feet, and eyes began to glow. Liset backed up and watched her man work his magic. Ton took two steps back and three steps forward, performing a straight high kick. His foot landed in the center top half of the door, sending it flying into the next hall. Ton and Liset rushed in to find robot bodies lying all over the hallway and around a corner. They followed the trail and found Jean just standing there. Poison, Tyton, and Silver Shadow standing at the other end of a long hallway. In the middle of the hall was an unknown shadow. He was fierce-looking with a long narrow football-shaped like head. The top of his head had three long, sharp spikes twisted and curved in different directions. A metal snake-like braid sprouted from the center of the spikes like a long vine. It dangled from the back of his head like a lock of hair. Who was he, and what was he after? Then he spoke.

"I'm here for the boy!" he demanded. His voice was deep, yet clear. Silver Shadow slowly pushed Tyton behind him. Poison put herself between the unknown shadow and her son.

"Who are you and what do you want with him?" Poison asked before anyone could answer. She seemed to be the only one who always asked the question on everyone's mind.

"My name is Viston; after today you will remember it."

"You know I will not let you take him," Silver Shadow advised.

"Make no mistake, the boy is coming with me!" Viston threatened. His eyes glowed but not like the other shadows. There was no smoke, and Viston's stayed lit. The very tips of the three sharp spikes on his head glow a little as well.

"You're gonna have to go through all of us!" Jean shouted. She edged closer to Viston with aggression. Her intention was clear, Jean was always ready for a fight. Jean snapped into smoke mode and flew toward him.

"Have it your way," Viston stated, quickly pulling some small device from his belt. It looked kind of like a metal whistle. Before Jean could reach him, Viston pushed a red button on the side of the device. Like a vacuum, it sucked Jean in and she quickly became trapped. The team now realized how much of a threat Viston really was. With his eyes and head still glowing, Viston turned around toward Silver Shadow, Poison, and Tyton. Ton and Liset saw this as their chance to make a move. Liset pointed her gun and pulled the trigger, but it jammed. Viston threw the whistle-like device on the floor like a piece of trash. It rattled around on the linoleum floor like an empty tin can. Ton glanced over at Liset, there were no words. They had the same idea. Ton began

"My name is Viston; after today you will remember it."

to reach for his size bracelet. Without warning, before his fingertips could grasp it, some shadow grabbed him from behind. It was Viston, but that was impossible. Viston grabbed Ton's hand, stopping him from removing the bracelet. Viston wasted no time pinning Ton up against the wall with his arm pressed hard on Ton's neck. Liset turned to see Ton almost helpless, she couldn't believe what she was seeing. There were two of them. Liset, along with Ton, did a double take. After thinking about it for a second, she threw her weapon to the floor and grabbed Viston's shoulder. It was her best effort to help Ton. With Ton still pinned, Viston looked back and did a backward high kick. It was so strong, and Liset was so small. The kick knocked her off her feet and back, sending her into an opposite wall. Ton tried to move, he could see her laying there on the floor. There was nothing he could do.

"I will destroy you and your friends if I have to!" Viston shouted.

"One way or another, you will pay for that," Ton replied. Ton's eyes started to glow, but he still could not break free. Somehow Viston remained stronger than Ton, almost like he was feeding on Ton's hidden strength. The other Viston started to walk slowly toward Silver Shadow, Poison, and Tyton. His walk became a run, Poison pushed Tyton behind her. Suddenly, Tyton was pushed to the floor and another Viston put Poison in a sleeper hold. He came up from behind them. Silver Shadow peered over to see Tyton on the floor and Poison being held up off the floor in a head lock. Silver Shadow knew his team was unprepared for this encounter.

"What's the matter, can't fight your own battles?" Silver Shadow instigated to the Viston running at him.

"I gave your team a chance to hand over the boy, you leave me no choice," Viston answered.

"There is always a choice."

"Not for me!" Viston argued. Filled with rage, he threw a punch at Silver Shadow and missed. Silver Shadow stepped to the side and countered the punch with a low sweep kick. Viston fell back onto the floor. In one motion, Viston flipped up onto his feet and did a flying high kick. His foot landed on Silver Shadow's chest, making his feet slide back a little. Viston was strong but not at his strongest. It was then Silver Shadow may have discovered Viston's weakness. The more of him there were, the weaker the original Viston became. Silver Shadow's eyes started to glow and Viston started charging at him once more. Viston did a mid-high kick and Silver Shadow batted it away. Then he quickly used both hands, punching Viston in the head. The impact sent Viston flying back down the hall, sliding across the floor. He was hurt, but the other replicas remained. A door at the end of the hall behind Tyton opened and another Viston stepped out. He was holding a large rocket launcher. "If we can't take him, he must be destroyed," Viston yelled, still laying on the floor holding his head. The Viston copy at the other end standing in the doorway shot the rocket down the hall right at Tyton.

"No!" Silver Shadow shouted. Everything was happening so fast. The rocket soared down the hall aimed for Tyton. Silver Shadow ran toward the rocket, and Tyton got to his feet in time to try and avoid it. Poison and Ton looked on, feeling regret, fear, and helplessness. Silver Shadow pushed Tyton back to the floor, and a large hot explosion followed. All the shadows felt the heat and pressure from the rockets' impact. After a few minutes, the smoke that filled the hallway began to clear. Poison could hear her son shouting for her. All the Viston replicas and the original were gone, leaving Poison on her hands and knees, recovering from the head lock she was in.

"Mother, Mother!" Tyton cried. Poison glanced down the hazy hall to see Tyton being dragged by Viston into the door at the end.

"Tyton!" she yelled in a panic. She jumped up and ran at the door. It slammed close and locked before she could stop it. A voice over the buildings intercom system sounded, counting down. The facility's fail safe had been activated. Some kind of self-destruct sequence was underway. "Ton, help me!" she yelled, banging on the door with her fists. Soon, the only sound in the hall was Poison banging on the heavy metal door. She looked back at the rest of the team. "What's wrong?" Ton was just standing there, looking down with his back to her. Liset was crouched next to him. They were whispering to each other. "What is wrong?" Poison repeated. She started to run back toward them. Both Ton and Liset turned and looked at her. Something was wrong, but Poison could not tell what. Sadness could be read in their eyes. As Poison got closer, she became aware of what had happened. "No...no...no!" she screamed. It was Silver Shadow. His lifeless body lay on the floor. Poison quickly became more frantic, "Silver Shadow...come on...snap out of it!"

"He is dead," Ton whispered.

"No, he's not, don't you say that!"

"What do we do now?" Liset asked.

"We have to get out of here. We have to fall back to base and regroup. Help me!" Poison was on the floor holding Silver Shadow's body tightly. Poison realized she would now have to lead the team if they were going to survive. The sadness consumed her heart and her mind. She felt weak, almost unable to stand. Liset could see Poison was having trouble. She helped Poison stand and walk. Poison had to show strength and be strong for the team. "Ton, grab Silver Shadow, he goes home with us!" Poison softly said in shock. Liset walked, holding Poison on her feet, down the hall back to the elevator shaft. Ton picked Silver Shadow's body up and followed. He saw the metal whistle rattling around on the floor with Jean still trapped inside. Ton grabbed it and put it in his belt. Jean would have to wait for now. Getting the rest of the team out of this facility would have to take top priority. Ton, Poison, and Liset made it back to the elevator doors, but the doors were closed. A loud alarm rang out and little red lights began blinking throughout the complex. The base was now on full alert and the self-destruction countdown had started locking down doors. "Ton, get these doors!" Poison ordered.

"I'm on it!" Ton replied. With one hand, he slid the doors open just in time to see CD and Cyber Ball coming down in the elevator. Surprise could be read on their faces almost immediately.

"What happened? Where is Tyton?" CD asked. Poison did not answer. She got in the elevator along with Liset by her side. He glanced at Ton for an answer. Ton just shook his head. The doors closed as the whole team entered. The elevator began to go up.

"We are going to face a heavy resistance force at the top," Cyber Ball said to Poison as they all kept staring at Ton holding Silver Shadow's body.

"I know," Poison answered with her head down.

"We will find Tyton. We will fight to the end for you!" Everyone shook their head, agreeing with Cyber Ball.

"I know." Poison was still in shock. She stared at Silver Shadow's lifeless face. She knew what he would do, and her sadness quickly turned into anger. "This is it, enough is enough. It's time we show them why they can't just do what they want. Before this day is over, they will understand who we are," Poison declared, letting go of Liset and standing on her own. The team started checking their ammo and reloading up whatever they had left. Poison remand reserved in the corner of the elevator. In her own mind, she could not let the sadness consume her every thought. This team is going to need her leadership now more than ever. "But…you will not just fight for me…" she whispered. They neared the top. "We will fight for the Silver Shadow!" Poison yelled as the elevator doors open. Ton ran into the extremely full hallway, still holding Silver Shadow. He pulled his bracelet off instantly, becoming his largest and activated Silver Shadow's shield. The robots couldn't stop him as he stepped on groups of them at a time. The rest of the team followed, unloading every bullet they had into what was left still standing. Ton made a hole almost as wide as the hall. CD and Cyber Ball took out all their rage on the robot army. With a member down and the youngest member missing, rage was all they felt. In the middle of all the chaos, Poison radios in. "SGD, we are ready for dust off."

"Affirmative, Poison, approaching emergency pick-up zone Alpha now."

"Alright, Shadow Runners, every shadow out!" Poison shouted, grabbing a gun from one of the fallen robots. With the self-destruction countdown time running out, they would have to move fast. Fighting their way outside, the team met the SGD aircraft in front of the building. SGD hovered there with the door open. CD and Cyber Ball covered the rest of the team as they climbed aboard one at a time. Ton put his bracelet back on, returning to his normal size.

"You ready?" Cyber Ball asked CD as they continued to hold off the remaining robots.

"Yeah, let's leave these trash cans something to remember us by!" CD answered.

"Drop that first line of troops and I'll take care of the rest!"

"I'd love to!" CD replied, pulling his most powerful dark blue disk from his back. He dropped his shadow shield long enough to cast the disk in a half circle motion using his whole body. The disk flew around, cutting down a line of 16 robots like a handful of twigs and a sharp ninja sword. Each robot cut in half at the waist. CD jumped backward onto the waiting extended ramp of the aircraft. He caught his disk on its return. Cyber Ball shut down his shield and ran toward the ramp as well. The SGD aircraft started its take off, elevating higher. The facility began to explode internally and the outside started crumbling. The entire place covered in smoke and fire.

"CD, shield!" Cyber Ball yelled as he released two bomb balls. CD reactivated his shield and Cyber Ball hit and bounced the last two bombs of CD's shield. As Cyber Ball ran and leaped for the ramp, the bomb balls hit the rest of the robot troops trying to follow the aircraft. Hanging there from the edge of the ramp, Cyber Ball looked back to admire his handy work.

"You sure know how to cut it close," CD said, pulling Cyber Ball up.

Hanging there from the edge of the ramp, Cyber Ball looked back to admire his handy work.

"That one was for the Silver Shadow." The aircraft closed the ramp door and flew the team to safety. Ton carried Silver Shadow's body to one of the last seats. He carefully laid Silver Shadow down and sat next to him. The team remained quiet, and still, there was nothing that could be said. The mood on the aircraft was sorrow and grief for their fallen leader. Poison could not bear her own thoughts of her love and her son out there somewhere alone. She got up and went into the cockpit, planting herself at the controls. She knew if she didn't keep herself occupied, her other feelings would take over her every action. Fear, despair, sadness would turn to anger, maybe thoughts of revenge.

"SGD, can you scan for Tyton or his location?" Poison desperately asked. Her tone of voice was soft.

"Negative, although my scanners did detect another aircraft leaving the underground facility just before the team did."

"Can you track it?"

"Affirmative, shall I set a course to follow it?" SGD recommended.

"No, keep tracking it on the long-range scanners, RTB."

"Affirmative, Poison."

"We must regroup if we're going to stop this new adversary, and I will make it my mission to find my son. This has gone too far, and it's not over!" The Shadow Runners were down but not out. This will be the biggest challenge they will have to overcome. In the end, this will bring them closer and make the Shadow Runners stronger. Silver Shadow's body lay alone in the back of the aircraft. Ton sits beside Silver Shadow's body. He glances over and something catches his eye. It was Sliver Shadow's hand, his index finger was twitching.

Michael Dunkley, Jr.

The Corrupt Shadows

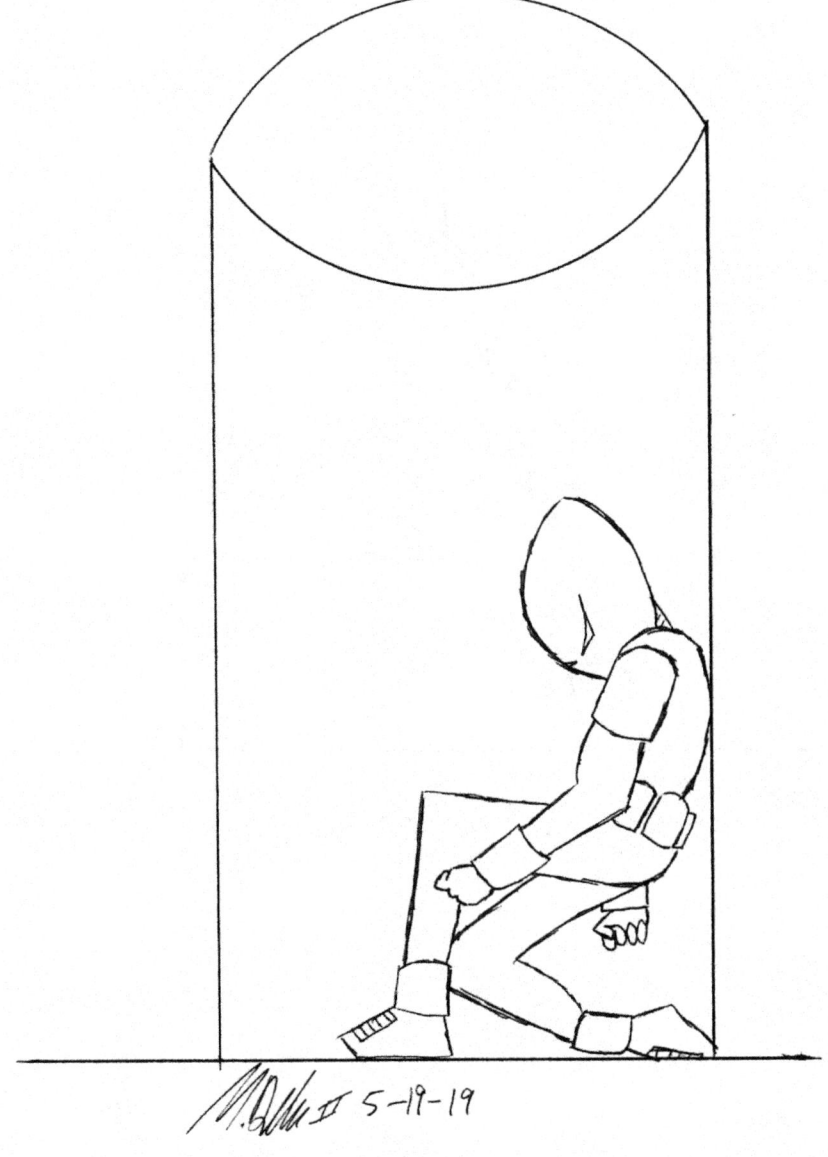

Michael Dunkley, Jr.

The Corrupt Shadows

Michael Dunkley, Jr.

CPSIA information can be obtained
at www.ICGtesting.com
Printed in the USA
LVHW052305080723
751829LV00003B/225